Rhys ap Gruffydd is a man accursed, his scarred
face hidden behind a black leather mask. When he
hears of a lass who can heal him, he acts without
honor: he kidnaps her. But Aileen O'Conaire
is no fey child; she is a woman, and she will resist—
and attract—the Welsh lord as no blue-blooded
beauty ever has.

Possessed with the gift of ancient magic, Aileen
perceives her fierce abductor as a fallen angel . . . a
man more afflicted in his heart than in his flesh. She
despises him for taking her captive, yet cannot deny
the desire he stirs in her blood.

In a war between a man and a woman, there can be
no victors. And in a land shadowed by bloodshed
and treachery, there is only danger—unless the fire
burning between Aileen and Rhys can
flame into love . . .

Books by Lisa Ann Verge

TWICE UPON A TIME
HEAVEN IN HIS ARMS
THE FAERY BRIDE

Published by Zebra Books

CAPTIVE TO HIS TOUCH

Aileen stood, sucking air into her lungs and trembling fit to shake her bones out of her skin, while Rhys ridged his teeth against the heel of her palm as if tasting a soft ripe pear. She stood snared in the blue blade of his gaze while her heart raced, raced, and all her body shuddered in the steely grip of a fierce, unyielding emotion.

He pulled her toward the tiny hut with its frosted thatch and pitted walls. She felt as if she flew across the ground, as if the wind itself pushed open the door for them. The light sifting down through the smoke hole dusted the edge of a crumpled blanket.

Every hard inch of his strong body pressed against her back, radiating heat like a kiln. He snapped off the netting of her hair. Burrowing beneath the tumble, he sucked his way down the line of her neck. She threw her head back at the shock of his lips on her shoulder, then curled fistfuls of her tunic in her hands as her mind separated from her body and her body fluxed to the commands of primitive instinct.

She hadn't come here expecting herb-scented reeds and tenderness. Such trappings were for beautiful women, gentle lovers, noble sentiments, none of which existed in this rubbled hut.

She had come for reasons she had not dared to acknowledge, not until now.

She had come for Rhys . . .

* * *

LISA ANN VERGE

ZEBRA BOOKS
KENSINGTON PUBLISHING CORP.

ZEBRA BOOKS are published by

Kensington Publishing Corp.
850 Third Avenue
New York, NY 10022

First Printing: March, 1996
10 9 8 7 6 5 4 3 2 1

Printed in the United States of America

I am a thief, a wound binds me,
thief of a fair girl, not a black stallion;
for tonight no thief of a ram,
thief of a maiden this happy time;
no thief of the cattle enclosure,
thief of her, wave-coloured, in the fair wood;
thief of a wonderful bold enchantress,
thief of a penance, not of a fulling mill;
thief to entwine a girl who's not mine,
thief of pure love, no thief of purses;
no thief of a hoofed heifer,
yet never was law so heavy upon me;
love's theft now overcomes me,
o daring pain, I am the thief of a girl.

—Gruffudd ap Adda
from *Lleidr Serch, Thief of Love*
14th century

Prologue

The Year of Our Lord 1275

Oh, it was a frightful visitor who came to us that strange Midsummer's Night.

It could have been yesterday, I remember it so well. Twilight had long blackened the crags of my lord's kingdom. The dying gasps of the pagan fires glowed red upon the hillsides. Now, I've been the keeper of this house for enough years to turn my hair full into white, yet never had a visitor come so high in the mountains in the midst of night. And none welcome for these past five years, mind you, with all the changes in the house of Graig. So you can imagine how I nearly leapt out of my skirts when someone banged at the door fit to split the wood.

I knew well enough that all the household was snug inside. They'd scurried back to their hovels from whatever pagan things they do at those fires on Midsummer's Night, like rats to their holes in a storm, not one of them brave enough to risk seeing whatever demons are set loose after the sun sets on this spirit night. And for the best, I was thinking, for I myself was hanging another sprig of St. John's wort over the doorway to the kitchens, to guard against demons and the like.

At first I thought to ignore the banging. No good news comes after dark, you know, and the master . . . well, it's no secret that the master wouldn't take kindly to having his refuge invaded. Faith, the master was no fit company for wolves these days. Oh, it was not always that way, you know. But now I feared, even not knowing who stood behind that door, for the poor unwitting creature's health. No man deserved the full wrath of this Lord of Graig.

But you see, I'm Irish born, Welsh bred, and Celtic to the bone, and I found myself padding through the rushes nonetheless, to pull open the door in welcome.

An Irishman, he said he was. Snarling and snapping at the delay, and me struck dumb with the shock of it all and wondering how to keep him quiet so as not to disturb the master in his chamber at the other end of the hall. I spoke as kindly as I could and ushered the visitor to the center hearth, offering him a bit of mead and oatcake all the way. Only then did I get a straight look at him. He was a strange spark of a man, too limber and sprightly for the wild night. There was a brightness to him, like to outshine the fire crackling in the hearth the girls work day and night to keep burning. I found myself lingering until he barked good and loud for the mead I'd promised him.

Then the far door banged open and my heart leapt to my throat, for the master tore out of his chamber breathing fire like the dragon that's said to live amid the caves of Snowdon. He caught sight of the visitor and I scurried out, not wanting to be burned by the hot edge of his tongue.

Faith, it's true I had no business lurking in the shadows with my ears cocked, me being no more than a servant in the house of Rhys ap Gruffydd, the lord of Graig. But I've earned my meddling, you see, having been with this house long before the present lord took his first squalling breath. I've known the family as if it were my own, I've watched through the good years and now, yes, now in the darkest. So I took little shame in peering around that splintered old wall. Surely it was my duty to stop the master from tossing the Irishman out into the cold. We're still Welsh, after all, no matter what curse God has put upon this lord and this house. I'll see myself begging

*in some English village before the Graigs deny hospitality to
anyone whose shadow darkens the door.*

*Oh, and the two went at it, the master and the Irishman,
my master roaring his displeasure and the little man talking
back with no mind to the danger to his own hide. Octavius,
he said his name was, recently come of Ireland, though what
he was doing wandering in this place so far from sea or road
was a puzzle to all. He was having none of my master's rude-
ness—none at all. Never did I hear any man talk to my master
the way this little tattered fellow did. He even made my master
pause a moment with the shame of finding such a harsh welcome in a fellow Celt's house.*

*Then my lord made to stomp off to that lair of his he lets
no one into, when Octavius called out and made a comment
on the lights he saw upon yonder lake. Ah, you know the one,
the enchanted lake with the faery isle my master has been
trying for years to build a castle upon. The Irishman was trying
to engage my master in conversation, after all the harsh words
that had passed between them! The little man began talking
of faery rings and dancing lights and all such things—true
enough, not a strange conversation for a Midsummer's Night,
for all the people of Graig had been talking of the old days
and the faeries on this night. But my master interrupted the
Irishman, as I knew he would. My lord scoffed as he does at
all un-Christian imaginings and mocked the little man, which
sent the Irishman to true temper at last.*

*"Listen to ye, believing only what you can see," the Irishman
said. "I'd curse you for your ignorance, but for all that leather
upon your face there's no hiding that you've been cursed already."*

*Ah, and didn't that set my blood to freeze! For no one dared
to make mention of it, though all men knew of the curse upon
my master. One look at that masked face set my heart to choking me. I thought my lord was to take the creature in his two
warrior's hands and strangle the life out of him. If it weren't
for the Welsh blood rushing thick in his veins he might have*

done the same. Instead he spoke quiet like the wind in the trees before a storm—like to make the hairs stand up on the back of my neck—and banished the creature into the night.

Before the words were full out of my master's mouth I made to hurry out and stop such discourtesy—take the Irishman aside and give him food and shelter in our kitchens, humble though they may be. It was no fit night for man nor hound.

But the Irishman stood his ground by the warmth of the hearth and smiled, he did; and it was the smile that stopped me—as did the look in his bright black eyes. My heart dropped to my stomach, for it was Midsummer's Night, after all, and Christian though I am, I'll not mock the old ways. This creature had come from the air itself.

The Irishman said that he knew a healer unlike any other, who lived on an island off the west coast of Ireland; a woman who had healed every ailment she'd touched. A woman with a touch of faery blood who could cure my master's curse with a pass of her hands. A miracle worker, like to be a saint.

I felt the heat of my lord's anger, for hadn't he made a hundred thousand pilgrimages and seen every charlatan and witch from Myddfai to Paris, all to rid himself of this curse?

On the Aran Isles, the Irishman continued, as thick as mud to my master's silent rage. By the name of Aileen Ruadh. Aileen the Red.

Then what happened I never could be sure, for it happened so quickly I wondered if my old eyes had deceived me, or if he had just moved so quickly that I'd not noticed the closing of the door. For one moment, the Irishman was there, standing as whole as you or me before the red glow of the hearth fire, and the next moment there was a sparkling around him, and suddenly there was naught but a wisp of smoke and an echo of laughter that chilled my skin from my scalp to my toes.

After a moment, my master was off to throw open the door and send the wind howling through the house, spewing bright red embers across the paving stones. Then he was back and glaring up at the smoke-hole while the wind tossed his black hair wild.

I saw a light come into his eyes. I'd seen that light before, long, long ago, before the curse, when the master was young and handsome and still full of blind ambition. It was like before he set off with Llywelyn, the Prince of Wales, to burn the English off Welsh soil for the last blessed time.

And a shiver went through my soul for the likes of Aileen the Red.

One

Inishmaan, The Aran Islands, Ireland
The Year of Our Lord 1275

Aileen let her eyes drift closed. She skimmed her hand far above her mother's shoulder, and it was like passing her fingertips through clotted cream.

"A right fine mess you've done of this, Ma." As dense as honey, it was, Aileen thought, as she shook out her fingers. "You should have told me about this sooner."

"It's not so bad as that." Her mother flattened a knife amid a tumble of vegetables upon the table, then rolled her arm through the stiffness. "It only started hurting this morning."

"Next you'll be telling me it wasn't the seaweed-gathering that got you in such a stitch. Ah"—Aileen arched a brow as her mother opened her mouth to protest—"don't deny it. It's no use, not to me, don't you know it."

"Aileen, my firstborn." Deirdre arched the same eyebrow that her daughter was arching at her. "You'd think *you* were the mother the way you do go bossing me about. Mind you remember it was I who set to your linens as a babe."

"There you go, talking about things passed well over five-and-twenty years. No." Aileen touched her mother's hand as her mother reached for the knife again. "Leave that be for now. I'll set my hands upon you. Then we'll have no more to argue about."

Aileen slid her hand over the injury again, then drifted her opened hand closer to the skin. A pressure pushed against her palm as if she were compressing a bladder full of mead. She touched the flesh. A ringing sounded in her head. In her mind's eye she envisioned the threads of sinew drawn overlong and frayed, stretched too far beyond their capabilities all by the will of a woman who tried to do much more than her age would allow her. It felt as if she strummed her fingers over her brother Niall's lyre, and the strings gave loose beneath her hand.

Wasn't it like the proud Deirdre of Inishmaan to get herself in such a mess? Well past her fortieth year, and still after every gale Ma heaped her seaweed-basket up well over the rim, then hefted the whole on her back to drag it up the steep limestone cliffs of the island of Inishmaan. Not a bit of sense in her, and she the mother of four sons and four able daughters, all healthy enough to do the work for her.

Aileen knew there was no use in scolding. The words would fall upon her mother's ears like stones. And where Aileen's mind wandered during a healing, there was no room in her heart for a sour thought.

It's God's blessing that you have one daughter destined to remain in your house a spinster, Ma, else who would look after you when Da's not about?

She began the long, languorous stroking in earnest. A bee buzzed in through the open doorway of the hut, circled the small room with its stone walls stained a mellow brown from years of peat fires, then wound its way upon its own path until it tumbled back into the sea air. The chill of the paving stones seeped through the calfskin of her slippers. The stinging scent of onion, the crisp sweetness of new-dug turnips, and the tartness of fresh greens wafted up from the table.

Her mind drifted away to a late Sunday afternoon. Aileen had long been in the habit of perching upon the rock-pile fence while all the islanders played games in the field just beyond, if the weather allowed. Often her cat would come and nestle beside her on the stones warmed by the day's sun, and she would absently stroke the creature while it purred and arched beneath her hand. Stroking, stroking, stroking, until something tingling collected on the palm of her hand, like the crackling of dry fur shed in autumn-time. She flicked it off into the air, before returning to the stroking . . . until all felt smooth and silky-warm beneath her palm.

"Och, lass. . . ."

Aileen blinked as the world rushed in upon her: The muted roar of the waves beyond the cliffs, the shouts and laughter of some children down the road, the sting of peat-smoke and the mist of water bubbling too hot. Her mother was gazing up at her, her hand laying upon Aileen's own.

"Lass, lass," her mother repeated, patting her hand. "It's done, the pain is all gone . . . You've a fine, fair gift, Aileen. You're like to outshine the skill of your own father someday."

"Listen to a mother's pride talking."

Aileen let her hands slip off her mother's shoulder. A lot of nonsense, that was. If Aileen ever came to the point of outshining the great Conaire of Inishmaan it would be because he'd never set his mind to healing with his hands. Sure, it came to her easily by virtue of her birth into this family where faery blood flowed, but she was convinced it was something anyone could learn to do, if they set their mind to it.

But no one ever set their mind to it, didn't she know that well enough? If they did, there would never be any trouble from it at all.

A tress of hair tickled the bridge of her nose; she swiped it out of her face, then strode to the hearth where the cauldron threatened to bubble over. Poking at the fire, she shook off the last of the lethargy which always fogged her mind after a healing. "No more gathering seaweed for you this week. It will take more than a pass of my hands to set that shoulder to right."

"God gave me two shoulders; I'll carry my burden on the other."

Aileen clattered the poker into the basket by the wall. "For the wife of a doctor, a body would think you'd be a far better patient."

"Where are you going, child?"

"To fetch your other daughters." Aileen whirled a cloak around her shoulders and set to the ties, casting her mother a strange look for the high pitch of her voice. "Not a bit of sense in them. Prancing about in the sunshine, they are, with no more care than newborn calves. And here you are, with a sore shoulder and a stew to make before sunset."

"Let them race about on such a rare sunny day and leave us free of their chatter." Her mother waved to the vegetables on the table. "You and I have enough hands for this."

The wool slid off Aileen's back. Her mother set to a turnip with quick, short chops. Aye, it was more than a sore shoulder that had her mother wanting her company. Ma had had an eye upon her since she came in from the milking, and a nervous eye at that. Aileen knew that look—just the sight of it shot warmth into her cheeks. Wasn't it a ridiculous thing for a woman of her age to be flushing as if Ma had caught her kissing Sean the son of the fisher again, in the cavern just beyond the southern shore? There was no reason for this sudden embarrassed guilt: It had been a fine long time since any boy had wanted to curl into that cavern with *her,* no doubt of that. Then, she'd been a girl of thirteen years and as flat-chested and boyishly hipped as all the others upon the island; but as the years passed and the other girls ripened, she'd remained as stringy and shapeless as a bean.

"What is it now?" Aileen swung the cloak from one finger. "It's been four years since Sean the fisher's son married that girl from the mainland with the long blond hair. I've no more need of hand-holding over that."

"Four years, has it been that long? You all grow up before my eyes, like the rye in the fields. Now come, and set to those cabbages. Don't be giving me that silver-eyed look of yours, daughter. Can't a mother want a bit of peace and quiet and the company of her oldest child?"

Not when there's a fine bit of work to do on the thatching, and a whole field of seaweed drying on the grass, waiting to be spread over the northern field, and butter to be churned before the setting of the sun.

There was never knowing her mother's mind, but Aileen had an inkling. A patch of brilliant sunlight stretched over the paving stones to lick the battered wooden trestles of the table. A sea breeze gusted in through the doorway, flattening her tunic against her shins. Aileen swung her cloak back up on the peg and squinted out into the blinding blue brightness of the open sky. No ocean gale muddied the clouds, no morning mist breathed a haze between the island of Inishmaan and the purple silhouette of the Connemara hills, no sea fog hung a veil across the sight of the salt-stained sails of foreign ships anchored in Galway Bay. Their island home of Inishmaan lay naked and vulnerable and dangerously open to the curious.

Aileen stepped back into the cool shadows. So the day was fine and clear. What matter, that? She and her family were safe here on Inishmaan—safe where the good island people knew who and what they all were, and understood.

Then, as if she'd summoned it with her own thoughts, a shadow darkened the room.

"Aye, Ma," she murmured, staring at the silhouette looming in the doorway. "We've a visitor."

Unexpected visitors were no surprise at the door to this house, but as the man stepped in out of the blinding white light, Aileen froze. A tall one, he was, and draped in layers of cloth the likes of which she'd only seen upon the backs of the English invaders on the mainland. Bright in shimmering hues of yellow, like the primroses which clung to the rocks in the springtime.

"This," he began in awkward Irish, "doctor's house?"

She didn't answer, not at once. He wasn't a mainlander, for though the mainland Irish was a garbled dialect, she could understand it well enough, and this man spoke with an unfamiliar accent. An Englishman, perhaps, but they mostly kept to themselves, the English. . . . And such a finely dressed one as this would surely send a lackey to do his bidding. There were several ships anchored in Galway Bay. No telling where they came from, or who sailed upon them. And any man who asked the mainlanders for a doctor would be told to come here, to the house of Conaire of Inishmaan.

An outsider.

Her insides rumbled in unease. A gift and a curse, it was, Da's skill. It brought too much of the world to their door.

"Need . . . doctor." The stranger motioned east, in the direction of the path that led to the shore. "Man hurt. . . ."

The stew popped and splattered a sizzle of broth over the peat. A briny breeze gusted, skidding a few turnip peels across the table, and upending a basket of wool set aside for spinning. Aileen glanced at her mother, expecting her to right the tumble of wool, but her mother sat still, her fingers curled around the cutting-knife, a crease of worry deep on her brow.

Then Aileen realized that Ma stared at the stranger, as transfixed as herself, without making a move to offer the man hospitality.

"This is the doctor's house." Aileen snagged a bladder of honey-mead off the wall and pinched the last oatcake in a bit of linen. She held the offerings out to him. Above the scent of the stew meat bubbling in the pot over the fire, she smelled him, some sickly sweet perfume—exotic and unnatural.

The man glanced at the offerings, then took the bladder of mead. He made a shrugging motion with his other sleeve. Aileen looked at his arm and realized that the sleeve hung loose below the level of his wrist.

An awkward moment passed while she stared at the nub where his hand should be. The man lowered the bladder of mead long enough to grant her the slightest of forgiving smiles.

Her wretched freckled skin grew warm. Wasn't she as skittish as a goat today, suspecting him without knowing his like? He looked honest enough, clear-eyed, open-faced, with enough humor to understand and accept her moment of awkward surprise. Aileen knew she'd never lose the tightening in her gut whenever she came upon an outsider—too much had happened to her to expect that. But she fancied that she had enough sense to gauge a man's character by looking into his eyes. How much of a threat to two strong women was a one-handed man?

"My father is off tending the cows on Connemara." She slipped the crumbled oatcake onto the trestle table behind her. "He won't be back until nightfall. You say that there's a man hurt?"

The man nodded over the neck of the bladder. He swung it toward the path to the shore. "Man hurt . . . bad."

"Then you'll have to make do with the doctor's daughter."

Her mother made a strange gasping sound as Aileen reached for her cloak. The bench scraped against the paving stones. Aileen ignored her and hefted a battered bag full of herbs and linens onto the table. Aileen always took her father's charges when her father was out and about. And this stranger hadn't asked for *her*, as some of the mainlanders did with a hush in their voice and a shuffle in their gait as if she would turn them into frogs with the strike of a single glance. The stranger didn't know the Irish very well, and there was a chance he'd heard Da's name and not the whispered tales of Aileen the Red.

Moreover, there was a chance a man lay dying upon the shore while she grappled with her own suspicions.

"What's he going to think of us, Ma?" She spoke to her mother in the thick Inishmaan dialect, so the stranger could not understand. "You didn't even offer him honey-mead."

"He's an *outsider.*"

"Wasn't it you who taught me never to deny hospitality to any man who comes to this door?" Aileen rifled through the bag and counted the linens. "He's not the first outsider I've set to heal, nor will he be the last."

The man slapped the bladder upon the table and wandered

out the door to wait. Aileen lifted a small linen of herbs and sniffed it before she nodded and tucked it back into the bag.

"You'll be careful, won't you, Aileen?" Her mother leaned over and righted the basket of wool. "Your gift . . . it's fine, but powerful, child, so powerful—"

"Don't I know that well enough?" It had been a good ten years since Aileen had discovered her faery gift, long enough for her to learn how to hide it well. And long enough to know that if she allowed herself to live always in a state of terror among outsiders, she'd only make herself as mad as old Widdy Peggeen who lived upon the cliffs and danced naked in the surf every sunrise. "I'm not like little Dairine, don't you know, foolish enough to teeter on the edge of cliffs."

"Och, don't I know it, no child more practical than you ever came from my womb. I'm full of foolishness today. Your Da has been away on Connemara for too long. Still, you'll be forty summers, lass, before I'll stop worrying about you. That's the burden and the joy of being a mother. You'll know it some-day."

Aileen dug her fingernails into the strap of her bag of herbs as she hefted it upon her shoulder. "Still hunting for grand-children, eh?" She tugged another bladder of mead off the wall so her mother would not see her face. "Look to your other daughters. I'll have no man bossing me about and telling me what to do. I'll live me own life, thank you very much."

"Life does not always take the path we've chosen, Aileen."

"Have you been drinking too much of the new honey-mead? You're sounding as maudlin as old Seamus in his cups." She tucked the bladder into her bag. "Why should my life be any different? I want it to be so; it shall be so."

"Och, wouldn't it be nice if the world turned upon a girl's whim. What a simple place the world would be, then." Her mother glanced out to the wide expanse of the island, and beyond to the sea, lost for a moment in the horizon beyond the stranger's shoulders. "But there are greater powers, Aileen, with wills of their own, and there's no telling how they'll weave the path of your life."

That set Aileen to stopping and staring. Ma's faery-gift was the Second Sight—it showed in the swirling green gaze her mother always hid from outsiders. It had always been an uncertain magic, its secrets not revealed for the asking. Now Aileen wondered if Ma had had a vision. But when Ma turned her swirling green eyes upon her, she did it with the softest of smiles.

"Och, don't go listening too deeply to me, Aileen, I'm all about today. Go." She kissed her daughter's cheek and nudged her toward the portal. "There's someone down there in need of your healing."

"I'll be back in time to help you with the spinning."

Aileen shook her head at the foolishness of it all. Ma was in a fix today, no doubt about it, as full of teary sentiment as a woman that had just given birth. Aileen shrugged it off and set off to follow the stranger's sure and long-legged pace.

It was thatching-time upon the island, and long ropes of braided hay stretched golden across the fields. Below the sheer cliffs, Galway Bay licked the ledges of rock with tongues of froth, siphoning up thinning whorls of sea mist. The milky vapor hugged the shore in a sheer white brightness. It was indeed a fair, fine day, she thought, looking about her at the rare sight of the sharp horizon, and at the bed of mist clinging to the shore below. She'd long convinced herself that the Heaven in the clouds the priest spoke of must be very like Inishmaan on the morning after a gale.

Aileen filled her lungs with the clean salt-spray as she descended the steep cliffside. On one part of the path she caught sight of a crescent mark dug into the mud. The faeries had been here this day, she thought, playing ball amid the rocks. When she returned home, she'd tell Dairine about this, and wind a fine yarn of a story around it, to get her wild youngest sister to settle before going to bed this evening.

The coarse sand sank beneath her *pampooties* as they finally reached the shore. Through the shifting sheets of mist, she caught sight of a single boat dragged up close to the cliff face, and a man pacing beside it.

Her steps faltered. A big man, this, as big as the one who had fetched her from her home. He seemed larger, though, with the sea wind slapping his cloak away from his body as if he felt no cold and the pale mists swirling around him as if he were some kind of Otherworldly visitor stepping out from between the veils. He ceased his pacing as he glimpsed them through the mist, then stormed toward them with all the force of a charging bull. It was then that she saw the mask, a leather mask tanned night-black and gleaming with sea-spray, slashing across half of his face, from forehead to jaw, making him look all the more like some inhuman thing.

Her throat closed in the grip of an uncertain fear.

Her guide gave way to the man, who stopped several paces before her, enough for only a breath of mist to pass between them. Sharp eyes the color of blue winter ice scoured her form, one from the shadows of the mask. She stilled the sudden urge to reach up and tuck a wayward sprig of her red hair back into the braid which snagged down her back. It would do no good; her hair never stayed in its bounds, even in the calmest of weather, and now the sea-breeze tugged it wild about her face. Still, he glared, a harsh, lingering look that made her feel as if he burned the clothes from her body and found her lacking.

And what was this? Aye, so she was no beauty, and aye, she didn't look like much of a doctor. She tilted her chin and returned the look in kind. She was well used to not being accepted for what she really was.

And *he*—he was a warrior. There was no doubt about it. She'd recognized the sure gait and the arrogant cast of his broad shoulders before she'd even noticed the beaten bronze scabbard of the sword hanging from his belt. The mask, too, spoke of a warrior's vanity. She'd seen his kind paint themselves up with blue woad and fancy themselves with chain mail and embroidery before they went off to do their killing. A battle he'd waged, no doubt, and killed enough innocents to satisfy his blood-lust for the morning. Now he brought a wounded man here, one of his own, hoping to patch him together so he could fight another useless fight on another bloody day.

She wondered why she was mustering so much hate for a man who had not yet said a single word.

"You are Aileen the Red."

It was a statement, not a question, and he spoke the Irish as purely as any mainlander. A shiver shook her spine, but she stifled the chill. Aye, those rumblings of distrust had been right. So he knew her name, and by the look in his eye, he knew the story behind it. She mustered the full of her bile,

"Aye, and what of it?" She jerked her chin toward the one-handed man. "He asked for a doctor. My father couldn't be here. You'll have to settle for me."

"You are the great healer." His lips curled in bitter scorn. "You, a bit of a girl."

That gaze scoured her again, from head to toe, and she cursed the wind which chose that moment to shift direction and flatten her woolen tunic against her body, leaving little to a man's imagination—and a man needed an imagination to see any curves in her, to see anything but bones with a bit of flesh clinging to them.

"It's clear enough you are not the wounded man." She yanked her cloak around her figure. "You've got too much air in you to be wasted on talking."

"You wouldn't have the stomach to pluck a bird for dinner."

"But it's not dinner I'm making here, is it?" She peered around him and saw no one else. She set her gaze upon the boat pulled up on the shore, thinking the wounded man must be inside. "I'll see to your man well enough, for it's either me or no one."

Then I'll see you off this island. We don't welcome killers on Inishmaan. She brushed by him, and it was like brushing by a ridge of limestone. She stilled the urge to massage her own bruised shoulder—she'd not give him the satisfaction. She would do her healing, masking the true nature of it as she always did, then she would return to the warmth of her mother's house, and curse this man and his ilk for their arrogance and their scorn.

The boat was cocked away from her so she could not see the inside until she seized the rim and peered over. Her pack slid off her shoulder, snagging the collar of her tunic. She clutched it to her arm until her knuckles turned white. Nothing but coils of hemp lingered in the belly of the boat.

A wave crashed upon the rocks near the edge of the cove, vaulting sea-spray over the sand.

She swiveled her heel into the muck. Her one-handed guide was staring at his master with an odd look in his eye. He muttered something in a garbled tongue—a strange language, like Irish but spoken as if through a mouthful of water. The warrior ignored him and kept his gaze fixed with piercing intensity upon her. His hands curled into fists at his sides.

Fear froze her feet to the sand. A thousand stories flooded her mind of pirates who seized women from the shores of Connemara, women who were never seen again. She'd heard the tales a hundred thousand times in her youth, and as she grew she scoffed at them as stories meant to keep young ones abed. Even as terror seeped cold into her blood she scolded herself for her foolishness. What would a pirate have with *her*, with all her thin and awkward height, her plain face, her tern's-nest of hair. Perhaps that was why this warrior stood so silent before her, brooding and fierce, eyeing her figure and wondering if he could find a price in some exotic port for such a shapeless, freckled bone of a woman.

What a joke it would be upon Aileen the Red, she thought with cold shame, to be cast back by the pirates in disdain like a rabbit too thin to be worth the work of slaughtering.

Pride rose in her, and she welcomed it to stem the thick seepage of fear. "The tide is coming. Are you to lead me to your wounded, or are we to stand here until this sand is beneath the sea?"

The guide said something again, but the warrior shook his head once. Then he came to her, his boots sure in the sand, his black hair rising above his shoulders by the force of the sea breeze and floating around a face that could have been carved from the stone of Inishmaan.

The scent of him filled her lungs: Leather. Heat. The rim of the boat dug into her thighs. Such eyes as his had never known the meaning of pity.

He reached behind her to heft up a roll of hemp, then seized her in a grip of steel.

"It's you or no one, Aileen the Red. So be it." The first coil of rope scraped her neck. "Say goodbye to Inishmaan."

Two

Aileen clenched her fist into the matted fur of the donkey as the beast swayed his way through a breach in the jagged mountain terrain. She'd been riding for half a day, since they'd set anchor off the shore of this strange land, and her stomach gurgled and dipped as if she were still locked in that dark hold while storms battered the ship like a simple *curragh*. For the hundredth time, she swallowed bile and set her sights on the men ahead of her, on the winding upward path, the trail of the pale white spot of sun across the leaden sky . . . on the world she'd been forcefully taken to, for reasons she still did not know.

In all her life, she'd never ventured farther than a few settlements along the mainland of Connemara. In all her life she'd never been away from the white-frothed blueness and the roar of the sea. Here, silence deafened her; a silence punctuated with the screech of unfamiliar birds, the rattle of wind amid the dry-leafed treetops, the echoing scrape of hooves on stone. Her head pounded with the teeth-jarring noises, with unanswered questions. And it pounded, too, with the cloying, musky scent of the wooden thickets which flourished in the crook of the valleys—a heavy perfume which choked her and made her ache with longing for the clean fragrance of salt-sea—

No. She yanked her woolen cloak away from her nose. *A good washing, this cloak needs.* Forcefully, she breathed out the last scent of salt clinging to the woolen fibers. A perilous path that, more perilous than these narrow ledges of crumbling rock. If she thought about the brisk Atlantic mists, if she thought about little Dairine waiting for a bedtime story while the peat fire crackled down to embers, she'd soon be hurling herself off the donkey into the froth of the river that scoured the valley below.

Aye, and she had more important things to do than wallow in her own fears. She had to remember every roaring cataract, every gurgling river, the pattern of the craggy horizon—for when she escaped this place, for when she returned home. Never mind that the jagged peaks loomed over her like stone palisades, and never mind that for all her skill, the ocean was a moat she couldn't swim. Never mind that in all her life, she'd never been lost or alone in a strange land, among outsiders who gave her long, measuring glances when they thought she wasn't looking.

I will survive this.

She chanted the words in her mind all through the afternoon. When she thought the air couldn't get any thinner in her lungs, when she thought the donkey couldn't get any harder beneath her seat, when the sun had set, casting the hills in shades of purple . . . then she glimpsed a black silhouette of a dwelling looming over the height of a crag, like a crooked crown perched to slip to destruction on the rocks below.

By the time they plodded, single-file, through the open gates of the wooden palisades, her exhaustion blocked out all but the hot crackle of pine torches, a vague sense of a throng of people, and the pungent stench of sweaty beasts still heaving in exertion from the climb. She slid off the donkey and jarred her heels against the paving stones, then stumbled after a man who beckoned her toward a small wattled hut nestled against the palisades.

The room reeked of fresh-cut rye. Her guard muttered something in his garbled tongue, clattered a tallow candle upon a cask, and shoved the door closed behind him. Pushing a rat's nest of hair off her forehead, she collapsed onto a bulging sack.

She woke to the crack of a door being kicked open. She tumbled off the sack of grain and slid into the rushes. She squinted at the silhouette looming in the portal.

Torchlight flooded around him and gleamed on the smooth leather of his mask. His tunic billowed unevenly from a studded leather belt, and the open neckline sagged as if he'd been tugging on it. The rolled leather of one boot sagged low on his shin, while the other cuff jutted out in a point. He choked the neck of a bladder in one hand.

"Comfortable, little captive?"

She blinked and struggled up to her elbows. No daylight filtered through the wattled walls. The tallow candle the guard had left her had long sputtered out, and streams of fat congealed along the wooden lathes of the cask. She wondered how long she'd been asleep, how long he'd been drinking.

"Welcome to Cymru. You'll know it as Wales." Liquid splattered on the ground as he swayed in an unsteady bow. "I see you find the accommodations to your liking."

She suddenly became aware of the bunching of her tunic around her knees, the raw imprint of sackcloth upon her cheek, the bits of straw knitted into her hair. She snapped her tunic over her ankles and struggled to rise.

"If there's anything else you need, my lady, to make your stay pleasant." He swung the bladder toward her as he swaggered in another step. "Some ale, mayhap, to quench your thirst after the long journey—"

"Don't you be mocking me."

"You mistake me."

She couldn't make out his features with the light pouring in from behind him, but there was no mistaking the scornful mockery in his voice.

"I'm showing you," he said, "some fine Welsh hospitality."

"The curse of the crows on you! If this is Welsh hospitality, I've no mind to see how you treat your enemies." She looked down her nose at the bladder swinging in his hand. "I see you've finally found the courage to face me."

He lifted the bladder to his lips. His throat flexed with each gulp, and when he was done he wiped his mouth with his forearm and held the bladder out to her. "In need of some courage yourself, Irish?"

"Not from the likes of *you.*" She pushed her hair out of her eyes. Bits of hay rained over her shoulder. "Not with the likes of a man who would rip a woman from the bosom of her family, and drag her across—"

"Good." He slammed the bladder on a cask. "It'll make the task easier if you're not trembling in fear."

He stumbled outside and seized something off the wall of the hut, then thrust a torch of flaming rushes before him as he returned, filling the room with harsh red light. An autumn wind dense with the scent of wood-fires whistled through the hut, buffeting the torch as he made his way unsteadily toward her.

She stumbled back against the jumble of casks which lined the far wall of the hut. His night-black hair hung wild, and locks of it lurched up from the ties that held his leather mask tight against the right side of his face, the same ties which dug angry red imprints across his forehead and neck. A sheen of moisture gleamed on his skin, stubbled from days without a razor's touch. He stopped close enough for her to feel the heat of the torche against her face, close enough for her to smell the scent of ale on his breath.

Show no fear. Aye, a thing easier said than done, with him breathing down on her, with that great big body of his looming over her close enough to blast her with its heat. Surely he could hear her heart pounding—surely like any wild thing he could smell the fear in her. Da had once told her that a man was most dangerous when he was in his cups, and now she knew why, truth be told, for there was a wildness in his eyes of so clear and so icy a blue, a terrifying savage light that spoke of a man with one foot in the air and the other on the edge of darkness.

That stretch of black leather stitched to fit the slash of his cheekbone wasn't a bit of help. A notch cut upward next to his mouth, casting the mask with a mocking sort of smile. One eye blazed bright; the other burned, hooded in shadows. A face half in darkness, half in light—and frozen to the bone.

"Who are you?" The words rushed out on a breath, too husky. She straightened against a cask and mustered more spit and venom. "A curse on your seed for generations. What do you want with me?"

She wondered if he was going to speak at all, or just stand there with the red glow of the rushes between them, all height and breadth of shoulders, breathing over her like to suck the air from the room. His gaze did all but burn away her clothes. Aye, so she was no beauty. A lifetime of being compared to her golden-haired mother and green-eyed sister had resigned her to that. There were other, more useful talents to thank God for. She was agile upon the cliffs, she could find more bird's eggs than any other woman on Inishmaan, she was strong, hard-working—these things were beauty to the people of Inishmaan, far more practical than a simpering pout or a fair tress. Even knowing this, she hated him for staring at her with such hot eyes, making her aware of every flat bony plane, every wiry muscle of her thin body, every itchy streak of dirt on her unwashed skin—when she wanted in her heart nothing more than to tear at this man with all the wit the boys of Inishmaan feared.

She grasped that indignant hatred as a sword against the fear.

"I am Rhys ap Gruffydd." He tossed the torch into his other hand. Drippings of hot tallow seared red across his wrist, a pain he didn't acknowledge. "I am the Lord of Graig, of all the land you passed through today. And you, Irish, are quick-witted enough to know why I've brought you here."

"In that you'll be wrong, *'Rees ap Griffith.'* " She curled her fingers around the rim of a cask behind her as her lips stumbled over the unfamiliar name. "For weeks I crouched in that stinking hold thinking you've gone to a fine bit of trouble for another slave for your fields."

"There is only one thing a man would want with you, and it's not for the plow."

She sucked in what she could of the thinning air. Sparks flooded her body at the gravelly sound of his voice, at the inference of his words. But no sooner had her blood risen—a strange and unfamiliar sensation—than a coldness washed over her and extinguished the pinpricks of heat. It couldn't be that. She scorned herself for entertaining the thought, even for a mite of a moment, that a man would want her as a man wants a woman.

"I've no ale in me to be knowing the ways of a stranger's mind. And I'm not vain enough to think it's my fair tresses and lovely figure that caught your fancy." The metallic rim of the cask sucked the warmth from her palms. She released it and sidestepped the bulk of him, away from the choking smoke of the torch. She thanked the red glow of light that masked the rising color of her cheeks, for at the mention of her figure his gaze roamed again, snagged on the rents in her surcoat, then lingered for a moment on the ratty bird's-nest of her hastily braided hair. "What else is there, then? I know you couldn't have captured me for ransom, unless you'll be wanting your ransom in mackerel."

"Your husband can keep his fish."

"I've no husband."

"Good." The features hardened. "One less man to seek vengeance upon me."

A rumble infiltrated his voice. It was no surprise to her that he had enemies. The chieftains of Ireland made a habit of stealing each other's cattle and torching each other's settlements and carrying off each other's women, then spent the lives of generations fighting each other over the resulting blood-grudges. Warriors were warriors, whatever their blood. "A man who makes a habit of stealing women shouldn't balk at facing their menfolk."

"You're the first, Irish." He swung one foot upon the rim of a cask and leaned into it. "Not the blackest of my sins, but the newest."

"You'll forgive me if I take no pride in that."

"Forget escape. This homestead is well guarded. Beyond this place are mountains which disguise their passes, forests filled with wolves, and not a single hospitable face for miles—for all the land belongs to me and the loyalty of the people upon it, as well. Were you somehow to make it to the sea, you'd have to bargain with the foulest Welsh pirates who scour the coasts for passage back to your island."

"Here I was after thinking you were the foulest of the pirates."

"I am." He laughed, a laugh that set the hairs on the back of her neck to standing, for it held no humor or warmth, but trickled down as cold as melting ice. "Remember that, while you conjure ways to escape."

"And *you* remember," she warned, "that I've a father and four strong brothers who'll seek me to the ends of the earth."

"Rich enough to hire a ship, no doubt. And full of knowledge as to where you are."

She tilted her chin. Her family was the richest upon Inishmaan, but rich in cattle and cheese, not by this man's measure. And truth be known, many a soul had disappeared off the shores of Inishmaan, stolen away by the caprices of the surf. Her people accepted such events as God's will and rarely searched beyond the ledges of rock which jut out into the sea. "You don't know the likes of my family."

"I found out all I needed to know about them before I sought you out."

"Sought me out?" She feigned surprise in the arch of her brows. "Should I be flattered, Rhys ap Gruffydd, that you sought me out in particular—*me*, Aileen the Red?"

"You've a reputation."

"Do I now?" A tremor of fear shook her bones. Didn't she know it was coming? Hadn't she spent ten years preparing for a moment like this? "I thought the tales of my messings with Sean the fisher's son never left his lips."

His voice rumbled with a growing impatience. "A reputation as a healer."

"Aye, well, it's no secret that I'm a healer." She shrugged one shoulder, still numb from where she'd slept upon it. "Learned it at my Da's knee, I did." She blinked at him, hoping she appeared to be glowing with a growing surprise, wondering all the while if she had the talent to fake her emotions like the bawdy itinerant acting troupes who occasionally wandered to the mainland fairs despite the priest's grumbling, and feeling as false and unnatural as little Dairine trying to tell a lie. "You're not telling me . . ." She shook her head in mocking disbelief. "You're not after telling me you stole me and dragged me clear across the world because you've need of a *healer?"*

The rushes crackled beneath his feet as he thumped off the cask. Two long strides and he'd crossed the room to thrust the butt of the torch in a sconce by the door. Aye, but she had some skill, to send him reeling away like this, and they had not yet gotten to the heart of the matter.

She clasped her hands together and let her voice drop to a whisper. "Is it plague, then?"

"No plague."

"A pestilence of some sort? Among the cattle—"

"No."

"A wasting sickness."

"No."

"Well, what is it, then? Aren't there any healers upon your own soil?"

"We've run through the witches of Wales." He seized the bladder of mead, leaned back against a cask, and fixed his eyes upon her. "I fancy an Irish one. With a witch's healing hands."

Outside the hut, a dog howled. The rushlight snapped and

sparked. She stepped back and her foot sank into the softness
of a sack of grain.

Once, she'd been collecting periwinkles along the slates of
rock which jagged out deep into the Atlantic from the shores
of Inishmaan, and a gale had rushed in on the wind so suddenly that she'd had no time to smell it. One moment, she'd
been prying a shell from the underside of a rock with the tip
of her knife, and the next the sea engulfed her hands in icy
sprays of froth, and the surf roared in and pounded against the
stone at her feet. A fog fell all around her so she knew not
which way the island stood, but only that she was lost in this
roaring world of stinging spray.

An expression, she told herself, even as her blood froze. It's
just a turn of phrase, meaning nothing.

All of a sudden she was fourteen again, standing in a Galway inn and staring at the blood on her trembling hands.

Da . . . Da . . .

*It's over, Aileen, a stoírín, her father had said. And no harm
done. We're away from the crowds now.*

*She couldn't stop trembling. She couldn't stop staring at the
blood on her fingers, the blood of the young boy who had
been kicked by an Englishman's horse at the fair. It had all
happened in a matter of moments. She'd seen the boy get
knocked aside, and she'd run to his side. Da had been teaching
her his medicine and she'd thought to help. It had seemed the
most natural thing in the world to hold the limp boy to her
chest, rock him, and run her fingers over the wound on his
head. . . . Da will heal him, she'd told the screaming mother
as she'd rocked him and stroked the wound. He'll heal him. . . .*

And then the boy had come to life in her arms.

"Your fame has traveled far, Irish."

She glanced up to meet sharp eyes of wild blue—bright
with expectation. She hadn't even heard him cross the room.
Tales had spread since that afternoon, wild tales of miraculous
healing powers, ugly tales of sorcery and devilry, but no one
suspected the truth: No one knew where her true power lay.

A bad bit o' luck, Aileen my girl, to be discovering your faery gift in the midst of a place running thick with outsiders.

It was my hands, she'd whispered, staring at them as if they belonged to another. I felt something. . . .

It's the gift of the healing hands, you have. Da closed his hands over hers and pressed them into her lap. But for the sake of your life, no one must ever know.

Those fierce blue eyes gleamed now with a growing triumph. She had hesitated too long. From some deep well inside her, she coaxed a laugh, a brittle, metallic sound as full of scorn as she could muster.

"Is that, in truth, what made you seek me out?" Though it sucked the strength from her bones, she forced herself to meet that fierce gaze. "Tales of my 'witchery'?"

The rushes crushed beneath his boots as he took one step closer. "Deny it."

"That I'm a witch, aye, I deny that well enough. Oh, I won't stand here and deny that I haven't heard the whispers about me." She hiked her fists on her hips, praying her knees of butter would hold. "Was it young Ternoc who told you stories? He always did have a bit of gall in his belly for that day I sent him sprawling into the sea. Or did you find a mainlander to give you an earful in an alehouse on a Sunday?"

He lifted the bladder to his lips. His eyes glittered over the neck, and she knew she'd drawn blood.

"By God, you've been listening to one too many drunken Irishman's tales. The Irish are full of tales, didn't you know? And what kind of man are you to listen to idle gossip—faith, let it send you clear across the world?" Her voice sounded shrill, even to her own ears. "Is there no more sense amid the learned folk, than there is amid the drunkards of Connemara?"

"Sense enough," he said, "to know you'd deny the accusation."

"Are you carrying a branch of the ash tree with you, Rhys ap Gruffydd, to guard against my sorcery, then? Have you nailed a horseshoe over the door?"

He turned his back to her. The bladder of ale slapped against his thigh.

"And what would you be wanting from a witch, as you would have me be?" She scoured his form with her gaze, noting the buttery leather of his boots, the fine weave of his tunic, the metal studs upon his leather belt, the woolen hose encasing the thighs of a man used to climbing mountains. "You've no need of riches, I see that well enough. Is it power over your enemies, then?"

He glared at her over his shoulder with a warning in his eyes, a warning she was in no mind to notice, a warning she *couldn't* heed, for words were her only weapons—and a sort of recklessness had seized her.

"Nay, I think not." She waved her hand up and down the length of his tall form. His hand curled into a fist by his side. "A fine warrior like you wouldn't call a woman to defeat his enemies, nay. Too much arrogance for that. Too much pride in your skill with that bloody sword of yours. You'd sooner see yourself dead on the field of battle, I wager."

"There are ways, Irish, to know the truth."

"Aye, and there's no doubt I'll tell you anything you want to hear when I've twenty stones weighing down on my chest."

He'd retreated into the shadows beyond the circle of light. Now she stepped toward him. She would mock him, aye, she'd mock him until his pride wouldn't allow him to keep her here—until his pride made him deny he'd ever thought such a foolish thing as witchery from her. Whatever tools she could use, she would use, for the sake of her life.

For it *was* her life she fought for in this tiny hut in this strange land. An outsider couldn't understand the truth of her gift. Outsiders would accuse her of devilry, kill her in fear, burn her, send her soul to Hell. She'd seen enough burnings in her youth at the annual *feis,* young women put to the torch for the sake of a neighbor's milk not churning into butter.

"If it's not riches or power, then what is it?" She tapped

her finger against her cheek, then straightened it into the air. "Ah, I know. I should have thought of it sooner. Men who hold the world in the palm of their hands often crave the one thing they cannot take by force—the love of a woman."

The bladder slammed with a splatter of liquid against the planks of the door. She froze as he footed a sack of rye out of his path with an animalistic grunt, then crossed the room in a few short strides. She'd gone too far. She waited for the *thwack* of his hand against her face. She waited for stars to explode in her head. As she closed her eyes and turned her face away she felt nothing but the heat of his breath upon her face.

He pinched her chin in his fingers and forced her to face him. Moments passed, marked by the heaving of his breath. She winced open an eye and dared to stare up at the dragon. His gaze scanned her fiercely enough to burn holes in her skin, and for a moment he looked like a man restrained by the last frayed thread of his tether. Murder burned in those eyes without spirit, as sharp a blue as the open summer sky—a summer sky without a sun.

Then, as she stared, transfixed, his features shifted. The blood-lust seeped from his eyes. The tight muscles around his lips eased by force of will. That sculpted mouth twisted up in a cruel and bitter smile. While her heart throbbed in her throat she found herself thinking that this was a far better mask than the leather one that covered half his face.

"Sharp little teeth you have, lapdog." He tugged her chin. "And I went to Inishmaan thinking you'd have none at all."

Fear froze her tongue in her mouth, fear and the surprise of her sudden reprieve . . . and something else. She felt like a lapdog now, lying upon her back with a wolf's teeth grazing her throat. She felt the blast of his presence through the thick fibers of her woolen tunic, but it was more than his body's heat that enveloped her, it was the intensity of his presence, the very essence of his character, the thinly reined danger of him choking her so palpably that she struggled for breath, struggled to think, while her knees softened like tallow in the hot summer sun.

"You should have been old, gray-haired, warted—that's what I expected when I landed on Inishmaan. There's no changing that now." He released her chin and stepped back. "A thousand pieces of silver. That'll be your reward for doing my bidding. Think on that this night."

"My family needs no money."

The words tumbled out without thought, a reflexive spurt of defiance. Immediately after she thought of all the things such an enormous sum could buy: a willow-harp for her brother Niall, to replace the battered one he played every night; fine clothes and a position in a good Irish house for her sister Cairenn who dreamed always of leaving Inishmaan; enough cattle and grazing ground to keep the family in meat and milk for a lifetime. A new bull to replace the aging one. Still, truth be told, they had all they needed upon the island. What more does a woman need but enough fish to keep her belly full and a warm summer day a few times a year?

And what, truly, was the price of her immortal soul?

"You won't see your island again, Irish, until you give me what I want."

She raised her voice as he headed for the door. "I make no deals with the devil."

"That," he murmured, swinging open the door, "would be very disappointing."

Three

Rhys rolled his fingers around the wooden shaft, then hefted the javelin up to balance it just above his shoulder. Spears angled the straightway between him and the target swaying in the distance. He bent his knees, gauged the force and direction of the wind by the way the scrubby grass flattened at his feet, and then peered down the shaved wood to the enemy.

With a grunt, he heaved the javelin, then straightened to watch the spear whistle through the air. The spear sank deep into the ground and splattered the target with clods of earth.

"Try throwing a few paces closer, brother."

A horse's harness jangled behind Rhys as Dafydd rode across the open tumulus. Rhys crouched down on his haunches to rub his palms full of gritty mud, stanching his anger at the unwelcome, uninvited company. His fool older brother was growing patient with the years. This time, it took a full day before his curiosity overwhelmed his common sense.

The mud oozed cold between Rhys's palms. "One learns nothing from an easy target."

"What are you learning here?" Dafydd slid off the horse and yanked the back of his shimmering blue silk tunic down from the beast's bare back. "We'd never fight the English on so much open land. Better to find a way for a javelin to twist past a tree, or—"

"Show me that trick," Rhys said, rising to hand a javelin to his brother, "and you sit by the fire this night."

Dafydd closed his hand over the spear. The light of challenge brightened his hazel eyes, but then he scanned the bare tumulus, with its even circle of lurching, lichen-covered stones. A wind slapped open the embroidered hem of his woolen mantle and rifled the tails of his well-trimmed mustache.

"I won't do it here. It's a wonder King Arthur doesn't rise from this grave of his and fight you for daring to disturb his slumber."

"This is a mound of earth, nothing more, nothing less. If I care to practice upon it and old King Arthur disapproves I urge him to come and give me a good sparring." Rhys's gaze fell upon the sword he'd abandoned on a nearby rock, along with all his clothing but for the *braies* now splattered with mud and sagging from the rope belt around his hips. "Practice with me, one-on-one. Your sword hasn't seen a dent—"

"Go back to your spears." Dafydd sank the point of the spear into the earth and grimaced at the grit on his fingers. "I've no stomach to strip down to my *braies* in this cold and practice swordplay on the grave of a legend."

"Get yourself a Christian bedmate, Dafydd. You've been spending too much time between the legs of that milkmaid, listening to her drivel."

"Easy, brother, else the devil will rise from hell to challenge you."

"If he had the courage to face me, I'd welcome him."

"What about a witch?"

Rhys slung his sword across the rock and tossed his brother a glare that would wither most men. Dafydd's eyebrows—well oiled this day—only arched a little more.

Rhys set off across the field, with Dafydd falling easily into step beside him. He clenched his jaw. Dafydd was his second in command, his older brother, and he owed the man too much to easily crack his hot temper upon his head. But why now, why *now* did he choose to interrupt? Dafydd knew better than to come between Rhys and his demons.

"This one has lost its point." Dafydd frowned at the bare

end of a javelin he'd yanked out of the ground. "Must speak to that blacksmith about the fitting. That's not the first time—"

"Out with it."

Rhys clattered a spear on his shoulder and strode still farther; a wind chilled the sweat which streaked his chest.

"Out with what? The arrow is already gone, buried somewhere beneath the dirt."

"I would have been back to the homestead for dinner, but you ride out here to confront me only hours before." Rhys yanked a spear buried halfway in the earth, dislodging a stone the size of a hen. "Have more cattle been stolen from the southern border? Or have they attacked from the English side this time, hoping to draw me into conflict with the Marcher Lords?"

"Actually, it's been quite an uneventful day."

"Good."

"It's your own household you must see to."

"You are the keeper of my household." Rhys seized the last spear and clattered it on his shoulder with the others. "Spare me the reports of cows which have stopped giving milk, or fires which refuse to be lit, or oatcakes burning in a cold pan—"

"Come to think of it, there was an odd fire in the stables this morning."

"Then carry a twig of mountain ash." He shrugged the weight upon his shoulders. "Or hang a horseshoe above your door."

An acrid taste burst in his mouth. His ears stung with a sudden heat.

"Too much burnt crust in the oatcakes this morning, Rhys?"

They reached the other end of the field. Rhys speared a javelin halfway up the shaft into the earth. "She's a harridan."

"She refused to heal you?" Dafydd reared back in mock surprise. "How ungrateful of the wench. After all you've done for her."

"I must have been crazed," Rhys said, "to let you talk me into going to Ireland."

"Only a fool would scorn the words of a man of *Annwn.*"

"He was a demon sent from hell." Rhys sank another spear into the ground. "And we've brought back his demon seed."

To mock me more.

"You'd best hope she isn't a witch, else with the way you've been treating her you'll find yourself croaking in the mud and eating flies." Dafydd leaned in close enough for Rhys to smell the orange-oil he used to dress his hair. "And remember: It was *your* idea to kidnap her and drag her here. Yours alone."

Rhys shrugged the rest of the spears off his shoulder and let them clatter to the ground. Sweeping one up, he whirled to heft the shaft upon his shoulder and squint down at the target, seeing nothing but the blood-red haze of his own foolish impetuosity.

He should have just done exactly what he'd gone to Inishmaan to do. He should have tossed a bag of gold at the witch's feet in exchange for her devil's sorcery. He should have bared his face upon that shore with only Dafydd and the witch as witnesses to the humiliation. All the roads to Hell were paved with such good intentions.

For he had known he couldn't do it, the moment he'd seen her striding through the mists, with the sea wind buffeting that wild hair. He had known the moment he'd glimpsed her gliding toward him as if she'd slipped between the veils that the peasants believed separated this world from *Annwn.* One look at her, with her hair blazing red and flying across a face so white, and her eyes the color of the Welsh winter sky, and all he could think was that such were the magical colors of the Otherworld. Surely *Cwn Annwn,* the hellhounds of that world, could not stare at him so levelly and so full of loathing—as if she knew already what he was, all that he had done.

For a flash of a moment, he had been of a mind to step back into that boat and leave that wretched witch's island in the fog without a word. But his feet stuck in the mud. In all the years of pilgrimages, at all the saint's shrines, in the stinking huts of women-charlatans, and under the bleeding-knives of too many physicians, he'd never once felt his throat so gripped by the presence of the unworldly.

What difference would one more sin weigh upon his soul?

"You always were overburdened with conscience." Rhys sighted down the level field to the target swaying in the wind. He envisioned that stuffed linen with a wild mane of hair the color of a Welsh summer sunset, with stormy gray eyes and a mouth full of venom. That was a witch, indeed, who could strike so close to the heart of the problem without even knowing its name.

Rhys heaved the spear back and lurched it toward the target. The lance sank into the earth wide of the mark. "I won't take the witch off bread and water."

"At least stop calling her a witch," Dafydd said, ignoring as usual what he didn't want to hear. "At least not aloud, in Welsh. The bondswomen would have her burnt to a crisp before Sunday if they thought you harbored a witch under your roof."

"Who else but a witch would a demon send me across the seas to fetch?"

"No one but us knows about our Midsummer's Night visitor. Marged has been uncharacteristically silent." Dafydd twisted one end of his mustache between two fingers. "I've spread the truth instead: Aileen the Red is a healer."

Rhys kicked aside a javelin, then bundled a fistful of his brother's silk tunic in his hand.

Is that what you told them? That their lord's own vanity drove him to this, that their lord's own pride had marked another sin upon his soul?

"The *llys* hasn't had a woman-healer since old Gwenffrewi died three years ago." Dafydd's hazel gaze glittered over Rhys's knuckles. "You've brought one back to us. Better than thinking their great lord makes a habit of stealing women from their homes."

Or has gotten so desperate for a healing that he'll heed the mutterings of demons.

If he were another man, oh, another man, he'd have beaten the words out of Dafydd's mouth. As it was he had to bite his fingernails into his palm so hard as to draw blood through the calluses and dirt so as not to knock Dafydd onto the muddy ground in all his silks and all his oils. But there was no vengeance in beating a one-handed man to the ground; there was no satisfaction in beating a man who spoke only the truth.

What a fool he was. Rhys would laugh at himself if it weren't so pitiful, he'd mock himself if there weren't already so many others to mock him—if the whole world weren't already laughing into their beards.

And leave it to this brother of his to smooth over the havoc he'd wreaked. Rhys owed him another debt now, another of many collected these past five years. With that thought in his mind he thrust his brother away.

"The bondsmen are wondering," Dafydd added, as he smoothed the wrinkles in his tunic, "why you're treating her so badly."

Rhys's sword flashed as he scraped it off the rock. "Think of some lie. You're good at that."

"There are other ways to bring a woman around."

You would know them, wouldn't you, my brother? You with your bright silks and easy smile, you with a list of conquests so long as to rival that of the Prince of Wales's best bull, in spite of that handless arm—perhaps because of it.

"You think," Rhys began, thumbing the edge of his sword, "that whatever tricks you use on the vipers of Llywelyn's court will melt that witch's heart?"

A few drops of rain splattered in the mud around them. "I think you might try a gentler persuasion."

Gentleness? He remembered the word, vaguely, a sense of soft woolen blankets on a mother's bed. It was as distant as the scent of summer, long shriveled and blown away.

"Some good food, a bath, a soft place to sleep," Dafydd continued, "they can work wonders on a woman's disposition."

There would be no making a kitten of this lioness, Rhys knew that, for he'd felt the tear of her claws. She knew nothing at all, yet with one look into those mocking, scornful gray eyes, he sensed she knew everything.

Rhys clasped the hilt of the sword in both hands. "I don't give a damn what you do to her."

"Yes, you do," Dafydd said, snapping his cloak around as he headed back to his horse. "You, my brother, just don't want to hope."

"By all the blessed saints, look at that hair!"

Cold air blasted into the hut as the door swung open. Aileen plunged deep into the bathtub, surging a wave of steaming water over the wooden edge. A tiny figure of a woman strode into the room.

"They warned me in the kitchens that you have hair brighter than a pelt of a fox, but I wasn't after believing them, I tell you, those girls talk until their teeth fall out, they do." The woman bustled in as the door slammed shut behind her. "It's sure I'll be sending someone else to see to your needs when the sun rises, my lady, no doubt of that. It's bad luck they say to meet a woman with red hair first thing in the morning."

Aileen lay in the tub with a bar of lye squeezed in her hand, wincing at the skin-pinking heat of the water, and blinking at the blur of woman darting here and there, laying bright bolts of silk and finely woven linen over the jumble of casks. All morning, servants had passed through this door to drag in the wooden tub, or lug pails of steaming hot water, or serve her a tray of some flat bread and watered-down ale, but none of them babbled on in a language she could understand.

"Course, that's only on the days I'll be off on a journey, I suppose it's no matter on any other day. It'd be worse luck to meet a cat or a dog first thing in the morning, though a hard thing that is to avoid in this place, with all the hounds wandering about the yard because of that lazy dog-keeper the master took in—"

"You speak the Irish."

"Aye, that I do, and a fine thing it is to be speaking it in the full again." Wayward edges of her turban flapped as she nodded. "It's true my lords do be using it now and again, when they're of a mind to tell me something they don't want to be telling the world. But most times I'm forced to twist my tongue around the Welsh, and a fine hard thing that is, don't you know, though I've lived here over thirty years now. My name is Marged, my lady. Let me set to that hair of yours now."

Before Aileen could speak Marged darted to the barrel and hefted a pail of water over her head.

"There's no need," Aileen sputtered, swiping the water out of her face, "for you to—"

"Thick, it is, blessed be, but it could be using a lavender rinse, if you don't mind me saying so." Marged plunged another stick of lye deep into Aileen's soaking hair and tugged and pulled it into lather while Aileen gripped the edge of the tub to keep from being yanked about. "Mind, I was thinking, looking at your hair, that it'd be as hard and springy as the wire the armorer uses to make his chain mail—no offense meant to you, my lady, it's just the look of it, all curled up so tight and wild, and mayhap the trials of the long journey did not leave it at its best—but despite its thickness it has a bit of softness in it."

"You're like to pull it straight out of my head," Aileen interrupted, seizing the lathered length of her hair and twisting to look up into the woman's eyes. "And I have two hands strong enough to wash my own hair, thank you very much."

"Don't be denying me the pleasure. It's been near twenty years since I've set my hands into a lady's hair. I came over from Ulster as a lady's maid, you know, with my master's sainted mother—may she rest in peace. She was Irish, too, like myself, and when the time came for her to go to God I stayed on, by the grace of the late master. He made me the keeper of this house in a lady's absence. But I'll have you know, it's no easy task seeing to a *llys*—that's what the Welsh call this place—the size of this one, with all the servants and the master's men to be fed and their clothes woven and sewn and mended and laundered and the livestock to be seen to. Lass, don't be getting out, the water's still warm."

"My mother didn't raise me to loll about in a bath until the water grows cold." Aileen twisted her hair to squeeze the water out of it. Water sluiced down her body and cooled in the autumn drafts sifting in between the ill-mudded walls. "You and the others can get in, now. You all worked so hard filling it up."

"The bath was for you alone. Faith, look at the figure upon you." Marged thrust a linen at her and looked unabashedly up and down Aileen's figure. "Like the leanest of the master's hounds, all bones and muscle, true."

Heat rushed over Aileen. For all the baths she, her sisters and her mother shared, never had she stood naked before an outsider. She seized the linen from the woman's hands only to pause as she felt the fine weave, as soft as butter.

"This is not for drying." The words came out with a chatter. She thrust the linen back at her. "Would you get me a fitting piece of cloth? I'm near frozen to death here."

"Aren't you a strange one? Dry yourself, now." The woman swept the linen around her, and rubbed it over Aileen's body with quick, brisk hands. "Wouldn't do for a healer to be catching the ague the moment she steps foot in Wales. I'll get another for your hair, now, just a moment."

Aileen swathed herself in the linen and stepped out of the cask as Marged bustled about, blathering on without taking a breath and rifling through the things she had carried in. Aileen watched her and rubbed the fine weave against her skin, thinking all the while what a waste it was to dirty such exquisite linen drying a body that hadn't been properly washed in all the weeks of the sea voyage. Wasn't that the way of the wealthy and the powerful, to put all the hard work of some expert spinner and squinty-eyed weaver to waste like this?

She pressed the soft linen against her face. She wasn't so weak from a few days' diet of bread and water not to know something was up and about. Life was hard on Inishmaan, and there had been more than one season in her lifetime when she'd felt the pang of hunger. Rhys ap Gruffydd had much to learn if he thought by sending her a bite of food, a bath, fine linens, and someone who spoke a civilized tongue, she would do sorcery for his whims.

Whatever those whims were.

"Here's another." Marged snapped out another linen, then tilted her head and scratched under the cloth of her headdress. "Faith, you are a tall one, I'd have to clamber on a cask to get to your hair. You'll have to do this yourself, unless you're of a mind to squat in the rushes."

"Five-and-twenty years I've done well enough without a servant." She twisted her hair into the cloth and cast her gaze around the room, searching amid the scatter of silks for her wheat-colored tunic. "Will you be telling me where my clothes are?"

"They're in the washing, of course. My lord brought you something else to wear. Now let me see if I can put me hands upon it, fine stuff, it is. A waste it was lying in that chest for so many years. It's good it'll see some use. . . ."

Marged had a walk like a cat in a hurry. She darted about here and there, and when she returned to Aileen two lengths of fine cloth shimmered across her breast.

Aileen stared down at the fine stuff, reeking vaguely of heather. "You're mocking me, are you?"

"Now why would I be doing that? Fine clothes, these are, though a bit musty, I'll admit, for they've been in a chest in the master's room for more years than I care to count, but they should fit you fine enough."

"Would you be wearing them?"

"Faith, I'm too old to be wearing such things, and such richness is not for the likes of me."

"Nor me, either." She tightened the linen around her and stepped out of the pool of water growing around her feet. "If this is your lord's idea of kindness, I'm of no mind to be accepting it."

Balancing one linen atop her head and gripping the other over a breast, she tiptoed through the rushes, plopped down on a sack, and curled her legs beneath her.

So now it's come to silks, she thought, stanching a shiver. What would Rhys ap Gruffydd be wanting, seeing her dressed in silks like some fine lady? She was no fine lady—he knew that well enough.

"Are you refusing our hospitality, lass?"

She avoided Marged's eye and arranged the edges of the linen around her legs. Rude, it was, to refuse a gift so fine, but she had no stomach for rich gifts from such a man as Marged's master. "I've had a bellyful of Welsh hospitality, truth be told. I'll wait for my own clothes, thank you very much."

Aye, her fine serviceable wheat-gold tunic, the fibers spun with her own hands from her family's own sheep, woven into cloth by her mother's hands, sewn into a tunic by her sister's quick fingers, and dyed along the edges with blue from woad. Aye, aye, she wanted *her* tunic, with its deep shoulders and comforting warmth and the lingering smell of salt-sea, with the tear in the hem where she'd stepped upon it looking for bird's eggs on the western cliffs.

"Very well, lass, I'll see to it, but I don't know what the master will be saying about this."

A short time later, dressed in her own wool which had been brushed to a fine clean nap, Aileen plaited her hair and fixed it with a bit of string that had unraveled from one of the sacks of grain. The door opened again, pouring the cold white light of day through the room, but this time a tall, broad-shouldered silhouette filled the portal.

With a quiver in her stomach she turned to him, only to

find herself face-to-face with the man who had come to her home in Inishmaan that fateful day, the one-handed Welshman who had aided Rhys in capturing her.

"I've met the devil." Her spine straightened as she faced him. "Now I meet the devil's right hand."

"I think," he began, dipping his head to step into the food shed, "that if a gaze were an arrow, I'd be standing here shot clear through."

"I see you've no problem getting your tongue around the Irish now."

"My mother taught both me and Rhys." He shrugged a broad shoulder under a silk the color of summer grass and spread his hand across his chest. "Our mother and Marged, that is, who rarely allowed us to get a word in."

Our mother . . . She narrowed her eyes. She saw the resemblance now. They were of the same height. His hair was a lighter black, the jaw not as sharp, the eyes not so light and piercing. As she stared, a smile lit those features. Of the same blood, this man and Rhys, but not of the same temperament.

"It took two of you to commit the treachery, then." She made the sign of the cross over her chest. "God save this world from the brothers Graig."

"I've seen prouder days than this. So," he continued, swiftly, casting his gaze over her tunic, "what of the silks I sent you? Did they not fit?"

"You sent the silks?"

"And the bath and the food and Marged." He shrugged again. "We've no woman in the house, so I plead with you to forgive the belated hospitality."

She turned away with a snap of her skirts, and wondered at the vague sense of disappointment. It all made sense, after all. Why had she expected any kindness, even kindness with a purpose, from the likes of Rhys ap Gruffydd? "I'm no Lady O'Brian of Connacht, to be painted in rich colors."

"The green would have done your coloring justice."

"Rich gifts wax poor when the giver proves unkind."

"I'd heard this about the Irish." His hazel gaze sparkled with repressed humor. "My mother was near as stubborn as you."

"Was she stolen from Ireland, as well? Do the sons follow the follies of their father?"

The smile hardened. "I hope not, indeed. My father sired nine sons, most on the wrong side of the blanket."

"If you're looking for redemption, *David,*" she interrupted, "don't be doing it with silks. Get me on a ship back to Inishmaan, and then mayhap your soul will find some peace."

By the love of God . . . She eyed the tall stranger. Could this be shame she saw darkening his cheeks? Aye, aye, there was a spot of it, but before she could be sure he shuffled his feet in the rushes and shifted his gaze to the horizon outside the door.

"Three days in a musty place like this will strain the disposition of even the most gracious of ladies." He twisted his mustache with his fingers. "Come and take a turn with me around the yard. The air is brisk, but—"

"Aren't you afraid I'll try to escape?"

"With mountains between here and the ocean, and an ocean between Wales and Inishmaan? No, lass. There is no escape . . . unless you can make a broom fly."

She should have been afraid of such words, should have spit back a hard reply, but the grin on his face disarmed her. Truth be told, she should jump at the chance to get out of this shed and take stock of her surroundings, find out how well she was guarded, how difficult it would be to slip out under the cover of night. But part of her cowered at the thought of leaving the safety of these four walls, of facing so many curious outsiders.

Aye, but Aileen the Red was no coward, and she'd not let them best her, she wouldn't.

"Pots, pans, and tempers—I've made them fly. But never a broom." She snatched her mantle off a cask. "At least, not yet."

She strode past him into the bright white light of day, then staggered to a stop. She'd never get used to a horizon that began so high that she had to arch her neck to look at it. Dizzying, it was, all those jagged blue peaks, they left her weaving in a state of unbalance that had her thankful for the hand Dafydd curled around her arm.

But only for a moment. As soon as the dizziness eased, she pulled away from him and strode around the perimeter of the yard, in the direction of the front gate. Dafydd fell into step beside her. The *llys,* as he called it, consisted of a circular enclosure of wooden palisades set in a clay-and-earth bank. Simple wattle-and-daub houses lined the inside edge—storage, Dafydd told her, for grain, hay, wood, weapons. One long shed sheltered the horses, another the butter and cheese. The mead-hall loomed in the center, a large building of thin layers of dry-stone, and shimmering with a thatched roof of reeds.

For all of Dafydd's polite babble about the buildings, it was the people she turned an eye to. A swarthy folk they were, dusky haired, light eyed, and she felt as if the sun set her bright hair afire amidst them. The blacksmith's clanging faltered as they passed. The stable boy lifted his head from where he worked polishing a harness to stare with vacant eyes. The chatter of the kitchen servants laboring over a spit ebbed to a whisper as they moved on. By the time they reached the front portal, she walked with a spine stiffer than iron.

A workman wattling a hole in the palisades wobbled on the ladder as he caught sight of her; Dafydd barked something in Welsh and curled a hand around her arm.

"Forgive us," he explained, leading her around the muddy trench leading from the front portal. "Living so far from sea or road, rarely do we have visitors. Even more rarely, visitors from so far afield. The people of Graig are but curious about the healer in their midst."

"Couldn't your mother have birthed you first?" She sidestepped a pile of tinder just outside one of the huts. "Had you been Lord of Graig, there would have been no woman-theft, I'd wager."

"Ah, but my lady, I am the eldest son of Gruffydd, the eldest of all his sons."

She stopped in surprise. He turned toward her, a smile twitching one side of his face. Nay, it couldn't be . . . not older than him. Those hazel eyes gleamed with too much wickedness, that smile came too easily.

"In Wales," he explained, "a father does not pass his wealth to the oldest son. He divides it equally among all his sons and dies praying they'll not kill each other over it. *Gavelkind,* it's called. The scourge of Wales."

"Then why does Rhys hold the title? Doesn't that go to the eldest son?"

"Sometimes." He lifted his other arm. Scarlet silk drooped over the knobbed wrist. "But it wasn't for a man like me to rule."

In all her years of healing, she'd seen many a child born without hand or foot, or with the limbs twisted. She knew Dafydd had to have been born with this lack, for the ease at which he used the stump. Suddenly she knew why Dafydd was not the Lord of Graig, for it was the way of the Irish, too. A maimed chieftain cannot rule. It was an ancient law, older than even Da knew, rarely spoken but always followed. Many an Irish warrior-chieftain had been unseated from power because of a disfiguring war-wound. A maimed man was thought of as less of a warrior; and a sick or disfigured one, bad luck to the health of the land.

Then she remembered Rhys's mask.

"Don't be talking like that. That arm of yours shouldn't make a bit of difference," she retorted, setting out to finish their circuit of the yard. "Lord Rhys manages to rule with that war-wound of his."

"War-wound?"

"The one on his face," she said, tracing on her own features the line of his mask. "How is it that he rules and you cannot, when he is just as disfigured?"

A strange expression flitted across Dafydd's face as his pace slowed. "That's no war-wound."

"Isn't it? Then what the devil is it?"

An odd light gleamed in Dafydd's eyes. All sense of mirth left his face. Grinding to a halt, he spat something in Welsh, and swung around with a snap of his cloak to stare up at the northern hills.

"I should have guessed," he snarled, in a voice that left no doubt in her mind that he and Rhys shared blood. "I should have known he wouldn't tell you."

"Tell me what?"

"Why you are here, why he dragged you clear across the world."

"I've been twisting in circles wondering that myself."

"I didn't lie to you that day, when I told you there was someone on that shore who needed a healing." His lips whitened into a grim line. "He needs a knock on the head as well. And if I had two good fists I'd be the first to give it to him."

Dafydd strode toward the stables, abandoning her in the bright open courtyard not far from a cluster of girls feeding a gaggle of squawking chickens from their aprons. Their curious whispers rode to her on the breeze, but for the moment she didn't care that she was the center of attention—she didn't feel the fear. For as she watched Dafydd's retreating back, realization washed over her.

So she hadn't been summoned to heal the three-legged dog she'd seen amid the hounds, or the falcon with the broken wing she'd glimpsed in the mews, or the young stable boy with the bloody linen upon his arm—the only signs of injury she'd seen among the people and the livestock of Graig.

She was here to heal Rhys. And the arrogant lord was too proud to admit it.

Aileen and Dafydd approached the tumulus from the south, skirting the shimmering brown stretches of ground too boggy to cross. Despite the chill filtering through Aileen's woolen cloak, the morning mist had long dissipated in the valley. From afar, she saw a solitary figure standing upon the barrow, wheeling a falcon through its paces within a circle of ancient standing stones.

She watched with scorn in her heart and more than a bit of horror. Wasn't it like this arrogant lord to play at falconry in such a place, as if he were the master of it—as if it weren't a sacrilege to do something so ordinary within the confines of a faery-ring? She'd mark it as stark ignorance if Dafydd hadn't informed her that the place was called King Arthur's grave, the resting place of a great warrior of ancient Welsh legend. In truth, even ignorance couldn't be used as an excuse, for in Ireland, such a circle of standing stones bubbled with invisible music, so much so that even those stone deaf to the ancient voices still veered away from the magical place, sensing what they could not understand.

Yet there he stood, wheeling the bloodied lure over his head to tempt the falcon off the soaring wind and back down to the ground. Aye, well she'd have a bit to say about that—she had enough words bubbling in her throat, a few more wouldn't make much of a difference.

When she reached the foot of the tumulus, those words faded in a tumble of confusion. She tilted her head, listening for the distant strains of faery music; she cast her gaze to the ground in search of faery footmarks in the mud. For sure, there should be some whisper of the Otherworld upon such a tumulus. . . . She struggled with the odd sensation of entering a familiar place and finding something gone, and not knowing for sure what the thing was.

Dafydd unwound the reins from his handless wrist, eased off the horse, then helped her dismount from her donkey.

"I'll wait here for you."

"You're not coming?"

"There are times, Aileen, when a man doesn't want a witness."

She tugged her tunic off the back of the donkey and made her way up the muddy slope. A fool of a man, Rhys was, so full of himself to cause such trouble. She'd seen pride in her brothers, aye, in her father too, but never so stiff-necked and destructive as in this man. She gathered her cloak in her arms so as not to drag it through the grass and mud, warning herself that she must watch her tongue; for if she let it loose and told him her mind he'd hide behind that shield of pride again and she'd be no better off than before. No, no, better that she set to the matter straightaway, as if there was nothing wrong with his foolish silence. Oh, what lengths a woman must go to tiptoe around a man's pride.

She let her skirts fall as she reached the top of the tumulus. Such a cold, forlorn place, with the wind howling between the standing stones and the sky leaden above. That strange sensation gripped her again. Surely, the sky of Inishmaan was as gray every winter morning. Surely, the wind of her island blew just as frigid over the bare rock, flattening the grasses to the rocky bones of the island. Yet even on the rawest day, there had always been a spark of spirit on Inishmaan. A whisper of laughter in the air; a patter of feet just beyond the mist. Here, the ground did not pulse, the air did not sing—the pitch of the wind, the scent of the earth . . . everything lay so different, so silent, as if she'd stepped through time to return to a familiar place, now age-worn and abandoned.

It was the time of year, she told herself, eyeing that figure standing within the circle of stones. *Samhain* was not a week hence; the beginning of the time of darkness. Or perhaps Rhys himself had driven all life away.

He wore nothing but a sweat-stained shirt, a loose-fitting pair of *braies*, and the mask. Swords and spears littered the circle, jutting out from the earth here and there like ragged palisades. She leaned against a lichen-covered standing stone and watched a goshawk descend from the sky, watched it stretch its talons toward Rhys's gloved arm.

Rhys swung around in one swift motion while the goshawk

landed, shuttered its wings and stilled. The bells of the bird's jesses fell silent in the ring of stones, like an echo of some sacred ceremony. She watched in growing fascination as Rhys murmured to the bird and stroked its golden breast with a strip of feathered leather. He stroked and murmured, stroked and murmured, dangerously close to that lethal beak, meeting the bird of prey's golden eyes with the same steady, unyielding, unemotional stare. The sight made something quiver deep in her abdomen.

Then he flashed the leather over the bird's head and with his teeth pulled two strips of leather tight on either side, and it was as if he were kissing the bird once on either cheek, only now the bird was as masked as he.

Only then did Rhys turn and face her, with eyes as cold and unyielding as the falcon's.

"I see," he said, "that you are free of your jesses."

That pride of his could fill all the valleys of Wales, it could. It would do no good to set him into anger again, she told herself. Da had always warned her to handle a wild thing with great and patient care.

A pity she didn't always have the patience to mind Da's words.

"Pardon my interruption, my lord, though I'm thinking it's you who should be asking pardon of me." Not even a flicker of remorse on his face, the arrogant warrior. "You've done more than enough, I'd say, more than many a person could forgive. But I've come here nonetheless, out of the goodness of my Christian heart, to tell you this: I'll help you with your problem."

His fingers paused on the goshawk's tawny chest. Something flickered in his cold blue eyes. His gaze skimmed down the slope, to where Dafydd put his gelding through its paces in the valley.

"Don't be setting your ire on your brother, I'm quick witted enough to figure it out for myself. It didn't take much, once I set my mind to it."

"Why now?"

"Why not now?" Why doesn't he do something with that shirt falling off one shoulder? Wasn't he rich enough to wear a good pair of hose instead of traipsing about in nothing but *braies*? And didn't he have any shame at all, standing before her near as naked as a babe and acting as if he stood before her in king's robes? "A mystery to me, it is, why you didn't tell me on the shores of Inishmaan. I would have healed you then, if I had the things I needed. If not, I'd have brought you to my house and seen to it—without asking for a single coin, I'll have you know. As it was, you left me guessing as to what you wanted—too puffed up with pride to ask me, even when you had me caught as surely as that bird—and then had me thinking you needed sorcery no Christian woman could provide."

"It's the sorcery I need, woman."

"Cock's feathers you do. Why a man insists on calling a woman's healing sorcery and a man's healing not I'll never know." She crossed her arms, but the fury burst through nonetheless. "All this trouble, for a man's vanity."

Rhys's arm hardened into cords. The falcon flapped open its wings and screeched.

"Aye, vanity," she repeated, forcing herself not to quiver under the fury of that ice-blue gaze. She'd found a sore spot, no doubt of that, but she didn't care anymore. "I'd hope it was shame that kept you silent, shame at what you did. But I know now it's vanity—vanity and pride. Now just take off that wretched mask, will you, and let me see the thing. I'll concoct some sort of salve to be rid of the affliction, then you and I shall be done with one another—and I can be home to Inishmaan."

Four

Vanity.

Anger swelled from that ugly place deep inside him, seething a fury so thick that a haze of hot red blood fogged his vision.

So she thought it was vanity that had driven him to the physicians of Myddfai and the charlatans of Troyes. So she thought it was simple vanity that made him suffer having his skin slopped with salves that burned, with unguents that all but froze his face. For vanity's sake he'd lain strapped to tables while men worked their knives and leeches upon him, for vanity's sake he'd allowed himself to be bled almost to the last drop of his life. He'd genuflected at every shrine from St. Dafydd's to Compostela, washed his skin raw in innumerable sacred wells, bowed his head to every saint who'd listen, felt the bite and glop of every liquid known to man, felt the sting of utter humiliation.

All for vanity's sake.

He'd laugh, if he could drag the sound up through the bitter gall clogging his throat. If only it were that simple. If only it were that simple.

"Don't speak to me of medicines." The goshawk tightened its claws deep into the leather glove. "Do you think I stole you here for *that?*"

The word snapped like a whip between them. The girl started, but kept her ground while those maddening all-knowing gray eyes widened. Setting his jaw, Rhys whirled away and swept the bird onto a perch he'd driven deep into the ground.

"My father," she insisted, "is the greatest healer that lives. And there is more medicine than can be found in Wales—"

"There are none unknown to me." No, none at all, not a single one, five years was a long time for a man to be educated in indignity. "It's your sorcery I need." He flung off his glove and threw it to the ground. "It's *these* I want."

He seized her hands and held them tight. He dug his thumbs over her palms to feel the rough surface of her skin, to ripple over the islands of calluses. He squeezed those hands as if he could squeeze out the sorcery that demon had spoken of. He crushed her fingers like kindling in his grip, milking them for magic. Ragged nails, hardened from work; a peasant's hands, as common as heather and just as tough—made for working.

She tried to yank her hands free. *Oh, no, Aileen, you're not leaving, not yet, not yet, not till I've felt the full of you.*

"Healing hands." He pried open her long fingers. "Like to be a saint, he said."

Some part of him realized that he'd not touched a woman's hands since . . . since a thousand years ago, in that vaguely remembered life before the affliction. The golden moment before the darkness. Now he felt the full length of these fingers, the knobs of each knuckle, and squeezed harder, searching for something, for anything, for some frisson of magic, a spark, a tingling, to show that these were more than just another peasant woman's hands better fit for wielding a scythe than conjuring demons.

He hated himself even as he yanked her closer, close enough for the wind to sweep the wiry ends of her hair against his cheek. Close enough to hear her breath soughing in her throat. Close enough to count the freckles splattering her nose and cheeks, close enough to see the terror in her eyes. She smelled of mist, but more than mist. A salt-sea fragrance steamed off her skin, mingled with the perfume of something else, something elusive, and it came to him on a filet of memory. . . .

It was the smell of woman, that dark mysterious love-smell he'd denied himself for so long, that potent feminine scent that even now caused a heaviness in his loins he would rather be without.

"There's nothing here, is there, Aileen the Red? Nothing at all."

His grip tightened on her hands. His nostrils flared as he drank in more of that forbidden fragrance, hating himself even as he sucked it in like a man starved. Look at her, a broomstick of a woman, all snarled hair and flatness. He'd felt this way the first day he'd seen her, on the edge of the sea, when she'd looked as untamed as the goshawk that spread it wings behind him, when she'd looked like the faeries the people of Graig spoke of in hushed whispers, the imaginary creatures of dew and ferns. He told himself then that she was a witch, for no one but a witch would tempt death so fearlessly with her defiance, no one but a witch could have *him* thinking faery nonsense, no one but a witch could dig up these dead yearnings of a youth passed.

"No, there's nothing here," he persisted, massaging those hands as if he could release the magic from them. "There's nothing here but a peasant's hands, nothing here but a wild bush of hair, a pair of gray eyes—no magic, no sorcery."

No hope.

He'd been such a fool. Again, he'd been taken for a fool, after all these years, after all this time. A man should know better—a man should *learn*.

"You're hurting me."

"It's part of the whole curse, isn't it? You . . . You're part of it, aren't you, Aileen Ruadh?"

Yes, he was beginning to understand. Finally, he was beginning to understand. Dafydd had insisted that there must be a *reason* for that Midsummer Night's visit—that only a fool would ignore it. This was Rhys's chance, Dafydd had said, mayhap Rhys's last. Now Rhys understood the full of it. Who else but a demon could trick Rhys into seeking out this witch-woman, full of spirit, full of contempt and mockery? Surely, this was the demon's most potent weapon—a young woman, all wild eyes and wild hair and defiance. Unworldly enough to give him hope to think she could change everything . . . that she could return the world to the way it once was.

"You speak madness." She spoke softly, as if to an unbroken colt. "Listen to yourself, babbling on about nothing. Now let me go and have done with this."

"Yes, yes, I do speak madness. It's a fine language, I've learned it well."

He hated himself for this, hated himself for searching for something that never existed—that would never exist, but that some wretched part of him still wanted to exist. He released her so abruptly that she stumbled back.

"Be off, Aileen the Red. *Go*. Go back to that rock whence you came, and take your secrets with you, God damn your soul." Blinded, he turned to his falcon. "As long as I live, I won't listen to the false voice of hope again."

He'd said too much. He hated the words the moment they left his lips. He nudged the falcon upon his arm, marched out into an open space, under an open sky growing as black as his own heart. There, with his teeth, he tore the mask off the falcon and spit it to the ground.

Then he launched the bird skyward, to glide naked and free.

The morning mist dissipated by the time the procession of horses lumbered its way down from the *llys*. A flaxen stubble gleamed in the narrow crook of the valley below, the golden remains of the harvest. The lowing of cattle echoed off the hills as bondsmen nudged the beasts down the slopes to the winter grazing grounds, close to the bondsmen's wattled huts.

Aileen swayed on the back of a donkey, huddled deep in her cloak against the wind. A thick layer of leaves crunched beneath the donkey's hooves, billowing the scent of dying vegetation into the crisp autumn air. By the end of the day she would shake her nostrils free of the stench of earth and wood-smoke, she thought. By the end of the day she would smell the brine of the sea again.

She took a deep breath and buried her nose in the wool. Aye, it would be the sea again, and then the sea-voyage, and then . . . *Inishmaan.* Her gaze passed over a cluster of peasants threshing some hay just beyond a rock-pile fence. Ma and the girls would have long finished the threshing by now, and would be full fit to hand-grinding the rye into flour and brewing a bit of it into the fresh ale Da liked so much. The boys would be off to the mainland, filling their *curraghs* with small wild apples for Ma and Cairenn to bake and press into cider. . . . Aye that was where she should be, she told herself, home helping Ma and Da through the harvest. Aye, that was where she belonged, she thought, even as her gaze strayed, for the hundredth time, to the straight-backed figure leading the procession.

The Lord of Graig could hang himself, for all she cared. He'd caused enough trouble, dragging a girl clear across the sea on a rumor and a whim. Disappointment was no more than he deserved. Aye, he deserved a far greater punishment, indeed! He'd left her family behind, thinking her dead or wondering if she could possibly have lived, he'd left little Dairine waiting for a nighttime story that never came . . . *Theirs* was the greater torture than ever this arrogant warrior could know. Aileen would leave him to his brooding and his pride, and good riddance to the man.

Aye, good riddance. She nodded her head and set her gaze to the narrow path that wandered toward the next mountain pass, a filet of pounded earth that snaked between the terraced fields and the first slope of the hills. Dafydd rode on a fine horse in front of her, his purple cloak flapping free as if the wind's chill couldn't pierce the chain mail draping his body. She saw the resemblance between Dafydd and Rhys much more starkly now, for since yesterday, when Rhys had ordered her back to Inishmaan, Dafydd had been as sullen and heavy browed as his brother.

Good riddance to them all, good riddance to this barren, lifeless place. She wanted home—Inishmaan; she wanted to feel the faery-breath on her face, and the thrum of magic beneath her feet. Aye, that was what she wanted, she thought, pulling her gaze once more from the back of the lead rider. She wanted her home, a land that didn't lay dead around her. Aye, it was true, cattle aplenty grazed on these softer slopes and huddled in the crooks of the valleys, and aye, there were homesteads here and there scattered about, smoke curling from their chimneys and chickens pecking in their gardens, and aye, there were deer enough, she supposed. She'd heard, once or twice, something large sprinting out of the glades when they'd passed through a patch of dense forest. But for all the life around her, she couldn't shake the sensation that she was riding across graves.

Mayhap it was her imagining. She wanted to go home and pretend that these weeks had never happened; pretend that a man had never grasped her hands in a fury of passion, pretend it was all a bad dream, that she'd never known a masked man with a voice as anguished as all the souls of hell and eyes as tortured as those of a caged thing.

Listen to her! So he'd looked, for one moment, like a man flailing in the throes of death. What reason did she have to take pity on a warrior-chieftain who'd caused her nothing but grief? What matter, if by some trick of fate he knew her power lay in her hands? She'd be three times a fool to admit to it— she'd be a dead woman, reviled as a witch, buried outside consecrated ground. It was not as if the man was in physical pain. He was healthy enough, for whatever was wrong beneath that mask. Aye, in good health indeed, she'd seen *that* well enough whilst he flexed his bare arms upon the burial-mound, wearing nothing but a bit of cloth around his loins. Da would say her soft spot was showing, if he could hear her thoughts now. It was Inishmaan she should be thinking of, and the moment she'd step upon the safety of that rocky shore and into Ma's fragrant arms.

So it was the ale-brewing and the cider-pressing she fixed her mind to as the procession followed the winding path through the brambled cleavage of the hills. The hard blue-gray rock pressed in on either side of them, opening only to reveal a steep crag or a rushing torrent of foamy water, or a stretch of heath or reed-choked valley. Aileen pressed her face against the wool of her cloak to shield it from the unexpected whip of the cold wind as they rounded one rocky promontory, then another. When she raised her gaze to the heavy leaden sky, she wondered for the thousandth time how anyone could keep spirit in such a soulless place.

Late in the day they marched single-file through a thicket of oak, the *clack-clack* of the horses' hooves dulled by the thick carpet of vegetation. The sky shed a hazy gray light between the lace of the bare boughs. Lulled by the rhythmic plodding of her donkey and the gentle ringing music of harness and chain mail, Aileen jerked out of her dozing at the sound of the first cry, an odd sound, like the whelp of wounded dog.

Dafydd scraped his sword out of its scabbard and swung it high to gleam in the hazy light. His horse pranced, frightening her donkey into skittering aside. Dafydd cried something out in his babbling Welsh, then pointed his sword forward. She strained to see around his horse through the thicket, but all she saw was faint movement through the mist.

Another cry came, mingled with the shouts of men, then another cry, and she recognized these—human cries. Human cries of pain.

Then the woods erupted.

Such faces as these, she had never seen. Aye, she recognized them as human, but barely so, with the way blood-lust curled their lips back from their teeth and crossed their brows over their eyes. And the hardness in those eyes . . . like chips of the slate mountains themselves, bereft of all emotion but for fury. The creatures burst from the darkness of the forest in a rush of sound, hurling their javelins with a whirr, then flashing knives out from their belts. They hurtled toward the line of horses and men so suddenly and so unexpectedly that she simply sat upon the donkey transfixed, not feeling fear, not at first, for surely these were but furies of some sort, ripped from the Otherworld—or more likely from the Hell the priest of the Aran Islands spoke so much about.

The horsemen around her scraped their weapons free and met the charge headlong. Dafydd screamed orders. Men cried out, screamed in pain. Had the men really carried so many weapons? There was a kitchen's worth of knives flashing in the gray light, and every man had his hands full. She hadn't noticed that when they'd left the homestead, though she had wondered why she had been granted such a royal procession back to the sea.

Still, she stared, only part of her mind registering the chaos erupting around her. Someone bumped her donkey; the beast skittered back to the edge of the woods, then picked his way down to the rounded stones of a dried riverbed. Left alone with slack reins, out of the center of the fray, the beast lowered its head to munch on a dry tuft of grass. A sound alerted her, like the whistle of a gust through a cavern. She turned and saw one of the attackers racing across the riverbed toward her, hefting a lance upon his shoulder.

She sat, transfixed, staring into blue eyes burning with a fierce wolfish glare. Blue woad caked his skin. Long fair hair flew out behind him and captured the pale white sunlight. Reeds strapped around his feet muffled his footsteps. A scream surged in her throat; then stuck. What use was there in screaming over the shrieks of wounded men, over the ear-piercing war-cries of bloodthirsty warriors, over the inhuman wailing of wounded horses? He splashed to the middle of the rocky riverbed, and curled his lips back from yellowed teeth. Sensing his victory, Aileen supposed, in the strange detached place she'd floated to in this unreal world where men took pleasure from spilling the blood of other men.

As he flexed his fingers around the shaft of the javelin and leaned back to launch it, a crack rent through the clearing. Air whooshed across the riverbed; a hot, humid gust that swiped her cheek but didn't rattle a single leaf amid the thousands littering the riverbed. A strange buzzing burst in the air, like the frenzied anger of a hive of bees. The warrior stumbled to a stop.

The trees rattled though the wind had died; tiny whirlwinds sifted up dust beneath her donkey's feet. An exotic perfume burst around her, like the distant smoke of fragrant wood-fires, and the riverbed clattered as if with the sound of a thousand tiny footsteps.

The warrior's javelin clanged against the stones. The man swiped at his head, then at his thigh, then, more furiously, at his arms. He stumbled back and raised his arms over his face, twisted this way and that, clawing the air, grasping his invisible tormentors. Aileen tightened her grip on a donkey grown suddenly skittish, a beast rearing back from the strange happenings on the riverbed.

Then the air filled with a louder clatter; the clatter of Dafydd's gelding as Dafydd urged the horse down the slope, Dafydd crying out a harsh warning. Steel rang as he pulled his sword from its scabbard. At the sound of the ringing of metal the leaves ceased their rattling; the whirlwinds died, the buzzing eased, and a cold autumn wind gusted away the last of the exotic fragrance.

The warrior sank to his knees in the riverbed and fisted his palms into his eyes. Dafydd cried out to him again. The warrior glanced up, started to his feet, and raced into the woods, casting a single backward glance at her—a glance that made her blood run cold.

A moment passed, a heavy heartbeat, as Dafydd chased the man into the woods. She flailed out and caught the rough bark of a tree. She flexed her fingers over the dampness. Her chest heaved. She twisted around at the sound of a twig cracking, to find nothing but the shimmer of light upon a clearing. She tumbled off the donkey's back, dragged her skirts off his rump, held the reins and pressed close to his matted coat while she scanned the darkness of the woods.

In the span of a heartbeat, it was over and done. She searched for signs of the *Sídh*, wondering why they tore through the veils that separated the worlds now, in this place, when not once before had she felt their presence upon this ground. Wondering why they had so soon retreated so far beyond her reach.

"Are you all right?"

Curt, clipped words. She glanced up into Dafydd's hazel eyes and saw in them that strange look she sometimes received after healing a mainlander; a look teetering between wonder, reverence and fear.

She tugged her tunic straight. "Of course I'm fine—thanks to you."

He nodded and kicked his mount back up the slope, leaving her alone again.

But it didn't matter; the battle was already over. A pall fell over the wood, pierced only by the fading shouts of pursuit, an occasional cry in the distance. All that fighting, all the grunting and the yelling, over and done with, and in the span of a few heartbeats nothing was the same. The neat line of horses, donkeys, and men scattered this way and that, like a line of stakes she and Niall had dug into the ground one day, to mark off the planting, only to have an unexpected gale scatter them into chaos.

So this was warfare, she thought, shock numbing her. She pressed her back against the donkey and curled her fingers over the reins. As unpredictable and fierce as lightning, as blinding and quick. A thunderous moment of men hacking away at each other with steel and iron, leaving a hollow silence stinging with the acrid stench of sweat and blood and trembling with the expectation of another attack; a silence punctured only by the moans of the wounded and the dying.

Aye, the wounded.

Her feet swept softly through the litter. She reacted by instinct—the battle, the swift arrival of the *Sídh*, the shock of mortal danger had stripped all else from her. A man lay across the path, his face contorted in a grimace. His leather cap lay like a broken eggshell in the grass. Warm wetness seeped through her tunic as she knelt in the dirt by his side. Her fingers slicked over his bloody brow, searching for the wound.

His eyes flew open.

"Don't speak." She lifted her tunic and seized the edge of her undertunic with both hands. "I'll bind your wound."

She tore free a ragged strip of linen. He didn't understand a word of her Irish, but as she pressed the cloth over the slash upon his temple and felt her mind fading to that familiar calm place, she knew it didn't matter that they spoke different languages. The words were not important. She rarely remembered what she said after a healing. It was the sound of the voice that mattered. Hers was a tone a man or woman or child understood even in the midst of delirium. She supposed it was the voice of a mother, the soothing lilt of lullabies and comfort-words, senseless soft syllables that echoed to some calm and tender youth, sounds that transcended madness and language, for she'd known wild beasts to calm at the murmuring.

She pressed the square of linen hard against the man's wound, to stop the bleeding. For all her skill, she couldn't mend such a wound with a touch of her hands—that would take thread, a needle, rest, and time—but she could ward off the shock. She stroked lightly with her other hand, willing the throb of good health into him, stroking and lulling, stroking and lulling, until the man's tight grimace eased, until she knew she could leave him for another.

She glanced down the path, and the sight struck her like a blow to the belly. She'd seen enough war-wounds in her lifetime. The Irish mainlanders often rowed their leaders out to Inishmaan when they'd been wounded so badly in battle that they couldn't care for the injured themselves. Still, nothing had prepared her for the sight of a battlefield. Men lay strewn all along the ground. Blood splattered bright red upon the dull brown litter, and ran in rivulets down the bark of trees. Moans filled the wind. As she watched, someone plunged a dagger into the neck of a suffering horse.

Too many. She began to tremble. *Too many.*

She staggered down the path. One man dead—nay, two. Another gone beyond her reach. She glided among them. They called out to her; she could not answer them all. She felt their pain like bruises upon her own body. *Too many.* Her palms tingled. Her ears roared with the scream of aching flesh. She must do something, she must start somewhere. She forced down the bile surging to her throat, she forced down the panic. The most seriously wounded first, wasn't that what Da had told her? She took a breath and fell to her knees next to a man with a hole gaping in his shoulder.

Time lost all meaning. She bound wounds and passed her hands across their bodies in the way she'd long learned by instinct, so that no one thought her movements strange, just the smoothing of a binding, the clearing of blood off a stretch of flesh, a search for broken limbs. She stopped their bleeding with her father's skill, then eased their pain with the stroking of her hands to ward off the shock that threatened—but only just enough for now, for others craved her skill, always others, calling out to her. Torn flesh, broken bones, the ravages of wood, iron, and steel—foreign invaders in tender flesh. Seeing to one after the other, she knelt again and again, working until her back ached, until jabs of pain speared down her neck, until the screaming within her head deafened her, and then she hefted herself up to the next cry of pain.

She stumbled upon a group of men clustered in a circle, their heads bowed as if in prayer. She shouldered her way through and knelt by the wounded man's side. She'd torn so much linen off her undertunic that stones bit into the bare flesh of her knees.

This wound gaped deep and ragged—and someone had made it worse by yanking the javelin out without thought to more damage. This one, well loved by the silence of the men around her, clung to the last threads of his life.

But he was not lost. She felt the strength in him, pulsing beneath the armor of boiled leather. Shrugging off her mantle, she tore at the laces of her sleeves and yanked her tunic clear over her head. Her hair, tugged out of its netting, sprang down her back in its tangled wildness. The cold air cut through her thin and tattered undertunic.

She winced when she pressed the thick pad of wool upon the man's shoulder, for the anguish of this torn bloodied flesh rang loud in her ears. No need for words here, for the man lay blessedly unconscious, his breathing short and shallow. She yelled at the men around her for hemp to tie the binding onto his wound, even as she passed a hand across his flesh, trying to stroke away the burning ache. She willed him to breathe deeper. His body screamed, screamed—she had to force herself to keep her hands upon him for the screams throbbed in her own head. This one was close to death, aye, for a body could not take much more of such pain before stopping, shutting down, ending life instead of keeping to the harder path and fighting to be healed.

Her palms tingled as she set herself to the healing. Someone dangled a strip of cloth before her blinded eyes; she took it only long enough to bind the padding, already soaked with blood, onto the wound. A harsh thing, this wound, it sucked upon that light that flowed through her as greedily as a hungry babe on a mother's breast. Sweat ran down her brow, sweat in the cold air of the mountains when she wore nothing but a thin slip of linen amid a circle of men. But all her pressing and stroking was working. She felt the drain ease. Around her, the men talked in hushed, excited whispers.

Then, on the pretext of searching for other wounds, she ran her hands across his brow and over his body, willing her own strength into the body of this wounded warrior, willing him to rest easy for now, rest easy, rest easy. . . .

Finally, she stood upon shaking legs and rubbed her arms.

A thin drizzle winnowed between the trees. She told the man standing beside her to move the wounded warrior upon a horse; he needed to be better tended to; his wound to be cleaned, his body to be strengthened against the fever to come. Somehow, the man understood her Irish and set to lifting the warrior upon a horse draped in boiled-leather armor.

"Will he die?"

Rhys loomed in front of her. Dirt streaked his face and his mask, blood dulled the shimmer of his chain mail. He gripped his sword in his gloved hand. In his eyes gleamed a knowledge that set her blood running cold—the sure knowledge that it was her hands, her *hands,* that had healed these men.

On the bloody ground of this battlefield, she'd given herself away.

"His fate is in God's hands," she said, digging her fingernails into her arms. "No thanks to the likes of you."

Anger surged in her then, born of pure cold terror. So he knew she had magic in her hands. At least she used it for good. What was *he?* She looked up and down this looming hulk of a masked man, and knew not all of the blood staining his tunic and chain mail belonged to him. He'd caused as much bloodshed today as any of the enemy. He was a killer, to the bone. A warrior skilled in the ways of hacking through human flesh—for aims undoubtedly not worthy of a dog. She trembled in impotence and frustration and fury and fear and the inability to comprehend all that had happened this day, while the stench of blood and death singed her nostrils.

"Are you proud of your victory this day, Rhys, Lord of Graig? Look around you." She stilled the urge to run from this place, from the knowledge in his eyes, the pools of blood and the cries of the wounded, the type of man who took pleasure in such battle. She knew only of healing, he only of bloodshed. He was all she hated of outsiders, the superstitious, ignorant destroyers. "See how the dead lie in piles—and mostly the enemy. How proud you must be. A fine warrior, you are, worthy of this glorious day."

"Listen to a woman's words." His gaze burned through her. She suddenly realized she stood before him in nothing but a filthy thin linen tunic, torn to her thighs, her mantle lost in the mud, her tunic padding for a man's wound. "I did not welcome this fight—they attacked."

"Does it matter? I see the cold light of victory gleaming in your eyes. Does anything matter but the bloodshed to one such as you? Does anything matter but piling up body upon body of your enemy? You and the men who attacked—you are of the same ilk," she snapped. "Bloody, greedy, heartless—"

"You've struck upon the truth there, woman." He stepped before her, his breath hot on her face, and his eyes as cold as the mountains. "We are the same, those men and I."

"Demons like yourself," she argued, her heart pounding in her chest. "Of the same cloth—"

"More than that. Of the same blood. Of the same flesh." He swept the point of his sword up to the dark woods whence the men had come. "Those men are my brothers."

Five

She made it all look so ordinary.

Rhys peered through his open door to the dim light of the mead-hall. Men lay on makeshift pallets amongst the reeds, shifting in their sleep. Aileen drifted among them, whispering orders to Marged trailing in her wake. She stopped now and again to pass her hand across a man's brow. A huge cauldron of something bubbled over the center hearth, tendrils of milky white steam curling toward the smoke-hole in the roof.

Rhys chewed on the end of a reed. She slipped among the wounded like some red-haired angel of mercy. Yet each time she lay her hands upon one of them, she transformed.

No one else seemed to notice. No one remarked upon it. It made him wonder if he was seeing something that wasn't really there . . . another bit of madness creeping in upon him. She had hands as slim and dexterous as an Irish harpist he'd once seen in the Prince of Wales's court. They fluttered over the wounded with the lightness of a leaf drifting down from a tree. And her face, as she touched . . . It wasn't natural for a woman with such freckled skin to glow with a pearly light. A half-smile curled her lips, a contented smile, and it nagged at him where he'd seen such a look until he remembered the statues in the great stone churches of Normandy, the serene expression of the Mother Mary as she held her child.

A woman who'd healed every ailment she'd touched. A woman with a touch of faery blood who can cure your curse with a pass of her hands. A miracle worker, like to be a saint.

Rhys closed the door and nudged his chain-mail hauberk off the bench. It slid into a heap of metal on the paving stones. Hiking his *braies*, he flopped down on the bench and brooded into the flickering light of his own hearth.

Like to be a saint.

He twisted the reed between his teeth. He'd seen enough battles with the Prince of Wales to know that at least two of those men sleeping in his hall should be dead, and another should die before the night was through. Yet all three dozed peacefully and showed every chance of recovery. From the devil's hand, or an angel's, the lass had power. A power she gave freely to heal his men, without hope for the meanest recompense. A power she'd refused to use upon him, though he'd offered her a fortune.

He tugged out the reed and tossed it into the flames. Hate and treachery, horror and betrayal. Familiar emotions these past five years. They bred around him.

The door burst open with a flash of light.

"You'll let me look at that wound now."

She strode in as bold as a wife, clean linens draped over her shoulder. A bowl of cloudy water swished in her arms. A faint flush swept away the pearly light of her skin. Up close, she looked painfully human—haggard and weary.

No, she wasn't saving any of that magic for him.

She clanked the bowl on the bench, splattered some to the paving stones, then leaned over to pick at the bloody cloth on his arm.

"No." He seized her hand and pressed it down flat against the bench. "My boy did a fine enough job on that. This is too simple a scratch for you."

"Fluff and nonsense." She tugged her hand out from under his. "Even the simplest wounds can fester."

"It's the deepest wounds you do your best work on, I've noticed."

"Are you as deaf as a pot? I told you I was a healer." She yanked a cloth off her shoulder and dunked it in the steaming bowl. "That's your sword arm, is it not? If you want use of it within the week, pull off that rancid rag and let me have at it."

Those wretched gray eyes, as stormy and unpredictable as the Welsh sky, glared at him as if he were a recalcitrant child. But he wouldn't settle for a dose of her broth, not now. Not when he knew for sure there was richer witchery to be had.

"You've taken a foolish gamble, Irish."

She wrung out the linen with a splash. "As stubborn as a bull. Well, don't be blaming me if you—"

"You must have tasted it. The salt-air of Inishmaan. Your mother's own cooking."

Something moved in those eyes as she shook open the cloth. "I'll taste it yet, I wager. Dafydd tells me the ship will stay—"

"Oh, the ship will wait. I owe too much money to the merchant who owns it. Castle-building is an expensive undertaking, and I need this man to ship me more quarrymen in the spring." He grasped the edge of the bench. The only thing this woman wanted was her freedom: The only thing he wanted was a healing. Fair enough trade to his way of thinking. "You'll not be with the Irish laborers when I send them back to Ireland. Not after what I saw upon the field of battle this day."

"What you saw this day," she began, stiffening her spine so hard that the points of her breasts pressed against her ragged linen shift, "was nothing any doctor in Ireland couldn't do if he was there so soon after the battle."

"Was it compassion that caught you, Aileen? Or was it an irresistible urge to use your sorcery after so many weeks of hiding it?"

The linen splattered into the bowl, spraying his face and chest with warm liquid.

"Sorcery, sorcery! Is that what you're wanting, then, Rhys ap Gruffydd?" She jerked up off the bench and hiked her hands upon her hips. "I'm sure if you call him, the devil'll show his own face here quick enough since he has you half in his pocket."

"You know what I want."

She was a sight. Her hair burst from the edges of the net she'd stuffed it in, dragged in tight curls over her shoulders. Blood streaked her tunic, making her look all the more like a pagan. She stood as stiff as a witch before a tribunal of priests deliberating over her sentence, the shadow of the scaffolding lying already upon her proud and defiant face.

Saint or sinner, he didn't know. He didn't care. Whatever she was, a power lay in her. He wondered how he'd ever doubted it. Look at her, broomstick-thin yet quivering from head to toe with some suppressed emotion, her cheeks flushed with blood, evening out the smear of freckles. And those eyes, those damned eyes, biting and snapping at him like a wolf-hound's. It came to him in that moment that she looked him square in the face, mask and all, without an iota of fear.

"I offered to heal you once." She crossed her arms over her breasts. "You refused me."

"You offered me salves and simple words." He stilled the urge to take one of those tight curls in his hand and wind it around his finger, to trap her here, to make her do his bidding. "Not a witch's sorcery."

"Who are you to call me a witch? Condemning me to the fires of hell on the strength of what? Some Irishman's tale in a Connemara tavern? If I *were* a witch," she said between clenched teeth, "I'd change you into a beetle. Then a woman could at least have a chance to crack the shell of pride you erect around you, Rhys ap Gruffydd."

"Call it healing if it pleases you—"

"I gave you a chance to take my healing," she interrupted, "and you scorned it, you did. May the devil take you by the heels and shake you, Rhys ap Gruffydd—"

"No curse you heap upon my head can do any more harm." Maddening, she was, staring bold-faced at him. She laid too much faith in a man's respect for woman. He jerked up and tugged his shirt from out of the rope-belt of his *braies*. "I don't care about your soul, whether it belongs to God or the

Devil. I want your witchery, for I've seen the truth with my own eyes—"

"Truth?" She jerked away and rubbed the center of her forehead with stiff fingers. "What do you know of truth, you, twisted with hatred? Men see what they want to see, rarely what is. I did no more than bind men's wounds, and gave them a chance at living today. No, I'll not hear another word of it!" She peered down at him. The linens slid off her shoulder and tumbled to the floor. "A destroyer, you are, Rhys ap Gruffydd. You know nothing of healing which is why you and your kind are so quick to call it witchery. Well, it's more natural than spearing other men upon your javelins like rabbits on a spit! Spearing your own *brothers*. That, aye, that's the devil's work, if I have my say upon it."

The pup had a bite—and small sharp teeth that could tear the meat from the bone. *I destroy, woman, yes, I destroy.* Everything his hand touched crumbled into dust . . . everything but one, and it was still but a half-built dream of stone and mortar.

Something moved in his loins, to see her like this. She was magnificent in her ire, her face flushed with color, leaning forward so the small nubs of her breasts strained against the linen of her shift. Indeed, there was much hidden under that shapeless tunic. She was all passion and wildness, like the island she came from, all roaring seas and spitting foam. This must be part of her sorcery, for him to notice such a thing in the plain face and thin body of a peasant woman.

"My brothers raised their swords to me—not me to them. Would you have me let them slaughter my men rather than spill their blood?"

"What kind of place is this," she argued, ducking her head to pick up the fallen linens. "What breed of men are you, for brother to set upon brother—"

"Gavelkind. You don't know of it in Ireland, but it's destroying Wales." He stepped over his chain-mail hauberk and spread his arms to the richness of the room around him, dark beyond

the meager glow of the center hearth. "By the custom of *gav-elkind,* every man's son—bastard or legitimate—has a claim to his equal share of the holdings. But my father did it the English way and gave it all to me." He tugged on the edge of the mask. The laces cut into his neck, his forehead, under his arm—a familiar tightness. "When this came upon me, my brothers challenged my hold. For all know that a Celtic king must be whole, unmarred, to rule."

He turned away from her. A log of peat popped upon the flames. It was none of her affair, such things of war. She didn't need to know it to work her wiles.

"Heal me, woman, and you'll stop the bloodshed."

She straightened, absently folding the linens as she narrowed her eyes in speculation. "You're asking me for a healing, Rhys ap Gruffydd?"

His nostrils flared. The fire had long dimmed to dull red embers, but her hair caught and held the glow. *You'll not make me beg for it.*

"You'll be amply rewarded for your trouble."

"Are you asking me for a healing?" She slapped the pile of linens back over her shoulder. "Or are you too proud to say the words?"

The words stuck in his throat. Damn the woman, damn her gray eyes to hell. She would have him break, she would have him bend a knee to her, a knee raw from being bent already too much.

It wasn't worth it, he thought. No reward could be worth the price of utter humiliation.

Then a flash of a memory came to him, of a time in Llywelyn's court at Aberffraw, on a feast-day when the mead flowed freely—a time before the affliction, bathed now in amber hues. Prince Llywelyn had given him a new sword, with a jeweled hilt, and the Prince had beckoned him to the seat of honor at his right hand in the feasting-hall. His brothers had urged Rhys up, laughing in their drunkenness. They'd hefted him bodily over the trestle-table and shoved him toward the Prince's table near the fire. Llywelyn had offered his own tankard of mead, smiled upon Rhys and called him son. . . . Aye, and Rhys had caught the eye of Elyned from across the room, as if to say, *Look at how high I've risen. Look upon the next Prince of Wales, my betrothed.* How golden her hair had looked that evening, shimmering down over her back, and her lips had parted in moist promise. . . .

"Yes." His neck stiffened. "Yes, I'm asking you for a healing."

A breeze sifted in through the smoke-hole, the wind of Craig Gwaun, whirling down from the icy peak and frosting the muddy earth of his exile. An exile as unjust as that of the infamous Emlyn ap Dafydd of Welsh lore, who dared to pluck a single flower from the land of the *Y Tylwyth Teg,* and thus was barred with all his kith and kindred from the magical land forever.

"Very well." The proud tilt of Aileen's chin eased. Her hands slipped off her lips. "I'll heal you, Rhys ap Gruffydd."

She must have drunk too much of the mead Marged had slipped her when they'd all staggered back to the *llys.* She'd emptied the bladder, she remembered, on a stomach that hadn't seen food since a bit of bread at the break of day. Aileen could think of no other reason why she'd just stood before her captor and agreed to give him a healing.

But the words were said, and there was no doubt by the look on his face that she could not take them back. Well, she was not the kind to mock a man who bent a stiff neck to ask for something, something she would have freely given under other circumstances. He'd swallowed a mouthful of bile to force the words out. She'd seen what it cost him. She stifled more than a bit of shame that she'd been so petty as to exact the price at all.

Truth be told, he could have forced her to stay in this war-torn, lifeless land, forced her to stay until she'd agreed to give him what he wanted. There was no shame, Da had once told her, in yielding to someone more powerful than yourself. The shame was in an excess of pride . . . or not having the sense to know when a man has got you trapped.

"I'll heal you," she repeated, flipping the linens off her shoulder and onto the bench. "But I'll have two promises from you, as well."

He turned away and strolled outside the red glow of the hearth-fire, into the murky shadows beyond. "The devil never keeps his promises."

"You would know that better than I, I'm thinking."

"I already offered you gold."

"And I'll be right happy to take your gold when it's offered, when the healing is done."

His footfall scraped in the rushes, a slow measured pacing. Chain mail crushed in a crunch of metal as he nudged his chausses out of his way.

"The first promise is this: You will cease accusing me of witchcraft." She sought out his gaze in the shadows, in vain; for all she saw was a flash of light upon the bare skin of his chest as he turned, all she heard was the rustle of his footfall in the rushes. "Your people know I'm a healer. What little I've been around them this day, I sense they accept that as it is."

"My brother's work." His voice filled with mockery. "Dafydd is a master at twisting a situation to his will."

"Then it's to him I owe my thanks. Still, one word from you could shift their sentiments. I would not have their minds warped with your foolish talk of witchery. It's a fine thing you only speak to me of such things in Irish, else your people would have me burned to bones by now. But Marged is a talker, and she knows the Irish, and if she overhears—"

"Your secret," he growled, "is safe with me."

"It's no secret. I'm no witch, whatever you think. If I were, I'd have made myself into a hare or a cat or a wolf or some other creature, and escaped from this place, long before now— and probably taken all the milk of your cows just for spite."

A spray of drizzle sifted down from the smoke-hole to prickle her skin. "I'm not a witch, nor am I God, Rhys ap Gruffydd. I know not God's ways. There are some afflictions that cannot be cured."

He stopped his pacing and took a step forward. Red light glazed his stony face, gleamed on the black leather mask.

She shook her head in slow warning. "Don't be looking at me like that."

"How easy for you to say it's God's will."

"And it might be, or maybe not. I won't know until I set to you. Only then will I be knowing the truth of it. I'll tell you that truth, too. Not all people are as treacherous as you, as treacherous as your brothers. In my world, there is nothing more sacred than a man's—or a woman's—word."

"We have a saying in Welsh. An oath made under duress is no oath at all."

"I'm making this oath freely enough; I don't see you setting fire to a pyre under my feet."

"But I could. I could do worse, and you know it."

He stepped farther into the light, so the deep red glow gleamed on his chest where his shirt lay open, so she could see the powerful muscles of his thighs beneath the sweep of his *braies*, so she could feel the hot steady stare of those icy blue eyes, and she remembered with stark clarity that moment on the windswept hill of Arthur's grave when he'd seized her hands and tugged her so close she could smell the sweat on his skin and the spice of honey-mead on his breath; feel the power throbbing beneath his skin and something else . . . a wide-open yearning she'd later attributed to his lust to be cured, nothing more.

Faith, what kind of woman was she, to stand here with her heart pounding in her chest, letting him try to frighten her? And if it wasn't fear coursing through her blood, what was it?

"I'll do what I can to cure that face of yours. That is my promise to you."

"And what is this second promise?"

"It's simple enough." She took a deep breath. "I told you, I'll do what I can for you. But no matter what happens, you'll send me back to Inishmaan by Christmas."

He shook his head once, hard. "You'll stay, healer, until the work is done."

"I told you—"

"Five years in the making, and you expect to cure it within two months?"

She flushed and cast her lashes down. She wasn't giving herself away, nay. Truth be told, she'd never spent more than a couple of weeks on even the worst of cases, nor more than a month on the weakest of the wounded. If it could be cured, she'd do it quickly enough, and she'd only decided upon Christmas to allow for ample time for arrangements to be made to board another merchant ship to Ireland.

"Which vengeance will you have?" He faced her across the bench. "Will you fail to cure it and blame it on God's will? Or will you cure it then disappear into the mists, while I remain here watching it return, inch by inch? That would be the sweeter vengeance, the more painful."

"I'm willing to buy my freedom with my own skill, an honest enough trade. But you can't see that, can you? Your brothers' betrayals have curdled your blood."

His fury blasted over her as hot as the air of a kiln fire, and just as suddenly. Curse her tongue, she knew better than to prod a man with his own weakness, aye, but this one set her senses so awry that she didn't know any better. He stood there stripping her of all strength with naught but the power of his gaze. She struck out with the only weapons she had— words.

No sooner had she sensed the roar of his fury than it ebbed, as if he were sucking it back within himself as he straightened and strolled too calmly around the side of the bench. The fire had died to naught but the smallest embers now. The cold night air sifted in through the smoke-hole, weaving its way through the ragged, dirty fibers of her undertunic. Strangely, she found herself wondering, for the dozenth time, what a sight she must make.

He curled his fingers around a bladder sagging upon a table by the door, and with his back to her he tipped it up. "If my brothers' weapons were as sharp as yours, and their aim as true, I wager not a single one of my men would have left those woods alive."

"Are you telling me you agree?"

"No."

She closed her eyes, fighting for patience. She resisted the urge to sink upon the bench, to ease the ache throbbing in her lower back, to give her weakening legs a rest. She should have curled up on a pallet against the wall of the mead-hall and saved this confrontation for the morrow, when she had more strength.

"You'll stay," he said, "until spring."

She opened her eyes to a face twitching with a wry smile, a face full of mockery but for the tightness in the lines fanning out from his unmasked eye. The months between now and spring stretched out before her like a hundred thousand years. She thought of Ma and the stored bales of wool to be spun and woven, with no one to help but a dreamy-eyed Cairenn. She thought of the long nights her family would lie awake, wondering what had become of her.

Then she looked upon Rhys, and knew there would be no bargaining.

"Done, then." She gathered the linens, then hefted up the bowl of water, sank the rim into her side, and headed toward the door. "We'll begin tomorrow."

"Oh, no, lass."

He seized her arm so swift and so hard that the cold water sloshed upon her hip.

"We start here." He drew her away from the door, deep into the room. "We start now."

Six

"Do you think it's as easy as that, then?" The edge of the bench bit into the backs of her knees. "I've salves to brew and herbs to dry."

"You didn't need those things this afternoon." He released her arm as swiftly as he'd seized it. "You don't need them now."

"What is it that you expect then? A wave of my fingers with a shower of sparks? Incantations naked by the full of the moon?"

"Whatever it takes."

She flushed and slammed the bowl of water back on the bench. A foul warrior he was, standing there making demands upon her when she'd spent the day tending to his men. Wasn't it like a man to care only for his own needs and not pay a bit of mind to the needs of others? Faith, it was a fine thing God made women the bearer of the children, else there would be no more people walking this earth. And faith, why didn't he lace up that wretched shirt of his like any decent man would?

"You want to start, then? We'll start by talking." She plopped down on the opposite side of the bowl of water, as far away from him as she could get. "I've no hope of curing that problem of yours unless I know something about it."

He swung his arm through the air in dismissal. "There's nothing to know that'll be any help to you."

"And I thought the Irish were a garrulous people. Are you to fight me every step of the way, Rhys ap Gruffydd? Or are you to help me rid you of whatever it is that plagues you so much you'll kidnap a woman from her home and keep her prisoner until she does your bidding?"

She made a fuss of scrubbing dry a spot of water on her hip, but she felt the heat of his anger anyway, and the action only drew her attention to how high the ragged bit of linen ended on her thighs. By God, what a mess she was. Her scalp itched, mud caked her knees, blood and earth streaked her undertunic, which did nothing to soften the angles of her body, or shadow what little she deemed personal. And why should she care that she stood all but naked before him? She was no beauty to inspire lust.

He jerked away so suddenly that the bench rocked. "It started five years ago last spring." He jabbed the middle of his shoulder, and she noticed the outline of more black leather under the gaping linen. "It started on my shoulder, and every month it spreads more."

"What were you doing, five years ago last spring?"

"Enjoying myself in the court of the Prince of Wales." He choked the neck of the full bladder with his fist. "We'd finished a round of fighting against the traitors of southern Wales, and we'd won."

"That got your blood up, I'm sure." The Prince of Wales, then! No petty baron, this Lord of Graig, she thought, remembering the silks and linens Marged had held out to her yesterday morning. "Were you wounded? Or did you—"

"I've searched for a *reason,* woman, every day for five long years." He spread out his arms. "Could it have been those foul cockles we ate on the march north, or the light of the full moon falling upon us when we slept in the open, or the leper I passed by without giving alms in Aberffraw?"

"How's a woman to tend to you spitting and roaring?"

"I tell you, it was none of that, for food was plentiful and the mead flowed thick. I'd begun to build my castle; the childless Prince of Wales called me son; and the first person to notice the thing growing upon my shoulder was a buxom tart of a woman warming my bed."

Her cheeks flamed at the image he conjured. "If it were another part of your body that had the trouble I'd know the source of it, then."

"There's never been any trouble there."

"I've no doubt you know how to wield your sword indiscriminately enough to sire a passel of bastards."

"Bastards." He spat out the word. "After what you saw today, you think I spill my seed so easily into fertile ground?"

Embarrassment coursed across her face. It was no business of hers what he did in his bed; she didn't want to hear of it, she didn't want to imagine it. It was the healing she would set her mind to, healing him and breaking free from this place. "Is there any pain to the affliction?"

"No."

"Does it itch, or burn?"

"It's as if nothing is there."

She dunked a linen into the bowl. This was going nowhere, and the fighting wearied her. She'd get no answers from him, at least none that would be of any help. "I'll look at the thing, and wash it, and tomorrow I'll have something for it. Now take off that mask, sit down, and stop prowling around like a wolf."

She whirled the cloth in what was left of the cloudy mixture in the bowl. Linen whispered as he pulled off his shirt and sent it flying across the floor. Aye, she'd seen a dozen shirtless warriors this day, she'd stripped the shirts off them herself, in fact. Then why was she staring into the bowl as if afraid to raise her head to the darkness?

She waited for him to sit, and when moments passed and still he didn't, she glanced up and bit the inside of her lip. For he loomed bare-chested at the other end of the bench, light gleaming off his skin, rippling over an abdomen and a chest so sculpted with hard muscles that it put all the Irish strongmen of the autumn *feis* to shame.

He was a warrior, she scolded herself, did she expect soft-ness in a man so hard? She'd stubbed her toe upon the likes of the chain-mail hauberk piled at her feet more than once, and knew the weight of the armor—he needed such broad shoulders to keep from collapsing under it. Still, for all her work on wounded men, she'd never seen so many muscles outlined so starkly against the skin. It was as if, because of the imperfections of his face, he'd tried all the harder to perfect his body. Any woman, she told herself, would feel a throb of excitement at the sight of such a fine specimen of a man. It was lust, pure and simple, and for all her common looks, she was still a woman and prone to a woman's momentary weak-ness.

Then she raised her gaze to his face. The mask still hugged his shoulder and head. He stared at her with unreadable eyes, though she sensed his mind going round and round with thoughts she could not begin to guess, whirling until she thought she could smell the effort, like the charring of the wood on a windmill whipped too fast in a storm.

What pride this man had. It was that—or shame—which kept him in the shadows. "Is that wretched mask sewn onto you then?"

"Would that it were."

"Aye, I'll have none of your vanity this night," she argued. "I've seen your men turned inside out this day."

"I know what you've seen. Not the likes of me."

"Shall you stand before me like a quivering boy hiding his wound for fear of my touch?"

He loomed before her, all naked flesh and bright determi-nation. "Your touch." A light came into his eyes. "Yes, yes, all you need is your touch."

With a swipe of his hands, he hefted the bowl of water off the bench.

"What . . . what are you doing?"

"The devil's work is best done in the dark."

He tossed the contents onto the flames. The embers hissed

and sizzled up a spray of steam. Darkness engulfed the room. Aileen stumbled up, backed away blindly, dragging her knee against the edge of the bench as a guide. No windows aired this chamber. No light winnowed through the smoke-hole above; only the vaguest hiss of light rain. A single strip of amber light splashed across the reeds, emanating from a crack between the door and the portal to the mead-hall.

His footsteps scraped across the floor. His bare-chested silhouette loomed against the light. Gold gleamed upon the leather mask which extended over his right shoulder, a massive shoulder, as stiff and unmovable as the mountains of Wales. He shoved something in the crack and plunged them both into darkness.

He moved restlessly about, she charting his movements by the scraping of the rushes. The hairs on the back of her neck prickled as the bench creaked when he gripped it and swung a leg over it. She probed the darkness in his direction, hoping to see something, a shape, a form, the limning of an arm by the light of stars . . . but nothing, nothing but the blackness of the grave and the memory of the curl of dark hairs dense on his bare chest.

But she *knew* how he'd sat. She knew he was struggling with something. She felt blinded in a wolves' den, and she was heaving as if she'd run clear across the island. Dear Lord, could *he* hear her breathing? He emanated a heat so intense that if it were light she was sure it would brighten the whole *llys*. There was no losing him in this room, nay, she'd know his every position with her eyes closed. She could smell him. The smell of man-sweat and warm iron, so pulsing and full of hot-blooded fleshy life.

Something *thwacked* to the floor near her feet.

"The mask," he said, "is off."

"This is foolish." The words tumbled out and she hated the quivering in them. "I've never known a more vain man, Rhys ap Gruffydd."

She sensed his anger, like the crackling of the air in an early summer gale.

"Get on with it."

"How am I supposed to know how to cure the thing," she asked, "if I can't see it?"

"Healing hands," he murmured in the darkness. "Healing hands."

"That's your folly, not mine." Suddenly she realized she had balled a wet linen in her hand, and she'd soaked a spot into her lap. "Now you expect me to act on it? As if by a touch of my hands you'd be cured."

It should be that simple. It should be simple enough for her to reach across the space that separated them, pass her fingers across his cheek a few times, and have it be over and done with. Aye, it should be that easy, but she'd be damned if she'd let him know that for sure. Damned if she'd give up the pretext.

Still, she hesitated, even as she slipped down the length of the bench and sat close enough to feel the heat of his body against her knees. What was this? She'd healed many a man she didn't like—all the warriors who raced to her father's house sobbing with war-wounds. Aye, she'd touched *them* and eased their pain whilst holding the distaste at bay, and she'd not been the least bit troubled by it. Why now, in the darkness with this growling caged beast, did she flex her fingers in her lap?

It was true that she'd never healed a healthy man. All that came to her were in pain or wounded, or in the throes of child-birth; all those who submitted beneath her touch bore wounds of the flesh and were weakened by pain. Now she sat across from a man pulsing with health, an outsider who knew too much about her gift, a man who claimed he needed a healing, a man whose flesh did not scream out in agony, a man who wanted her touch and was clear headed enough to *feel* it.

If she healed him with her touch, what would he do? Would he truly set her free? Or would he turn upon her as soon as he was healed, call her witch and see her burned? And if she didn't dare to trust this contrary man, would she ever smell the grass of Inishmaan again?

She held out her own hand to the darkness. "Give me your hand."

"My wound," he growled, "is on my face."

"Are you to be the healer, then, telling me how to go about my business?"

A moment passed. Anger and hesitation pulsed from him. Then, suddenly, she felt the scrape of his palm against hers.

A shock reverberated up her arm, as if it were he who was to give the healing and not her. She absorbed this sensation while their palms lay intimately upon one another, pressed hollow to hollow, his fingers stiff against her wrist, while something tightened in her throat. His pulse pounded against the pad of her fingers. When the shock passed she blinked her eyes and focused her thoughts upon his hands. Hot hands, he had. Hot and large and strong, heavy upon her own.

She looked up, where his face must be, and knew in that moment that their lips were only inches from each other.

A strange feeling, this, to stare into utter darkness and know someone was inches away, know the position of his lips, know that his eyes were probing the darkness. His breath fell upon her mouth, and a raggedness hitched it into his lungs. Stubble upon his cheeks—aye, she sensed that, too, though they didn't touch, for she sensed him with her own skin as if their skins were pressed together.

Here was the intimacy she needed for the healing; his skin felt as rasping as sand against hers. Oh, he was pulling at her own insides when it was *she* who was to pull upon his and drag out the poisons.

And listen to her! She was in no state to heal, what was wrong with her? Leaning up to a man, offering her face like a harlot at fair-time. She drew back then, flipped his hand over so his palm faced up. He scraped against the bench as he moved closer, and she felt a flush rise to her neck as his knee brushed against hers. She scented, vaguely, the hazelnuts he'd had for dinner and realized she must smell them on his breath, that they were still close enough to breathe the same air.

She pulled his hand down, to the bench, and with her other hand began to trace the skin on the back of his arm.

Soft, downy hair tickled the pads of her fingers. Dark hairs, she remembered, on a forearm leathered from sun and wind. She'd watched the muscles in that forearm flex like so many taut-stretched ropes as he held his falcon that day. An elbow. There wasn't a bit of give in this arm, each ridge as hard as stone, but the skin as smooth as her own except for the ridge of a scar here and there. She trailed her fingers up over the ball of his arm, then around the ridge of the muscle. A strong man, this, with muscles as dense as rock. She started as he flinched beneath her touch.

So he was a strong man, what difference did it make? Rhys ap Gruffydd was not the sort of man to put these muscles to good use; nay, he'd spend all this strength on killing before he'd hew a stone to make a fine house. She'd seen the strongest of men brought down by the meanest of wounds, crying and sputtering whilst her father stitched them up or lathered some soothing salve over their meager bruises. Then she'd seen women wracked with the pain of labor bite through their lips rather than bring shame upon themselves by crying out. There was no telling *her* who was the stronger sex. It was time for her to purge her mind of foolish thoughts and set to the task at hand.

She trailed her fingers higher, to the curve of his shoulder, to a sudden ridge in his skin.

She felt his discomfort—it made her think of the hardening of a brick in the sun—though her only contact with him was on the palm of his hand and the ridge of his shoulder.

"It feels," she murmured, tracing the edge of the affliction, "like a burn."

"It's no burn."

"Well, I wouldn't be knowing that, would I, not seeing it myself?"

"Just get on with it."

As if it were that easy, as if he didn't do what he could to make it impossible for her to concentrate, looming over her, growling words onto the nape of her neck. She squeezed her eyes shut harder and waited for the quiet to come over her, for the soft slipping into peace. Faith, she was surprised it hadn't come already. She flattened her hand over the edge of the affliction. She took a deep, deep breath . . . and waited.

The rain hissed harder into the thatch above. Outside, in the mead-hall, a wounded man cried out in his sleep, then rustled deeper into his covers. Somewhere beyond the walls, a horse neighed and a man shouted across the yard.

Aileen's brows twitched together. She stroked higher, her fingers rumbling over the rippled skin. Smooth ripples, no more heat emanating from them than the rest of his skin, the rest of his body; as if his skin were water and this part was but frozen ripples in a pool. She traced the affliction to the curve of his neck, to the throb of a pulse, searching for pain, for something, and there she waited, the pulse throbbing, throbbing, throbbing beneath her fingers.

This couldn't be.

She took another breath, deeper this time. The fragrance of his skin filled her head, the fragrance of man.

You must concentrate, Aileen, on the task before you.

The pulse throbbed, throbbed, throbbed.

She blinked her eyes open and stared blindly where she knew her hand lay. She jerked up from the bench, then scattered back from him. She squeezed her fingers together.

This couldn't be.

"Enough for one night." She fumbled in the dark for the wet and dirty linens, giving up the overturned bowl as lost. "I'll make you up a salve for it, I will, then we'll set upon it again another day."

She stumbled her way through the dark to where she supposed the door was. She pushed it open. The dim red glow of the mead-hall blinded her, but she did not stop her pace. Her feet scraped through the rushes. Her lungs ached for fresh, clean air. Now, bereft of touch, the palm of her hand tingled as if she'd scraped it upon a bed of nettles.

But when she'd laid that hand upon Rhys ap Gruffydd . . . she had felt nothing.

Nothing at all.

"Pay no mind to these girls, my lady. It's not that you don't know the language that they be bringing you water when you want lard, or hemp when you be wanting linens. They've not a wit of sense in them these days, that's all."

Aileen took the linens Marged offered and sank to her knees next to the pallet of a sleeping warrior. The morning light seeped in a white haze through the smoke-hole. On the next pallet, one of the wounded found the strength to sit up and tease a maidservant enough to send her skittering off, giggling.

"All they do be thinking about is the coming of *Nos Calan Gaeaf*—All Hallows' E'en to good Christians. It's the only word out of their mouths from morning to night. They be racing here and there, collecting nuts to be thrown in the fire and fighting over the blade bone of a shoulder of mutton and choosing leek beds to be walking about nine times in the night—all to conjure up the sight of their future husbands. . . ."

Aileen plucked at the crusted linen strapped across the man's belly, listening to Marged's monologue with half an ear. The Irish boasted some of the same *Samhain* rituals as the Welsh; she remembered more than one night in her youth raking out the ashes of the hearth-fire, hoping to find the footprint of her future husband marked in the ashes the next morn, and finding nothing but the scuffs of sleepy children who'd scuttled across the flagstones on the way to the chamber pot.

She'd given up those rituals by her fourteenth year, about the same time she'd given up all pretense of finding a husband.

". . . peeling apples and tossing the peels over their shoulders. Do you know we've lost a sack of apples already, and *Calan Gaeaf* three days hence?" Marged twitched; Aileen felt the brush of Marged's skirts against her back. "Oh, my lady, look at that girl, yawning without even making the sign of the cross over her mouth, does she want the Evil One to jump in and take abode in her?"

"Could you hand me the water, Marged?" Aileen had quickly learned that the only way to communicate with the voluble housekeeper was to interrupt at will. "And will you stop calling me 'my lady'? Did I not bed down with you in the kitchens last night?"

"That was but for a night. It's sure I am the master will have you set up here, in the mead-hall, as soon as he sets one of his men to make the partitions."

"I'll be sleeping in the kitchens, thank you very much." Aileen scrubbed a streak of dried blood off the man's abdomen, avoiding the padding stuck to his wound. "I'm the oldest of a family of eight, Marged. I've boiled soup and spun wool and tended cows all my life. 'Tis sure I'm no highborn guest, and I'll not play the pretense from now until spring."

"And a glorious thing that is, that you'll be staying for so long. We've lacked a good woman healer in Graig for too long, I'll tell you. More than one woman has died or watched her babe die in childbirth for lack of an experienced hand. Your ears must have been burning all night, for the freemen's wives have done naught but talk about you, my lady."

"Did you not hear a word I've said?"

"What will I be calling you then, you, a fine healer and a guest in this house?"

"My Christian name is good enough. In all my five-and-twenty years it has not worn out yet."

Aileen wrung the blood out of the linen and tossed it over her shoulder, then swiftly retrieved it before it wetted the wool. Aye, she hoped this wretched rain would stop soon. She had given her own tunic to the launderer last night, to be pounded free of soil and blood, but in this dank weather it would take a fortnight to dry. Now, Marged's own best wool draped her figure, and she felt awkward doing common chores in such a fine, borrowed dress. But it had been this or the silks Marged had again offered her. Her only concession had been to borrow from amid the fine stuff a tightly woven linen shift, for her own was all but useless. Now, the butter-soft length of the chemise brushed against her thighs and belly with a disturbing intimacy.

"I'd best be learning the Welsh, myself, I'm thinking, seeing that I'll be staying here for a while." Aileen gazed upon the wounded man while her palms itched. "With no woman to run the house, you've got your hands full. I can't have you following me about when you've your own chores to see to, Marged."

Nor can I have you watching too closely, seeing too much, suspecting there's more to this healing of mine than wood-anemone plasters and herb broths.

If there still is . . .

"This man will be needing some of that plaster I had one of the girls make up yesterday," she said, glancing over her shoulder. "You remember, with the wood anemone?"

"Aye, I'll be telling them, though only God will know if they'll set to it, with their minds all a-flutter."

Marged marched away. Aileen dug her fingernails into her palms and returned her gaze to the sleeping warrior. The tumble of healthy men who'd laid their pallets along the edges of the hall last night had long dispersed to their chores outside. Now, the hall murmured with the rustle of the wounded testing their sore limbs, with the banter of soldier and maidservant.

Shielded by the huge fire which roared in the center hearth and crackled the spice of wood-smoke into the air, Aileen stretched out her hand. She let it hover, trembling, over the man's blood-encrusted wound. Then she curled her hand into a fist and jerked it back under the folds of her tunic.

Aye, what a coward she was, as skittish as kite under the shadow of a hawk, too afraid even to try her hands again. She felt like the Widdy Peggeen, who in her increased age had taken to leaving the laces of her tunic undone, not out of lack of skill but out of fear that if she made a habit of lacing them then one day she'd set to the task and find she couldn't do it at all.

I was exhausted, Aileen told herself, for the hundredth time. She'd spent the night tossing and turning, wondering what was wrong with her, and by morning's light she'd convinced herself it had been simple exhaustion. She'd witnessed a bloody battle, had her own life threatened, felt the sudden presence of the *Sidh*, and spent a whole afternoon and evening in healing. It was no wonder that she'd no strength left for the likes of Rhys ap Gruffydd, no wonder she'd felt nothing but the power and intensity of a man beneath her hand.

The breath she sucked in burned all the way to her lungs. *Look at yourself Aileen, with no more sense than these young maidservants flipping their hair and batting their eyes at the warriors scattered about.* The coming of *Samhain,* that was what was causing her blood to roil so. She'd be fooling herself to deny that Rhys, for all his faults, was a fine cut of a man, and everyone knew there was no controlling the burn of one's blood with the coming of the time of darkness. She'd long seen it as rutting season for humans, and she was human enough to be swept along with it all, while sensible enough to see it for what it was.

She unfurled her fingers. There was only one way to know for sure whether she still had the power, or whether this bloody and lifeless land—or this fierce and contrary man—had sucked it away from her. Clenching her jaw, she let her hand drift down upon the wounded man.

Without a heartbeat of hesitation, she felt it: the sensation of dipping her hands into a thicker medium, the resistance against her fingers . . . and then the subtle current of life rippled through her into the man, as if the sluice gates of a river dam opened upon a dry lake bottom. Relief shuddered through her so fiercely that she didn't sense the woman standing over her until the unexpected visitor said something in Welsh.

Aileen glanced up and found herself staring past a protruding belly to the hesitant smile of a very pregnant Welsh woman. The Welsh woman bobbed her head and began babbling in a soft, gentle voice, then thrust a package at her as Aileen stood up, leaving Aileen no choice but to grasp the gift against her abdomen lest it tumble atop the wounded man. She listened to the gurgle of the woman's words, thinking she'd have to learn some Welsh—and soon.

"She's thanking you for saving her husband's life. Roderic ap Ceicyll—the one with the javelin wound in his shoulder." Dafydd sauntered to the end of the pallet and snapped his fur-lined mantle free of drizzle as if it were a pair of wings. "A leg of lamb, apparently. Much prized in these parts."

"Tell the young woman that I'm moved by her generosity." Aileen's gaze skittered away from Dafydd's clear hazel eyes. In the rush of transporting the wounded yesterday, she'd managed to avoid him, but now he stood before her with knowledge in his gaze, a dangerous knowledge. She fixed her attention on the young woman dressed in homespun, a girl no older than her sister Cairenn. "But tell her that it is my gift to her, and her growing family, that she keep this lamb."

Dafydd translated swiftly. The young woman smiled, bobbed, then lumbered off toward the doorway.

"Wait."

Dafydd seized Aileen's arm before she could catch the young woman's attention. "You don't want to insult her."

"What," she asked, pulling away and shifting the weight of the package in her arms, "did you tell her?"

Dafydd grinned and tugged a hazel shoot out of his mouth. "I told her that you were moved by her generosity, and that you wish her health and happiness with her growing family."

"A bit got lost in the translation, then."

"Would you shame her by refusing her gift?" Dafydd shifted the weight of the quiver of arrows strapped across his back, and shouldered his purple mantle open to reveal the embroidered blue tunic beneath. He nodded as she cast her gaze away. "Ah, I knew the custom was the same in Ireland, as well as Wales."

"Aye, but in Ireland I was mistress of my own." She hefted the package out to him. "And will you be telling me what I am to do with this thing?"

"I'm partial to having it basted within a suet crust and served with mountain-ash jelly."

"I'll give it to Marged, then."

Aileen turned on her heel and headed toward the door. Dafydd's soft leather boots made no sound in the rushes. He shot out an arm to open the door before she could do it herself.

"You'll be getting plenty more of that before the week is done," he said, falling into step beside her as she made her way through the faint drizzle toward the kitchens. "It has been years since we've had a healer here. The Welsh don't live clustered up in towns and villages like the English and most of the Irish—our people live on small homesteads scattered about these hills, hills that don't make it easy for travel. This *llys* is the largest settlement in half a day's ride." He stepped around a pile of gorse and straw undoubtedly destined for the *Calan Gaeaf* fires, and tossed the hazel shoot into the pile. "All our people are grateful for what you did yesterday. You're needed here."

"I'm needed on Inishmaan, as well."

"But you're staying until spring."

"What choice did I have in it?" A couple of hounds, scenting the lamb, trailed in the mud behind them, their muzzles in the air. "Your brother didn't give me much of one."

"My brother is not one for diplomacy these days."

"Your brother," she began, rising to a good Irish temper, "is the most arrogant, undeserving, con—"

"He is my brother," Dafydd reminded her. "And the lord of this place."

She felt the heat of a flush rise up her cheeks, followed swiftly by indignity. Perhaps she shouldn't speak badly of the lord of this house—especially to his brother—but she'd been too ill-treated to grant her host the respect he would normally deserve, too ill-treated to take the words back.

Dafydd reached over his shoulder and scraped something out of his quiver. "See this?"

Aileen suffered a glance at the bow and arrow gripped in his fist, then looked at the unusual bow more closely.

"A clever little device, isn't it?" Dafydd paused in the courtyard. He trailed his stunted wrist down the length of the bowed wood, then nudged his wrist into a molded leather cup hanging from the center. "I was nearly fourteen, and Rhys was ten, when he returned here one day from the house of Gerwyn ap Rhain, where Rhys was being fostered." With a twitch of his leather-covered wrist, he turned the bow flat and nudged the arrow across it, upon a small wedge in the wood. "Rhys overheard our father threatening to give me up to the church."

She frowned at him, wondering what this was leading to, and sensing she didn't want to hear it. She gestured to his fine purple mantle, trimmed in soft gray fur growing matted in the drizzle. "You like your comforts too much to be any kind of priest, I'm thinking."

"Indeed, I was an unlikely choice, but our father thought a one-handed man would make a better priest than a warrior." With a twitch of his wrist, he twisted the bow level again, then dragged the tail of the arrow back with his good hand, and curled his fingers over the bowstring. "For though I could shoot a lance as straight and as far as any man, a warrior needed two hands to use a longbow. And a Welshman isn't a man if he can't shoot a bow."

With a twang, he launched the arrow. It cracked into the doorpost of a food shed, clear across the courtyard.

"On that day of Rhys's return," he continued, calmly fisting the bow back into the quiver, "I shot my first arrow alone. And my father relented."

Her eyes widened. "Are you telling me Rhys made that thing for you?"

"A cruder version of it."

"Don't be talking foolishness." She swiveled in the mud and set her foot back on the path to the kitchens. She knew as sure as she breathed that the child who'd fashion such a thing for the sake of his brother was not the same as the man who'd stolen her off the shores of Inishmaan. "A fine, pretty story. And it explains better than anything else why you stay loyal to him when your other brothers have rebelled. But will it get me to Inishmaan any faster by knowing it?"

"No. I suppose not."

Aye, and it was Inishmaan where she wanted to be at this moment, instead of under the clear hazel gaze of an outsider who sensed too much; it was Inishmaan where she wanted to be, instead of in a world where generous intelligent children grew up into raging, senseless men.

"We welcome you here, nonetheless, Aileen." Dafydd clasped his arm behind his back and shrugged. "Inishmaan's loss is our gain."

Aye, wasn't that the truth. She thought of Ma and her sore shoulder, hefting a basket overflowing with seaweed upon her back. She thought of the pile of wool tumbling in the corner of the house, waiting for long winter's night spinning by the fire. She thought of the soft white sea mists pillowing around the island, cutting it off from the rest of the world, from the eyes of outsiders, from warriors and their bloody battles and all the ugliness and pain of this world. She thought of briny fogs swirling outside the house fragrant with a peat fire, with stew bubbling in the cauldron. . . .

The homesickness cut through her sharper than the cold mountain drizzle, so sharp and so sudden that she stumbled in the mud. She shot out an arm to clutch a handful of Dafydd's fur-lined mantle to right herself, then blinked her eyes open to the prickle of rain, to a slate-gray sky, to a horizon lost in the clouds. Thinking of spring with its green shoots and bright sunshine was like thinking of a leaf buffeted farther and farther away by the wind.

The dogs took advantage of the ebb in Aileen's pace to leap up and nip the coarsely woven fibers wrapped around the meat.

Dafydd's voice cut through the fog in her head as he yelled sharply at them.

"Does the sun never shine in this wretched place?" She hugged a bundle of Marged's tunic up out of the mud. "Enough to make a woman mad, it is."

"Hiraeth."

"Don't be cursing me in your wretched Welsh."

"Hiraeth," he repeated. Dafydd reached over and relieved her of the burden of the package so she could hold up her skirts. "There's no translation for it in Irish. It means . . . longing. A yearning for your birthplace."

Too perceptive, this one. Far, far too perceptive. The kitchens lay just ahead, a woman's place, and so she lengthened her pace toward sanctuary.

"It can be a sort of sickness, *hiraeth,* enough to drive some-one mad." His voice deepened. "I pray you never know the depths of it."

"It's sure I wouldn't have known it at all if a certain Welshman hadn't taken me off the shores of Inishmaan. With your help, I remind you."

"If you look hard enough," Dafydd continued, as if she hadn't spoken, "you'll see that every man, woman and child in this *llys* is infected with *hiraeth.* And has been, since this thing happened to Rhys."

The kitchen blasted a strip of heat and light over the muddy paving-stones, and it was here Aileen swiveled and held out her arms for the package. But Dafydd paused with it slung upon his shoulder and stared off to some point beyond the prickled horizon of the wooden palisades.

"It's a strange thing," he continued. "Five years ago I first noticed it. A sharper chill to the winters, a staleness in the air. It's as if the spirit of the place withdrew and left us all here. Instead of being banished from Eden, Eden has been banished from *us.*"

She stanched the quiver in her belly. So it wasn't her imag-inings then, the odd silence of the woods and valleys, the deathly stillness of Arthur's grave. For the moment, she didn't know which struck her as more unusual; the silence, or the fact that an outsider had the sense to hear it.

"I've always held this fanciful thought," he mused, "that if Rhys is healed, then so is the land."

"Aren't you a strange one, talking such superstitious nonsense."

"Indeed." A wry grin spread across his handsome face. "Rhys would flay me with the sharp side of his tongue if he heard this talk. He has no use for anything he can't taste, touch, see, hear, or smell." His half-smile faded as he drew his gaze from the horizon and fixed it upon her. "But the truth is, Aileen, I haven't felt the soul of this place in so long. Until yesterday, during the battle. On the riverbed of Nantfechan."

The sounds of the kitchen roared behind her—the bubbling of cauldrons and the chatter of women, the crackle of fires and the squeal of turning spits. Drizzle gusted beneath the doorjamb and sprayed her face with icy rain.

Her skirts sifted out of her arms to swish around her legs. He'd heard. He'd *seen*. And he'd understood what he'd seen on that riverbank.

For the second time since she'd come to Wales she stood naked beneath the gaze of an outsider. Those hazel eyes cut through to the truth—more, perhaps, than Rhys's had; for Rhys called her magic witchcraft and cared not of whence it came. But Dafydd stared down at her with all the knowledge of the world in his eyes. She knew she should rise up and ask him with scorn in her voice what he was talking about, but she also knew it would all be in vain. Those hazel eyes had cut through all her denials and mockery before they were even spoken.

Though she stood before him, frozen by shock, and though words of denial quivered on her tongue, she knew—from a knowledge born of some deep instinct—that she could trust this man. The certainty made no sense. She knew no more about him than she knew about Rhys. But Rhys was mocking, scornful. Dafydd *believed*.

"You are going to heal him, aren't you, Aileen?"

Horses' hooves clattered over the wooden bridge that lay over the hollow of the trench just outside the palisades. Hounds swept out of their shelters as a cluster of horses galloped into the yard, with Rhys at the lead. Rhys yanked his mount to a stop, spraying clods of mud over the stableboy who'd raced to be the first to seize the reins.

She watched Rhys swing off the horse. Rain plastered his hair to his head, and streamed down the black mask which hid all but his scowl. He slapped his crop against his thigh and strode toward the mead-hall

In all the years she'd tended the men of Inishmaan, she'd always sought out the boy in them—in the ease of their smiles, the tumbles of their hair, the quivering of their lips as they bit them against the pain. She'd come to the conclusion that nothing could separate the boy from the man.

Perhaps nothing . . . except bitterness.

"Marged was after telling me," Aileen began, "about the chaplain of this parish."

Dafydd watched her with clear, intense eyes, full of so much hope that she almost didn't dare to meet them.

"He's partial to herb-gardening, I'm told. This kitchen is shamefully bereft of herbs, and the season is too late to find much of what I need on the land. If I'm to make any medicines—for your brother and the wounded—I need to pay the chaplain a visit."

A slow grin lit Dafydd's face. "I'll take you."

"Good." She wiped a wet tress off her forehead, then seized the leg of lamb. "Be off with you now, I've work to do."

Aye, a day's worth of work to do; salves to brew, broths to boil, plasters to mix. She entered the red heat of the kitchens, her heart quivering in trepidation. When it was all done . . . the time would come to test her hands again.

On Rhys.

Seven

Rhys yanked his gauntlets out of his belt and tossed them into the corner of the room, then struggled with the buckle. The door squealed behind him and soft footsteps sounded on the reeds.

"Leave." With a growl he tossed his belt and his sword upon the bed. The footsteps faltered, but did not retreat. He seized his tunic by the scruff of the neck. "I said *leave.*"

"I will not."

He jerked his head out of the neck of the tunic and glared at the intruder. He'd expected Marged with food, for he had had no stomach for the dinner she'd had laid out upon the trestle tables this day, and she'd long made it a habit to follow him with a tray of leftovers like a clucking hen. He hadn't expected *her,* standing just inside the doorway with defiance in her eyes.

So she was still here.

"Marged tells me you're done with your dinner, and you've sent your men off to new duties." Two bowls clattered upon a chest by the door. "If you've a moment, I'll see to you now."

"While you still have the courage?"

He eyed her as he tugged at the buckles of his hauberk. Those smoky gray eyes cleared to the sharpest silver when she was in a fury. Granted, the woman had courage. More courage than his brothers, whatever that amounted to. They'd vanished into the hills as quickly as they'd appeared, rather than face him again; yet this woman came to his chamber on her own will after tearing out of it last night as if the devil were after her. By the rigidness of those narrow shoulders, she must have spent the day bracing herself for the ordeal.

Poor little wretch. Forced to touch the monster.

"I'll not stay awake till the wee hours of the morning for the likes of you, Rhys ap Gruffydd." She slapped a pile of linens beside the bowls. "We'll do this now, before you set off for that castle of yours again, or roam the borders of your wretched kingdom in search of your murdering brothers."

"I admire your eagerness."

With a stiffening of her shoulders, she hiked a bowl onto her hip and plunged a pestle into it. "I've made you a salve of a sort. It's the best I could do with what little I could find in your kitchens."

He jerked open another buckle of his hauberk. "You disappoint me, Irish, by playing the pretext still."

"Aye, Lord Rhys, you won't be happy until I powder a newt for you, will you?"

"I expect better than that. I've had powdered newt."

"And the bitterness lingers on your tongue, I see."

He jerked open his hauberk. The lass gave as well as she got—sometimes better. "What is it you have in that muck? Frostwort? Celandine? Or have you fried cabbage leaves to deaden the pain? Hung house-leek to the thatch of the roof?"

"If you let yourself be talked into eating a bit of powdered newt, Lord Rhys, then I'm sure you've tried all sorts of useless things. Who have you been seeing?" She scraped the pestle across the rim of the bowl. "I would expect better medicine from the Prince of Wales's own doctors."

He wrenched the hauberk off his shoulders and launched the iron links across the paving stones. The chain mail spit sparks as it scraped across slate and slammed into the stone wall. He glared at her, but she'd turned her profile to him and now wiped the pestle clean on a linen scrap. He wondered how she'd heard of his relationship with the Prince of Wales, and wondered if she'd been talking to someone—Marged, perhaps, with her wagging tongue, coloring the whole story with the softness of a woman who'd nursed him into manhood—or Dafydd who'd spent dinner staring down at his trencher bread rather than discuss the building of the castle. Dafydd who believed in all the superstitious rot that infected this country, these people.

Then Rhys remembered that he had mentioned the Prince to her, only last night. Just as swiftly he wondered why he cared what she heard. She'd hear the whole story sooner or later. Everyone knew of the public humiliation of Rhys ap Gruffydd, the leper-lord of Wales.

"Rich doctors are no wiser than poor ones," Rhys said, "just better born, lighter of tongue, and more clever." He tore at the buckles of his gambeson until the padded shirt dropped to the floor. "You fool no one but yourself with these salves."

"Believe what you will, it's sure I'll not be able to change your way of thinking." She marched to the bench and clattered the bowl upon it. "I suppose it's better you believe in something, else you'll never be cured."

He snorted a humorless laugh. He'd tried that, too. Believing in God. Trusting in man. He seized his shirt at the nape of his neck and tore it over his head. "Shut the door."

She stood up and scraped the door closed, then took the bowl of water lying upon the chest and poured it over the center hearth. No arguments this time, Rhys noted, as steam hissed up to the smoke-hole. No mockery, no hesitation. He wrestled the shirt off his arms and tossed it onto the bed. She'd learned her lesson last night, as she touched him in the dark then reeled away as if burned, racing out of the darkness into the light.

He tore at the ties of his mask. One beneath his arm. Another on the side of his neck. The third above his ear. A cool breeze siphoned down through the smoke-hole and chilled his face as he crumpled the leather in his fist and then tossed it aside.

An exhilaration seized him. *Now, woman, you're in my land. You're in the darkness where we are both equal.*

Not even the endless Welsh drizzle could completely cut off the afternoon light, a beam of hazy gray sifting down to gleam on the stones of the hearth. Aileen sat upon the bench, her lap jutting into the haze, her face a mere ghost in the darkness.

"Come here," he said.

Her legs stilled; her hand drifted into the light to rest upon her thigh. He sank upon his bed. Her hand curled into a fist as the straw mattress crinkled beneath his weight, as the bed-clothes rustled. With a flash of memory, he thought of a time when a woman would eagerly cross the rushes at such an in-vitation. He remembered a time when he'd not even had to command a woman to his bed. Now this skinny witch-creature stiffened in terror when his intent was no more prurient than to draw her into the darkness so she could wield her magic.

Yes, Irish, I am the creature of your nightmares, of all maid-ens' nightmares—the monster who would take an unwilling woman, laughing at her screams.

"I've eaten my pound of human flesh today," he said. "It's unlikely I'll get hungry again before Vespers."

She jerked up from the bench. He caught a flash of silver eyes before she turned away to gather her bowl and linens. She stomped across the room, cursing as she tripped over an article of his discarded armor. She faltered and flailed out an arm that knocked against the bedpost.

He reached out and caught a fistful of woolen skirts, then dragged her toward him. He hiked a knee upon the bed and turned his back to what little light remained in the room, swung her in front of him so that light gleamed in the whites of her eyes, on her lips as her tongue darted out to wet them.

She yanked her skirts out of his hand. "I could have found my way myself, thank you very much."

The bedclothes drew tight beneath his knee as she set the bowl of unguent upon the bed. He heard her ragged breathing, the rustle of linen under the wool. She shuffled closer. Her skirts brushed his legs. He sensed her hand in the air between them and lifted his face. His gut wrenched into a knot the moment he made the motion. How easy it came, this motion of a supplicant, a beggar. At times he wondered if he were born in the wrong class—if he'd have made a better pilgrim or priest. He was ever on his knees. Ever submitting himself to humiliation.

Her fingers curled into his hair. Her breath caught in her throat and her hand shot away. He reached out and seized it, then crushed the fingers in his grip.

Oh, no, woman. I sit here before you, the last time I will sit before any healer, and you will have the stomach for it, if I have to make you touch me. If I can contain my shame, then you will contain your horror.

"No one has contracted the disease from me." He loosened his grip. "At least, not yet."

"Isn't that a risk every healer takes? And aren't you full of mockery today?" Her voice sounded shrill. "Now be still. This might burn."

She twisted and leaned over the bed. He heard the sop of liquid as she dipped her fingers into the bowl. Something soft and silky trailed across his bare arm—a strand of her hair, one of the long kinky strands which always sprung from her plait as if too wiry to be held down. She straightened and the strand of hair trailed away, catching on the hairs on the back of his arm.

She leaned closer, then dabbed the cold grease in the hollow of his shoulder. He probed her face in the faint light falling upon it, but the haze only glazed her features and cast dark shadows in the hollows of her cheeks and eyes. He sensed her instead, sensed the shift of her legs beneath her skirts, smelled the onion and wood-smoke clinging to her clothes—the smell of kitchens. But as she leaned closer, another scent wafted to him from the gap in her tunic. Floral. Sweet. Mixed with the warmth of her body. Heather-soap. Heather on the warm hills in the late springtime.

He remembered that scent. The scent of youth, the scent of a woman writhing naked in the grass.

He found himself sucking it in as her fingers lingered in the hollow between his neck and shoulder, as she smoothed the cool unguent into his skin with tight circular strokes. She warmed it with the swiftness of her touch so the lard softened into liquid and seeped deep into his skin. She should be trembling, but she stroked with a remarkably impersonal touch, professional and efficient, and a dark thought flitted through his head . . . of another swelling which could benefit from such swift and heated stroking.

How long had he gone without a woman now? Two years . . . three?

If he raised his hands and held them out just beyond his knees, he could grasp the bones of her hips. Between those hips rose the rope-belt she tied, letting the ends hang down to one side; the flat stretch of her belly, the mound of her sex. All within his reach. His palms itched.

Her fingers left his shoulder momentarily, then returned to spread more unguent upon the side of his neck, beneath his hair. Her body swayed as she rubbed it in his skin. He stared straight ahead, his blood pounding with the knowledge that her breasts peaked a breath away from him. Small, he'd noticed, nearly flat. But he'd caught sight of a nipple poking hard beneath and the hard curve of the side. He wondered if a woman of such unusual coloring would have nipples that were a bright and bold raspberry-red. Or would they be tight and smooth and the palest pink. . . .

Time for you to reel away, woman. Go ahead. Fear me. Fear me so I can lash out and grab you. So I can feel a woman's flesh against my mouth.

She didn't stop. She didn't stumble away. Fine sorcery, he thought with a grimace, to fill him with the fires of common lust while stroking him with the burn of a common salve. The woman had magic, but not of the sort he'd expected. He'd yet to feel anything he could attribute to healing, yet to feel anything more strongly than what was happening within his *braies*.

He spread his knees higher on the bed to ease his growing discomfort. A fur brushed his bare knee. Soft stuff, like a woman's long hair. He remembered that. He remembered too much. He remembered the feel of silk giving away under his hands. He remembered pearly flesh against his dark thighs, he remembered the heat and the tightness, the bulging ache, the stroking.

The stroking.

The stuff she pressed into his flesh tingled hot all over from his shoulder to his neck, and now her hand trailed over his jaw. His mind raced with images of where he'd like to stroke this salve on her, and with what part of his body . . . and into what part of hers.

By God's Nails. He was hard, standing straight up in his *braies*. The scent of her was in his nostrils now, fevering his mind. She shifted on her feet, an uneasy restlessness, but she did not draw away. The darkness shielded him; yes, the darkness was still his friend. Perhaps she couldn't sense the rising of his blood. Perhaps she didn't know the danger of a man long denied.

She scraped her fingers against his cheek and followed the line of the affliction to the edge of his mouth. All he had to do was turn his head. All he had to do was open his lips, take those fingers into his mouth . . . and suck. Suck the slickness off them. Suck her hands onto the heat of his tongue. Taste her, taste the woman.

His blood surged.

He needed a woman.

Her fingers made their way around his mouth, tempting him. Her face hovered close to his, close enough for him to smell the heat of her breath, to notice the catch in her throat.

He could have her. She was his prisoner. She would do his bidding—he could make her submit. He'd been too long without a woman. The blood roared in his ears. *Seize those hips.*

Rip the wool from them, rip the clothes from that flesh, bury this burning rod in the sweet heat of her loins. There's the release I need, there's the healing, the only "healing" I'll ever get from any wench.

Her fingers skittered away. She leaned over to dip her hand in the bowl. She missed in the darkness. The bowl tipped, sloshed its contents onto the bed, onto his knee. A quiver shook her body; it vibrated the air between them as she skittered back.

Her terror washed over him like icy rain, sizzling dead the heat of his lust. There were some horrors, it seemed, that not even the darkness could hide.

"Leave." He wiped the unguent off his knee with the butt of his hand. "Unless you want to be my next meal."

"Aye, will you sit still, man? I'll never get your dressings back on if you keep squirming about like a boy of four years of age."

Aileen knew the burly wounded Welshman couldn't understand a word of her Irish, but there were certain tones of voice that transcended language, she'd learned that well enough in the fortnight she'd spent here in Wales. The man shifted on his makeshift pallet of hay, barked something in Welsh, then frowned at his wife who giggled behind her loom on the other side of the room.

Aileen beckoned the wife over to watch as Aileen wrapped clean linens around the man's chest and shoulder. She showed her where to place the pad soaked in the brew of *Mead Cailleath* she'd made for her, and how to knot the binding firmly but not too tightly. The fair-haired young woman watched with half an eye. Her dancing blue gaze was fixed upon the wounded warrior who'd only come back to this dry-rubble house at the base of the cliff this morning, and a smile quivered about the girl's mouth as another sort of wordless language passed between her and her husband.

Aileen stood and gave up the lesson. She'd forgive the couple their distraction, for after all, it was *Samhain.* Let them stare at each other like deer in rutting season by the light of burning pine cones. She'd just hoped the man's bindings lasted through the rompings to come this night—and he didn't split his wound open anew.

She gathered her things in the basket she'd acquired from Marged for her healing needs, then hooked it over her elbow and muttered her farewells. The wife clutched her arm just as she reached the door and slipped a knotted linen full of fragrant soul-cakes into the basket. Mumbling her thanks in halting Welsh, Aileen dipped her head beneath the door frame and left the lovers to their passion.

Outside, a chill breeze rustled the thatch and flattened the grass of the yard. She lifted her face to it, let it carry the loose tendrils of her hair aloft and chill the nape of her neck . . . and she caught sight of the flare of an orange fire amid the black slate of a jagged peak.

On Inishmaan this night, the fires would rage on the highest point of the island, fair weather or gale. Da and the boys would have spent the day gathering straw, thorn bushes, gorse, whatever they could find to heap up and burn. As twilight cast its murky hand over the land, all the island would gather to dance around the golden light, and do the sorts of things no one spoke of in the light of day.

Calan Gaeaf, the Welsh called this night. *Samhain,* to the Irish. The Christian All Hallows' E'en.

Clutching the basket close to her side, Aileen set her feet upon the path toward the palisades looming on the crag above. A hen squawked and flapped its wings as she strode by it. It was as natural as breathing, her mother would tell her, for her woman's blood to be racing in her veins at a time like this. After all, Aileen was not so different from the Welsh woman she'd left behind, staring at her husband with such lust. They were both slaves to their own flesh. Wasn't it this very night, long, long ago, when one of her own ancestors raced to the

Samhain fires to meet her destiny? That ancestor had known there would be a price to pay for going to the fires—a price that succeeding generations still paid. She'd gone nonetheless, driven by a heat stronger than her own human will.

Aileen burrowed deeper in her woolen cloak and hiked the hem above the dirt of the path. She'd not expected to find fires on these bare and barren hills, and for all the burning in her blood, she scented no magic rising from the ground, not even the faintest perfume of the Otherworld drifting on the wind. Why should she hurry her pace, to make the safety of the *llys* before dark? Would the dead truly rise to walk on earth this night, joined by the faeries and all the creatures of the Otherworld, to do what mischief they could? She couldn't imagine such a thing, not here, where the veils which separated the worlds seemed as hard and impenetrable as mortar and stone.

A rumbling rose from the ground beneath her feet and she thought, for one crazed moment, that perhaps she walked upon a holy burial ground and the dead would rise up as the sun began to set. But then the rumbling grew more distinct, and she recognized it as the clatter of a horse's hooves coming down from the *llys*. She knew even as she lifted her head, even before the horse and rider rounded the curve, that the rider was Rhys.

She knew those wide shoulders silhouetted against the deep purple sky—she knew them by touch. Knew the way the hair whirled on his arms, how it thinned and disappeared over the curve of his shoulder, how his strong neck flexed when she touched it as if he stiffened against the healing magic she still could not seem to muster in his presence.

Aye, for all the deadness of this land, the fires burned far too hot in her blood this night.

"The fires are upland, Lord Rhys."

"So you told my brother." Rhys jerked his mount to a stop, spraying her ankles with pebbles and soil. He thrust out his hand. "I'm not so easily sent away, Irish."

"You grant me more power than I own." She strode past him and ignored his hand. She had been certain when she'd told Dafydd that she could find her own way back to the *llys* there would be trouble coming from it, but had not thought it to be so soon and so fiercely. "Your brother knew well where the fires would be burning this night. Faith, I'd say he'd set a few of them himself."

"He left you. Alone."

"Aye, and what of it?" She turned with a swish of her tunic. "He was scuffing about, pawing and gazing out at the hills, like a stallion with the scent of a mare in his nostrils. Doing nothing but knocking things over and blocking out the light from the door. He was not of a mind to wait for me while I tended the wounded."

"He thinks with his *braies* and not his head." He kicked his horse closer and stretched out his hand again. "Get on this horse."

The black beast snorted steam into the cold air. On all of Inishmaan, there was only a single horse—a gentle Connemara pony that the priest stabled with one of the islanders, a small and sturdy mount which carried the elderly man up the hill to the chapel every other Sunday for Mass. She'd ridden that pony once, on an Easter Sunday when the priest generously offered rides to the children of the parish. But she had no trust of this pawing war-horse, which stood far above her own shoulder, and less of the man losing patience upon him.

"I'll keep my feet to the ground, thank you very much."

He dismounted with a jangle of metal. "You'll walk right off a cliff. The *llys* is too far to make before dark, on foot."

"I'll take my chances."

"It's *Calan Gaeaf,* Irish." His voice turned wry as he trailed the horse's reins through his hands. "The dead rise tonight. Hellish specters walk the earth. Beasts beyond all your imagining."

"I know well enough what night it is, and I'll walk just the same."

"Clutching your mountain ash twig, no doubt. And mumbling prayers to an empty sky, like all the fools cowering in the mead-hall right now."

He fell into pace beside her while the wind snapped his cloak off the broadness of his shoulders and the purple haze of twilight glazed the leather mask and shadowed his stony, impassive features, broken now by the most cynical of smiles. He was as dangerous as any creature of the night: impenetrable, threatening, dangerously attractive.

"We have something in common, after all, Irish."

"Something in common, with you?" She hiked her basket higher on her elbow and kept her gaze to the uneven path. "There'd sooner be ducks on the cliffs of Craig Gwaun in January."

"You have no fear of this night."

She stepped over a narrow fissure in the rock. Fear was not the word. She had wary respect for the night, for the thinning of the veils between the worlds, for the Otherworldly creatures who unwittingly stumbled through to walk in Earthly darkness. She knew better than to get in their way.

"Any man or woman with a bit of sense knows better than to mock the darkness of *Samhain*."

"Ah, but we both belong here, in the darkness."

"I'll take the warmth of the kitchen fires, thank you very much."

"This night, your creatures wait for you up there"—he waved to the fires flickering on the inky silhouette of Craig Gwaun—"to dance around the ashes of the fire with the dead in their shrouds. And I," he mused, humorless laughter deepening his voice, "I ride among my own, the hellish creatures of my people's nightmares."

"Careful, Lord Rhys." Such scorn was more than enough to rile the spirits of the night, wherever they hid. "If you believe I dance with the dead, then you'll believe I can turn myself into a mouse, cross to the sea and stow away on a merchant ship."

"Be warned: Hawks thrive on these mountain peaks. Foxes teem in the wood. And sailors can get very hungry at sea." He leaned toward her and whispered close enough to ruffle the hair springing from her silvered hair net, another item borrowed from among the silks. "Try a broom, Irish. You'll have better luck."

"So full of mockery, are you?" She swiveled. Pebbles tumbled down the path. "Then why did you see fit to race down here and make sure I didn't disappear in the mists?"

"You're alone, on an evening when my best guards are quivering beneath the bedclothes."

"Thinking I'll not honor my promise, are you?"

"Adam once trusted a woman in the face of temptation."

"A wise man would know I'd prefer an escort to the sea and a captain paid well to see to my safety," she snapped, "than a journey alone through foreign countryside and putting my faith in pirates. I made a deal with the devil. You were there, remember?"

"I'm here now to see you keep it."

She shook her shoulders deeper into her mantle and swiveled back to the path. "You gave up the pleasures of the fires, to chase after me? I'm flattered, Lord Rhys."

"Don't be. I've never taken well to playing the part of a ghoul. What's your excuse for avoiding the fires?"

"Don't I have my hands full tending to your wounded?" She swung the basket up the other arm and hiked the knee of her tunic up as the path grew more steep. A faint heat stained her cheeks. For all the excitement roiling in her blood, even at Inishmaan she'd never dared do more than stand outside the circle of light at the *Samhain* fires. An outsider, looking in, watching the others pair off, not daring to step within the light and give rein to the throbbing of her senses, for fear she'd be left alone, partnerless, shamed. Why should she act any differently here? "I've no time to be racing off to the fires, but you're lord of this place, it's your duty."

"A fine duty—to dance around a fire and choose a comely wench fired up enough to roll in the bushes with me."

"A man could do that well enough any feast night, I'm thinking. There's more to the fires than that, don't you know it."

"Just superstitious rot. Faery-stories to justify the crop of bastards we'll have in nine months."

She sucked in a shocked breath, for his talk bordered on blasphemy. "Listen to you talking, you who thinks I'll fly my way out of here on a broom."

"Ah, but I believe in sorcery."

"It's a fine thing you believe in something!"

"You know what sorcery is. Evil done by humans. I believe in the evil of the human soul."

"But not in the good? I pity you, then."

"You wouldn't be the first."

How could he not believe in the magic of the spirit nights, the magic of this, the strongest? How could he not believe in the truth? Maybe that was the problem between them. He didn't believe in anything. There was no healing a man so utterly bereft of faith.

She increased her pace, but he only mocked her with a laugh and lengthened his stride. She glanced up, past the palisades, to the looming mountain Marged called Craig Gwaun. The first stars glimmered around its snow-capped peak. A night wind rolled down from its steep sides, blowing a gust chill enough to cut through to the bone.

He was talking rot, he was, she told herself, shaking her head. No man could deny the magic of *Samhain.* Surely, it transcended the earthly trappings. Aye, it was true, in this land the air did not breathe with an Otherworldly perfume, and the ground did not tremble with the dancing of spirits as it did in Inishmaan. But she knew the Welsh still felt the rumbling in their blood, as she did. They still felt the call of the fires, every last one of them. And the presence of the fires flickering like orange stars against the black rock of these hills bore witness to that magic.

Besides, she'd felt the surge of his blood. She'd felt it under her hand just yesterday eve, when she'd traced his throat and the vein had throbbed under her finger, when she'd smelled the man-smell of him rising hot and urgent from the bareness of his chest, when she'd heard the hitch in his breathing, and the roar of her own blood had filled her ears.

"You've mastered the art of cynicism, haven't you, Rhys ap Gruffydd?" She took a deep breath to calm the racing of her heart. "But there's no telling me you feel nothing at the coming of this night."

"I smell rain on the wind." He tilted his head to the sky. "A herd of cattle reached the northern pasture—"

"Any man with blood in his veins feels the coming of *Samhain.*"

"I feel lust, Irish. That's not from *Samhain.* I'm capable of that every night of the year."

"You can't stop it anymore than you could stop the moon from waxing or waning." Anger flushed her cheeks warm. "You can't deny it, not to me."

He yanked her to a stop. The heat of his fingers burned through the layers of wool. She'd said too much. Damn her tongue, damn her loose tongue. *She* had felt it in the darkness with him, aye, she'd felt it well enough. But what did she know of men other than of Sean the fisher's son? The excitement of those awkward fumblings in the caverns bore no resemblance to the hot liquid yearning born into life in Rhys's presence.

He loomed over her. All mockery washed from his features. Beyond his shoulder she glimpsed the flicker of a distant fire, one of a string of fires that lit the night, fires of a stubborn belief in the ways of the world long, long passed . . but never forgotten.

"Do you feel something?" He pulled her so she faced him. "Are the tides rushing in your blood? That is the better question."

She licked her lips, suddenly dry, while her senses screamed *no no no*. Not now. Her senses were not her own, in truth, they'd not been hers for many a day, and she couldn't seem to put a rein on them. Her blood had roiled since she'd set foot here in Wales, as if every night were *Samhain,* so much so that she wondered if the lack of the sense of the Otherworld made it burn all the hotter. Why couldn't her blood burn for Dafydd, kind and handsome and a believer? Why did it burn for this cynical, contrary, faithless warrior?

Her basket slipped down to her hand; she curled her fingers tight around the handle. His mantle flew off his shoulders like a falcon taking wing, baring a chest as solid as the stone behind her back. Aye, so he was a fine cut of a man, there was no denying that. But for the mask which hid half of his face, he had fine enough features; clear skin ruddied by the cold wind, bright eyes intense under a slash of a dark brow. But the heart of the man was hidden from her. Only a lust-driven simpleton would succumb to these fierce basic urges with a man she despised.

Even as these thoughts passed through her head, they were pushed aside by the memory of all those years she'd stood outside the *Samhain* fires, afraid that the shame of not being chosen would follow her, afraid to live with the sight of girls cackling behind their hands, of boys edging away from her with a smirk. Here, she was an outsider, living far away from all who knew her, far away from the world which would someday be her home again. Dark thoughts flitted through her mind, dark, tempting thoughts.

She could do things here, things that she would never have dared at Inishmaan. The failure would not haunt her beyond the coming of spring.

"Aye," she heard herself whisper. "The tides run in me, Lord Rhys."

A flush cooled by embarrassment swept over her face. Starlight fell upon his shoulders, gleamed on his mask. She sensed the swift hot intensity of *him,* the same intensity she'd felt as she'd set to healing him in his room. As if his life-force vibrated at a pitch she could sense not with her ears but within some secret place deep in her body.

Who was this man, to make her quiver like this? He'd shown her no kindness, he'd shown kindness to none but a three-legged dog, a falcon with a broken wing. This yearning . . . this was about the young couple she'd left behind in that tatter of a wattled hut, about tangled linens and sweat and flesh slick against flesh . . . and something more, something much more.

He stiffened like rock. Hot breath billowed down to brush a tendril of hair across her forehead. She couldn't catch her breath, and every time she sucked in the thinning air her nipples scraped harder against the constraint of linen and wool, sensation whirling and circling on each peak in two excruciating aches.

"It would be a pity to waste those tides." He dropped the reins to the ground, seized her hips with warrior's hands. His thumbs pressed in the hollow of the juncture of hip and thigh, a brush away from the place in her body where the molten heat smoldered the hottest. "You don't need *Samhain* fires for this, Irish."

He dipped, suddenly, as if he stood upon a *curragh* which had sunk in the trough of a wave. She flattened her hands against his chest as he hefted her up. His knees wedged between her legs, then jerked them open wide, wide enough for him to sink his hips between her thighs and grind his loins— once, twice—against hers.

She gasped, too choked with the waves of sensation rising from the joining of their loins to do anything but open her mouth and soundlessly gulp lungfuls of air, full of the scent of him, horse and leather and steel and something sweetly fragrant he'd rubbed into his hair. He scraped his hands around to her buttocks to flatten her hips against the tumescence straining against his tunic. His hardness brushed against that throbbing molten point nestled at the apex of her thighs.

"I feel you."

He spoke into her ear, ruffling tiny hairs on the nape of her neck. Her body pulsed from throat to foot, and her skin flooded with tingling.

"You're hot, woman. Hot and ready." He lifted her hips a fraction and sank them down harder on him, rocking her so the hard ridge sank deeper between her nether lips, driving the smooth linen against her most tender flesh. "Is this the magic that you speak of? The magic of *Calan Gaeaf?*"

She knew she should say something, she should tell him to stop, but she was a prisoner. Not by chains, not by his will, not even, now, by his hands. She was a prisoner of the building ripples of sensual pleasure which lapped through her body with every tiny movement of his loins against hers, with the trembling heat roiling between their bodies.

Twenty odd years she'd lived, and not since this very moment had she ever felt alive, right down to the last quivering strand of her hair.

He growled, deep in his chest—a fierce, animalistic sound that rumbled against the flat palms of her hands.

She felt it, then—a single sensation in a sea of sensations but distinct enough to draw her notice. It was a movement of a sort, as if a rock she'd been straining against suddenly budged beneath her hands. Something burning and molten flowed out from behind it.

Pain.

A scream rang through her mind, piercing the heavy waves of sensual languor, too loud to ignore, too insistent, even as she fought it and clung to the quivering sense of life pulsing between her thighs, it screamed and howled, fierce and unyielding until she shook herself from the first wave of pleasure to focus on the sound, the sound she heard not with her ears but with the vibrating hollow of her palms.

Pain. Her eyes flew open. Her hands flexed with the jabs of sensation as if her fingers had been stabbed with a thousand tiny daggers. She stared at her fingers and felt the suck of light course through her body into that hollow of his chest,

The thought had just pierced her consciousness, her fingers had only begun to flex with the unexpected sensation of the healing, when, abruptly, he thrust her away.

She scraped her hand against the cliff, stumbled to keep her balance in a place where all had turned asunder. The stars, the vague jagged peaks of the hills, the distant orange fires . . . they all merged into one until she didn't know which was up and which was down and whether she stood still on the earth on her own two feet or whether she'd somehow stumbled into the faery lands where all was not as it seemed. She fixed her gaze upon the only focal point in a swirling world: Rhys. Rhys with his hair wild in the wind, Rhys glaring at her across the darkness, his shoulders heaving as if he'd run all the way up the slope.

"It's rutting you feel. Lust. Only a woman would call it magic." His mantle snapped as he turned away. "You're old enough to know that a man feels lust every night of the year."

Her palms ached. She scraped them against the rough surface of the stone behind her and scrambled to make sense of it all while he seized the reins of his horse and swung himself up. The place between her thighs burned, the sensation still throbbed up her arms. It had been the healing she'd felt, in the midst of the madness. *Healing,* after all the nights she'd set herself to it, when she least expected it, when she'd nearly given up, it had jarred up her arms.

"Guard yourself this night." He swung himself upon the horse. "Lest you rut in the dark with a demon."

His horse's hooves pounded in the distance, fading as he cleared the ridge and entered the homestead just beyond.

She sank against the cliff as her knees softened beneath her. Realization sapped her of strength. Her hands had not been laid upon his shoulder, nay, nor upon his face. In the midst of the strange passion that throbbed without reason between her and this warrior, her hands had strayed to the part of Rhys from which emanated the most pain.

His heart.

Eight

Rhys swung his leg over the horse and tossed the reins to a stableboy. Hunting dogs vaulted into the yard, yelping at the houndsmen who rounded them toward the pen. The bailey rang with the voices of the hunting-party regaling each other with tales of the morning's foray. In the midst of it all Aileen stood like a blazing red fire, arms akimbo, deep in an argument with Dafydd.

Rhys strode to them. Boys skittered out of his path, grown men averted their eyes and tugged their horses out of his way. Like Moses watching the parting of the Red Sea, he imagined.

Aileen jabbed a finger in the air. ". . . as full of excuses as a drunkard, you are, but you promised today, you promised—"

"I promised," Dafydd argued, "before I knew we'd be hunting."

"Well, you're back from hunting now." Aileen tugged an empty sack under her rope belt. "Marged was after telling me there's time enough to get there and back before nightfall."

"A fair lass you are, Aileen, but my time is not set aside for you."

"Shall we give her a sword," Rhys interrupted, "and let her fight it out?"

"And give her the advantage?" Dafydd tossed the reins of his horse to a boy hovering nearby. "She already has a mace in that tongue and a lance in her words."

"Your brother was after promising to take me to the chaplain today," she explained. "Father Adda at Bwlchcapel."

"I will," Dafydd insisted, "once the cattle are herded in and the tenants' tribute counted."

"Apparently," Rhys said, "the lass can't wait until Sunday to confess."

"It's herbs I'm seeking. Your larder would put the meanest midwife in Ireland to shame."

"You, boy." Rhys gestured to a stable boy who froze like a deer sensing danger. "Saddle my palfrey."

"You're not thinking about taking me to the church?" Aileen settled those wild gray eyes upon him. She brushed her cloak out of the way of the milling hounds. "Aren't you afraid the holy ground will open up and swallow you?"

"No. Are you?"

"Why would I be? I've no sins on my conscience."

"And I," he retorted, "have no conscience to be burdened."

Color flooded her cheeks, evening out the spray of freckles. The memory of *Samhain* throbbed between them. It was always there, a living thing, rising whenever their gazes met in a flash of heat.

Damned witch of a woman. She'd stuffed that wild mane of hair into a net of some sort, a silvery thing. Still, sprigs of hair burst out all over. The chill wind riding down from the crag buffeted the loose hair across her cheek and the pale nape of her neck. That wretched peasant's mantle she wore swathed her figure, but he knew that body well enough—lean, strong, full of heat where the pulse throbbed close to the skin.

He could have had her. She'd been ready for a man, that All Hallows' E'en, hot and open with nothing separating their loins but a few layers of linen and wool—and even that seemed to burn away with the heat between them. Even now he didn't understand what instinct had sent him reeling back from her, back from a lust so intense that he'd spent the last days in bone-jarring activity; dragging his men half dead with lack of sleep, over the hills, driving the hounds beyond endurance, and felling two stags in an attempt to shake the erotic dreams from his head.

Erotic dreams about a broomstick of an Irish woman throwing her head back as he plunged himself into her tightness.

"You told me," Dafydd said, dragging his attention away from Aileen, "that you planned to ride to the castle this afternoon."

"It makes no difference which fool's errand I make." Rhys slapped the knee of his tunic with his glove and billowed up a cloud of dust. This morning, one of his men had ridden in bug-eyed and babbling of strange lights dancing on the scaffolding of the construction site; faeries, he'd claimed, elves dancing to the whirr of the *crwth*. "Cledwyn drinks too much of his wife's bad ale," Rhys said. "And whoever camped on the site is long gone by now."

"One lord or another, it makes no difference to me," Aileen said, turning toward the stables. "I'll see to the donkey."

"Forget the donkey," Rhys said.

"In this cold?" she said. "I think not." A three-legged mutt nuzzled her skirts and she absently swept down to pet its head. "I didn't think you so pious, Lord Rhys. If you want to play the penitent and walk your way to the church, then you'll not find me stopping you. But I'll ride a mount."

"You will ride, but not on a donkey."

She straightened and glared at him. A stable boy tugged a fresh horse into the yard.

Her chin puckered into stubbornness. "I won't climb on that huffing beast of yours."

"I won't have you trailing after me like Mother Mary."

Ride with me, woman, with your loins against mine and your hair in my face, ride with me. Even if it's only a mockery of the rutting, it's better than waking with sweaty linens in the night.

This is what it had come to, then. Luring a woman onto his horse just to feel soft buttocks pressing against him. Demanding a "healing" every night just to feel a woman's hands stroking his face and shoulder, glopping useless, pungent lard on his skin in the darkness of his bedroom. He was no better than an old man agreeing to launder the linens just to sniff the perfume of a woman's undertunic.

"You ride with me." Rhys snapped his leather glove out and tugged it back on his hand. "Or we don't go at all."

"Listen to you." Her footsteps scuffed in the dirt as she made a beeline to his side. "For days on end I've brewed you salves and mixed you unguents from what meager stores you have in your kitchen. It's for your own good I'm going to this priest to ask for herbs."

"You forget to whom you speak. It's for you we do this. You can't mask what you are from me, Irish."

"Aye, it's like talking to stone. Let's make a bargain, shall we?" She yanked a piece of hair out of the corner of her mouth. "I won't mock your mask, if you won't mock mine."

"No bargain." He flexed his fingers into the glove. "Not until you start taking off your mask in the dark."

Stormy gray eyes sharpened to silver. *Yes, woman, it's not so easy, is it, to drop the mask?* He scoured her features while a second wave of a flush rose up her neck. She lowered her eyelids, the fairness of her lashes stark against her freckled cheeks. He scoured her features still, and the questions which had tormented him all these nights rose with sudden fierceness, *Who are you, Aileen? What are you?* It had been more than lust he'd felt that *Samhain*'s night, more than a primitive carnal urge—else he wouldn't have let her go.

Like to be a saint.

She was no saint. She banked too much molten passion in that lean body to be a saint. Some sort of enchantress, for him to be staring at her in the middle of the bailey whilst his own people watched, staring at this Irish witch who was all angles and bright red hair, all prickles and defiance.

He turned away from her and seized the reins of his palfrey from the stableboy. "I ravish only one woman a day. Feel like taking a chance?"

"Here I was thinking I only had the horse to worry about." The horse tossed its head. She eyed the great beast as if it were some strange mythical creature, and he remembered she was peasant-born. She hadn't been raised on the back of a horse like a Welsh noble. She'd probably sat on nothing bigger than a plowhorse.

A wry grin stretched his lips. What a twist of irony. She was more afraid of the horse than of him.

"A pity this palfrey is so fierce." The horse snorted, bared his yellowed teeth, and thrust his muzzle into Rhys's side with bone-jarring force. "We have no choice but to mount him. All the others are too exhausted from the hunt."

The horse nuzzled an apple out of a pocket inside his cloak, tossed his head, then neighed in soft thanks as it chewed the apple's flesh.

"I warn you, watch for his hooves," Rhys continued, as the horse rubbed its snout lovingly against his cloak. "He's been known to give swift, clean kicks. And to bite, too, if you don't please him."

She twisted her lips in a frown and eyed the horse, which was making soft snorting noises and bowing its head to be scratched. "For all your mockery, the horse seems tame enough."

"I've got a strong hand upon him." He drew the reins taut. "But a single sudden move from you will send him bucking and bridling."

"Are all horses so skittish? Or is this one more prickly than the others?"

"The finest breeds are the highest strung."

"Is that what it is?" She drew herself up, then strode around Rhys to where the lackey kneeled. "Then war-horses are like men of war, determined to frighten without cause."

"This isn't a war-horse."

"All the better, then." She planted her foot in the lackey's knitted hands. "I've no use for them."

Clutching the saddle, she cried out as the lackey all but launched her into it. Her seat met the leather with a jar, then she grasped the saddle as the beast skittered.

Her knuckles whitened. "Not a war-horse, you say?"

"Any horse would be uneasy with the feel of a new weight on his back." He pried her fingers off the edge of the saddle and planted her hand on the pommel. "He has to get used to the feel of you, to the smell of you."

Ah, yes, he thought, breathing in the scent of bread and woodfires rising from her skirts. They'd wandered far from the subject of horses.

"Is that why they buck and prance like this?" She fumbled to swing her leg astride. The cloak parted to show a length of wool and fine white linen before she cast her cloak over her legs. "Foolish, stupid beasts they are, then."

"By the way you're talking, the horses of Inishmaan must be as tame as lambs."

"What need do we have for a war-horse upon Inishmaan? There isn't enough land for such a beast." Her knuckles whitened on the pommel. "He'd eat up all the grazing in a month, and do no work, all full of spit and snarl and nothing but trouble."

"A spiritless horse is worth nothing."

"Me, if I were to have a horse," she said, keeping an eye on the beast below her, "it would be a Connemara pony, strong-backed and docile."

"You want a common workhorse."

"Better than one who bucks and bridles out of a simple fear of the unfamiliar, I'm thinking."

"A rare horse that would be." Rhys swung up behind her as the beast settled. "You should know, Irish, there's no greater fear than that of the unknown."

Fear of what hides beneath the mask.

He thrust his hand under her arm, and flared his fingers across her flat belly. Her buttocks slid against his loins.

"Easy." He spoke into her hair, half to the horse clopping in impatience beneath him, half to the woman stiffening against his chest. "The ride will be easier if you relax."

Easier for her, yes, but not for him, no, not for him, as he kicked his mount and turned it toward the open gate of the *llys*. By God, the woman did have an ounce of flesh upon her and now it pillowed his loins as they rocked in rhythm with his horse. That hair . . . spraying out from all sides of the net and smelling like warm heather as it flew in his face.

He nudged the horse faster across the short yard and down the path toward the base of the hill, but the pace gave him no ease, it just increased the brush of her behind against him, the sway of her stiff back against his chest. The wind eased in the valley and he brushed his face free of the clinging tendrils of her hair. He caught a strand through his fingers. As bright as new brass, as soft as down, and radiating an inner heat.

He flicked it from his hand. Foolish fancy. It was just hair, just a woman's hair, of a color and texture he'd never seen before Aileen the Red.

The valley opened up to winter grazing grounds, flecked with cattle and sheep. Rhys veered his horse west, toward a pass that wound its way around a ridge of slate gray mountains to lower ground. The birds had long abandoned these lofty slopes, and the boughs of the dense oaks and birch rang with silence. Beneath a sky striped with reedy gray clouds, the land lay brown and black with winter heather, gray with exposed stone.

They rounded a cut in the hill and cantered out into a patch of woodland surrounding a near-perfect circular lake. A peasant woman, kneeling by its edge, upended a basket full of hazelnuts as she stumbled to her feet, and turned to watch them crashing through the woods.

The woman's ruddy face paled to the hue of porridge. With a hiss of a command, she thrust her arms out to a small boy playing with sticks in the mud. The boy glanced up under a flop of bangs, then darted like a squirrel behind his mother's skirts. The two stood, frozen like sentinels, as Rhys kicked the horse into a gallop and swept by.

"Aren't you a haughty lord," Aileen muttered, as they continued on through the thin forest. "Not even stopping to greet your own people, leaving them standing there as frightened as if they'd seen a ghost."

"No, not a ghost. *Y Tylwyth Teg.* The faery folk." He barked a wry laugh. "I wager the story will reach the *llys* before we even return."

"What story?"

"The story of the black-faced beast." With a brush of his hand he sent his cloak snapping behind him. "The beast and the flame-haired faery he carried off upon his winged mount near Llyn Dyffryn."

"Llyn Dyffryn?" The lake lay as still as silver, shattered only by the reflection of yew branches stretching out from the shore. "Don't be telling me that, it's as cold and dead as a witch's heart here. Marged tells me Llyn Dyffryn is a sacred place."

"There isn't a lake or a cataract or a crag on all of Wales that doesn't stink of faery-stories, and Marged knows every last one of them."

"Something about a man who abducted a faery." She ducked her head as they swept under an overhanging branch. "He bound her in chains of silver so she couldn't slip away to her home."

"Makes the mind reel to think of how that story came about."

"What," she asked, ignoring him though her face flushed bright, "do you call the Otherworld—*Tir na nOg?*"

"*Annwn.*"

"Yes, *Annwn.*" Her tongue tangled in the word. "She longed for *Annwn* so much that she sang a song of sorrow until he was moved to undo the chains."

"And then he sang a song of sorrow so sweet that she chose to stay." He snorted. "The moral being to sing for forgiveness after cruelty."

"Faith, that poor woman must have thought we were creatures of the Otherworld riding past like that. No wonder she looked as if she'd faint on the spot."

"I have that effect on women."

"There are times," she said drily, "when I think you take pleasure in playing the beast."

Rhys yanked the reins to one side, leading the horse around a stretch of muddy ground. *Yes, woman. I take pleasure in the sight of men turning their faces away, of the flutter of hands as people make the sign of the cross as I pass. There's a joy in watching children race screaming to burrow their faces in their mothers' skirts.*

"Fighting superstition is as futile as fighting the wind." Rhys's knees tightened into the horse's ribs and the beast took a rise. "A lesson you should learn."

"I'll have none of your lessons, thank you very much. Your people have taken to me well enough."

"My people don't know the truth."

"Your truth is a twisted thing, Rhys ap Gruffydd."

"How long do you think it will be," he argued, curling his fingers into her abdomen as her weight slid harder upon him, "before they see what I see with my own eyes? How long will it be before they bring you gifts in trembling hands, as if you were a sacred pool nestled in these hills somewhere."

"You'd have me dancing at midnight by the light of the moon and digging up graves."

"You should revel in their adoration, instead of fighting it."

"Adoration." She let go of the pommel long enough to tuck a tress of hair into the net. "Such a pretty word . . . for saints."

"It's a finer face than fear, Irish."

"It's but a mask for fear. You do know of masks, don't you?"

A fox exploded from a lichen-covered log and darted across the path. Wind rattled clutches of dried leaves clinging stubbornly to the upper branches of the yew and beech. His palfrey snorted the hot mist of its breath through the cool air.

A pity she hated him so much. In many ways, they were two of a kind; both outcasts in a world rife with superstition.

"I know of masks, Irish." He splayed his fingers upon her abdomen. "We have that in common, at least."

"Nay, nay. Don't you be thinking that." She stiffened against him, and he felt the heat of her ire like the flash of a spark in dry hay. "We've not a *thing* in common—not a thing. I have nothing to hide. I have no reason to fight superstition. Still, after all this time, you cling to those stories told by drunken men. Twenty-five years I've lived on Inishmaan. Do you really think I spent my days receiving gifts from frightened people and denying the superstitions of the ignorant? Nay. There I'm adored, aye, but not for the reasons you think. I'm adored as the daughter of a good man, a strong woman; as the sister of seven siblings who don't wage war with me over marriage-portions."

"You're a lucky woman."

"Lucky?" She shoved an elbow in his gut as she twisted on the mount. "Lucky? To be ripped from the bosom of my family? To be dragged to this lifeless land of yours, against my will; to be forced to heal a man I despise; to be all but accused of sorcery?" She turned away as her voice broke. "I left behind an ailing mother, a babe of a sister who's come to expect a story from me each night, and others. All have long given me up for dead. Such luck as this I can better do without."

She sat stiff in the saddle, her back as cold as a slick of ice. Poor, misused waif, he thought, as a strange emotion knotted in his gut. So he'd abused her. He was well used to hatred. His presence bred it. And he'd taken her from her family. She'd be well rewarded for her trouble in the end. What was done, was done, and there was no going back and changing it. He'd long given up the luxury of regret.

He brooded in silence as he urged the horse through a steep, narrow pass which led to a sliver of a valley. The church was little more than a chapel of rubble-and-stone snugged between the jagged edge of a mountain and the trickle of a stream. Deeper in the elbow of the valley, a wattle-and-daub hut served as the chaplain's quarters, surrounded by a stone fence made of lean layers of slate. The chaplain, a stringy man with a ruddy face, emerged from the doorway and gaped as they approached.

Rhys yanked his horse to a stop and dismounted. He seized her by the waist and dragged her down off their mount; setting her on her feet while she struggled to dislodge her tunic from a loose stud on the saddle. He held her longer than he had to, with her back against the horse, whilst she glared up at him with accusing eyes and he wondered what it was about black robes and the sight of a polished wooden cross that had a man grimacing under the weight of all his sins.

"I'll send a message to your family."

He felt shock ripple through her frame, saw the fury hard upon it, and caught the wrist of the hand set to slap his face.

"Is there no end to your mockery?"

"Call it a miracle."

"From a man who doesn't believe in them? I suppose you'll be telling my family where I am, too."

"I don't welcome war."

"How, then?" She scoured him with her sharp gaze. "How are you to achieve this miracle, oh great Lord Rhys?"

"Money is a powerful thing."

It would buy a man willing to travel to Galway on the whim of a woman, then pay someone else to deliver the message after he was safely at sea. The how was easy. The better question was *why.*

"A *simple* message," Rhys warned. "You are in good health. You shall return in the spring."

"And you expect me to believe you will do this?"

A gust of cold mountain air snapped between them. Only a fool would expect gratitude from a woman who'd done nothing but spit defiance at him, a woman whose healing hands had saved the lives of his men, a woman who held her power back from him even now; for in all the weeks she'd been here, there had been no change in his condition. None at all.

He tightened his grip on her wrist. For all her snarling wit, she had the fragile bones of a bird, and now they quivered, from more than the cold swirling around them. If he held too tightly, he could crush these bones like kindling.

"I see no silver chains on these arms." Her linen undertunic shimmered, exposed above the snarl of her tunic. "And the fine chemise you wear was woven for a lady."

"I wouldn't be wearing it at all if I hadn't used my own as linens for your men's war-wounds."

"You eat well, you sleep close to a fire, you grow rich with my people's gifts. Yet you fight me and fight me, and wear a cloak that would better serve as a sack for oats. You're an intelligent woman, Irish. Stubbornness will avail you naught. A practical woman would see the prospects winking in her future."

"We've already made a bargain."

"Then call it a bribe." He stepped back and shook her hand away, then shoved her toward the priest waiting nervously just outside his door. "Mayhap my generosity will increase the power of your salves."

Aileen cracked a branch off the end of a pine bough. A cinnamon-spice scent burst from the wound. She scraped off the resin beading along the bark, and let it ooze off the sliver of wood into the bowl put aside for the purpose. Later, she vowed, she would coat short wicks in the sticky resin and float them in bowls of oil. When she was finished decking the mead-hall, she'd set them aflame, to fill the room with the fragrance of Christmas.

"Higher," she said to a maidservant teetering upon a stool and gripping a braided garland of holly. She searched her growing Welsh vocabulary as the girl blinked at her blankly. *"Uchel."*

A blast of air swept her hair off her shoulders as the door swung open. Marged marched in with another maidservant trailing behind her. The housekeeper made it halfway through the mead-hall before she took note of her surroundings. She stumbled to a stop and her hands flew to her face.

"By God, may the Saints preserve us!"

Marged swept the room with her gaze, following the drape of the plaited spruce bows upon the walls to the heap of cut boughs snugged in a corner, then going to the waxy ivy twined around the roof-beams and the bits of holly scattered in the rushes.

Aileen uncurled from the pool of her skirts. "Finally, Marged, you're here." She scraped her sticky hands down her thighs and met Marged's gaze squarely. "I'll hear nothing about hares to spit or butter to churn or laundry to be boiled today. This job is far more important."

"Aileen, faith." Breath eluded the older woman. "What are you doing, lass?"

"Putting a little life in this place, that's what I'm doing."

"By the blood of Christ—"

"Don't you be thinking of stopping me." Spruce needles bit into her palm as she blindly fisted a pile of boughs and stomped over to where the maidservant labored with the long festoon. "The meanest peasant in Graig has his house filled with greenery by now, and don't you be telling me otherwise. I've spent enough time traveling among these valleys and checking on the wounded men to know. It's shame on this house to remain as bare as a cave, and bad luck as well, you should know it better than any other."

She twisted the narrow bough onto the end of the festoon and fastened it with a bit of hemp, bracing herself for the edge of Marged's tongue—expecting it, welcoming it, and chafing at the unexpected silence.

"Lost your tongue, Marged? Aye, and you should, for the shame of it. I'll hear of none of this nonsense about not celebrating the season. Are we Saracens, to ignore the birth of Jesus Christ? I think not." She glanced over her shoulder to the two men whittling by the fire, their ears cocked to the argument. "You two. When are you going to be after getting that plough, hmmm? I fear my Welsh is sorely lacking, Marged, for if I understood correctly, the girls were after telling me you Welsh have a tradition of placing a plough under the trestle table during the season, and wetting it with ale when you drink. Is it true, then?"

Her palms stung with the bite of nettles. Still she worked the boughs, one after another, lengthening the garland until it curled upon the rushes, while waiting for Marged's explosion. Aye, it was a brash thing she was doing, going against Marged's orders and luring the kitchen servants into helping her, as well, but what was this nonsense about not celebrating Christmas? Wasn't it bad enough that not a single bard had drifted to this remote corner of the world in all the time she'd been here? Weren't the evenings dreary enough, sitting by a sputtering fire whilst the winter howled outside, with no poet to recite the histories or no bard to pluck a harp? Was Christmas to be no better?

Nay. She couldn't bear it. With every drift of a snowflake against her skin, every breath of the snapping cold air, every bell rung at Sunday Mass, the memory of Christmases past roared back to her. The blaze of a peat-fire crackling high in the cottage, the spice of fresh-cut greenery. Niall plucking his harp and Cairenn singing sweet as an angel. Ma and Da dancing wildly in bare feet, each of them savoring a precious cup of the sweetest, most potent honey-mead, and all of them staring curiously at the gifts wrapped in oilcloth piled up in a corner; wondering what exotics Da had bartered for over the year with the men on the foreign ships that drifted into Galway Bay. Remembering the fine things of years past, the gray fur, the cask of wine from Aquitaine they'd shared over two weeks, wrinkling their noses as it turned to vinegar; and once, the tang of a strange fruit, one sweet orange orb for each of them; and always the stories, the stories told by the fire whilst they dozed in the warmth of family.

Something hot dripped onto her hand; she opened her eyes and watched a tear sluice off her wrist. She unclenched her fingers from the spruce and set to winding more hemp around its base, to bind it to the garland. She had wanted to be back in Inishmaan by now, damned the day she'd promised to remain here until spring. He was supposed to be healed—she had counted upon it. How was she to know her gift would fail her with him? How would she know Christmas would come and she'd still sop his skin with salves that did not a bit of good, still stand in the darkness with that living breathing blaze of a man and hurry through the healing; unnerved by the lack of power in her fingers. Because of that wretched promise, she would miss Christmas in Inishmaan—the first she'd ever missed.

Hiraeth, Dafydd had called it. The ache cramped like an empty belly. Three weeks had passed since Rhys had sent one of his men off to Aberffraw in search of a merchant ship to Ireland. Three weeks. Her family may have received the message by now, if the messenger found a ship quickly, if the weather permitted, if the ship anchored in no other port along the way. She seized the vision in her head of her mother rejoicing at the news, of Cairenn's rampant curiosity of the world beyond Inishmaan's shores, and Da's silent, stoic relief.

"Take it away." Marged hissed the words loudly enough for her voice to carry to every corner of the room. "Take it away, I say!"

"No." Aileen swiveled a heel into the rushes and thrust out a hand to prevent the servant from descending. "We've been at this far too long to be stopping it now. What's done is—"

"What's done must be *un*done, and quickly, quickly."

Marged charged across the room. The girl stumbled off the stool and sent it clattering across the stones.

"You, start on this. And you"—Marged jabbed a finger at a servant winding ivy around a roof beam—"unwind that, and set it out to be burned."

Marged's urgency infected the hall. As she barked orders, each guilty-looking servant dropped their duties and raced to her bidding.

"Now look what you've done." Aileen seized the stool and

set it upright as she climbed upon it with the garland draped over her shoulder. "Will you let the gloominess of that wretched lord of yours ruin the season for the rest of us?"

"We have our own Christmas in the kitchens. We have these past three years. Now stop that and help us undo this before we feel the bite of his fury." Marged seized the end of the garland and glared up at her. "What gave you cause to defy me, Aileen? Have I ever given you cause to do me harm, have I ever given you a reason not to believe my words?"

"If ever I knew a house that needed the spirit of the holiday, it's this one."

"And it was *your* place to bring it here, then?"

Aileen flushed, but held her gaze steady. She'd known it was presumptuous; she'd known Marged would take exception, but for all Marged's calm acceptance of the state of things, the housekeeper had refused to give her any rational reason to leave this place unadorned—nothing more than that Rhys wouldn't take kindly to it, which was no surprise to her at all.

"We're wasting time jabbering. The ivy upon the door—you get that." Marged wound up the garland, the nettles scraping pink lines upon her cheek. "By God's Mercy. Look at this place. Any moment now he'll be back, and oh, Saints alive, if he sees . . . if he sees—"

"Listen to you, acting as if the walls will come down upon our ears if Rhys ap Gruffydd so much as crushes nettles beneath his feet."

"Listen to you, talking when you don't know the half of it."

"Put the blame upon me, then." Aileen followed a darting Marged and rounded to stand in front of her. "Leave this place as it is, and I'll feel the blast of his ire."

"It's not his anger I fear. The holly, the holly," she cried out to another servant, jabbing her finger at a pile amid the rushes. "I'll tell you why in good time, if you insist upon it, but for now get out of my way, before it's too late."

Marged shoved by her, then halted as a shower of pine net-

tles skittered across the paving stones. A cold draft sifted over
Aileen's ankles as afternoon light poured into the room, and
she glimpsed Rhys's silhouette against the light, a hazy steam
rising from it as if he strode through the veils with the mists
of the Otherworld still clinging to his form. Three long steps
into the mead-hall and he ground to a halt.

He reached up and fingered something which trailed over
his shoulder. It was the ivy, knocked off its perch around the
door with the force of his entrance. He stared at the waxy leaf
blindly.

Good, she thought, *he's here. Now we can have it out and
I can show him the face of his own childishness, I can mock
him for being such a miser, shame him for allowing such in-
hospitality in his own mead-hall.* She seized her skirts and
stepped over the pile of spruce which had slipped out of
Marged's hand. Words bubbled in her throat as she raised her
eye to face him . . . and she choked on her own spittle.

Her heel sank into a pile of spruce. She'd seen him angry
before, aye, with his fists tight and the veins throbbing on his
temples, the muscles of his arm as tight as rope. She'd known
his anger. That she could fight, as one fought the advance of
fire with more fire. But the man who stood staring at a strand
of ivy in the midst of his own mead-hall was reddened with
more than rage. Nostrils flaring against the smell of pine, he
flushed all the way to the tips of his ears, his color brighter
than any she'd ever turned in all her life.

She told herself it couldn't be, that her mind was playing
tricks upon her, that surely it was not *shame* she saw stiffening
those proud features. He flexed his fingers over his chain mail
gauntlets, thrust out his chest, and flared his nostrils as if to
snort the stench of pine from his nose; and she found herself
thinking of the legendary Irish warrior Cu Chulainn, who in
the heat of battle strapped himself to a tree trunk, determined
to die upright, determined to avoid the shame of being slain
with his face in the mud.

Woolen skirts whispered as servants rushed out the side

door. Dafydd followed Rhys in, his footsteps scraping to a halt as the door slammed closed behind him, a bang that echoed through the room and left in its wake a stinging silence. A garland whooshed off a peg, and the weight of the end snagged the rest down to scrape against the floor. A bird descended amid the thatched roof and crackled its way through the braided hay.

Marged clutched her hands, took a tentative step toward him as she poured out a torrent of words. Snagging the ivy off his shoulder, Rhys scanned the room, then he turned his eyes on Aileen.

She sucked in a breath through parched lips. Wasn't it strange that she couldn't move a limb as he strode toward her, winding the ivy around his hand and elbow as it trailed behind him and snagged a path through the rushes. It was if she stood beside her frozen self, watching this muscle-bound warrior set upon her with a fierce intent in his eye. She knew the truth as he neared and his breath fell upon her face with all the heat of a dragon's breath. There would be no mercy for her, not this time. She'd seen eyes like this once before; on a mainlander who'd nearly killed his own son as he'd raged with the brain-fever.

She'd made a mistake. A terrible, terrible mistake.

Spots of mud dotted his mask. A welt marred his cheek where his man had dug the razor too deeply that morning. *A bit of celandine salve will help that tonight.* What a crazed thing to be thinking as she waited for his fury to burst forth. Whatever shame he'd felt had subsided under a torrent of rage. Impotent rage, by the way his hands spasmed over the ivy.

The vein on his temple throbbed, then throbbed again. A wonder he could see her at all in this state. The pupils had contracted to pinpricks in eyes as bone-cracking cold as Galway Bay after a gale. She wondered at her own frozen calm as the moments passed, and realized she had no choice but to wait. To fight was to increase his rage. She'd unlocked something dark and hideous. Da had told her always to remain still at the sight of a bull.

The hearth-fire popped behind her as a breeze sluiced across the smoke-hole and sucked up the flames. A hound lying in a corner scraped his claws upon the paving stones as he changed positions in his sleep.

Then it happened—fast enough to know that he'd made this transformation many, many times before, yet slowly enough for her to see the effort it cost him. His pupils dilated. The muscle of his cheek stopped flexing by sheer force of will. His chest expanded with a breath of air sucked in through thinning nostrils. A grimace stretched his lips, a stiff emotionless smile so well proportioned that only someone standing as close as she would notice it did not reach his eyes.

She realized with a strange sense of irony that he was putting on a mask.

"Such a conscientious Christian." He bruised the ivy in his hand. "Determined to bring me back into the fold, Irish? Don't you know satyrs grow nervous in a holy place?"

Words gathered and lodged in her throat. She stared at him as she once had looked upon the masked actors in a Christmas mummery, knowing each merely played a part yet swept up in the fantasy nonetheless.

"Tell one of my men to cut you some rivets. The ones in these walls are rotted." He thrust the coil of ivy into her arms. "It's been many a year since this hall has seen Christmas."

Tugging off his gauntlets, he stepped around her and headed leisurely back to his room, nodding at the men staring openmouthed by the fire, their knives poised over rough blocks of wood. The door swept closed behind him.

Marged's sob broke the silence. Dafydd muttered something and placed a hand on her shoulder. The ivy in Aileen's arms unwound to the ground.

"*You!*" Marged's sharp word rang out in the silence. The older woman tore away from Dafydd's grip and her foot pounded the ground between them. "Look what you've done!

I told you this was folly, I told you we didn't celebrate. Why didn't you listen to me? *Why?"*

Aileen shook her head. She stumbled back and kicked something—the bowl of resin. She picked it up and hugged it to her belly.

"Only three years have passed—three. Each year, we did well enough pretending the holiday didn't exist . . . until now. Until *this."* Marged jutted her fists into her bony hips and rounded to face Aileen. A strand of fine salt-and-pepper hair slipped out of her wound linen headdress and sprang over her forehead. "In one act of folly, you ruined years of work. Do you think a man could forget after so short a time? Can a man *ever* forget?"

Dafydd's voice rose in warning. "Marged—"

"Nay, she'll be hearing it. She'll be knowing what she did this day." Marged wagged a finger at Aileen. "Three years ago this Christmastide, do you know what we were all doing? We were dancing in Prince Llywelyn's court, at the feast of Lord Rhys's wedding."

Wedding. The word rang in her head like the clapper of a bell. She raised her gaze from the sheen of the amber pool of resin.

"Marged, *enough."*

"A wedding, mind you," Marged continued, her breath coming swiftly, "an event of great joy for most. But blood had been shed to bring the Lady Elyned to the church steps, and we celebrated with gritted teeth, with the mead-hall decked for Christmas like I've never seen."

Dafydd seized her and dragged her back, but the words spilled out of her as freely as her tears.

"And when the time came for all the great lords of Wales to carry Rhys to the wedding chamber for the bedding, do you know what they found? Do you know what they found, Aileen?"

Her head pounded with pain and horror, her mind screaming *no no no no,* the stench of pine resin turning bitter in her throat.

"They found his wife, Lady Elyned, lying on the blessed

marriage bed, sure enough." Marged shook off Dafydd's grip. "Lying there as pale as snow with blood soaking the linens and dripping to the floor. She'd slit her own wrists, nigh to the elbow. Do you hear me, Aileen? She chose eternal damnation over marrying the leper-lord of Graig."

Nine

It had been a moment of triumph.

Rhys strode through his room, startling a maidservant setting the fire. His chain-mail gauntlets slipped from his hand. He kicked by a pile of kindling, snapped a branch beneath his foot, then cracked his knee against the chest at the end of his bed.

Noise deafened him—distinct and vivid, undiluted by time; the shouts of his drunken men, Dafydd's complaints as he grunted under Rhys's weight, the scrape of noblemen's swords along the stone walls of the narrow hall, the ringing of unbuckled chain-mail hauberks, the snap of pine torches choking the hall with resinous incense. A smoke so thick he felt buoyed by it and the sweet taste of triumph.

She waited for him in that room at the end of the hall, the woman promised to him seven years ago, when she was still a girl of fourteen in the first bloom of womanhood and he, a young man rising in Llywelyn's court. *She* waited for him in that room, the rich beauty whose father dared to deny her to him on the grounds that as a man diseased he was no longer fit to rule.

That father now stood by the door at the end of the hall, his gnarled hand trembling as if it itched for the feel of a sword-hilt. Rhys had rained wine upon the heads of his men as he tipped a golden goblet up to his betrayer, before laughing and weaving the rim toward his mouth. An old Welsh proverb rang in his head. *The best revenge, contempt.* In the wine-craze of his triumph, he even considered thanking the man. If this foster-father of his hadn't betrayed him so foully, Rhys would not have returned from the pilgrimage to find his lands under siege by black-hearted brothers, his position in Llywelyn's court usurped, his world ripped asunder—all because of a stubborn rash.

The wine burned a path to his belly. By blood, by battle, he'd proven his worth to them all, all the drunken hypocrites now shouting bawdy jokes as they reeled behind the crowd carrying him aloft to the wedding-chamber. Aye, there would be no cure to this scourge rising over his jaw—and he'd be damned if he kneeled before another shrine—but woe be to the man who dared to defy the Lord of Graig again.

He lurched as the men set him down. Wine darkened his tunic. He laughed and tossed the empty goblet away; it spun through the rushes and clanged against the wall. The screams of women rose from behind the iron-studded door. The men chortled at such maidenly fear, and in that moment his senses came to him. He'd known Elyned for years, had watched her grow from a girl to womanhood as he trained in her father's house. He had watched her that day stumble through the wedding ceremony and sit stiffly by him at the feast like a stunned doe. Elyned deserved finer treatment than this, because for all the bloody beginning of this marriage, she was still to be his wife.

So he turned to the crowd and raised his hands to fend them off, but it was too late. In the darkness of the narrow hall the latecomers surged, anxious to view the bedding revels. They shoved Rhys and his men against the door until the hinges squealed and the door burst open to the heat and blazing golden light of the wedding chamber.

Rhys spread his arms wide to contain the crowd, but they tumbled in, reeling around the edges of the portal eager to get a glance at the canopied wedding bed draped in the shimmering hues of virgin white silk and at the beauty lying naked upon it. And one by one they stumbled amid the rushes and froze, a look of stark horror on their faces.

He swiveled. The rushes crackled beneath his heel. In a billow of skirts, the maidservants dropped to their knees at the side of the bed as their screams gave way to wrenching sobs. A blur of blue silk charged him; fingernails sliced the flesh of his cheek. Someone gripped the fury and tore her off. His mother-in-law rained curses upon his head through foaming lips as he looked upon the waxen figure lying upon his wedding bed.

His mind groped for reason. A sick jest, he thought, his gut wrenching. That woman lying on his bed was but a servant wench paid to take his wife's place, to dress in fine linen and stretch out on bedclothes soaked in pig's blood to mock the imminent loss of his wife's virginity. He'd witnessed worse jests in his years at Llywelyn's court.

A stream of blood gurgled its way along the gullies of the paving stones. The mother's crazed screams echoed against the hall as she was dragged away. The gasps of the crowd faded. The pine-cone torches crackled in the heavy silence. He stiffened as the gazes of the crowd behind him shifted, one by one, to stab into the nape of his neck like a hundred tiny daggers dripping with poisons—horror, angry blame, a craving for vengeance—and that most potent poison of all, gleeful, contemptuous pity.

Within him, triumph twisted and flexed and mutated into something sulphurous and evil that curled out of him like smoke, leaving him shuddering with a mix of impotent rage and something else, something he'd never felt before. It burned up from the ground and seeped, hot, through him to flame his face and sizzle in his scalp.

There lay the last victim of his foolish arrogance. There lay his proud victory bleeding on the wedding-bed.

And it was as if the earth cracked open beneath his feet and let loose the hell hounds of *Annwn*. A smoky red haze blurred his sight; his ears rang with snarling and snapping as shadowy shapes darted in a tightening circle around him. The scourge throbbed on his face like an ulcer. Its roots curled around his heart. *Go ahead, demons, drag me down to your black Hell, you who have cast this curse upon my face, upon my life. Drag me away from this chamber stinking of blood and humiliation, in Hell, at least, I can be among my own kind.*

In his mind, one of the shadowy shapes leapt for it and crushed his throat in its jaws. . . .

"Marged is after getting you supper," Aileen said. "Best we be doing this before she arrives."

He curled his fingers around the bedpost as the voice shattered the silence. The shadowy shapes stilled and faded; the bed hangings darkened to violet; the figure lying upon the mattress twisted into a tangle of linens and furs. The scent of burning pine haunted the room like the faded notes of an ancient perfume.

Footsteps crackled in the rushes behind him. Only one person was foolish enough to invade his privacy at such a time, only one woman would dare. *Get out.* His mind screamed the words. He bit down upon them. Not even here could he be alone in the darkness anymore. Nor could he take off the mask. To think he'd invited this woman to invade the deepest heart of his exile, to stir up things he'd spent three years trying to forget, to cut him to bloody bits with pine boughs and the mirrors of her silver eyes.

"Did you tire of garland-making so soon, Irish?"

"Oh, the servants are clattering and clanging, setting up the trestle-tables for supper, all beside themselves with the activity." She perched a bony hip upon the bench and dug a pestle into a bowl streaked with a thin salve. "I gave up. There's no joy in decorating alone."

He glanced up to the smoke-hole and saw that the afternoon light had died. The makings of a fire lay scattered across the paving stones, where he'd kicked them in the blind heat of his retreat into this room. Two tallow candles flickered low by the floor, where the servant had abandoned them. He wondered how long he'd been standing blind in the darkness, paralyzed by memory.

"I thought we might try something different tonight."

Her voice sounded bright and thin. She sat straight-backed upon the bench, finding the smooth tallow-based unguent of particular interest.

Somewhere in the muddle of his senses he realized she'd come for another healing session, just like any other night. She'd come to slop more useless lard upon his face with quick, businesslike strokes in the darkness, as if nothing had happened out there in the mead-hall, as if the days didn't revolve around the few minutes they spent together in this room, in the darkness, standing close enough to touch, close enough to hear the pounding of her heart. He forced his lips into a cynical smile. "You'll be using your hands, perhaps?"

"Don't be talking foolishness."

"I'm disappointed, Irish."

"You haven't even given it a chance—you don't know what I'm talking about. It's not a new salve, mind you, although I am making a liquid of the leaves of absinth, but that won't be ready until tomorrow eve, if all goes well." She swallowed the last words on a breath and flushed a warm color. "Are you going to douse the candles and take off that mask, or shall you stand there and glower at me all night?"

The beast lurched at its thin and brittle tether, writhing inside him like an incubus. Every instinct screamed to send her away, but his fingers found their way to the ties of his tunic. Yes, he'd sit in this bedroom with a woman, while the scent of pine swirled around them. Yes, he'd suffer this healer's trembling, frightened touch in the darkness, and do it all with a smile on his lips. What choice did he have? To refuse her healing was to show weakness; to refuse was to admit the smell of Christmas had unnerved him; to refuse was to prove that even a monster could be human . . . could feel pain.

No one would ever make him feel pain again.

"Dafydd was after telling me," she said, her voice still unnaturally high, "that there was a bit of a chase this afternoon, not far from the scaffolding of your castle."

He tossed his tunic across the bed. "My brothers are well-versed in the game of cat-and-mouse."

"He told me you have a wounded man from it."

"Bruised pride and addled senses, no more." He jerked on the last buckle of his hauberk. "Owen ap Roderic fell off his horse. Claimed the beast had been spooked by something in the woods near the river. We left him at home babbling to his wife about the Blessings of the Mother—the faeries."

"I'll see him this evening, then."

"You'll stay in the *llys*. Winter is here. The herds are huddled near the homesteads." Chain mail clinked to the floor. "My brothers and the wolves circle close."

"And if the man dies of brain fever before I can—"

"The women of Graig tended well enough to their men before you came." He wrestled his way out of his padded gambeson. "They don't need you to see to every scratch, bump, and bruise inflicted by a bush of gorse."

"Aren't you the prickly one this night?" She clattered the pestle in the bowl. "I suppose there's nothing like chasing family into the snow-covered hills to bring on the joy of Christmas."

He tossed the padded garment onto his bed and ignored her words. Let her think that was the excuse. It was safer than the truth, easier than the truth. He swept up the candles, blew them out and set them upon the table near the portal, then slammed the door closed.

"Let's see your new trick."

It was blacker in the room than the caves of Moel Cefn he and his brothers used to explore in their happier youth, but he knew every move she made nonetheless. Tonight, his senses sang shrill and high. There was a vibrancy to her presence, as if she gave off a dark light of her own. He heard the rustle of her skirts as she stood up, felt the warmth of her shoulder as he brushed by her and settled on the bench.

He untied the laces above his ear, on his neck, then reached into his shirt to undo those beneath his arm. He yanked the leather out of his sagging collar and tossed it to the ground, then spread his knees wide, to welcome her between them.

Come, Irish. Come close this night.

His loins ached long before she moved into him. He closed his eyes as the cloud of her scent inundated him; the spicy perfume of spruce and cold winter air riffling long-ago memories of cold nights in abandoned *hafods* with milkmaids and servant-girls of a time when they'd have a piece of him gladly. Wool brushed his thighs, rubbing on the strip of bare leg where his *braies* met his stockings . . . scraping tender skin, razing the thin veneer of his control. Warmth pooled in his loins and began to harden.

"You'll have to take off your shirt."

He stared up in the darkness, imagining the gleam of her eyes, the tongue darting out to lick her lips, while that warmth surged hot and rock-hard between his legs.

His throat parched. "I might like this healing."

"Stop your talking," she said, her voice trembling, "and take off your shirt."

The words shivered between them, innocently erotic, and he let himself for a moment imagine she'd spoken them in the heat of passion. He let himself imagine as he wrestled the shirt out of his belt that she wanted to touch his body for the sheer joy of it, not with a healer's impassivity. He despised himself for the weakness, even as he allowed himself to drown in the illusion.

He sucked a breath into his chest and felt the sharpness of the air course through his blood. All his senses focused with fierce intensity on the woman standing before him. Something shifted between them, something hot and eager, as she laid her hands upon his shoulders. Their skin met in a shower of sparks.

She stroked, a long, languorous brush of her palm against his shoulder, and he told himself that illusion was a pretty thing, for he imagined she used the open palm of her hand this night and not the swift efficient pads of her fingertips; he imagined she leaned her body into each long stroke, and tilted her head so a tress of her hair slipped out of whatever kept it up and brushed his cheek as she swayed.

How pitiful he'd become, letting himself swim in this illusion, letting his loins burn with it. His palms itched to be filled with more than the roundness of his own knees, and he felt his own breath warming the fibers of her tunic as she leaned close. All he had to do was shift forward, seize this woman by the hips, and thrust her against the ache between his legs. Yes, there would be relief, to feel her wet warmth pressed against him as he had that Hallows' night . . . all he had to do was open his mouth and take that nipple between his lips—all he had to do was seize what stood before him.

Can't you sense it, woman? Can't you feel the danger? He flexed his palms over his knees, remembering a story his Latin tutor had told him whilst he stared out into the yard of his foster-father's *llys.* Something about an ancient Greek forced to stand neck-deep in cool spring water, but never be able to take a drink; and to gaze upon a cluster of gleaming grapes, always just out of reach.

He closed his eyes on a growl. How long could a man take it, night after night? He knew the answer to that, fool that he was. He would take this self-inflicted punishment over and over, again and again, for as long as she would give it. For as long as he could make her give it. And the only way to keep it coming was to stay as still as a stone. For if he moved, if he showed her the beast raging beneath the man, he knew she'd startle like a sparrow and flap her wings in a desperate attempt at freedom.

Then, suddenly, she trailed a hand down, far below the last ridge of the affliction, to snag over the flatness of his own nipple and finally rest against the hollow in the center of his chest.

He stopped breathing. He heard her heart pounding, he

sensed the rush of hot blood through her veins. He felt his own heart move beneath her hand; a loosening, an unfurling, a step off a precipice into thin air.

Something snapped within him. He closed his thighs and trapped her legs between his. She gasped. He seized the bones of her hips and drew her flush against his loins before she could struggle away. Off-balance, she stumbled forward and he buried his head in her chest.

I was once a man who dreamt of being a beast, Aileen. . . . Now I am a beast who dreams of being a man.

Blood roared in his ears. He'd trapped her good. The sparrow was captured. He took advantage of her shock. Her chest heaved against his face. Her nipple beaded hard beneath his cheek and with one turn of his head he could have it in his mouth. . . .

Hard. Hard and taut and as small as a raspberry. He sucked on it and the wool, wetting the fibers hot. Blind to all but the taste of it, he held her tight while he feasted on the rarest of delicacies, sucking and licking and all but nibbling the wool from the flesh.

Irish. His loins throbbed. He pressed her thighs against him harder but the pressure only thickened. Her hair brushed his face, tumbling down from whatever she did to keep it up. Soft, soft, all that curling mass she could never control, swirling fragrant around them. He yanked the neckline of the wretched wool to get at her womanflesh, felt the burn of her skin, found the nipple, and suckled it deep into his mouth.

She gasped and he held her tighter. *No, woman, you'll not get away, not yet. You think I don't know the fear roiling within you now? I've seen it in a hundred thousand faces since that Christmastide when I recognized it for what it was. You should have known better than to enter the sanctuary of a beast, should have known better than to tease him, to touch a man starved for the feel of another's flesh. Now you shall pay the consequences. . . .*

What was this? His arms tightened reflexively on her hips.

He scraped his hands across her buttocks to crush her in his embrace. She was all molten heat, all give and suppleness, a spine bending easily beneath his grip. He struggled out of the fog of sensation to realize she made no resistance to his embrace. She didn't struggle—no, more than that, she *pressed against him.*

Her fingers raked over his head, through his hair from forehead to nape, then trailed down flat against the center of his back.

For one brief, shining moment he stilled in the awareness of the heat of a woman's flesh against his cheek; in the smell of her gentle woman's perspiration, in the taste of willing flesh. He drank in the shimmering moment, sucked it down to a place parched and cracked from lack of it, and felt the sustenance through his body like a throbbing heavenly white light seeping in, pushing back the darkness. He knew this was more than the carnal need for a woman, knew that she was feeding a different hunger, a more basic one, a more necessary one— knew, too, that *she* knew his need.

That, in the end, was what gave him the strength to drag his hands back to her hips and thrust her body away from his aching one. That, in the end, was what doused the heat in his blood as effectively as if someone had changed it for mountain water. Yes, he could have her; he could tear the wool and linen from her body and ease his tightness in her heat. He was lord of this place, she was his captive, and she stood willingly enough before him, bared nearly to the waist. He'd taken women for lesser reasons.

But he hadn't fallen so low that he would take a woman who felt no more for him than *pity.*

With a grunt he thrust her away from him. The bench rocked beneath him as he stood up. She knew of Elyned. She'd heard the story. For what other reason would the woman come to him after all this time, a woman who'd snarled and snapped at him at every turn? The taste of her turned bitter in his mouth, everything turned bitter, even the scent of her turned as bitter as that of pine resin. So he'd fallen so low that only a woman full of pity would willingly give herself to him.

She should give thanks to the darkness, he thought, as rage thrashed within him. For if he saw pity in her eyes, he'd have to kill her.

"Are you the kind," he said, his voice as hard as gravel, "who likes rutting in the dark with satyrs?"

"R-Rhys?"

"I don't want your pity-kisses, woman."

She rustled frantically, arranging her clothing, knocking a stick of tinder across the paving stones.

"Yes, leave. Run." He turned away from her. "Tomorrow, when your senses are restored, you'll thank me for not planting a demon seed in your belly."

Light poured into the room as she swung open the door and stumbled out. He fisted his hands and dug the butts of his palms into his eyes, squeezing them shut against the illusion he'd held, for one fleeting moment, of something he would never have: The feeling of a woman who, for want of him, gave herself, open and willing, in his arms.

Ten

Aileen trailed a scowling Dafydd across the yard. A herd of cattle poured through the narrow gateway of the palisade, lowing and bumping as they splattered through the opening. Dafydd barked orders to a young man herding the cattle toward a pen, then stopped to turn upon her.

Aye, Dafydd's veins ran with the blood of his fathers, Aileen thought, as she slowed to a stop. With a scowl marring his pleasant features, he had the look of Rhys upon him.

"A wise woman," he said, "would have stayed in the kitchens today."

"In the kitchens I have nothing to do but suffer Marged's silence." Color flooded Aileen's cheeks, a common enough occurrence this past night. "Is there to be no forgiveness for me from either of you?"

"You didn't seek me out so early in the morning to ask forgiveness."

Dafydd edged on the outside of the herd and ran his hand over one cow's back. So he, too, had turned his heart against her, Aileen thought. Aye, decorating the mead-hall against Marged's instructions had been a foolhardy enough thing to do, but not near as foolhardy as what she'd done later that evening.

She dug her fingers into the edge of the mantle flapping in the cold wind howling down from Craig Gwaun. Her Ma didn't raise her to slink away and hide when she'd done someone wrong. Aileen knew she had to set things to right even though the slight had been unintentional. Truth be told, she'd not soon forget the look in Rhys's eyes when he'd first stepped into the mead-hall—or the tale Marged had told her afterward. For the first time since she'd been dragged to this craggy *llys,* she saw the real festering wound she should have been trying to heal all along.

"Dafydd, I need your help."

Dafydd sank to his haunches and probed the cow's underbelly. "I've heard this before."

"I need but a moment with him."

"A man doesn't want company," he said, as he thrust his head beneath the beast's belly, "when he rides off alone."

"I'm not after keeping him company. I'm going to say my piece and have done with it."

"Say it when he returns."

"When he returns, you'll be bending his ear about these cows," she argued, waving to the milling chaos in the yard, "and the slaughter to come and the salting of the meat, or whatever you two chatter about in the evenings."

"You had plenty of time to say your piece last night, when you were alone with him in his room." Dafydd glanced up from his crouch and elbowed his mantle over his shoulder. "Whatever did you do to him in there?"

Color flooded her face; the warmth seeped clear to her scalp. Aye, the walls between Rhys's room and the rest of the hall were thin enough, nothing but wattle and daub and a lean wooden door. And aye, she knew the servants had noticed the cold wicks of the tallow candles, the dry tinder of the fire, the closing of the door during each of their healing sessions. But no one could know what mischief went on behind that closed door. Surely they speculated, weaving wild stories from the thinnest thread of truth. But no one—*no one*—could have witnessed the blinding lightning that had cracked through that room last night. No one else could have heard the roar of her blood.

It had all been in her head.

"He was of no mind to listen to me last night." Nay, and

she of no mind to speak, and having no tongue for it after the way he'd touched her. Clutching her cloak closed, she pressed her forearm against her breast to stop the tender throbbing. "What I've to say can't wait any longer."

Nay, not a moment more. She couldn't live in this place any longer with the shame creeping up on her with every breath, with the memory playing over and over again in her mind. She wanted to be done with him, with this place; she wanted to run home to Inishmaan where the men didn't thrash and fight and growl when they set to kissing—and where there were no men willing to be kissed by her.

"The Irish never know when to keep quiet, do they? Or is it just the women?" Dafydd slapped the rump of the cow and sent him bolting toward the pens. "Leave the man alone, Aileen."

"Is this your mouth I hear these words coming from?" She trailed after him as he singled out a calf amid the herd. "It was not my choice to come to this wretched place. Don't you remember it was Rhys who dragged me here? With your help, mind you. It was Rhys who insisted I stay after he promised me safe passage back to Inishmaan. And it was you who was after asking me to set things to right."

He whirled on her. His mantle flared out over a cow's back. "There was a time, Aileen, when I believed you could do just that."

"Then you were the fool."

She met those hazel eyes, bright with frustration and angry thwarted hope. She wondered if Rhys saw what she now saw. She wondered if Rhys knew the depth of this man's love, or if he waited for Dafydd to show the same blackness of heart as his other brothers. She knew even as the thought came to her that Rhys had blinded himself to that, too. What did it matter? She could not open a mind so twisted with bitterness; she could not ease a heart encased in stone, no matter how rightly so. Her hands did not work on his face. And when she dared to touch his heart, the healing muddled with something else, something fierce and reckless that rebounded upon her and turned her into a creature she did not recognize; aching for things she had no right to feel, for things she'd never expected to have.

"Maybe I was a fool." His jaw tightened. "If so, I'm damned for that, too." He brushed by her and skirted a cow patty steaming in the frosty air. "But I won't be doing the man any more wrong today."

"Are you saying you won't be taking me to him?"

He waded his way through the herd of cows and gave her no answer, and she knew the set of those shoulders well. There would be no give in the man, none at all.

"Very well." She swiveled a heel into the mud. "I'll go myself, then."

The walk through the frosted valley would do her good, she told herself. She needed the slap of the cold air on her face, she needed the weave of the icy wind through her hair. Maybe the journey would help her forget what she'd nearly done last night. Maybe she could figure out what it was in the darkness that urged her to throw herself upon a wealthy Welsh lord—a thief, a killer, an unbeliever—when in the brightness of day she could not even find a civil word on her tongue for the likes of him.

"There's no end to a woman's wiles, is there?"

Dafydd's voice rose above the lowing of the cattle. She glanced over her shoulder to find him striding after her.

"Don't look at me like an innocent." Dafydd snapped an order to a boy, who raced off to the stables. "Do you think I'm going to let you wander these hills like a stray calf, with Rhys's enemies roaming the woods?"

She blinked and the color drained from her face. She'd forgotten. Rhys's brothers had ravaged the borders these past weeks. What had the man done to her, to have her acting so addled?

"I'll take you. You won't give me any peace until I do, I see that." He seized her arm and dragged her toward the stables. "I won't have your death laying more woman's blood on my brother's hands."

It was a silent and uncomfortable ride across the frosted valley to King Arthur's grave. Dafydd rode the palfrey with a vengeance. She clenched the pommel of the high saddle praying for safety with each leap over a fallen log and each clatter of pebbles beneath the horse's hooves.

She saw the falcon soaring high above the tree tops long before they broke through the woods into the valley that sloped up to King Arthur's grave. Under the gray sky, virgin frost gleamed on the heather, its sheen broken by only one set of hoofprints. They trailed the flight of the winged bird beyond the rise of the tumulus, over a rocky outcropping. By the banks of a shallow stream, Rhys stood alone, his red leather glove the only spot of color in a landscape of grays and browns and pale blue slate.

Dafydd yanked the horse to a stop on the height. "You go alone." He slid off the horse and hefted her down with little gentleness, then remounted while she found her footing. "Do what you've come for, and have done with it."

How cold it was this day, how frigid the wind which howled down from between the slopes of two peaks in the east. The frozen grass crackled beneath her shoes. Once she slipped on the slope and cracked the butt of her palm against a tree trunk, then picked her way more carefully until she reached level ground.

Rhys swung the lure in a wide circle as the falcon hovered overhead, its attention on the bits of feather and meat arcing in the air around its master. With a spread of its wings, it swooped down and seized the food in its claws, then landed to tear at it with its beak. Rhys's cloak billowed as he sank to one knee and swept the falcon onto his thick leather glove.

Her steps faltered as she stared at the man she'd touched so intimately last night, at the wide drape of his mantle over his shoulders, the proud line of neck and jaw. His powerful thighs flexed as he straightened with the bird upon his arm. All the words she'd mustered to throw at him in the bright of morning clogged in a throat grown as parched as winter.

"She's a fine hunter," Rhys said, holding the falcon aloft. The bird's jesses jingled in the air. "I've seen her take down geese twice her size, but there's no challenge for her here today." He toed a pile of fur on the ground. "Nothing but rabbits."

Rhys's long hair, unbound and the bluest of black, flew in the wind. She squeezed her frozen hands tight, remembering the slipping of that hair through her fingers . . . as soft as the swan's down she'd gathered one day off an abandoned nest in the caves of Inishmaan. She wondered what he was blathering on about, when she could think of nothing but the feel of his hot mouth upon her breast.

"She was raised on Ramsey Island. She learned to fly in winter gales, and to hunt on sea-birds. There isn't a better falcon in all of Wales." An odd half-smile twitched on his face as he brushed the bird's breast with a knuckle. "She was a wedding present, Aileen. From my wife."

Shock jolted her, and for a moment she wasn't sure whether it was from the talk of his wife or the sound of her own name rolling so easily off his lips.

"My wife's dower lands, her riches, her cattle—I returned everything to my father-in-law, everything but this." He reached inside his cloak and palmed out a bit of feathered leather. "You must think it appropriate that she would gift me with a falcon—a bird who hunts and kills his own kind."

He stared deep into the falcon's unblinking golden gaze as he stroked the bird's breast, the bit of leather hugged in his palm. With a movement so swift that the bird didn't flinch, Rhys slipped the leather over the falcon's head to blind him.

"She even," he said, tugging the leather tight with his teeth, "wears a mask."

Listen to him mocking himself, she thought, when she could barely muster enough strength to speak. She fisted her tunic and made her way across the frozen earth. He was just a man.

She wouldn't live in fear of him. She could be as cold-blooded as he, if she willed it so.

"Easy," Rhys murmured, as the bird bristled her wings at Aileen's approach. "She smells you on the wind, Irish. Always approach a wild thing with caution."

If only she'd thought of that last night. Aye, when this man now standing with his profile to her had worked a sort of magic upon her senses that she'd never had the imagination to dream about. The fumblings of Sean the fisher's son seemed childish and laughable, now, as did the uncertain feelings of a young girl compared to the yearnings of a woman. And aye, aye, she told herself, that was all it was, the yearnings of a woman who had lived too long like a bride of Christ. Was it any wonder that a strong man with so much skill could make her lose her senses so easily? Thoroughly enough for her to forget that he'd found her lacking once before. Now twice.

"I've been thinking," she blurted, hugging her elbows above the cloak, "about our bargain."

He tugged the rope of the lure from under the hawk's talons and slipped it in a bag sagging from his belt. "You've a way with my brother."

"What?"

"Dafydd." Rhys jutted his jaw to the silhouette of horse and rider upon the outcropping. "He's stubborn to a fault. When he chose to join me in my little . . ."—Rhys waved vaguely to the hills around them—" . . . my little exile, he discovered that some of my tenants were cheating me on the yearly tribute. From that day on, he made it his personal responsibility to count the cattle himself." Rhys absently stroked the bird's breast. "Yet you get him to agree to drag you all the way out here, when I know the cattle-counting is today."

"He'll tell you I gave him no choice." What was Rhys babbling on about, standing there with his masked side to her, talking to his falcon and not paying her a bit of heed? "Did you not hear a word I said?"

"I heard you." He swept up the rabbits and strode to his

horse, tethered amid the brambles. "I'm not sending you back to Ireland, Aileen."

Her mouth opened but no words came out, for he'd spoken her heart as if he could hear the thoughts rolling about in her mind. By God, was she so simple, then? Aye, it was true enough that she had little experience in these tangled matters of men and women, true enough that she floundered about as if she'd swum out too far past the ledges. It was clear enough, too, that he'd gotten involved in such affairs whilst she was still cutting teeth on wood-blocks. Still, she'd not expected to be manipulated so easily.

Why did she feel like such a coward, hearing him speak those words? Aye, she wanted to go back to Ireland, was that any wonder? She'd been taken here by force, whatever the bargain they made afterward. She missed Ma's loving arms, Da's gentle understanding. She missed all that was familiar, predictable, controllable. She was not running away, she told herself. She just wanted to go back to where she belonged.

"I didn't come up here to ask for that." What a good liar she could be, when Rhys wasn't staring her in the eye. And what was she thinking, changing her mind just out of the pride of the moment? "I'm a woman who sticks to her bargains."

"Good."

"Not that I'm doing you any good here, mind," she added, trailing to the bank of the stream. "Despite all the weeks I've tried."

"You're doing a fair enough job of it."

"Who is the doctor now?"

"You have," he said, hooking the hares to his saddle, "until spring to do your work."

"If I had until midsummer I'd do no better." She filled her lungs with brisk air and raised her voice. "It's of no use. I've tended to your affliction long enough to know it is not within my power to cure it."

The moment the words left her lips she wanted to bite them back, chew them up and rearrange them so they wouldn't fall as hard as hail in the clearing. Fine healer's manner you have, Aileen Ruadh, blurting out such a thing. Why not tell him he'll die within the week, and strip him of all his hope?

Why should she care, *why?* So the man had a reason for his twisted, cynical heart. Many a man had been betrayed and had not turned bitter. What could she do? Did he truly think that by healing the scourge on his face, the world would come to rights?

"You know so soon," he said, over his shoulder. Oh, he was a hard man, standing in front of his horse with his back to her and his hands loose at his sides, those shoulders stiff as rock. "It's been barely a season."

"I suspected the very first day."

"Yet you made the bargain with me."

"I'm not a woman to give up hope so easily. Besides, you gave me little choice."

"I suppose I did."

She blinked at him. So easy an admission, after all this time.

"Nonetheless, you shall continue trying," he said. "You will keep to your side of the bargain."

"I'm telling you, these healing sessions are doing no good." She pivoted and took two steps toward him, holding out her hands in growing frustration. "What do you think I can do for you? If I cured your face, what do you think would happen?"

"I could take off the damned mask."

"Aye, and what else? Do you think it will bring your brothers back to you?" *Do you think it will bring back your wife?* She dug her teeth into the flesh of her lip to stop herself from slinging that stone. She turned away from him, and stared blindly at the black trunks of the denuded trees; then her gaze followed the path up to where Dafydd waited. "You should thank that curse on your face. It has shown you who your friends are. Dafydd is the only true brother you've ever had. You haven't lost anything that you had in the first place."

"It's not the past I want back—it's the future." The falcon

cawed as Rhys swung around too swiftly. "This conversation is finished."

"No, it's not. You're no doctor. For all I know, I'm doing you more harm than good."

"If there's any harm here," he snarled, "it's to your vanity."

The shock of humiliation stung her. He fished his horse's reins from the brambles and yanked the mount out of the shelter.

"Don't curse me for pushing you away, Aileen." His lips curled in a mocking smile. "I was just saving you the horror of waking up next to me in the bright of day."

Her breath gelled in her lungs. "Of all the vain, p . . . pompous . . ."

"Easy. If your face gets any redder, you'll be caught in a fit of apoplexy, and I'm no healer, you keep telling me."

"You think. . . ." Words bubbled to her throat. "It's you who's full of vanity, not I, to think . . . to think I came here because . . . because . . ."

Because he thrust you away as if disgusted by the bones jutting from your hips, as if you weren't enough of a mouthful, as if you smelled of fish and sweat. And you can't bear the thought of seeing the mockery in his eyes every single day for all the months to come . . . hearing in your head the whispered words of the girls of Inishmaan spoken loud enough for you to overhear . . . poor Aileen the Red, mother to all but of child she'll have none.

"Why else would you lie?" He wound the reins of his horse over his wrist and led it toward her, holding the goshawk to the wind. "You told me your healing doesn't work."

"Don't I know that well enough," she said, sweeping a hand through the air, "all these weeks, and no change in your condition."

"Ah, but there has been a change."

"Now who is the one full of tales?"

"It has stopped spreading."

She looked up and met his clear blue gaze and felt the jolt

of it all the way to her toes, and thought that *couldn't* be. The salves couldn't be doing him any good, he'd admitted that himself a hundred times before. She'd only felt her hands working on him twice, and then on his heart and not his head. . . . But even as her thoughts tumbled over one another they faded under the rise of a stronger sentiment. The awareness of his strong, warm body so close to hers in the crisp morning, the mist of his breath between them, the oddly boyish tumble of a lock of black hair over his brow, the fierce intensity of his presence . . . and strangest of all, most unnerving of all, the gentlest twitch of a smile upon his lips.

The falcon cooed a throaty sound. Its wings rustled in the silence.

There was a breath of a moment when she thought, Rhys is going to touch me, and a tingling raced over her skin from her scalp to her feet, a wild, reckless sense of anticipation— *He's going to touch me*—her heart leapt like a hare charging across an open field—*he's going to kiss me*—and her lips throbbed, throbbed, throbbed, throbbed, throbbed. . . .

"Don't talk to me about stopping the healing, woman."

Kiss me. Why didn't he just do it, instead of staring at her mouth so fiercely? Why didn't he just do it so she didn't have to think about it, so she didn't have to listen to that voice screaming in the back of her head to pull away and break this tension drawing taut between them. *Kiss me—kiss me and let me know the taste of a man's mouth.*

A shout shattered the moment. Rhys glanced up the slope. Dafydd's mount struck sparks on the stone, then splattered mud as he pulled him to a stop.

"What is it?"

How easily Rhys slipped back into the stance of a warrior, how even his voice, how easily he turned his attention to Dafydd. While she stood trembling beside him like a leaf in the wind.

"There's been a raid. At old Dunwyd's place near the salmon stream." Dafydd's voice sounded hoarse and unnatural. Aileen noticed the other rider on top of the hill and the steam rising from his mount. "They're heading west. We might be able to cut them off. Aileen, we'll be needing you."

"Her?" Rhys's falcon screeched and unfurled its wings. "What do you need from her?"

"It seems our brothers are no longer satisfied with stealing and slaughtering cattle." Dafydd yanked the reins to control the stamping of his horse while his teeth flashed bright behind a grimace. "Come, it might already be too late."

A plume of smoke hung over the valley, scenting the breeze with the stench of burnt thatch and charred clay. A blackened house tumbled its stones toward the bank of a stream, a toothy hole gaping in the one-room structure. The hoofprints of horses and cattle trampled the mud around the smoking building, and wove a river still farther west, into the woods.

Rhys stiffened against Aileen's back as he jerked his horse to a stop. "They're heading west," he said, as Dafydd rode to their side. "To the next *cantref.* Gerwyn's lands."

He spoke swift Welsh, but she understood it—just as she understood the darkness in his voice. She knew that the Gerwyn of whom he spoke must be Gerwyn ap Rhain, the foster-father who had denied Rhys his daughter. Now she knew that his lands lay just over that ridge.

"So Gerwyn has taken up my brothers' cross." Rhys's laugh sent chills down her spine. "The fools think to draw me into another war."

A boy emerged from behind the building. Sighting Rhys's colors, he raced barefoot across the field, as leggy as a newborn foal. He skidded to a stop. His bony chest heaved beneath the muddy rags of his tunic. He sputtered in loose-tongued Welsh, his thick-jointed elbows flying every which way.

She picked up enough of his words to scan the grounds around the house. Cloth fluttered amid the mud, and she made out the limbs of two people, lying side by side. His grandparents. Tugging her mantle across the horse's withers, she slid down the beast and splashed into a puddle. One of the men kicked his horse toward her. It was Roderic ap Ceicyll, the warrior whose shoulder she'd tended after the battle last fall, the husband of the woman Aileen had just helped through a long and difficult labor in birthing a son. He fumbled behind him, then swept down her basket of herbs and linens. She seized it from his grip and mumbled a swift prayer of thanks that Marged had had the foresight to seize this from its hook in the kitchen and deliver it to one of the men before they rode out in search of Rhys.

The boy looked up at her from beneath a shock of dirty brown hair. How big his eyes, and gray as the sky above, and how full of desperation. He set off with a spray of mud toward his wounded grandparents.

"I'll send someone back to you by nightfall."

She glanced up at Rhys's impassive face, hidden behind a mask far stiffer than the supple leather he wore. His gaze had already slipped away from her and focused on the craggy line of the western ridge. The singular moment they had shared by the banks of the stream drifted away like a mist. She wondered if Rhys even realized he'd just spoken to her in Welsh.

The ground rumbled as the horses tore up new clods of earth as they set to the path. *What did you expect? Loving words of farewell?* What a fool she was becoming, aye, and she was old enough and wise enough to know better. She had far more important work to think about this day.

The boy danced impatiently near his guardians. Neither of the wounded moved as she approached, not even the faintest twitch of a finger or a bare, muddied foot. She dropped her basket and crouched down between them.

The boy babbled something in Welsh. Aileen didn't look at him. She couldn't. Aye, both of the wounded were breathing, and the man's heart throbbed faintly beneath her hand, but she knew the chances of dragging either of them back from beyond were slim. The essence of them, the life's-spark she always sensed when she approached the wounded had faded to naught but the faintest breath.

She fingered a lock of peppered hair off the man's face. He bore the rewards of a smile well used. Lines carved his features in the most blessed of elderly beauty. Beneath the torn and bloodied tunic swelled a strong chest, round and thick-muscled. How like the leather-skinned fishermen of Inishmaan, whose arms and shoulders bulged from all the years of hefting weighted fish nets out of the sea and upon the boats, yet whose legs jutted spindly from beneath their *braies*.

Aye, this man wouldn't be fishing anymore salmon out of the stream gurgling behind them. The moment she flattened her hand upon his brow, she knew it was too late. His spirit had slipped beyond the point of drawing it back into life. All that remained were the feeble tremblings of a body too strong to surrender without a fight. She ran her fingers over his brow, hoping to ease the last of his pain.

Then she turned to the lady. The woman reminded Aileen of old Widdy Peggeen. The set of her jaw revealed a strong spirit in defiance of a body as frail-boned as a sparrow's. Now, lying here bloody in the mud, she even had the look of a sparrow who'd been caught in the narrow-walled caves during a gale.

The woman clutched something in her reddened hand, a frothy bit of cloth, the ties of which siphoned up with the breeze. Aileen fingered one of the charred ties. It was a baby's bonnet, the sort of fine linen cap an infant wore at a Christening.

Her innards twisted. All the riches of the world lay within the cup of that carefully stitched linen, the memories of a lifetime; and Aileen felt them pour out into her hand, though she knew nothing of the lady.

Nay, she *did* know. She knew of babes born, of children dying, of keening over graves and of dancing at the *Beltaine* fires. She knew the smell of the newly turned earth and the warmth of frothy May-milk on her tongue. These two people lying in the mud before her were simple cattle-herders like Niall, like her Da, like old Seamus. Aileen understood more of their lives than she would ever understand of those chain-mailed warriors living in the *llys*.

For a moment she despised herself for lusting Rhys's kisses, for forgetting in this bloody land amid a prince's palace who she was and where she'd come from.

She squeezed her eyes closed against the heat of tears and flattened her hand upon the woman's head.

Then her eyes flew open. There was life here, there was still some life.

The boy hovered behind her.

"Bring water," Aileen said through a throat suddenly tight. *"Dwfr."*

She spent the afternoon kneeling in the mud, sending the boy off to search for firewood, to rifle through the smoldering ruins of his house, and to clear up a corner within the roofless building for shelter against the cold. Aileen cleaned the woman from head to foot with a strip of her torn chemise. She stroked all of her aching flesh, the burns, the lacerations, the bruises just beginning to streak her arms blue. She murmured nonsense-words, comfort-words, and sensed the course of the healing flow through her hands as warm and thick as honey. She willed the woman back to the living, to the grandson who hovered over Aileen's shoulder between tasks, watching with tears streaking his face.

He knew, despite all Aileen had done to hide it from him, that he'd lost his grandfather. His chin puckered with the effort to keep in the pain.

Dusk cast a haze over the valley when Dafydd and three men galloped down from the western ridge. With the boy standing as stiff as ice, Dafydd wrapped the boy's grandfather in his own cloak of silken embroidery and eased the old man's body over his horse, to bring him to the church where he could be buried in consecrated ground. Dafydd argued for fashioning a litter to carry Dunwyd's wife to the shelter of the *llys*, but

Aileen refused. The frail woman would never survive the trip. Dafydd left provisions and blankets, along with the three men as guards, for they'd not yet caught the murderers.

The men cleared some rubble from inside the house and made a fire in one corner, where two walls still stood strong against the winter wind. For two days Aileen stood vigil over the elderly woman, fussing with poultices and strips of her linen chemise for the sake of appearances and laying her open palm upon the woman's chest for the sake of healing. Determination fed her strength. The flow of life rushed through Aileen as palpable as the current of a river in spring flood. Yet it was as if it flowed into a great gaping hole that would not fill. The woman still lived, still lived. At the end of two nights, Aileen finally left the woman's side and settled down, to replenish her own strength with sleep.

She woke to a valley dusted with snow, sparkling pure in the first rays of the cold sun. She sifted the powder off her woolen blanket and trudged past the three sleeping guards, through the silence broken only by the gurgle of the river. She kneeled down by the stream and splashed her face with the frigid water. Only then did she hear the sobbing.

The boy sat by the stream, on the tumbled stones of his home. His spine ridged the thin wool of his tunic, and it shook with grief.

She rose to her feet, whilst water still dripped off her chin, and stumbled her way back to the fire.

A dusting of snow had blown its way under the makeshift roof of reeds, and lay like the breath of faeries upon the grandmother's pale face.

Aileen hugged her body against a cold that came from her bones. It was over, then. She'd lost her. It had been nothing but arrogance, thinking she could keep her here. She had done nothing but hold the woman to earth by the wisp of breath. For as soon as Aileen had loosened that hold upon her, she'd drifted away to join her husband in *Tir na nOg*, the land of peace and pleasure, the Welsh *Annwn*.

The boy emerged from the ruins, red-faced but stoic, to help wrap his grandmother in a horse's blanket. The guards stood in reverent silence while the boy heaved the body across a saddle. Then they all mounted and rode for the *llys*.

All along the way, the boy stared sightlessly ahead of him. He should be marveling at the strength of the war-horse beneath him, she thought, he should be gazing about in curiosity at lands he'd undoubtedly never crossed. He was but a lad just stepping into manhood. But the light that burned in those gray eyes was one she'd seen before. The light of a blind, furious vengeance.

She buried her cheeks in her cloak and closed her eyes against the bitter, biting cold. Was there to be no end to it? Was bloodshed to breed more bloodshed, and still more bloodshed? Could she blame the lad for wanting to strike a blow against the men who had done this to him?

Dafydd met them just inside the gates to the homestead. He glanced at the boy and at the bulky blanket held across the other mount as he helped Aileen dismount.

"It's done then," he said.

She nodded; her throat was too full to manage words.

"Then there will be no mercy."

He mumbled the words. A scruff of a brown beard stained his lean cheeks. His cloak was rumpled as if he'd slept in it for days. His eyes were soft with a deep and unbearable sadness.

"Come, Aileen." He turned and headed across the yard. "We have yet another patient."

A breath of winter wind siphoned between the edges of her cloak. She stumbled her way through the horses snorting and pawing in the yard, as eager for their dinner and some warm straw as she was for the same. Dafydd led her to the storage shed where she'd been imprisoned the first few days after her arrival. A guard stepped aside as they approached.

"We found him this morning herding two of Dunwyd's cows that had strayed from the herd. He was wounded fighting and couldn't get away from us." Dafydd swung open the door and stood stiffly in the portal. "His name is Edwen ap Gruffydd." She paused. ". . . ap Gruffydd?"

"Yes, Aileen. My half brother." *And Rhys's.*

Eleven

Rage flooded through her, rage as she had never known it. It shuddered her limbs, blinded her, closed up her throat. One of Rhys's half brothers; one of the pack of wolves. One of the warriors who had beaten an elderly man and his frail wife to death, and left an orphaned boy to nurse a blood-debt in his eleven-year-old heart.

The bark of her basket-handle dug into her palm. Amid the shadows, a body unfolded and stumbled to a stand, then swayed like a crazed beast tethered to the back of a cage. Was she to heal this *thing*'s wounds, while the blood of his victims still clung to her fingers? Was she to lay her hands upon a man who fed on another's suffering? Better that his wounds rot; better that he suffer, as his victims had; better that *he* taste the dirt of the grave.

She started, shocking herself with the trail of her thoughts. She knew the herbs she needed for such a thing. Who would know? Then the vengeance would be complete and a young boy could rid himself of blood-lust and get on with his life. Even as the thought was formed, it died. The blind fury that had surged through her, hot and bright, faded like a comet across the sky; too foreign to live long in her heart, but strong enough to leave bitter ashes.

With that bitterness biting at her throat she stepped into the musty shed. Never in all her life on Inishmaan had she felt reason to turn away from a wounded creature. Yet here in this cursed place she found herself regretting the very urge that

HERE'S A SPECIAL INVITATION TO ENJOY TODAY'S FINEST HISTORICAL ROMANCES— ABSOLUTELY FREE! *(a $19.96 value)*

Now you can enjoy the latest Zebra Lovegram Historical Romances without even leaving your home with our convenient Zebra Home Subscription Service. Zebra Home Subscription Service offers you the following benefits that you don't want to miss:

- **4 BRAND NEW** bestselling Zebra Lovegram Historical Romances delivered to your doorstep each month (usually before they're available in the bookstores!)

  - 20% off each title or a savings of almost $4.00 each month

  - FREE home delivery

  - A FREE monthly newsletter, *Zebra/Pinnacle Romance News* that features author profiles, contests, special member benefits, book previews and more

  - No risks or obligations...in other words you can cancel whenever you wish with no questions asked

So join hundreds of thousands of readers who already belong to Zebra Home Subscription Service and enjoy the very best Historical Romances That Burn With The Fire of History!

And remember....there is no minimum purchase required. After you've enjoyed your initial FREE package of 4 books, you'll begin to receive monthly shipments of new Zebra titles. Each shipment will be yours to examine for 10 days and then if you decide to keep the books, you'll pay the preferred subscriber's price of just $4.00 per title. That's $16 for all 4 books with FREE home delivery! And if you want us to stop sending books, just say the word....it's that simple.

It's a no-lose proposition, so send for your 4 FREE books today!

4 FREE BOOKS

These books worth almost $20, are yours without cost or obligation
when you fill out and mail this certificate.
*(If the certificate is missing below, write to: Zebra Home Subscription Service, Inc.,
120 Brighton Road, P.O. Box 5214, Clifton, New Jersey 07015-5214)*

Complete and mail this card to receive 4 Free books!

YES! Please send me 4 Zebra Lovegram Historical Romances without cost or obligation. I understand that each month thereafter I will be able to preview 4 new Zebra Lovegram Historical Romances FREE for 10 days. Then if I decide to keep them, I will pay the money-saving preferred publisher's price of just $4.00 each...a total of $16. That's almost $4 less than the regular publisher's price, and there is never any additional charge for shipping and handling. I may return any shipment within 10 days and owe nothing, and I may cancel this subscription at any time. The 4 FREE books will be mine to keep in any case.

Name _____

Address _____ Apt. _____

City _____ State _____ Zip _____

Telephone ( ) _____

Signature _____
(If under 18, parent or guardian must sign.)

LF0396

Terms, offer and prices subject to change without notice. Subscription subject to acceptance by Zebra Home Subscription Service, Inc.. Zebra Home Subscription Service, Inc. reserves the right to reject any order or cancel any subscription.

A $19.96 value.... absolutely FREE with no obligation to buy anything, ever!

ZEBRA HOME SUBSCRIPTION SERVICE, INC.

120 BRIGHTON ROAD

P.O. BOX 5214

CLIFTON, NEW JERSEY 07015-5214

made her what she was. She could not refuse to heal. To turn away from any wounded man was to turn away from herself, to leave a nagging ache in her head, a throbbing sensation of a task left undone. Aye, she'd tend to this man, but she'd not be blamed if she prayed to God to block the power of her healing hands.

He stood as tall as all the sons of Gruffydd, but thinner, more lanky, and the jerkin of skins which hung from his big-boned frame bore witness to the difficulty of the capture. Blood stained one sleeve and trailed onto his hose. Mud matted his fair hair. He watched her as she approached, then cocked an elbow on a cask and leaned into it.

He said something to Dafydd in Welsh. She understood only one word. *Dewines.* Witch.

Dafydd snapped back at his brother so hard and fast that all she heard among the gurgle of his words was *meddyg.* Healer.

The prisoner's gaze settled on her with new speculation. He rubbed a clean-shaven chin while a contemptuous smile lifted beneath his hand. "Witch . . . try . . . heal . . . Rhys."

"Tell the prisoner," she said, "that he should be pleased I'm not a witch. For if I were, he'd be sitting in a bog somewhere catching flies with his tongue."

Dafydd repeated her words while she swallowed the bile thickening in her throat.

"This woman—" Edwen nodded, the grin not faltering— " . . . temper."

"You tell the prisoner," she continued, "that if he chooses not to be healed, it will be my pleasure to let his wound fester."

Edwen picked at the laces of his jerkin, and managed a shaky bow. The words were nearly incomprehensible, but the sarcasm wasn't.

"I . . . not scorn . . . Rhys's . . . generosity."

Dafydd bridled behind her. His voice dropped dangerously soft.

"Rhys . . . like father . . . gifts . . . horses . . . sword . . .

clothes . . ." Dafydd gestured to the fine boots Edwen wore, a rich contrast against the tattered linen shirt he tore off his back with some difficulty to reveal a young, well-formed chest and a bloodied arm. "You . . . fool. You . . . black heart."

Edwen shrugged and retorted in a string of lazy Welsh, never losing his careless grin. She stopped listening. She didn't want to hear, she didn't want to understand. Snapping her cloak out of the way, she tossed her basket on the rushes by his feet and yanked his arm straight, ignoring his wince of pain. Along his elbow lay a deep gash. He ignored her as she prodded the ragged flesh.

She would concentrate on this, on something she could heal. Then she would be out of this hellish place, away from the words these two brothers threw at each other like daggers. Living in a house full of brothers, she'd heard enough arguments in her day. She'd even seen them come to blows. But always when the noise ended there was easy laughter and bravado and slaps on the back and other such things that she never understood, after all the harsh words. She'd long attributed this to the strange ways of men, incomprehensible to all but themselves.

But this was no churchyard argument, no spat over the dinner table. Dafydd's voice dropped, raw, and quivered with repressed fury while Edwen's filled with more and more wicked sarcasm. She understood enough of the rapid Welsh to know Dafydd rained upon his half brother accusations of all the treachery of which he was the cause; and she knew that Edwen scorned them. More than once she heard the word *gavelkind* fall from his lips. It was his birthright, he claimed, to have part of this land. *My land. My land.* She heard the words over and over, hating the man who said them with that sick smile frozen upon his face. He repeated the words like a jaded monk repeating his paternosters. As if it were something he'd memorized and now spoke so easily that he no longer listened to the meaning of the words.

Then the door slammed open and Rhys tore in with the

wind in his hair and lightning in his eyes. Aileen reared back as Rhys shouldered Dafydd aside, scraped out the length of his sword, and lodged the point in the hollow of his half brother's throat.

Her breath snagged in her lungs. Eye to eye, the men were of the same height, a distorted mirror of one another. Though steel pricked his neck, still, *still* Edwen wore that arrogant grin, his eyes dancing over the length of the sword that with one push would mean his death.

She shook her head at Rhys. He couldn't see her though she stood only inches away. He couldn't see anything beyond the face of his half brother. *No, no, no* . . . Her insides screamed the words though no sound made it past the thickness of her throat. Why should it matter so much to her? What did it matter if Rhys killed this creature right here, before her eyes? She'd seen bloodier deeds on the day of battle, and none so deserving as this.

Then Rhys spoke. Sharp, biting words rumbling with accusation, in a voice that sounded like gravel grinding over rock. This was not Rhys talking—not the controlled, cynical Rhys she knew. These words roared up from that tightly locked coffer of anguish, then burst open in a man's angry wail of *Why? Why? Why?* which put her in mind of the banshees who raged in warning at the coming of a death. At the crack of his voice, he shut his mouth against all emotion whilst he stared down the gleaming sword stretched between him and his treacherous half brother.

Still that arrogant grin froze on Edwen's face though his skin had paled to the color of tallow. And Edwen stood proud and straight, not bending a hair to the man he'd wronged, not lowering his chin against the steel.

Rhys, don't be doing it, you'll never forget the flow of your brother's blood over your own hands.

Dafydd clamped a hand on Rhys's shoulder and said something swift and low. Rhys scraped his sword back into the scabbard. His cloak snapped as he turned back to the wind flowing in through the door.

Dafydd followed. Aileen stood motionless, shaking from the moment, glaring at Edwen with venom enough to kill, if one could kill with one's mind. As she rounded to give him a piece of her own heart, he sagged down against the cask, laying out one of his legs and folding the other under him. She glared at him. The pallor she'd seen moments ago had intensified. She had assumed that the blood staining his hose had dripped from his arm, but by the awkward angle in which he held his leg she wondered if he bore more than one wound.

Damn her heart. She crouched down and yanked a lock of his hair away from his face and noticed another gash, just above his ear. Against her knuckle his cheek was as smooth as a child's, sprayed with the faintest first down of a beard. With his eyes closed, lying against this cask, without the cocky stance he'd taken so proudly, he had the look of a young boy in the first flush of manhood. He couldn't be more than sixteen or seventeen years of age.

Nay, he was man, she told herself. Boys killed squirrels and rabbits with slingshots. A boy was no longer a boy once he killed a human in cold blood.

She tended him. When she was done, she went in search of another man, more deeply wounded.

She emerged into the light. Snow sliced down from the gray skies and disappeared in the muddy yard. Rhys sat atop his palfrey near the open gate of the *llys*. Dafydd stood in front of him, his fist in the bit, arguing. Rhys's horse stamped and jerked its snout high in the air. Rhys yanked the horse free to gallop around Dafydd and shoot out the gate. The last thing she saw was the flick of a horse's black tail.

She joined Dafydd as he stared out at the empty path whence Rhys had disappeared. "Where is he going?"

"Away." Dafydd seized her arm as she turned toward the stables. "Leave him be."

"But—"

"He'll be back. Edwen guaranteed that, by being foolish enough to get himself caught."

She looked up at Dafydd's stubbled, impassive face. Snow melted in his hair, dulling its usual sheen, and shadows dug caverns under his eyes.

"That idiot half brother of mine is no better than a child seeing a pretty toy in a hound's jaws, and having no sense to leave it be." Dafydd released her and flexed his hand. A welt slashed across his palm, the bite of Rhys's horse's bridle. "Do you know how we caught him? Edwen had his eye on a bull, and he galloped right past our camp to try to steal it instead of having the sense to stay with his brothers. That was an arrogance we couldn't ignore."

"His folly is your triumph."

"Is it?" He cast his gaze upon her. "For all the years we've been chasing those wretched brothers of ours, Rhys made damn sure we never caught them."

A hound skittered by, its head lowered against the snow. The dampness of mud seeped through her shoes.

"Don't look so surprised, Aileen. You may have no love for my brother, but you don't know the man. You don't know how he was before all this. Rhys didn't want to catch them. He knew what he would have to do, if he did."

She followed Dafydd's gaze across the yard to where some men hammered at a structure rising near the gate. The spindles of wood creaked and snapped in the wind.

"If we release Edwen, we invite the whole pack of them to raid and kill again, and we lose the faith of every man living under Rhys's protection. If we imprison him, we show weakness, for there is only one punishment for treason."

Snow sluiced across her cheek. A hound bayed within the kennels. Her blood ran cold.

"Edwen gave us no choice." Dafydd closed his hand over the burn. "Come morning, Rhys will hang him."

* * *

Rhys shaved off a sliver of oak. It curled over the blade into a bed of bark and chaff piled around his feet. Against the stone walls of the *hafod* bristled a line of other spears, the pale wood browning from exposure to the cold sun. A scaffolding of oak branches webbed the ground before him, waiting their turn to be transformed into weapons of war. Somewhere beyond the murky mist clattered the hoofbeats of a single horse.

Come, Aileen. Yes, come. Find your way here, through a mist as thick as milk. Pass the grass-covered mound on the precipice walk of the hill, the grave of a giant serpent who had lived on this mountain hundreds of years ago. Think upon that fabled snake, Aileen, that snake with the power to paralyze anyone who stared into its eyes too long. A serpent who devoured human flesh for supper. Then come and find me sitting before this wretched summer hut, the fable made flesh and blood, a beast capable of frightening women into suicide and hanging young boys.

The shape of a mare formed itself out of the mist. Aileen's hair blazed so improbable a red, a bloody streak of color in this hazy world of stone and fog. His loins swelled at the sight of her, as they did the very first day he saw her crossing the shore of Inishmaan with the sea-spray pounding upon the rocks and her hair flying about a face as Otherworldly as any creature of Marged's imagination. His blood pulsed, pumping life through a body grown sluggish and unwieldy.

He forced his concentration on the flash of his knife as he dug into another layer of wood and eased the curl off the oak. He circled the shaft of the spear and ran his fingers down the length. A splinter pricked him and left a reedy trail of blood upon the wood. No bumps, no ridges, no cracks. Only perfect instruments would rise from his hands, beautiful in their lethal strength, staunch in their loyalty—leaving no chance that they would fail him in the heat of battle.

Her feet scraped against stone as she awkwardly dismounted and wound the horse's reins around a branch of fir. Out of the corner of his eye he saw the wind steal the hood from her head as she strode across the hard earth. She crouched by the fire and shifted her shoulder. A sack slid off her back and thumped to the ground.

Suddenly she was standing before him, thrusting a flagon under his nose. The cork dangled below the neck of the bladder. The scent of mead choked him. His gaze drifted past the mead, toward the woman.

Yes, the woman, staring at him as steady-eyed as a falcon, those gray eyes as open as the winter sky and rippling with challenge. A woman, despite the sag of her tunic from her shoulders, despite the all-enveloping mantle, for he knew what lay beneath; strong, lean muscle and a woman's curves sparsely formed—the meat all the sweeter for being close to the bone. Hunger stirred amid the black muck of his bleary haze.

"Are you going to take it?" The breeze whipped a few strands of hair across her face. "Or must I stand here and suffer your glaring until the sun goes down?"

She nudged the mead at him. Something in the gesture whirled up a memory from the wool clogging his head.

His voice wheezed out of him. "This is the same honey-mead that you offered Edwen, before I had him hanged."

Edwen had taken the mead, too, he remembered. The boy had had enough self-possession to raise the bladder to Rhys in mock salutation, before drinking his fill. Just like the twelve-year-old Edwen that Rhys remembered returning from the salmon-stream one summer's afternoon, battered from a fight with two older boys—and grinning about it through a chipped and bloodied tooth.

"What kind of Welshman are you," she said, setting the bladder by his feet, "to refuse my hospitality?"

She retreated out of his range of sight, like some dream-creature melting into mist. His spear clattered to the ground. He curled his fist around the bladder and forced his stinging eyes to seek her out.

"By the look of you," she said, "you don't even know that it's New Year's Day, do you?"

She crouched by the fire. Her spine ridged her wheat-colored tunic as the wind tossed her mantle aside. He wove the bladder to his lips, wondering why she'd bothered to lie. He'd only just ridden from the sight of his youngest brother swinging on the scaffold. His body still ached from the cold, hard ride. Yet with the first icy trickle of mead down his throat he found himself choking it down as if he'd not tasted liquid for days, noticing through the clearing haze of his eyes the carcasses of hare and grouse scattered across the ground. He wiped his mouth with the back of his hand and felt the give of stubble flowering into beard.

"Two weeks you've been gone," she said, "and not a word to any of us in the *llys,* not knowing if you lived or died."

Such was the way of the Otherworld, *Annwn,* where time ran differently. One moment amid the mists of that land and a man would return to find a hundred years had passed in his own. The man who had created that faery tale must have had sins weighing heavy on his mind, Rhys found himself thinking, to dream up a place where a man could hide for a moment, and then return to a world which no longer knew him.

"You should have had the sense," she muttered, her face in the sack, "to return to the *llys* by now."

"You should have had the sense to stay away." The bladder sank out of his hands. He looked upon it sagging on the ground, and noticed the stains on his silken tunic, once a deep shade of scarlet and now streaked with offal. "Have you brought New Year's water to sprinkle me with, woman? To give me luck?"

"You'd be needing the luck, that's sure enough, but it's a Welsh tradition and I know naught of it. Still, I do know this." She clanked a pot out of her sack. "Your people believe, as mine do, that how you spend this day will reflect the year to come."

"Marged," he said, groping for the half-carved spear, "would be proud of you."

"Mock me, mock Marged, too, if you must, but there will

be no mocking every man and woman in Graig." She plucked a stick out of the wood piled on the ground. "You're the lord of this place. This land's health relies on your health. It's the same in Ireland, as well. Though you may scoff at it, your people don't." She seized another branch. "What you do this day you'll be doing for the remainder of the year."

"I should have hanged him today, then." He sliced off a curl of wood so thin it lay transparent against his hand. "By Christmas next I'd be rid of my enemies."

"Have done with that." She cradled the wood in one arm and snapped off the twigs thorning their length. "Nothing can change what's done. It's the future you should be thinking about."

He speared the knife into the earth and heaved himself to his feet, leaning into the spear as the blood rushed out of his head and left him reeling and dizzy. Leave it to a woman not to have the sense to forget a man's words. Leave it to a woman to bring up things best left unsaid.

"No recriminations for me?" He fisted the splattered silk of his tunic. "The warrior, the cold-blooded killer you so despise?"

She jabbed a stick into the ground, knocking a chunk of frozen sod into the air. "What difference would it make, would you be telling me that?"

"I killed a man." He tucked the end of the spear under his arm and leaned into it, feeling his lips crack as they stretched into a grimace. The tether upon which he'd held the beast within him threatened to snap with a single tug. *Speak, woman. Throw those words of hatred at me. Let me hear them, let me hear the condemnation of the world in your voice; let me face it here and see the disgust in your eyes. I've heard it often enough before, and no time so worthy am I of your disgust, no time do I better deserve it.* "I spilled my own brother's blood that day."

"Don't you think I saw with my own eyes what Edwen did to those defenseless people?" She struck the third stick into the earth, avoiding his eye. "I watched them die while I stood helpless."

"Am I receiving absolution?" He wove the sign of the cross in the air before him, swaying drunkenly off the support of the spear. "You've committed fratricide, Rhys, but it's the New Year so I forgive you?"

"Don't mock me."

"What honor, to be forgiven by a saint."

"I'm no saint. I can hate, just as well as any man, I wager."

"I've felt the sharp edge of your tongue often enough."

"Aye, you have, and I'll not be apologizing for it." She clattered the three sticks into a pyramid and hugged them against her breast as she wound a string of hemp around the joint. "But I've come to think that there's good and evil in this world." She muttered the next words into her mantle. "And I'm beginning to think there might be something else in between."

The ground shifted under his feet. He heard the stamp of his own foot as he straightened himself by reflex. What trick was this? he thought, watching her hang a pot on the makeshift tripod and, deft as any soldier far from home, stoke the flames. She stood there peeling wilted leeks out of the bag and stripping them into the pot, as calmly as if she stood outside the kitchens and not amid an aerie in the wilds of ice-topped mountains, with him losing his grip on sanity.

He should have kept this woman chained in the storage shed. He should have allowed her out only for the healings, then bound her in silver and locked her in irons. But no, he'd seen fit to set her loose to throw her spear of human kindness. He wheeled away from the sharpness of its point.

"Go back to the *llys.*" The dried bones of a long-eaten rabbit crackled beneath his feet. "You're not wanted here."

"Are you a man who doesn't honor his bargains then?"

"Pack your riddles with your leeks and go."

"I will not." She knotted the hemp tight and fished a knife

out of her pocket. "You promised me passage back to Inishmaan in the spring, but only if I set to trying to heal you."

"Pretty words and salves do me no good."

"That's not what you told me before all this business happened. You told me I had stopped it from spreading."

He didn't have to grope deep into the muck of his memory to remember what she was talking about. The lie surged to the surface to mock him before he could force it back down, with the other sins he kept hidden in the mire. In his head a demon's laughter singed his ears. This was his punishment, then, for craving pity-kisses; this was his punishment for lusting for yet another taste of this woman.

"There'll be no going back to the *llys* for me now, Rhys, unless you'll be taking me there yourself. Dafydd watched me from yonder rise until he was sure I had set upon the right path, but he's halfway to the *llys* by now." She cut the hemp and tossed the knife to the ground. "I'll go, if you insist."

"To be caught by my loving brothers?" He stared into the mist curling down through the valley. "They'd hang you. Or burn you. I'd be forced to hunt them down until all of them lay dead at my feet. Would that please you, woman?"

"I shouldn't have had to make the trip at all." She slung the pot over the tripod. "You have a fey habit of running away from the world whenever it pricks you."

"And you," he said, as rage hazed the world red, "have a fey habit of running to the wolf's den while the blood still clings to his teeth."

He strode to her. Branches snapped beneath his feet. Damned fool woman, straightening to stare at him with widening eyes. Didn't she know there came a time when a man no longer cared for the sanctity of his soul?

There was only one hell, after all.

Now she stood before him, her lips quivering with some repressed emotion, her hands sliding up to fix on her hips even as her back straightened.

Lisa Ann Verge

"Edwen had committed treason," she said. The freckles stood out stark against her skin. "You had no choice."

There you are wrong, woman. There was always choice—always. He could have submitted to his brothers' wishes, divided up his holding, let them build and marry and have their own children subdivide the holdings even more until nothing was left of the lordship of Graig but a string of tiny homesteads that the English and the Marcher Lords could roll over with a single incursion into the North of Wales.

But he'd made the choice to fight, long ago, to hold these lands strong and unified. And he'd done it for the Prince of Wales, for his own father, for the dream of Wales itself—to keep the Gwynedd free of the English. His father had cursed him with this duty when he'd made him the chosen heir, bucking all Welsh traditions in the process; and now Rhys paid the price in his own brothers' blood.

The irony of it all was that he no longer cared if the English conquered the *cantrefs* around him and built their churches and villages and castles, and burned the sound of Welsh off every man's tongue. Now he fought for himself. He could not live out in the world, and so he fought to hold this place of his exile—he fought to survive.

And here this silver-eyed woman stood, talking to him of choices.

Go away, woman. Run away before the monster forgets he was once a man.

"It would be so much easier for you, if I hated you, wouldn't it, Rhys?" Her chest swelled. "It would be easier for me, too."

Something snapped; a gray film hazed over his eyes. He yanked at the tie which held his mask against his neck, then at the leather that stretched across his forehead. A flush crept up her neck and spilled over her cheeks.

Yes, woman, you'll see it now. You'll see what children fear in the shadows in the darkness.

The wind which howled over the hilltop tore the leather from his hands and battered it against his shoulder. A rumbling sounded in the distance. A horse whinnied and scattered back from the whip of pine boughs, and the frail housing of firewood collapsed in on itself in a shower of sparks.

Neither one of them moved. He stared into her eyes, waiting for the horror to transform her features. That had become a familiar sight in the days before Dafydd had fashioned him this mask. The widening of the eyes. The sudden slackness of the mouth. The stiff hand upraised, not quite reaching the mouth, before the lips rounded and a cry tore from between them. Brows trembled together. Then the shoulders collapsed in, the entire form flung itself back and away, the other hand flew out, palm up, to ward him off. Then came the quick sign of the cross, the kissing of holy relics, the stumbling steps away, the flutter of perfumed handkerchiefs to ward off plague and sometimes, sometimes, the clink of alms falling at his feet—payment against a curse no man would wish upon the foulest of his enemies.

"Ever see a scourge like this, Aileen?"

The blood drained from her face, but she didn't step back, she didn't step away; and with a strange softness to her eyes she stepped forward—she stepped toward him.

He felt as if he'd raced headlong across long flat ground and lurched off the edge of a cliff. He waited for the signs, waited even for the subtler looks of horror the doctors would set upon him: the surge of nausea in the throat, the sudden whirl, the bustle and talk to hide the trembling of their hands, talk of worse cases, of other men's scourges.

She raised her fingers to his jaw. He seized her hand in his grip before she could touch flesh.

No.

She ignored his silent scream and raised her other hand to trace the edge of the affliction over his cheek, up past his eye to where it raged upon his forehead. Bare fingers on bare skin, and in the bright of day.

"I've never seen anything like this." Her gaze drifted from his cheek to his eyes, and her voice fell, as husky as rustling leaves. "I've never seen a man walking with so many open bleeding wounds."

His breath slammed hard into his lungs.

She is looking at me.

Not at the bubbling boil of his face, but at him, at his eyes, and deeper still. His throat parched. The world shifted around him, the horizon tilted, the mist changed color, even the wind shifted its pitch. This was a dream, a crazed dream of madness. That, or enchantment, magic emanating from this woman with the nest of fiery hair and the skinny arms and eyes too big for her face.

And her hand upon his skin . . . it was doing something, drawing away a veil of darkness so that the world around him turned brighter; the fir trees glowed a deeper green, the sky a lighter white, the oak spears glowed golden against the silvery sheen of the hut's stones. His heart floated up from his chest as if a great stone had been pushed off it. He could not look away from her—he could not.

He crushed her fingers in his grip. He raised her hand to his face, watching her over the curve of her fingernails, and sucked her thumb into his mouth.

Twelve

There existed in Ireland an herb called *Faud Shaughran,* the faery grass. Whosoever was fool enough to tread upon it would find herself tearing mindlessly across the land through night and day, through brambles and woods too thick for sun to penetrate, over choppy seas and up the cliffs of mountains, so fast and furious it was like flying, it was said—a mindless headlong flight that paid no mind to exhaustion but forced the enchanted one on, for the herb rendered her powerless to pause or to change the course of her flight.

Here Aileen stood, sucking air into her lungs and trembling fit to shake her bones out of her skin, while Rhys ridged his teeth against the heel of her palm as if tasting a soft ripe pear. Here she stood snared in the blue blade of his gaze while her heart raced, still raced, and all her body shuddered in the steely grip of a fierce, unyielding emotion.

He pulled her toward the tiny hut with its frosted thatch and pitted walls. For all her stumbling, she felt as if she flew across the ground and the wind itself pushed the door open for them. He thrust her forward. She banged her foot against his sack, stumbled over the cold black ashes of an evening fire, and scraped to a stop before a makeshift pallet of fir boughs. The light sifting down through the smoke-hole dusted the edge of the crumpled blanket.

He snapped off the netting of her hair. Burrowing beneath the tumble, he sucked his way down the line of her neck then came up short on the edge of her mantle. Throwing an arm

around her shoulder he pinned her against his back as he tore
the ties asunder, then yanked the mantle out between them and
sent it flying across the room to thud against the wall and
crumple into a pool of wool. Every hard inch of his big body
pressed against her back—heaving, as she heaved, and radiating heat like a kiln.

Aye, and was this *her* leaning back into him, savoring the
feel of his body so close, savoring the touch of hard man's
muscle against her woman's flesh? She threw her head back
at the shock of his lips on her shoulder, then curled fistfuls
of her tunic in her hands as her mind separated from her body
and her body fluxed to the commands of some primitive instinct, doing things with a shift of her hips that she'd never
dared imagine. Doing them, no less, to a man who had spent
weeks living like an animal, a man with half a face and a
slipping grip on his soul.

Oh, but hadn't she spent the last fortnight weighing the risks
and the consequences of seeking out the man she couldn't
seem to shake out of her thoughts? Hadn't she brooded all
through a gloomy Christmas while her heart battled with her
mind, her instincts with her sense? She'd told herself, aye, he's
a warrior, an unbeliever, a man she should hold in contempt . . .
but her heart screamed to heal the wounds that festered inside
him. He'd not brought the hatred of the world upon himself,
but for all her healing gifts, it wasn't in her power to wipe
away a thousand whispers of contempt, the sword-slice of betrayal, the unhealed bruise of constantly witnessing fear and
disgust in people's eyes. Da's teachings rang in her ears: *There
are many ways to heal, Aileen—with your herbs, with your
hands . . . and with your heart.*

So she'd come to this place ignoring Dafydd's warnings.
She'd come to this place knowing the moment she laid eyes
upon Rhys's grizzled face and unfocused eyes there would be
a price to pay. No healer could open herself up to the fire of
another's agony and remain unscathed.

In the end, she had come for reasons she had not dared to

acknowledge, not until now. She reached up, scraped past the scruff of his jaw, stubbed her fingers on the ridge of his ear, then buried her hand in the tangled silk of his hair. She arched her back to draw his lips deeper into the nook of her shoulder, to press the stretch of his arm against a breast grown tender and bottom-heavy.

She wanted him. Her legs buckled. Her knees sank in the pallet, and he sank with her, their bodies spooned. Even like this, she wanted him, even with his fingers digging into her side and his teeth against her shoulder. A sharp edge of a pine bough dug into her shin. She hadn't come here expecting herb-scented reeds and tenderness. Such trappings were for beautiful women, gentle lovers, noble sentiments, none of which existed in this rubbled hut. None of which existed as he peeled himself away from her, flattened a hand on the small of her back and forced her belly-down on the pallet.

A twig snapped as he yanked at her tunic. The wood reeled off her hem and spun across the floor. Cool air washed her calves; then seeped higher . . . to chill the bare skin of her thighs above the edge of her stockings. The hem of her tunic rode up under her, bumped past her knees, scraped over the ridge of the rope garter, and settled in the hollow of her hips as he doubled the tunic over her back and left her bottom as bare as the day she was born.

His bare hands shocked the hollow of her back, and razed down, down, shamelessly down, molding her buttocks into the shape of his grip. Before she could even release the breath she'd gulped at the first feel of his callused hands on her bare flesh, he kneed her legs apart and trailed his thumbs into that part of her grown hot and liquid. She bucked at the intimacy. Her thoughts whirled too fast for her to sort out whether she'd moved to get away from the sweet invasion of those hands, or to grind up against them in the grip of a passion she'd never known.

He nudged her legs wider. Those fingers probed open a part of her that had never felt the breath of an open breeze. His warmth left her, and for long agonizing moments she lay trembling on her belly with the blanket crushed in her fists listening to the snap of his belt, the clang of his sword on the ground, the harsh drag of his breath into his lungs. *So this is to be the way of it then.* How fitting it was that he'd take her like this, so she couldn't look into his face. How fitting that even in this most intimate of human relationships, he hid from her still.

Then his weight crushed her to the pallet and all rational thought fled. His hands seized her hips and dragged her down, closer to that solid throbbing root of him. He pinned her at the source of the heat and lurched against her hard enough to bring a surge of tears to her eyes. She'd been summoned to enough pallets the morning after a bedding to know there would be pain in the first joining, so she braced herself for the sting of it. With each hungry lunge, with each stretch of her own body accommodating him, she braced for the inevitable.

And it came, the pain, aye. She'd not expected him to be so *big*. But it wasn't the pain which gripped her when finally loins met loins, when his harsh breath warmed the nape of her neck and one hand curled into her hair and yanked her head back so he could suck her earlobe into his mouth—nay, not pain. That came and went and though the healer in her knew she'd feel it again when the thing was done, right now that made no difference. His breath rasped through his lips. His hips surged against hers. His hands dug into her with urgency and she knew with a sort of delirious joy that he wanted her, he wanted *her,* with each swift deep stroke.

She began to shudder. A shuddering that had nothing to do with cold. It thieved her of speech, blinded her to the splattered walls, dulled the stench of horse rising from the blanket, and then launched her into such a blinding white place that for all she knew she could be lying amid a bed of feathers in the grandest castle in all of Wales.

With a grunt he collapsed upon her. She lay smothered under

the crush of his weight, drifting down from that high, white place, thinking, this is life.

This is life.

Rhys slept the sleep of the dead. When he woke, he shot up from the pallet to the clatter of something falling outside. He groped for his sword, then spied it gleaming across the hut, still in its scabbard, at the edge of the long skid mark it had made after he'd torn it off his waist.

Images inundated him, hazy uncertain images of a woman's pale flesh, of hair scented with heather, of hot moist yielding flesh. He flung his arm across the pallet, but only her imprint remained upon the wool grown cold.

He jerked up, fully awake. He probed beneath the blanket for his mask, but no leather caved beneath his hand. He spied one of the ties dangling across his arm and realized he'd lain bare-faced beside her during the night, dead to the world, dead to the revulsion which must have spread across her features in the bright cold light of morning. *So the wench's courage had failed her.* Twisting the leather up over his head, he stumbled up from the pallet, expecting to hear the sound of hooves galloping away down the slope.

Bitterness cut through the dry wool which filled his mouth. He swung open the door. Could he blame the woman for tearing from his side? She'd enjoyed last night. He hadn't slipped so far away from the world that he didn't feel her response and know it for what it was. He still had that, then—a rod which could give a woman pleasure, if a woman ever dared to get close enough to use it.

He strode out into day and blinked at the sharpness of the blue sky. The whole of Wales stretched out beyond the clearing of the *hafod*. Patches of green spruce spotted the brown hills, and blue-white ice frosted the tips of distant peaks. Just outside the shadow of the pine trees, his horse whinnied a greeting and stamped the frosted earth. Aileen stood by the fire, flexing one of his newly carved spears underfoot.

"So you're awake, high time for it, I'll be thinking." She set her weight upon the middle of the wood. "I set to checking your breathing hours ago, to make sure you still lived."

"What the hell are you doing?"

"Making soup." The wood cracked and yawned open with splintered teeth. "I'm famished, and the only way this soup is ever going to be done is if I build a bigger fire."

She had crushed her hair back into the netting, but half of it tumbled across her face as she pulled on the spear until it snapped in two. Her cloak sagged over one shoulder, revealing the skewed neckline of a creamy linen tunic. Patches of red flared at the nape of her neck, over her shoulder, upon her ear.

"This soup," she said, poking the pieces of the spear into the flames, "will be done a lot faster if I've a man breaking this wood for me."

"Those," he said, "are my spears."

"Is that what they are?" She glanced up at the row of spears, tumbled down off the wall of the hut. "I was after wondering why they were so smooth and straight and sheared of their bark. What a waste of good oak. At least I'm giving them a better end than you planned for them."

He stared at her stirring the soup bubbling in the pot while the fire streaked the sky gray. He stood there wondering what she was about. Any other woman would be sobbing upon the pallet or screaming her way across the land in search of someplace safe, someplace where she could hide from her own memories. He'd expected her to disappear into the air like that creature Octavius did on Midsummer's Night, he'd expected to wake alone to the echo of distant laughter and a mind grown silly; for there were said to be places in these hills where it was dangerous to sleep, lest the faeries steal off with a man's soul.

This was too long a way for a woman to go for pity's sake.

"Don't just stand there looking at me." She clattered another stick under the bubbling brew. "I assume you have snares set around and about, by the looks of this place, why don't you be going and making yourself useful? I've never had much of a belly for soup without a bit of meat in it. And I'll not have us setting on the path back to the *llys* with empty bellies."

High above his head, a hawk screeched, then tilted its wings and dipped down past the edge of the hillside, into the black crease of the valley below.

For one fierce, angry moment he wished he believed in faeries, for then he'd have an excuse for the bright-eyed trail of his thoughts. As it was he could only blame them on the thinning fog throbbing in his head. She'd stayed, oh yes, she'd stayed. Aileen the Red was far too practical even in her horror to leave this place alone and bumble her way back to the *llys* through a countryside crackling with cold and quivering with threat. Far better to stay with the devil you know.

"It's not the soup I want."

The words came out husky and raw—a reflex of tongue and jaw. Her bright gray gaze flew to meet his, and new color washed out the evidence of the lovemaking upon her skin.

"You'd have red meat if you could, I see that in your eye." She swung the edges of her cloak closed. "But it's soup you'll be getting, and herbs to—"

"Come here."

He wanted her. He wanted to feel her writhing naked beneath his own naked skin, to know he hadn't dreamed the night. He wanted to see the hesitation, the revulsion in her eyes, to know he *had* dreamed it; to know for sure that it had been an illusion born of madness, no more.

"What makes you think I'm going to snap to attention at your merest call?"

He thrust out his hand and summoned her with a regal curl of his fingers.

"I'm no hound to be summoned at your whim, Rhys ap Gruffydd." She whirled the stick in the soup. "And I won't be, wherever this leads us."

The air thinned. "This will lead us to my bed. Early and often."

"Did you think I didn't know that?" She showed him her profile. "Did you think I didn't know that by coming up here, I'd be taking a lover?"

A breeze whirled over the edge of the hill and flattened the scrubby grass. The mare neighed and stamped her foot on the ground. The chill sifted under the loose edge of his mask, and flattened his tunic against loins grown as hard as rock.

He found himself thinking of the faeries of *Annwn* again; the way they dazzle a man's eyes as they wile them into the danger of the faery-dance.

"You look so surprised." She raised a brow at him. "Don't be telling me you believed I'd give myself to you purely out of the goodness of my heart?"

"If you wanted a lover," he said, his jaw hardening, "there are men enough in the *llys.*"

"Now you'll be mocking me with false flattery." She cracked the stick on the rim of the pot. "Did you think I chose you out of hundreds? Truth be told, you're the first man who's shown any interest."

Now the mockery starts. What would she tell him next? That mothers burrowed their children in their skirts as she passed, that penitents tossed alms at her feet to ward off curses? That men lived in fear of this reed-slim creature of fiery hair and eyes of silver; they'd sooner kill themselves than lie down with her?

"I never could take a lover on Inishmaan." She scraped the side of the pot, and peered attentively into the froth of the brew. "There wasn't a man on it who fancied to look at me in that way."

"Your island is but a spit of rock."

"Where else was I to look? Did you think I'd be seeking a man amid the mainlanders? There wasn't one of them who would dare to look me in the eye—never mind bundling me off to the bushes. You know that. The stories they do be telling about me found their way all the way here."

He found himself remembering the day he and Dafydd had sailed into Galway Bay and set ashore to ask about Aileen. He found himself remembering the sudden silences that greeted their inquiries, the gazes sliding away, the voices dropped to whispers.

He watched her scrape her palm down her side, watched the wind pick and tug at her wild hair. He remembered the day on Inishmaan when he'd first seen her emerge out of the mist like some sort of faery-wraith—ethereal, exotic, Other-worldly to those who believed in such things.

So she knew what it was to live both inside and outside the world. Even as the thought formed, he hated the bond that tightened between them, hated the twist of that shriveled organ in his chest, like the painful throb of a muscle unused.

"The Welshmen know nothing of you." Something snapped beneath his feet as he swiveled away. "Nothing more than we've told them."

"Aye, but a lofty lord of Wales is a finer prize for a poor peasant lass."

"There was a time when you cursed me to the bowels of hell."

"Who better than a demon," she said, turning the silver of her eyes upon him, "to lay down with a witch? Now there's an explanation that should please your cynical heart."

She leaned over the soup. The steam curled tendrils around her flushed face. Her tunic gaped to show the tight nipple he'd sucked into his mouth one night . . . and other urges overcame him, more intense, more immediate.

He strode across the distance that separated them and knocked the stick out of her hand. "Forget the soup."

"Listen to you." A sheaf of wild hair fell to hide her face from his gaze as she bent to retrieve the stick. "Faith, a man has no sense when it comes to a woman and his lusts, I'm thinking."

He seized her arm and forced her straight. She gifted him
with the fury of her eyes. He breathed down upon her, thinking
she could be a striking woman when the mood was upon her,
strong and tall and bright-eyed. He'd set Marged upon her so
she would learn to do her hair in the ways of the Welsh no-
blewomen at Aberffraw. He'd send a man to Aberffraw to purchase silk—the blue-green of spruce, the red of deepest wine.
Let the men at the court of the Prince of Wales sit back and
wonder what lady Rhys ap Gruffydd adorned, let the men wonder what woman found the courage to lay with the leper-lord
of Wales.

Aileen.

Oh, there were a thousand ways he would suck upon this
woman's body, a thousand ways to taste her skin and her hair,
a thousand ways he'd make her moan. When they returned to
the *llys,* he'd treat her to smooth linens and the softest of furs.
He'd smear honey upon those sensitive nipples of hers and
suck off every drop.

He filled his lungs with the crisp air of the New Year, with
the scent of Aileen.

"Come, Irish." He curled his fingers in her hair. "I'll show
you the way it should be done."

Aileen had always considered herself a woman of iron
strength, of principle, but at the look on Rhys's face all those
sureties shattered into nothing. With his hand lost in her hair,
he nudged her toward the *hafod.* She stumbled with him on
liquid limbs. She trailed him in a dreamy sort of dance as the
horizon shifted, as they twisted past the fire, edged around her
pack, and wove their blind way toward the hut. His eyes glowed
bright with an expression she'd never seen before, something
beyond the mind-numbing lust which had seized them both
this past night. She thought, he is going to kiss me. He's going
to kiss me.

The silence of the *hafod* enveloped them. He loomed before

her, all heat and clear blue eyes too bright for the darkness. He tugged something between them. Her cloak slipped off her shoulders and whooshed to the floor. He yanked at the ties of her tunic.

"Take it off."

She smelled him—warm wool and sweat—as she set her clumsy fingers to the knots at her neck, the ties of her sleeves, the knot of her belt. She fixed her gaze upon a pulse throbbing in the thick column of his throat as the wool crumpled to her feet, revealing a fine linen undertunic as sheer as mist. Even swathed in the stained and ragged silk, and wearing boots caked in mud, Rhys cut a royal figure. She knew well the muscles that rippled beneath his clothing. But she was raised on thin fish stew and hard work—and her body showed it. Tremors riddled her skin, from much, much more than the cold.

"All of it, Irish."

She plucked at the ties of her undertunic. She was new to this, but she didn't grow up amid a family of eight children without coming upon Ma and Da more than one time fixing their clothing with a flush upon their faces. The deed could be done well wrapped.

Her voice came out a whisper. "It's as cold as the morning here."

"We'll be making enough heat."

"We can make it well enough, without stripping down to flesh and bone."

"Take it off, Irish."

She gazed up into that masked face. Yesterday he'd torn off that strip of black leather and exposed the ridges and puckers of his ravaged face. He had bared himself to her. Now he expected her to take that same risk.

She gathered the tunic in her hands. *Now he can see my knees, knobby bony things that they are, and the cut upon one of them from kneeling down in the rocks by his wounded bondsmen. Now he can see the freckles clustered on my thighs.*

And now . . . Fresh color burned her cheeks. Now he'd know that she didn't wash her hair with some root to give it the hue which had earned her her nickname.

She was the daughter of Conaire of Ulster, she told herself, even if she did look as skinny as a cat caught in the rain. With a defiant snap, she wrestled the cloth over her head and tossed it in a ball to the floor.

"Am I to stand here and freeze all day," she whispered, leaning into him, "or are you going to share that heat you've been promising?"

She let her eyelids flutter shut and tilted her head back. Surely now, *now,* he'd kiss her. Aye, a kiss, a kiss unlike any other, the kiss she'd been aching for since *Samhain* in the darkness when the moon-tides had throbbed in her blood and he had spread her legs with his thighs and mocked the loving act that before this day ended she'd know for real—again.

His lips found the base of her throat instead. He trailed a hot tongue across her pulse as his callused hand scraped across her belly. She gripped the rolling bulk of his shoulders to support legs suddenly turned to water. The perfume of his hair inundated her senses, fresh winter air and oak-spice. The bristles of his beard scraped the line of her jaw.

He did things to her with his hands and fingers and lips as the gray circle of light hazing through the smoke-hole crept across the ground. All the unimaginable, forbidden, unspeakable joys of hungry flesh revealed to her, all the voluptuous pleasures of a world she'd never thought to know. She feasted. The exotic food charged her blood with a heat that burned away every last shiver of shame. The trail of his fingers across her breast, the rasp of his hand through her hair, all transformed her into a ravenous creature, greedy for more, ever more, so eager for him that she found herself tasting the warmth of his salty skin, trailing the tips of her nails across the hair whirling on his chest. She tasted that, too; scraped her tongue against the coarseness of it, closed her eyes as it tickled the tip of her nose. She gently dug her teeth into the hard swell of his chest and felt the vibrations of his groan shiver against her mouth.

The pallet sank as he lifted himself atop her, blocking out the light, blocking out everything but the sweet heavy pressure of his naked body on her naked flesh, the fullness of him as he pressed inside her and their loins merged, the breath-stealing rhythm of a stroking so much more powerful than anything she'd ever known. Then it came again, that quivering sensation that had taken her so much by surprise—it swelled in her now, a wondrous confusion that tugged her deep, like the suck of the sea, into the powerful, into the dangerous—for this was uncharted country, a stranger's land, and Rhys her only guide through the darkness.

She thought perhaps she had screamed. She didn't know, she didn't remember as she lay beneath him on the woolen pallet listening to the rasp of their breath, their bodies pressed so close they could be one flesh. She flexed her fingers over his broad back as the world drifted to her: The soup bubbling over the pot, the trill of a winter bird swooping over the hut. Her body throbbed. Her lips throbbed—but with a painful, sore kind of ache.

Then she realized that despite all the loving, he hadn't kissed her.

Not even once.

Thirteen

It was the mornings Aileen liked best.

Aye, the mornings after the long winter nights, when the fire in Rhys's room had long sputtered to ashes. The mornings when a fresh breeze siphoned in and swirled the stagnant smoke, when the hounds barked for their food and the cows moaned outside the *llys* for release from the ache of their udders. The mornings when she and Rhys lay cocooned beneath a mountain of soft furs, a pocket of human warmth amid the brisk chill of the outside air.

This morning was no different. Though she'd stayed up late at the Candlemas feast, years of rising with the cows had long stolen from her any urge to snuggle beneath the furs. At the first distant lowing of the cattle, she blinked her eyes open. But Rhys, aye, Rhys could sleep like the dead, he could; she'd never seen such a thing. It was no wonder. He spent nearly every night thrashing about and grinding his teeth and spewing meaningless broken syllables at his invisible tormentors, while she lay cooing and stroking him, understanding it all.

Now she turned to find him blind and deaf to the world, lying on his side, his arm curled under a pillow. She reached out in the pale light and dared what she'd never done in his waking moments but what she'd dared every morning since she'd taken her place by his side in this bed. In the calm silence of the early morning, when all was fresh and new and possible, she slipped her hand up between them and pressed her palm flat against his chest.

Didn't she feel like a thief, laying her hands upon the man at his most vulnerable. But during the month they'd been lovers, all those rough nights and languid mornings, she'd discovered that only in these few predawn moments could she feel the essence of Rhys seep out from the edges of his battered heart, like a light around the frame of a door set ajar.

Today, as on every other, tears pricked the backs of her eyes as she set to the healing. She wondered at this strange reaction, for before, as she had lain her hands upon the weak or the wounded, she'd sensed the pain as a separate thing—a density or a weakness. With Rhys, the pain drove nails through her heart.

It set her to thinking of last night, when they all had feasted in the mead-hall. The meal had teetered close to merriment, for Lent was only a week away. A bard had wandered his way here through the hills of Wales, a well-dressed bard from a place called Aberffraw, filled with news of the outside world. The men had gathered around him and listened, rapt, to his stories all day, then set loose their heels in the night to the trill of his harp. At one point while she'd scrambled about making sure every man's cup was filled, Dafydd, his head turned with the drink, had pushed the bard away from the harp and summoned Rhys to it.

To her surprise, Rhys had strolled to the instrument and trailed his fingers over the strings. Amid the hall she could hear the sound of mead dribbling into the rushes, the crackle of the hearth-fire, the held breath of two dozen men.

He played with the rusted perfection of a man who once knew well the lay of the strings. The shimmer of the music filled the room. By some trick of light, it seemed as if Rhys's mask dissolved into shadow, and he sat as whole as any man in the room. She saw clearly, for the first time, the strong, stunning beauty of the man—how breathtakingly handsome he must have been, before all this.

Now with her hand pressed against his heart she stared at the skin of the right side of his face, bubbled and boiled and swirling on his bones. She thought about her sister Cairenn, the beauty of the family. She remembered how the Widdy Peggeen sewed finer clothes for her than any other, how old Seamus gave her the best of the catch when she set off to fetch some fish for dinner. Cairenn was the one to whom all eyes turned wherever they traveled, the lass everyone had a smile for. Aileen imagined what would happen to Cairenn, if she were ever afflicted. She imagined her sister's bewildered confusion, if the approval of the world suddenly turned to disgust, for no more reason than a rash.

Rhys shifted beneath her hand. She loosened her palm and let her fingers trail down the ripples of his abdomen. Aye, she loved this, too, the feel of his hand scraping down her side, the warmth of his palm cupping her breast, then his hot lips upon her shoulder. The furs shifted, cold air sifting in, then closed again to contain them in their cocoon of warmth.

There would be no more sleep this morning.

His hands worked their magic upon her, without a word spoken between them. So much warmth, so much comfort, with fur tickling her nipples and his hair soft upon her belly, flesh sliding against flesh . . . and she found herself dreamily spreading her legs as he lodged his warmth against hers, as he eased himself between her thighs until she gasped with the pleasure of it all, feeling a fullness beyond the joining of their bodies. She wrapped her arms around him, loving the rhythm of his movements, loving what little surrender he ceded when his hands flexed over her hips, when all spiraled out of control into that blinding white light.

Aye, Rhys . . . She lay in abandon while he lifted himself off her. In the muddle of her contentment she felt something soft trail across her lips.

She blinked her eyes open. The light of the smoke-hole gleamed like a halo around his tousled black hair. His finger stroked her lower lip, back and forth, back and forth, a slow tender stroking. Air frozen in her lungs, she stared into those shuttered blue eyes as the moment stretched.

Kiss me, Rhys. Kiss me.

She lifted a heavy arm and curled it around his neck, urging him down with the lightest pressure. She arched her neck and lifted her lips toward him.

Kiss me.

His finger trailed off her lips, down her chin, then away from her. The bed moved as he shifted his weight and flapped the blanket back. The chill morning air seeped in and destroyed the warm cocoon they'd made for themselves during the night. He swung his legs over the bed, padded naked toward the door, and splashed his face with water from the bowl on the table.

She lay back against the pillow staunching yet another prickle of disappointment. The morning was over. Now the day would begin, with all its duties. Now, they'd both put on their masks. She had never known it possible for a man and woman to lay flesh to flesh, loin to loin, their legs entwined like so much fishing rope, and still not be joined at the heart.

That was fine with her, she told herself, sitting up and pulling the linen to her breasts. She pitied the woman who would dare to love Rhys ap Gruffydd.

She dug under the pillow for her undertunic. "I wonder if that ewe had her lamb by now," she said, to fill the silence as they dressed. "Last night, Dafydd was after telling me that her pains had begun." She eyed him as he pulled on a shirt over his *braies.* "Will you be going boar-hunting again today?"

"No. To the castle."

"Again?" Her toes curled as she set her feet upon the cold flagstones. "The master mason isn't due for three weeks at least, and you and Dafydd have talked of nothing else since St. Agnes's day."

Aye, too many days she'd sat by the fire with her wretched spinning whilst Rhys and Dafydd pored over sheets of parchment riddled with draftsmen's lines and scribbled Latin, whilst they talked of masonry and scaffolding, of mortar and stone, whilst her gaze drifted from the spindle in her hand to the sight of Rhys's dark head bent over the drawings.

"I'm taking Tudur Aled to see it."

Cold seeped up her spine at the sound of their guest's name. "What interest would a minstrel have in a pile of stones and mortar?"

"Purely mercenary. He wishes to see the castle, to gauge the true measure of my wealth."

"As if we hadn't given him a taste of that at the feast we laid out for him last night."

"In Wales, we don't disappoint our guests."

"Are you scolding me, Rhys ap Gruffydd? Didn't I lay out a good enough table for you, even slaughtering a fatted calf for that leering poet?"

"That leering poet is one of the bards in the court of the Prince of Wales. Equal in stature to the King's doctor."

"If ever I am blessed with a visit to the Prince's court, warn me never to get bored or sick."

She tugged the leather tie from her braid and let her hair spring over her face. Aye, well, she'd make no bones about it: She didn't like the man, she hadn't liked him from the moment he'd sauntered into the *llys* with his harp slung across his back and a sneer on his face. His worldly, black gaze had drifted to where she stood by Rhys's side, and his lips had twisted in the slyest of smiles. For the first time since she and Rhys had returned from the mountain *hafod*, she'd felt like the whore of Babylon.

Dafydd had assured her that Welsh law recognized such a relationship as hers as an honorable liaison, despite the dictates of the Church. For the first awkward week sleeping in Rhys's bed, while making her initial bumbling attempts to take on the domestic duties of a mistress, she tried to take some comfort in that knowledge and not think of sin and shame. Truth be told, no one had made a protest, or openly insulted her—probably out of fear of risking Rhys's fury. But a bard was beyond vengeance. His place was sacred in any man's home. This bard of Aberffraw had a way about him that brought a stiffness to her neck.

Well, the Irish knew of courtesy as well as the Welsh. She'd bite through her lip before she showed him any ebb in her hospitality. She padded across the room and yanked her old woolen tunic off a peg.

"No." Rhys's breath brushed the nape of her neck as he loomed behind her. He fisted the wool and tossed it back up on the peg. "I won't have you dressed like a peasant while that bard prances around in his silks."

"By the way he clung by the fire last night, chattering his teeth, we should be giving him a wool tunic."

"There are silks enough in that trunk. Wear them."

"I've no stomach," she snapped, eyeing the dusty old trunk, "to wear another woman's clothing."

She had rifled through that trunk one day, wondering if there was anything within besides fripperies, and had realized it contained a bride's trousseau. She had stepped away and slammed the lid down. In that trunk lay the musty, unworn trousseau of the Lady Elyned. Rhys must have had the cloth purchased and cut, long before the disaster of the wedding. She wondered why he hadn't burned it all.

"You're a practical woman, Aileen. If you don't wear them, they'll be nothing but food for moths."

"Would you have me on my knees in the storage shed, wearing some fine stuff—"

"No. I'd have you ordering others to do that work."

"You're trying to make a silk purse out of a sow's ear, Rhys ap Gruffydd—"

"I will have you looking like the lady of the Lord of Graig."

Lady. Wasn't that a pretty word, respectful and so cunningly vague. She glared up at his masked face, at the shadow bristling along his jaw.

"It's no use." She swept her fingers down the length of her undertunic. "Dress me in silks, if you will, but Tudur Aled will still be the prettier."

"Let me be the judge of that."

She flushed, for she'd meant her words as a slap to the bard and his preening ways, not a beg for a compliment. As if he sensed her discomfort, his lips twitched in the faintest of smiles. She wondered if she actually saw humor in his face, or if she was just losing her senses. She felt a lot that way lately. Half-adrift, bobbing on a boat at the end of a frayed thread. Pulled in at one moment, sucked away at another, always waiting for the tether to break, praying with bated breath that it wouldn't.

"What have you planned today, Irish?"

He tucked a lock of hair behind her ear. The unexpected, affectionate gesture disarmed her.

"I . . . the spinning, as usual. Always enough flax and wool to keep me busy at that." She shrugged, and felt the neckline of her undertunic slip down her shoulder. "I thought I might set to the soap-making before the day is done."

"That mare you rode, New Year's Day. Do you think you can handle her?"

"You're making no sense with your questions."

"I could use better company than Tudur Aled on the ride to the castle."

Her pulse jumped. If she had any sense she'd refuse him downright. Already the chill of the day was seeping in through the stones. The last freeze had made the passes icy and uncertain. She'd not yet mastered the art of riding a horse, and she had no stomach for the company of the bard.

Aye, but it would be a fine thing to get out of the smoky mead-hall, she told herself. Her wrist throbbed from spinning and sewing. She'd welcome a day's reprieve from the duties which had been thrust upon her when she'd become mistress of the place. That was why she was considering the journey . . . not because Rhys was looking at her as if her answer mattered.

"I'll go with you." She curled her fingers around the wheat-gold tunic. "But I won't wear the silks in the cold."

"There's more than silks in there." He crossed the room, threw open the trunk, and yanked out a stretch of blue wool. "You'll wear this, instead."

She eyed the deep blue mantle with its edging of soft gray fur, and bit down upon her reflexive refusal. It *did* look like a warm cloak, and her woolen mantle was seeing the wear of the years. Surely she'd need all the warmth she could muster for the ride through the hills. . . .

"Very well." She slipped her arms through the cloak. "Don't let it be said that I don't know the meaning of compromise."

Ice crusted the patches of snow which spotted the hillsides a glittering white. Their horses's hooves cracked the veneer, and the sound echoed across the hills. Aileen clung to the mare with her thighs and let her hands lie loose upon the reins, giving the gentle horse its head as she followed Rhys's gelding. The sharp breeze tore her hair from its netting and sent it flying wildly behind her.

Her heart flew as wildly. It was a fine thing, to be sitting atop a strong horse cantering across the hills. The clean snap of the frosty air filled her head. Trickles of mountain streams spilled here and there from melted pockets of snow, winding their crystal clarity down to pools where ice stretched transparent fingers across the surface. Rhys rode with all the straight-backed assuredness of a lord upon his own lands, but more than once she caught him glancing over his shoulder to check upon her progress through an icy pass.

She found herself thinking of what Ma, Da, and all her brothers and sisters would say if they could see her now. Aye, Cairenn and Niall would turn green with envy, they would, so eager they always were to make their way to the mainland, so hungry for what lay beyond the shores of Inishmaan. Yet it was she, the spinster sister, who sat upon a fine noble horse and galloped in mountain snow behind a nobleman. She, the second mother of the family, who spoke now another language, who knew stories of a strange land and its people, and who lived the adventure she'd never really wanted.

Where was the homesickness now? A flush of guilt did little to heat the numb cold of her cheeks. It was the day, no more, she told herself, the fine crisp air and the novelty of it all and

the look in Rhys's eyes as he'd invited her in his casual way
to see the half-built castle he and his brother had spoken so
much about. Later she'd feel the homesickness, later she'd
worry about her family. Now she would breathe in this rare
and unusual excitement, and thrill to the sinfully luxurious feel
of soft gray fur against her cheek.

Rhys halted his beast at the top of a rise and waited for her
to join him. Steam emanated from his horse's shaggy brown
coat, bathing him in mist. Her mare edged close to the palfrey.
Aileen glanced behind her and discovered that Dafydd had
taken another route with the bard. They headed into a dim
pass through the hills.

"There it will be."

She followed the path of Rhys's outstretched hand to a wide
river which split around a mound of an island and headed in
two creeks down the gentle slope of a hillside. A skeletal tracing of rocks poked up amidst the snow; the outline of a large
square building flanked on each corner by round towers. On
either side of the river, tree stumps poked out of the snow
where the workmen had cleared the wooded valley nearly up
to the elbow of the hill. The black, leafless branches of alder
and oak rimmed the valley.

"The far tower," he said, pointing toward the southernmost
stone ring, "will be built this spring. Twelve feet across on
the inside, the walls five feet thick." His fur-lined sleeve swung
as he gestured to a craggy gape in a nearby hillside. "The
masons quarry the stone from there, good Welsh rock, it splits
straight and even, as if God himself deemed the stone worthy
of the castle. There, do you see that break in the northern
wall? That will be the front entrance. The bridge over the moat
will rise, and an iron portcullis will close up inside. It's being
smithed even as we speak. And there, that southern tower . . ."

Aileen listened as he talked of carpenters and scaffolding,
of mortar and measurements, gesturing here and there, discussing details worthy of a craftsman's skill. She struggled to
keep up with his words. Excitement animated his voice.

"Four towers—at each corner—and one in the middle to act as a guard tower at the entrance. Arrow-slits all around. Huge living quarters—enough for all my fighting men if need be. The mead-hall will be in the southern exposure, and kitchens in the courtyard. We're even building staircases which lead to pockets where men could be isolated, if the enemy managed to get in at all. I've seen that done in a castle in Normandy. . . ."

He spoke of war matters, and her attention wavered. Her gaze trailed from the black etching of the castle in the snow-covered valley to the sight of the man sitting straight upon his mount. She'd never heard him speak this way before. She had never seen him so animated.

"It'll be a fine, strong castle, I've no doubt," she said, as he paused, "but why are you building such at thing when you've a good strong house in the shadow of Craig Gwaun?"

A wry smile stretched his lips. "You think this is a nobleman's conceit."

"I think no such thing." She knew for sure that there was more to this castle than stone and mortar. He spoke of it as a bard would speak of a lover. "It's true a body can't be in two places at the same time, so there must be another reason for such effort and expense."

"There is. The English."

"The English?" She sucked in a cold breath. She knew of the English; Ireland knew of their atrocities. "Surely the *llys* is well protected against them?"

"The *llys* would keep us safe from the English, but this castle will stop their march before they come that close." He swept his arm over the eastern horizon. "The river grows shallow here, but beyond it is deep enough to carry boats full of Englishmen straight into the heart of Gwynedd, once they climb the first set of hills."

"Is England so close, then?"

"Close enough for the Prince of Wales to commission me to build a castle on this river."

Her brows shot up. "You're building this castle for Llywelyn?"

"Of course." His lips twisted in a smile. "Every stone laid in the name of God, Gwynedd, and the Prince of Wales."

It was a good thing his attention lay upon the terrain before them and not upon her face, for though he had spoken the words as if he'd repeated them a hundred thousand times, she heard the dry sarcasm beneath.

"North Wales has yet to be conquered. These hills have protected us." He shifted on his mount and straightened his shoulders under the layers of chain mail and padding. "But this place is the breach in our natural defenses. If they dare to try to conquer us yet again, it is here they will thrust their arrow."

And I will be here to ward it off.

She heard the words though they lay unspoken. She saw the truth of them in the rising of his chest, in the way he unconsciously clutched the hilt of his sword.

"This is a lot of trouble to go to, for the sake of another man." She knew something of the troubles in building the castle. Dafydd and Rhys had argued over the plans loudly enough for her to hear about the difficulty of finding good laborers, the problems with the mixing of the mortar, the sogginess of the island ground. And Marged was full of stories about the strange happenings the people of Graig whispered of whenever the subject of the castle rose among them. "How long have you been making such effort for Llywelyn's sake?"

"Five years." He kicked his horse around. "Don't look so surprised. It may take twenty-five. Or thirty. Or forty. Something that will last forever cannot be built in a day."

Aye, she thought, nudging her mare behind his gelding. Perhaps he'd started building this castle for the prince who had forsaken him. Perhaps he'd begun building this castle to ward off the English threat. But anyone with eyes could see that the castle had become much, much more than a fortress for a faraway prince. Down in that valley lay the physical manifestation of Rhys's power, the proof that he had not yet been defeated by the world.

How convenient that the bard of Aberffraw was to see this monster of stone rising from the valleys of North Wales. She hoped that perfumed puff of a minstrel scurried back to the Prince's court to tell the tale of what the leper-lord of Wales had wrought.

She snuggled deep in the fur-lined cloak, wondering why she would feel so much joy at this, Rhys's quiet triumph.

They eased their mounts down the side of the hill into the edge of the woods. The boughs closed over their heads, forming a lacy canopy against the pale blue sky. The horses's hooves thudded in the snow, softened upon a soil spongy with leaves. They passed a dark cave overhung with ivy, snug in the curve of the path. The sight of the cavern set her to thinking about the dragons who were said to live in these hills, it set her to think of the tales Marged had told whilst they broke from their work to share a meal across the battered table in the kitchens, before she'd become mistress of the place and thus been barred from that kitchen sanctuary.

Marged spoke of the *Y Tylwyth Teg*, small, handsome creatures in human form, very kind and generous to those who treated them well but who took revenge on people who dared to ill-treat them. Aileen had recognized them as the Irish faeries. Marged said the Welsh believed they were the souls of virtuous Druids, who not having been Christians cannot enter the Christian heaven. Such a cave as this one would be a fine doorway to the Otherworld. To the Welsh *Annwn*.

Aye, Aileen thought, as they passed the ivy-covered rise of an old *cromlech*. Their worlds . . . they were not so different. Somehow, today, she could almost sense the rustle of faery-life in the crystalline snow. A wind sifted its way through the tree-trunks, musical in its whispering, though no leaves remained upon the trees to rustle or hum. Strange . . . she'd never sensed so much life in Wales, as she did now, in these winter woods.

She closed her eyes. Aye, was that faery music she heard

upon the wind? The rustling of the *Sídh* in the snow, frolicking amid the cold and tossing grains of crystal ice at one another in play? She must be imagining things, surely. She'd been too long away from Inishmaan. Only once before had she sensed the faeries in Wales, and then only for a moment, during battle.

She blinked her eyes open. Rhys rode through the woods as if nothing had changed. It was her imagination, for surely even Rhys could sense the vibrancy of the air around them, if it were anything but a trick of her heart. As she watched, he swatted something away from his ear.

She laughed aloud. No flies sang through this crisp winter air, no birds whistled down from these branches. He glanced over his shoulder at the sound of her voice and something in her expression made him rein in the horse.

"What are you doing, stopping like that?" She dared to nudge her mare beyond his horse. "Do you want the faery-folk to start pelting you?"

"Not you, now. You're not going to spout foolishness, too."

Snow sifted down from a branch set a-shaking by some airless wind, and blew into his hood to melt upon his mask.

"Come." She grinned at him as he brushed away the snow, then she kicked her mare forward. "There will be more mischief than that if we linger in such a place as this."

Her horse's hooves crunched on the narrow path. She heard him behind her and she bent low over her mare's neck, daring to kick the horse into a faster gallop, giddy with the reckless race. Ahead, the trees thinned. Her horse shot out into the cleared land littered with tree-stumps.

And it was as if she'd slammed into a wall. Aileen jerked back and yanked so hard upon the reins that the mare whinnied and reared up on her hind legs. Shock and a tight grip kept her upon the saddle, but the mare struggled and shook the reins loose just as Rhys caught up to her and seized them from Aileen's stiff hands. He spoke softly to his mount as the mare stamped and pranced, and he struggled to get her settled.

Aileen clung to the horse's back while her mind reeled. She

sucked in air and tried to shake the throbbing in her forehead, for as sure as she was living and breathing she felt she'd slammed into stone. Around her lay nothing but clearing, oaks cut to the quick, their moist hearts exposed to the snow and sky.

And silence. Deathly silence. The dead silence of the most frozen of winters, the coldness of the grave.

"What were you doing?" Rhys nudged his horse closer. His black brows thundered over his eyes. *"Aileen."*

The pall stole her voice from her. She twisted on her saddle to look back upon the forest, searching for the lost music, the sweet playfulness she'd sensed only moments ago beneath the boughs of the trees. Now a silent screaming sounded in her ears. It rose from the ground beneath her, it was like the screaming she sensed in her fingers when she placed them upon mutilated flesh, but this she sensed with more than her hands. She sensed it with every fiber of her being, every inch of flesh and bone and muscle, and the screaming seemed to come from all around her; from the open hearts of the trees, from the ground frozen over, and mostly, *mostly,* from the mound of the island in the midst of the river.

"Aileen."

She heard his voice from a faraway place. She could see the island better now. The walls of the castle shot as high as a man's shoulder, and they dug deep into the soft earth of the island. She nudged the mare with her knees, but the horse only bucked, setting Rhys to cursing and holding firm to the reins. Such an island as this, Aileen thought, was far too round, far too evenly made for God's unsymmetric hand. . . . Then she saw something that set cold teeth sinking into the back of her neck.

She seized the reins from Rhys and dug her heels into the mare's flanks. She crushed a path through the snow to the banks of the river. In the mud lay a series of long stones, marked in black with the lines and crosses of an ancient language. They lay in pockets of melted snow, as if too hot for any ice to harden upon them. She nudged the mare along the banks of the stream, counting the standing stones which had been pulled out of the ground and laid aside for later building, shaking, shaking as she had last autumn as she'd stepped over the bloodied bodies of Rhys's wounded men.

Suddenly Rhys loomed before her. He seized the reins from her trembling grip. "Off that horse, woman."

He dismounted and seized her by the waist, then dragged her forcibly off the back of the mare. She clutched his arms and stared up into his face, searching those eyes the color of the winter sky for any hope of understanding, seeing only a thundering confusion, an angry concern.

"By Christ, woman, you're as pale as ashes."

Couldn't he hear the screams? Couldn't he feel it? No man could be so deaf, so blind, to the world around him. No man could commit such blasphemy.

"Speak to me, Aileen." His fingers dug into her arms. "What ails you?"

"You can't . . ."

The words croaked out of her throat. She licked her lips, gasping for breath like a woman in labor.

"You can't," she continued, wincing at the shudders of pain rising up from the ground beneath her, "build . . . this." She swallowed and glared at the black stones around them, at the scaffolding for the castle. "You can't . . ."

"I can't what?"

"Rhys . . you can't build this castle."

Fourteen

Rhys tightened his grip on her arms. Her lips pulsed blue. Her eyes rolled wild in rings of shadow. She stared at the island as if it were some river-dragon roaring into life.

"Enough."

He shook her. Anger mounted in him along with something else, a fear he didn't want to acknowledge. Moments ago she'd been laughing, sitting upon that mare straight-backed, swathed in fur, looking like a noblewoman and laughing like a peasant on a feast-day. Now a sheen of moisture frosted her skin and she was babbling nonsense and trembling. A coldness washed through him. He'd seen old men and children die of sudden fevers—he'd lost his own mother to one in the midst of Lent, fifteen years ago.

She couldn't become sick. She was the healer. There would be no one to heal her if she took ill, no one to seek the right herbs or tell Marged how to brew them. He'd have to send to Myddfai for a doctor, a delay that could stretch into days, days when death could steal her breath away while he stood over her and watched.

"*Enough.*"

Her head lolled back under the violence of his shaking. She struggled to focus her wild gaze upon him. She curled balls of his woolen cloak in her fists. "Can't you . . . can't you hear it?"

"Hear what?"

"The *screaming.*"

Around them the day lay silent and cold but for the bubbling of water beneath a sheen of ice, and a crack, now and again, of an icicle snapping and spearing into the snow. "I hear nothing but your raving, woman, listen to yourself."

"Even the horses can sense it." Her mare skittered, its hooves scraping through the snow. "Even your own palfrey."

"They can smell your fear."

"They can sense the pain."

"Are you hurt?"

He probed her body for injury. Her horse had snapped to a stop so suddenly that he'd almost collided with her. She could have pulled something, she could have broken a finger in the reins.

"Not me," she said, "the earth. The world."

"You're talking nonsense."

"I am not." She toed the edge of one of the stones lying around them. "There were standing stones, *menhirs*, on that island."

"A dozen of them." Covered with ivy and arranged in a circle, outside an ancient ring of oaks. He remembered the trouble he'd had finding men willing to pull them up from the earth, so many of his own full of mindless fears, so many of the Irish workers, too. "And a *cromlech* in the center. It took fifteen men to pull off the capstone."

"You broke down a—"

"I did." Was this the cause of the madness, then? "I broke it down and used the stones in the foundation of the castle. They are there now, mortared in."

She made a sound like a wounded animal. Flexing her hands open, she recoiled from him and bumped into her mare. "And you, you accuse me of having no sense. What were you thinking, tearing such a thing down?"

"They were made of good rock. I put them to better use than standing forgotten under a coat of ivy."

"Forgotten?!"

"Forgotten. Abandoned. The work of a people long dead and gone."

"And their sacred place had no more sanctity?"

"Not for anyone living and breathing." He yanked his hood off his head. "I thought you too practical to take to petty superstitions."

"Then I'm not the first to tell you."

"And not the last, undoubtedly, for such nonsense spreads among simple people like disease." He spread his arm toward the island in the midst of the river, his cloak slipping off his shoulder. "What do you see, woman? A faery circle? Inhabited by little people who dance under the moon every night until dawn?"

Her breath caught. "You scorn what you don't understand."

"I scorn the workings of idle minds." He seized her shoulders and turned her forcibly to face the island. "Look at it. *Look!* It's an island, a mound of dirt in the midst of a river. No more, no less."

"You're blind." She jerked her shoulders out from under his grip. "Those people you spoke of—the ones who built such a thing—is that all you think they saw?"

"They saw just what I see." Rhys's nostrils flared as he swept the landscape with his gaze. A sheltered valley. A river which ran in from the East and out to the West, navigable on both sides, a path into and out of the heart of North Wales. A perfect place for a castle strong enough to hold off the world. "A good meeting place. Easy to travel to. A sheltered island—"

"A sacred place," she argued in a voice that trembled with emotion, "full of strange music, full of mystery, full of magic—"

"Magic." He spat the word between them. For all the magic that the doctors and charlatans of England could muster, none had managed to cure him. Magic was wild, unreasonable hope. Magic didn't exist. So what matter if he built upon a place too many idiots held sacred? "Magic is for fools. You have spent too much time listening to Marged's stories."

"Tales, is that all they are? Then everyone in Graig is a fool . . . but you."

"You can dress a peasant in furs, but you can't drive sense into her."

What had he expected? She was a woman sharing his bed, yes, the first for years to do so willingly, the first with the courage to stare at him without a mask and to show a nobility of character that went beyond the circumstances of birth . . . but beneath that fine fur still beat a peasant's heart. More skilled at milking cows and fishing and sowing the earth . . . more susceptible to a mother's wild stories told by the hearth-fire than anyone gently born. "For a woman with enough cold-blooded self-possession to take a lover away from home, I expected more."

"And I should not have expected anymore," she retorted, "from a man arrogant enough to take no other man's counsel."

The true mystery of it all was why he cared. Inviting her had been just another impetuous gesture, like playing a harp, like opening that chest of silks and furs—he was full of such foolishness these days. What would a woman know of the thrill of watching stone rising under his direction, faith, under the very palms of his hands? What would this woman know of the beauty of stone and mortar, of the power of creation?

The sounds of horses' hooves cracked the heavy silence. Dafydd and the bard headed across the field. Dafydd reached them first and pulled his horse to a halt, his brow creased in worry.

"What's wrong, Rhys? Is it the horses—"

"Dafydd. *Dafydd.*" She skirted a stone and raced to him, then clutched the harness of his horse. *"You* must hear it. You must."

"Hear what?"

"The screaming, of course." Rhys met Dafydd's eyes. "Can't you hear it, brother?"

Wind whistled over the plain of the cleared land, clattering ice crystals along the sheen of frozen snow. The river gurgled beneath a veneer thinner and clearer than any glass made by man. Dafydd wrapped the reins around his handless wrist, then leaned down to lay his hand on Aileen's shoulder.

"Aileen, lass,"—Dafydd dug his fingers into the fur of her cloak—"this place has a way of playing tricks on a person's mind."

"You *do* hear it!"

"Aileen—"

"You do. I can see it in your eyes." She jabbed a finger at Rhys. "Tell him he mustn't build this castle. Tell him he must put it all to rights."

Go ahead, brother, tell me what you've told me every spring for the past five years, that the place is cursed as I am cursed and our efforts are futile. Tell me to put an end to it. Condemn me to sit in that mountain llys *and brood in exile for a lifetime. Such talk as that will only make me more determined to see this castle done, see it rise upon that island, sturdy and strong, with me in it as its master.*

The ice cracked beneath the hooves of the bard's mount as the bard tugged him to a stop. Tudur Aled watched the scene with a wry smile curving his pale lips, the embroidery of his tunic bright against the winter snow.

"There's no going back now, Aileen." Dafydd's hand curled into her shoulder. "Sometimes, there are more important things than—"

"Don't you be talking like that," she said, "not you, who knows better."

Rhys's nostrils flared as Aileen's silver eyes searched Dafydd's face, as she pressed her breast against Dafydd's leg. Never once did she speak to Rhys like this, nor did she look at him so full of trust and understanding or lower herself to plead for anything. Dafydd's hand lay so casually upon her shoulder—the shoulder of *his* woman.

Rhys snapped the crop upon his thigh. He was not blind. Dafydd, despite his handless arm, was a handsome man, an untitled, unlanded man with little ambition—and a softness for the Irish witch.

He'd been waiting for this last brother's betrayal.

"She's feverish." Rhys snatched the dragging reins of the skittish mare. "Five years of work and she wants me to tear it down on a woman's whim."

"I want you to put back together what you've torn asunder," she argued. "I want you to rip those sacred stones from the mortar and place them upright in their holes, I want you to remove the weight of those rocks from that island—"

"You want me to build a home for rats and rabbits and abandon the Prince of Wales's commission." He managed to tilt his lips up in a scornful smile. "Or would you have me build it for the faeries?"

She stumbled back, away from him. He knew that look. Instinctively, he reached up to brush a knuckle against his face and was surprised to find the mask intact.

"Take me away from this place."

She spoke the words on a breath, and though she did not lift her head Rhys knew they were directed at Dafydd.

"Yes, Dafydd, take her back to the homestead. I'll show Tudur Aled the castle." Rhys hefted a leg over his palfrey. His lips stretched in a mocking smile. "But I warn you: Beware. Or you, too, will find your wits addled by a faery."

"Take care of the water!"

Marged heaved a bucketful of dirty water out of the door of the kitchens, then gasped as it splattered at the feet of a frail wraith.

"Saints be blessed! Oh, Aileen, lass, it's you!" Marged clutched her chest. "I thought I'd splattered water upon the spirits of the dead last buried, I did, and doomed myself to be haunted for the rest of my life. What are you doing standing in the twilight like a ghost, with your cloak flapping open like that and the air frozen enough to crack in your lungs?"

Aileen stared at the figure standing in the doorway. The warmth of the kitchens spilled out into the darkness, a golden glow of welcome. She had stood here with her feet on the frozen mud watching Marged bustle here and there, seeing the servants one by one pass her and head toward the mead-hall where the men were taking their evening meal. She had stood here breathing in the smell of poached fish, wanting with all her heart to press forward and be a part of that warmth. But her mind held her feet frozen to the ground, for it had been a month since she'd walked easily among those who toiled in the kitchens.

"Aileen, my lady?" Marged clattered the pail to the floor and scurried out, her hands buried in her apron. "Is the master back yet from the castle, then? I thought I'd heard horses, but I wasn't sure they—by God, Aileen, you look as if you've seen. . . ." Marged curled her fingers around Aileen's wrist. "You just came from Aberygaun, didn't you, lass?"

She nodded, though she hadn't known the name of the place before now. She knew by the tremble of Marged's hushed voice that she could be speaking of no other place, that no other island in all of Wales could engender such reverence.

"Come, lass, come into the kitchens. There'll be no one the wiser, with all the girls in the mead-hall now, and you've a look upon you that sends chills to me heart, it does. Faith, your hands are like ice. What were you thinking standing in the cold like that?"

Aileen stumbled after her. She blinked against the stinging smoke swirling in the building, and blindly found her way to a stool by the hearth-fire. She sank into it as a tired babe would sink into a mother's arms, then listened to the lullaby of the kitchens: Water bubbled in a pot slung over the fire, burning logs crackled and sank into themselves. The fragrant breath of warm bread, onions, and roast drippings nourished her battered spirit.

Marged thrust something warm between her fingers. "Drink that, and quickly now. We've got to be warming you from the inside out, I'm thinking. Did the master even warn you before you rode off to that place? No, he wouldn't, would he? He wouldn't see any need to, but I'd expect better of Dafydd. Now you didn't do anything to anger the *Y Tylwyth Teg*, did you? They're fair enough to those who treat them well, but it's sure they take revenge on people who ill-treat them, you know. Haven't I seen that enough in all my years here. There was once a shepherd who wandered into that valley one day and set free a strange little man who'd got his clothes caught under a boulder. . . ."

Aileen winced as she wiggled toes thawed by the heat seeping up from the hearth stones. She hadn't realized how cold she was. Funny, she'd felt no chill when riding to the castle behind Rhys earlier in the day, watching his straight, proud head, thinking of the moments in the bedchamber that morning when she'd curled her fingers into all that hair. . . . She hadn't felt the cold of the brisk February day until she'd galloped out into that cleared forest land and felt death all around her. Only now, in this warm and sacred sanctuary, did she begin to thaw it from her bones.

". . . And later, two old men thanked him and gave him a walking stick, and don't you know, from that time onward every sheep in his flock bore two ewe lambs, until he lost the stick and his luck vanished with it. . . ."

Aileen sucked on the rim of the cup and filled her belly with fresh buttermilk, still warm from the churn. She stared into the flames flickering under the iron pot. Now and again a blue flame would flare up and then die, like the ghost of Rhys's eyes.

Magic is for fools.

He didn't believe. She'd known that since the beginning, hadn't she? She'd known he was a man whose senses had long been deadened to the mysteries of the world. Yet this morning he'd walked on that riverbank amid the corpses of mangled trees, blind deaf and dumb to the agony screaming up from beneath the snow. Had she come upon him destroying a cathedral to build a tavern upon holy ground she'd not have been more shocked. Holy ground was holy ground, and that mound was not the place for man's mortar.

". . . Years ago I remembered a woman telling me about a white cow that wandered from that valley and no one knew who was the owner." Marged spooned broth into a bowl. "The farmer that found her took her into the herd just like all the others, though she be a faery cow and didn't they all know it. When the cow grew old and the farmer set to have her slaughtered, didn't the cow just up and leave, and take every calf she'd ever had with her? And then there was that young girl who disappeared by the lake. . . ."

Aileen clunked her cup down by her feet, took the soup Marged absently thrust at her, and nestled it on her knees. Her stomach twisted at the swirl of meat in the soup.

Or would you have me build it for the faeries?

". . . Never saw that poor lass again, truth be known. Oh, I could tell you a dozen stories of that place, Aileen—dozens and dozens, good and bad. But since the master set his mind to building a castle upon that island there's been nothing but bad luck. Nothing, I tell you—talk of faery-rings and swarms of bees and the like." She clattered the ladle back into the pot and jutted her chin to a small clay tumbler by the hearth. "Every night I put out a bit of milk for the wee folk, don't you know, and not once in all these years have I woke to find it emptied. Now what kind of house is it that the faeries won't enter when given a little hospitality, will you be telling me that?"

The audacity of it, that's what chilled her bones; for he'd torn up a ring of standing stones and destroyed a *cromlech* without a blink of his eye, in the face of his people's own horror. To Aileen such an act was like striking a stone cross with a sword in a church . . . Surely the very stone would bleed, surely screams would rise to the heavens and sting the ears of God.

". . . It's as if the faeries have disappeared from Wales, or they've turned a dark eye onto us all. I can't remember the last time I heard of a young man falling in love with a lovely girl he saw combing her hair in the reflection of a lake, or an old man gifting some luck in return for a kindness. Except for one time, of course, the night we learned about you." Marged rifled through the debris on the table, searching for a spoon. "But even that was a strange visit, and I won't be the one saying whether it was for the good or—"

"Marged." Aileen straightened on the stool as Marged's words penetrated the fog of her thoughts. "Marged . . . did you say something about the night you learned about me?"

"Aye, that's what I was after saying. I haven't heard tell of a single encounter with the faeries for years and years now, with the exception of last Midsummer's Night." Marged seized a spoon hiding amid some dirty bowls and wiped it clean on her apron. "Didn't you know lass?"

"Know what?"

"Aye, that's no surprise, either, the master being as hard as rock, swearing me to secrecy. Well, I didn't really take that oath, don't you know." Marged handed her the spoon. "It was a faery who told us about you, Aileen. As surely as I stand before you now."

Fifteen

Aileen pinched the strand of wool and rubbed a lump smooth. She stretched the scratchy hair across the back of her hand then twisted the length upon the wooden spindle. The winter wind swept down through the smoke-hole and battered the wood-fire at her feet. She watched the flames flicker lower and lower, until naught but a glowing mass of embers singed her slippered toes.

Suddenly he was there, looming over her across the red embers, still muddy from the ride back from the castle. His blue gaze fell fierce upon her face as he tossed his cloak back to reveal the strong body which could do such things to her. A weakness invaded her limbs. She fought it off. Aye, she was as much a slave to her own needs as any woman full of red-hot human blood, but she had work to do this night.

"There's blood in your cheeks." He tugged at the ties of his cloak. "Has it yet reached your head?"

She straightened upon the bench and bit down on the angry retort. So he thought she was daft, and no wonder, with the way she'd behaved at the castle. But it had been no less of a shock than if she'd come up suddenly to a friend's gaping grave. She fingered the bulging woolen thread of the spindle as he tossed the cape to the floor and seized the bladder of mead upon a tray by the door.

"Have you lost your tongue, woman?"

"You must be weary from the journey." She speared the

spindle in the basket of wool by her feet. "Sit, and I shall serve you."

He froze with the mead halfway to his mouth and stepped back as she brushed by him. His wariness shimmered in the air. She peeled the linen off the tray and the pungent scent of pepper sauce rose from the poached fish.

"I'll be asking you to forgive my behavior today," she said. Calm logic, aye, that's a thing the man could understand. She had enough brothers to know something of the working of a man's mind. She hefted the tray on her hip. "There's no doubt I should have controlled myself in the presence of a guest."

He stood still as stone in half-shadow, the flagon gripped in his hand, the laces of his boots trailing upon the floor, those blue eyes burning holes into her back as she made her way around the fire to the bench.

"You sound like a pickpocket who is very, very sorry she was caught, but not sorry in the least for the crime."

"You sound like a man disappointed that his horse did not prance to his liking before the King."

"My mistake." The bladder crinkled under his hand. "I forgot that beneath the noble trappings beat the heart of a simple mare."

"Have I ever put on airs, Rhys ap Gruffydd?" She clattered the tray onto the bench. Her hair slid over her face as she bent over the steaming white fish. "It was your idea to drape pearls on a sow. Wearing a princess's clothes isn't going to make me into a princess. I am what I was when you stole me off the shores of Inishmaan—a simple peasant girl."

"Wealth doesn't give a woman sense. And the woman who offered her body to me on New Year's Day was not a woman to flinch at shadows."

"Aberygaun is no shadow." She slammed the plates onto the bench, then scraped the tray out from beneath them. She couldn't think of him in that way, not now, though she sensed his presence behind her like the throbbing heat of a kiln, though she sensed the desire stretching between them. She needed a clear head. She needed to think not of things of the flesh, but of things of the spirit, after all she'd discovered this day. "In my world, such a place as Aberygaun is as sacred as a church. To disturb it is blasphemy—"

"You are not in your world anymore." His voice rumbled low, in a way she'd long become familiar with, dangerous and seductive. "You are in *mine.*"

"Listen to you, as if our worlds are so different."

"Oh, they are, Irish. I don't understand yours, and you cannot enter mine." Suddenly he stood behind her. He curled his hand around her waist and dragged her back against the hardness of his chest. "Only in this bedroom do they meet—"

"There's a bit of arrogance." She elbowed out of his grip, then skittered away to sit on the end of the bench. She seized the spindle, to have something to look at other than his bulging arms, to have something to occupy her nervous hands. "To think you have a world of your own, separate from all others."

He swung away from her. His boots scraped in the rushes. "My world isn't peopled with little mischievous creatures who live in flowers, or dragons who breathe fire—"

"Isn't it now?" She tugged up threads of wool with shaking hands, thinking of the faery footmarks that spotted the cliffs of Inishmaan, thinking of the dribble of snow off still branches in the woods around his wretched castle. "Haven't I heard stories about Arthur's Grave and Aberygaun and that lake up in the heights of Moel Cefn that I can't put my tongue around. Marged has told me—"

"Is Marged," he asked, as his tunic sailed through the air and crumpled in a ball near her feet, "the goddess of this world of yours?"

"Every home I've entered in this kingdom has a bowl of milk set by the fire for the faeries, and a tale or two about the woods nearby or a sacred yew tree or a curve of river." She pinched the wool into a strand of thread between her fingers, wishing she could mold this man's mind as easily. "This

Wales of yours is peopled by the *Y Tylwyth Teg*, as Ireland is peopled with faeries. Your disbelief won't make it otherwise."

"We've had this argument." He slapped the bladder back on the table. "And you've grown no wiser these past hours."

Oh, no, Rhys, there's where you are wrong, in these past hours I've grown as wise as Solomon. Now I know why I've been dragged into your world. I know the task the faeries have given me as a price for my faery-gift.

"Listen to you talking of wisdom," she argued, "you who stand in the midst of snow and insist it is not there."

"Snow, I can feel, I can see, I can hear it falling in the quiet." He snapped open a buckle of his chain-mail tunic. "My senses tell me it is real."

"A poor man is he who believes only the evidence of his senses." She crushed the spindle into her lap. "If you were deaf, would you insist there was no such thing as music?"

"I would feel the vibrations of the harp-strings. That's a deaf man's music."

"What of this stuff around us?" She whirled the spindle in the air as his chain-mail shirt clanked to the floor. "This stuff that fills our lungs with each breath? Can you see it? Can you smell it?" She rolled her fingers into her palm. "Can you hold it in your hand?"

"The wind blows it against my skin. I can feel it when it's hot, when it's cold."

"And what of a thought? A dream," she added, pressing her temple. "Can you see, smell, or touch that?"

"I've had lessons in philosophy, Aileen, more than you, I wager." He yanked the collar of his shirt wide. "My castle was once a dream, but now it is real—more real than any of your faery-creatures."

"What of *my* thoughts," she retorted. "You can't see them. Does that mean they don't exist?"

"The workings of a woman's mind are one of the world's greatest mysteries."

Didn't he have an answer for everything, standing there and

peeling off his clothes until only the loosest shirt and the sweep of his *braies* remained for decency's sake? Well, in spite of the fox's cunning, many a woman wears its skin.

She jabbed the spindle in the cloud of wool. "What about God, Rhys? Can you feel Him?"

A grin spread across his lips as he toed the heel of his boot and nudged the leather off his foot. "Best you don't ask me questions you don't want the answers to."

"All of Christendom believes in him and have never seen him, heard him, or felt him; and God thinks the better of them for it." She swept behind the bench, to put distance between herself and that dangerous smile. "Are they all ignorant peasants, too?"

"Some must stick their fingers into the nail-holes before they believe."

"You've done just that, yet you stand before me talking nonsense."

He kicked the boot to the floor. "How your mind works is one of the world's great secrets."

"I'm talking about the faery." She swept his linen tunic up off the ground and crumpled it into her midriff. "The one who told you about *me.*"

Aye, that did it, that froze Rhys's smile upon his cynical face, that put a stop to his mockery. He hadn't known she knew about *that,* it was clear enough in the way he reared up from untying his boots, then granted her the masked side of his profile.

"Marged," he said, with an edge to his voice, "has been tapping into the ale."

"What were you thinking, trying to keep such a story hushed?" She shook out his linen shirt and hung it on a hook by the bed. "That's a tale for generations—a great honor—and such a thing won't be kept quiet."

"He was nothing but an Irish traveler." He kicked off the boot. "Fleet-footed and full of foolishness."

"He disappeared into the air." The boot skidded to a stop by her feet. "He left not a single sign of his passing."

"The jongleurs of Llywelyn's court make a living from disappearing behind a puff of smoke. Ask Tudur Aled, if you can face his mockery."

"Are you telling me you thought he was a trickster, then?"

"A wily Irish one."

"If that's the truth, why did you travel across oceans on his advice, in search of me?"

"Dafydd's idea." He nudged the metal pile of his chain mail shirt and retrieved the bladder of mead. "Dafydd has no more sense than you, and less excuse, having been better born and better educated."

"Oh, such a hard man you are, Rhys, as cynical and worldly as that wretched bard sleeping in your hall. And an answer for everything. Blame my kidnapping on Dafydd, then. But in the end, it was you who insisted I stay here." It would be many a year before she forgot that moment on Arthur's Grave when he'd taken her hands in his and demanded a magic she was too afraid to show. "It was you who claimed I had magic in my hands."

"I saw what you could do." One shoulder rolled in a massive shrug. "There is evidence of your skill."

"What kind of evidence?" She twiddled her fingers while anger made her bold. "Light coming from my fingers? The singing of hosts of angels?"

"I've seen you bring men wounded unto death back to the living."

"I just wield linens and herbs better than any other healer you've known, isn't that the truth?"

Frustration made her bold, and she found herself standing before that looming hulk of a man with her feet spread and her fists planted on her hips, staring into that face as stiff as stone and wondering what it would take to make it crack, what it would take for her to see the pith of the man, to get him to kiss her.

"Maybe," he said, his voice dropping, "I had other reasons for keeping you here."

The intensity of the man roared over her like a blast of heat pouring out of a kiln's open door.

"Don't." She could not melt, not now, not when the spider struggled in a web of his own making. And she couldn't bear the arrow-points of his lies. "Don't be telling me pretty things, I'll have none of that."

"You need some of that."

"Do you think I'm so blind that I can't see what my reflection shows me?" Her voice broke; she hated herself for it. "It was I who went to you, in the end, not the other way around, so don't you be twisting the truth." Her tunic pressed against her chest as her breath came too fast, too hard. "By the love of God, Rhys, is it so hard to admit that you believe in magic?"

"I don't believe in magic, Irish."

She closed her eyes. Stubborn, wretched man. What did it matter? If the Lord himself descended upon this room in all his radiant glory, no doubt Rhys would call him nothing more than a trick of the light.

It was beyond her comprehension what the *Sidh* thought she could do to stop a man from building his only dream.

"But," he said quietly, "I am human."

Her eyes flew open. A muscle twitched in his cheek, mocking the ease of his smile.

"That's where I'm damned." He trailed his fingers down her arm, then raised her hand, palm up, between them. "Damned to look for miracles in the hands of an Irishwoman. And fool enough to hope."

Hope.

The word chimed between them. Oh, how easily he could keep that smile on his face, that cynical smile, as if his words meant nothing to him, when she saw in the tight crimp of the skin around his eye the price he paid to say them. Anger and frustration drained from her like mead from a punctured bladder.

She'd finally got an admission from him, aye. She'd come here after hearing the full of Marged's story, in a rage at his hypocrisy. Oh, he could talk a fine tale about not believing in anything, but she knew the truth now: He had listened to the words of a faery to find *her*. And had believed enough in the possibility of miracles to keep her. So sure of herself, she was, so sure she could finally trap him in his own hypocrisy. Now she stood in the midst of her triumph trembling with shame.

He didn't want to hope. Hope was a flame that flickered faintly, oh, so faintly, in his heart, threatening with the next breath of pain or betrayal to flicker out and plunge him into the darkness. Those eyes staring at her, the one through the mask hungered for the darkness; for in the darkness there is no pain.

"You want me to believe in faeries, Aileen?" His voice rustled like bed linens in the morning. "There's a way to make me believe in anything you want."

He whirled a lock of her hair around his finger. A familiar warmth suffused her limbs, softened the fists on her waist and sent them sliding down over her hips. That veil descended upon them, that misty sort of magic she felt whenever they drew this close, that small world of their own where nothing mattered but the easing of the needs of the flesh, the secret wordless sharing of the needs of the spirit, that world they disappeared into every night only to emerge in the cold bright light of morning and pretend it never existed.

She wanted to hold him. She wanted the hurt to go away. "Tell me."

The air trembled between them. Her gaze fell to his mouth, to those lips always twisted in cynicism, and she found herself rising to the balls of her toes, wanting to kiss them soft, wanting to kiss him and be kissed by him with a fierceness that gripped her deep, deep inside.

"Heal me, Irish." He slid his fingers down her throat. "Prove to me that strange little visitor spoke words of wisdom. Then we'll talk of magic."

She moved by instinct. Hadn't she thrown all caution to the winds New Year's Day at the *hafod?* He needed this, as no other man, woman or child had ever needed it from her. She found the ties of his mask on his throat, at the back of his head, and pulled them free whilst his pupils widened, whilst his gaze set upon her with new intensity. *Aye, Rhys, the trials of the sons of Tureen this is not, for in your eyes there is magic in my hands, if God will let me summon it.* The tingling began in her palms as she peeled off the leather and let it cave onto his shoulder. Without hesitation she lay the moistness of her hand on his ravaged cheek and, waiting for the healing current to course through her, willing it to do so, praying for it to do so, pressed her lips against the throbbing of his throat while he stood as stiff as rock.

No salves this night. No more hiding behind pretense. Perhaps that was what had prevented her healing from flowing all these months. Perhaps she had to trust this man who trusted no one, had to show him the true face of trust, as she was doing now, baring her gift to him in the haze of orange light.

He slid a hand around her waist and drew her up against him. She bit down on the moan that rose to her throat at the feel of his body hard against hers. Aye, she'd wondered during all those years tending women in childbed how a woman could let herself suffer through such agony over and over again, why she would let a man near her after tasting death in the midst of life. Now she knew why; now she knew the heat-madness that boiled a woman's senses, the yawning ache of an empty womb, the fire that only a man's touch could quench—only this man's touch.

But she mustn't think about that, not now, not while her fingers stroked his ravaged cheek and ran along the ridges of his jaw. She must think of the healing. She must show this man the faery-gift that she'd loved and hated, the faery-gift that had set her apart from others and brought her both reverence and fear, the faery-gift she now must pay the price for having.

But in the darkness of this corner, with the murmurs of the men in the mead-hall drifting in through the crack, with the faintest heat rising up from the center hearth, Aileen struggled with frustration as he bent his strong neck and tasted the skin of her forehead.

Let me heal him. Let me heal him.

Please . . .

She curled her fingers, and her palm slipped off his cheek and trailed down his chest. Her fingers scraped through the whorls of hair and tugged the open edges of his shirt. She kissed the hollow of his chest and pressed her forehead against him, to hide the tears surging in her eyes. To hide her failure.

She wondered why the faeries had brought her to this god-forsaken place, then had stolen from her the one gift that could save a dying man.

He swept both arms around her and hefted her up against his chest, caught up in that other sort of magic. She hid her face in his shoulder. Let him believe this was part of the healing, she thought. *Don't let him know that my magic has failed.* He knocked the bench as he strode by, the tray skidding to the floor. He lay her on the bed. She sank into the softness of fur and linen and his weight sank atop her. She closed her eyes as the frantic tugging began, of tunics and tangled laces and garters, the kicking of slippers off her feet. A breath of cold air kissed her breasts, her naked belly, and rolled over the powerful stretch of his back as he nudged her legs apart.

She buried her hands in his hair as he kissed his way across her breast. His fingers played her body as skillfully as a bard the quivering strings of a harp. A yearning swelled inside her, fierce and unrelenting as the need to feel the kiss of his flesh. She wanted to *give*. She wanted to grant him something to believe in, someone to believe in—wanted to peel that mask off his face. Not the one stitched of leather, the one stitched with threads of anger and bitterness that he wore even now, in the sweet heat of their intimacy. She longed to see him smile. She ached deep in her bones, for the breath of his kiss.

She clutched his head to the nook of her throat and squeezed back tears. Her healing had turned in upon itself.

She'd fallen in love with her captor.

Sixteen

The wench didn't know how to be a mistress.

Rhys scowled as he watched her stride around the trestle table of the mead-hall. She hiked empty flagons of ale in the crook of her arm and replaced them with full ones, while keeping a sharp eye on the platters of trout and nodding silent directions to the maidservants. She wore that colorless tunic again. She had scorned the silks he'd purchased from that peddler who'd found his way through the hills to the *llys*. Instead she wore the shapeless dull brown wool that gaped every time she leaned over to serve a man, that damned muddy wool which dulled the blaze of her hair.

Not that he could keep his eyes off her. They'd spent the evenings of Lent matching wits over a game of chess, arguing over the existence of faeries, and making good use of his bed. He'd spent the winter drinking ale in this mead-hall and watching her glide around the room as sylphlike as any creature of a pagan's imagination. Were she dressed in a sack of oats he'd still be staring at her, as bewitched as any fresh-faced boy. Now he sat amid men who chattered like hens, wondering if she smelled of flour or onions, imagining how he'd take her when he finally got her alone and away from this noisy crowd, lusting for the feel of her hot-blooded in his bed.

He curled his hand over his knife and took a bite of the pale flesh of the fish. It tasted like sand. Everything tasted like sand but for her skin, her hair. Her breasts.

Now where was she going? By God, weren't there enough

maidservants here to fetch ale for these wretched men? He sneered at the women idling up and down the length of the mead-hall, joking and cajoling the Irishmen he'd shipped over to labor at the castle. That woman of his needed a lesson in her duties. Before the thought passed through his mind he'd already tossed his knife upon the table and stepped over the bench.

He scowled as he thrust the door to the mead-hall open into the crisp evening air. He would think she had bewitched him, if he believed in such things. His throat was dry except when he had a mouthful of her flesh against his lips. He spent his hours crunching through the snow around the castle, listening to the master mason babble on about details that once had been the only things to excite him, finding instead his thoughts drifting off to the delights of the evening before. Now he'd left a fine supper for one reason only—to taste this peasant-lover of his who scorched the sheets with her passion.

He swallowed a mocking laugh. *His* woman, indeed. She was his but to borrow, and now they lived on borrowed time. He was no fool. One day she would discover what he'd been hiding these past weeks.

Not tonight.

He strode into the steamy kitchens, thrust the door closed behind him, and squealed the iron bolt into its sleeve. Aileen whirled around with a flash of hair.

"No more hiding from me, Irish."

She slapped a full flagon down upon the table with a never-you-mind and picked up another to be filled. "Don't you have a head full enough to burst," she muttered. "I'm mistress of this house—and there's food and ale to be served."

"There are servants for that."

"Aye, and not enough, I tell you, with the master mason and his carpenters and stone-cutters all filling out the table. Let the girls twitter about like birds, it's no pain for me to do the serving."

He leaned the butt of his hands upon the other end of the

table and peered at her through the fragrant steam. Aye, she had a bit of a fit upon her, he knew that flash of her gray eyes. His blood rushed at the thought of it. "So it was the conversation that set you flying out of the mead-hall."

"Me? Fly out of the mead-hall for such a thing?" She frowned at him, then started scraping the leavings of the leeks into a basket for the pigs. "I was quite interested in that stone-cutter who said he'd been set upon by a swarm of wasps just the other day, so early in the season, with not a flower blooming in all the hills of Wales."

"What about the building of the north tower? Did that set you to temper?"

"Aye, and why would it? When the master mason said it'd never stay up if the stone-cutters didn't start finding rock that wouldn't crumble into dust as soon as it was brought over the bridge?"

His loins throbbed. She never backed down from a confrontation, no, not Aileen the Red with those bright eyes and that temperament to match the fiery hair upon her head. His blood rushed at the battle, his loins hardened at the sight of her so proud before him despite the woolen tunic and the streak of soil across her cheek. Mayhap that was her witchery over him—to give so much and yet still hold true to herself, while he floundered about trying to find the strength she sapped from him every morning they lay together. He didn't recognize himself anymore. He found himself thinking she was a *Lian-haun-shee,* the Irish faery-creature she claimed lived upon the vitals of the chosen, until the host wasted away and died.

Then he dismissed both ideas. After all these nights when she'd lain her bare hands upon his bare face, he now knew for sure that this woman wielded no magic.

"What brought you across the cold yard into the heat of these kitchens?" She tossed a lock of hair off her shoulder, where it had clung to the perspiration beading on her neck. "Is it serving yourself you're after? I saw you eat enough bread to fill two men's bellies and enough soup to drown—"

Her words caught on a gasp as he rounded the table and seized her by the hips. With one lunge he hefted her up on the kitchen table.

A ghost of a smile played about her lips. The wench. She knew her own power over him. She'd known it since that day she'd cornered him and made him admit things he could barely admit to himself.

"If it's not dinner," she said, "then it must be a game of chess you're hankering after. Careful, Rhys. There will come a day when I beat you yet."

He ignored her and set to the ties of her tunic. Her skin smelled earthy, as if she'd been rolling around in the garden she'd just ordered plowed, all green and fresh.

"If it's not a game of chess," she continued, as he yanked the last knot undone, "then it must be more talk of scaffolding and mortar-making—"

"You talk too much, Irish."

With a clatter of bowls and spoons he swiped the table behind her free of clutter, then he pressed her down upon it. A cloud of flour rose up around them as he kneed open her legs and set himself firmly between them.

She got over the shock quick enough. That smile widened, her arms went limp like the rest of her body, and a heat intensified at her core—he could feel it through the layers of linen and wool. By God, this woman stole the strength from him, she sapped it with each spilling of his seed into her. He shouldn't do this and he damned well knew it. Look what he'd turned into, suddenly caring about his next act of betrayal, suddenly caring that he'd have another black mark on his soul, at the price of this woman.

He bucked against her to clear his mind of thought. That did it fine enough, with her arching her throat and moaning and bending her knees to feel him better. He traced his knuckles down her throat, then seized the neckline of her tunic to yank the wretched threads off the body he needed to see. She hunched her shoulders and in one pull the cloth slid to her

waist. She arched like a cat, lifting those tip-tilted nipples toward him, two ripe raspberries floating on cream.

He dragged his hands over her flesh, pearly in this rosy
kitchen light. How dark his hands against her flesh, how big
on her body. He stared at the sensitive nipples beading between
the knuckles of his fingers, never more aware than now of
how easy it would be to hurt this woman, how fragile she lay,
how trusting, how open, how soft and yielding.

He wondered who was more the fool, himself for letting
this creature dazzle him beyond all reason, or her for thinking
he could be something more than he was—a man without conscience.

He squeezed his fingers together, teasing her nipples until
she bit her lower lip and moaned. Over the weeks he'd discovered every secret she'd freely given him, secrets best kept
for a husband—how she liked to be sucked and kissed and
touched, he knew it all, knew how to elicit the most exquisite
of sensations from her body with the lightest touch of his fingers.

He swallowed his own mocking laugh. There was some
value in that, wasn't there? A few moments of sensual pleasure
for her to remember. That he could do—that he would do willingly.

Steam swirled thick in the room. It beaded upon her skin
and raised a flush beneath the freckles. He rubbed the moisture
over her body, on the underswell of her breast, into the hollow
of her belly. Then he caught sight of a pot upon the table, a
pot full of golden liquid.

He dipped his fingers into the fluid, passed it from one
nipple to another, and lowered himself to suck the honey from
her flesh. With a groan, she tangled her fingers in his hair, as
her legs tangled around his hips.

The sweetness exploded on his tongue. No honey had ever
tasted so fine. He trailed his fingers in a line down her mid-
section and drew circles around her navel. His tongue followed
the sticky path.

"Rhys, *a stór.*"

Darling. She called him that in this madness they made together, in that breathless voice, enough to make a man forget all reason—enough to make a man do anything, say anything, promise anything, just to hear it one more time again.

"Rhys, if you keep . . . Glory, I'm going to melt away into nothing."

Melt into me, woman. That would solve his problems, if the boundaries of skin faded, if they were one flesh. Then he couldn't do what he must.

He disentangled her legs, lifted her hips, and dragged her tunic and undershift off her legs. The last of her clothing puddled to the rushes. The heart of her lay open and exposed to him, moist and throbbing.

He dipped his fingers into the honey again and trailed the golden fluid over her ruby red flesh. She made a sound he'd never heard before, a sound beyond a gasp. He lowered his head to feel her heat quivering against his tongue.

No meal was more exquisite than the very last.

Marged strode into the mead-hall with two baskets slung over her arm. Aileen jerked up and dumped a cloud of unspun wool off her lap.

"Are they coming?" Aileen asked.

"Aye, they are; and making enough noise to break an old woman's ears, I tell you." Marged thrust one of the baskets at Aileen. "Come, we'll be meeting them just outside the gate to the homestead, and mind you hand them the eggs with your right hand, else there'll be nothing but trouble for Easter."

"So you've told me three times already." She slung the basket on her arm and ran her fingers over the eggs. "Just as you warned me not to break one, either."

"Don't even say it, lass!" Marged's hands flew in the sign of the cross. "Saints preserve us from such a calamity."

"Saints," she said, pushing the door open into the sunshine, "and the sure grip of my hands."

Aileen trailed beside Marged across the quiet homestead. A three-legged mutt loped from a comfortable curl in the sunshine to tag at her heels and sniff at the basket. Owen, the eleven-year-old whose grandparents had died in Edwen's raid, stumbled up from his seat near the hound's hurdle to nod at her before returning to his leash-mending. Dusk threatened on the western horizon, a faint dimming of what had been a bright March day. Aileen smiled at the rosy pink clouds streaking the sky above the western hills, a heavenly promise of an even finer tomorrow.

As if there could ever be a finer today.

Must be the coming of the spring that had put such a fever in her brain. She had no right to be striding with such pride through this muddy yard, skittering around a clutch of chickens pecking in the thawing mud, glancing at the hurdles of the hounds's pens she'd ordered mended over the winter and thinking that the ewe-house needed some work before the full of the spring planting began. When had she gotten so accustomed to nodding at the men who gave way to her, with a lowering of their heads? All her life she'd been used to people's eyes following her as she passed . . . but never with such gentle respect, never with such open-heartedness, and she no more than the lord's mistress setting on a task better made for a lord's wife.

She lowered her face to hide the flush of her cheeks from Marged's sharp eyes. It wasn't shame, nay, not shame that set the color to her face, it was memory. Memory after memory. For a time of contemplation and denial, she and Rhys had spent the season of Lent making merry as if they were marked for death on the fortieth day.

More than once this winter she'd sat close to the hearth-fire warming her toes, snug against the Welsh wind, while men shaved arrows or wove fishing creels or whittled toys for their children, while Dafydd and Rhys lingered over a flagon of ale talking of plans for the castle or the doings of his brothers or of the goings-on of the distant Welsh court, which a peddler had told them about when he'd stopped here for a while. Many a time in the gentle folds of that domestic warmth, she had heard the rough sound of Rhys's unexpected laughter and had glanced up to find him hand-feeding that three-legged dog the remnants of his trencher-bread. Many a time, she'd looked up from her spinning to find Rhys's gaze upon her, the unshadowed eye bright with lovers' secrets.

Once, on Inishmaan, when she had been collecting periwinkles on the ledges, a gale blew in and sent her skittering for the shelter of the cliffs. Amid a knot of stone she'd discovered a crevice in the rock that burrowed deep into the granite. Squeezing in between the slick walls, she'd stood for hours feeling the vibrations of the waves crashing against the sheer rock face. The salty mist of the sea had curled in and brushed silken hands against her skin, then eddies of surf had trickled around her ankles, and she'd pressed herself against the rock at her back knowing the danger but trembling nonetheless with a wild emotion teetering between fear and blind exhilaration.

She'd always attributed that strange elation to how close she'd come to death; now she knew it surged when she was feeling most *alive*.

"Listen to them, my lady. Have you ever heard such a sound?"

They neared the opening to the palisades. An unholy rattling rose up over the walls. "Marged, don't be telling me that's the children?"

"It is, and they'll be clattering for eggs the whole night through, I tell you. It's been a long Lent, and there isn't a one of them not looking forward to the Easter feast this Sunday."

For years, Marged had told her, the children had come rattling for eggs every Monday before Easter. The gate yawned open, and the two bondsmen who guarded it grinned at the noisy crowd winding its way toward the small wooden bridge over the ditch. The men swung back, lowering their eyes to

Aileen as she and Marged clattered across the bridge to await the procession amidst the soggy earth of the other side.

"Faith," Aileen exclaimed, picking her calfskin boots out of the mud. "There looks to be three dozen of them."

"There's more than just the bondsmen's children here, but no matter, they're all spawn of Rhys's men."

"Well, unless you be thinking these eggs multiply like the loaves and the fishes, we'd best get more."

Aileen ordered one of the bondsmen to send Owen to scour the hen-house. The last of the sun wavered warmly upon her hair, and cast an amber glow over the field in the valley, a small nook of it churned up from the first pass of the plough. She plucked one of the brown eggs from the pile, then curled her fingers over the vague warmth as she watched the procession of children near. Beyond them came the first of the bondsmen, plodding their way to the homestead and their duties to Rhys after a full day of planting leeks and beans and peas in the tiny garden plots by their own houses.

Aye, and she wasn't fooling herself that she was searching beyond these children with their sticks and rattles full of dried beans just to gauge the number of men who'd be partaking of the leek soup tonight. Nay, she'd long given up that pretense. If she gazed longingly toward the southern horizon, she was waiting for a certain proud chestnut steed and its wide-shouldered rider to appear on the horizon.

The children crossed the field and stood before her singing a Welsh song, clattering and banging their rocks and sticks, their legs wrapped in coarse wool still dirty from the harrowing they'd done in the fields that afternoon. Their thin faces lit with delight as they jostled each other in competition to be closer to her. One by one they pushed each other up to receive an egg, bowing or bobbing in thanks before racing around the crowd toward the path to the valley, their precious burden—not to be enjoyed until Easter Sunday—clutched in their dirty hands. Toward the end came the toddlers, too small to compete with the wilder children, and last the gangly older children, faintly embarrassed to be partaking in this child's ritual, caught at that ephemeral moment of growth when one yearns to be thought of as a man or woman while clinging to the traditions and security of childhood.

Her gaze drifted over the blond head of the girl standing before her to fix upon the silhouette of a rider topping the rise. Rhys slowed his mount to a canter as he reached the children turning back toward the path down the hill. The dusk cast an amber halo around his hair, and his cloak flapped behind him.

Even the children, she thought, *pause to stare at such a regal lord.*

The rattling stuttered to a few clatters of sticks, then died to a ringing silence The blond standing in front of her gasped and stumbled back. Aileen heard something crack behind her.

"Owen, look what you've done!"

Aileen followed Marged's horrified glance to find the jelly of an egg splattered at Owen's feet, and Owen staring pale-faced at the oncoming rider.

Only then did Aileen notice the black flap of leather slapping against Rhys's shoulder; only then did she notice that Rhys rode unmasked.

Crack. An older girl seized her younger sister and shoved the child's face in the coarse wool of her skirts. *Crack.* A pregnant woman with a babe in arms twisted away, shielding her eyes with a hunched shoulder. *Crack.* White hands fluttered in the sign of the cross.

Crack.

A child screamed. Another raced toward the path down the cliff. Then it was if some great monster sucked them past the man who rode stiff-necked toward the lowered bridge of the *llys.*

She stepped forward to greet him, but he rode past her as if blind. A thin line of blood streaked his face. His mount clattered over the bridge.

Tears glimmered on Marged's cheeks. Aileen thrust her basket into the servant's hands and strode through the sucking mud while the air still rang with the screams of children. Shoving by Owen, she pounded across the bridge and watched men pause in comic terror as Rhys dismounted and swaggered into the mead-hall.

Aileen tore her way across the yard in his wake, and threw open the door.

"A fine show that was, Rhys ap Gruffydd."

A servant collided into her. The girl stumbled back, then skittered around her to escape out the door before it swung shut. Rhys paused at the trestle table and made a silent motion with his arm. The hall came alive: Men whittling by the fire dropped their work and lumbered up; the servants shuffled through the rushes; even the hounds skittered to the shadows of the corners. The mead-hall closed them in silence.

"It's your brothers, isn't it?" She curled her fingers into the edge of the fur-lined mantle she'd taken to wearing with more ease than she'd ever expected of herself. "You said they always emerge with the first thaw. Did they attack the castle today? Are there many wounded?"

Rhys clinked his chain-mail gauntlets onto the trestle table while the fire popped in the center hearth.

"I forgot," he said, in a smooth, even voice, "that the egg-begging was today."

"What difference does that make, will you be telling me that? Where's Dafydd?"

"There has been no attack. Dafydd will be arriving soon enough." He raked his fingers through his hair and hung onto the nape of his neck. "Had I remembered the day, I would have delayed my arrival until after dark."

He spoke the words quietly, as if to himself. With a start she realized he was standing with his stiff back to her and apologizing. For frightening children.

Her heart moved. Aye, he could play a fine game, he could, mocking himself and his mask and the scourge that raged over his face. She remembered a time, not long after she'd been captured, when she had stared him in the face and accused him of vanity. The heat of shame stung her cheeks. Hasty, thoughtless words. She should have known better. She knew how important it was to hide that which most people could not understand. She could hide her own gift through artifice and open denial. Rhys needed a far more palpable method.

He suffered the vanity of the mask for one reason alone: For the sake of the ignorant, for the sake of the innocent. For the sake of the children.

"You've done every mother in Graig a great service this day." Aileen trailed her fingers over the battered wood of the trestle table as she made her way around it. "You frightened the love of God into them. There won't be a single child in all of Graig who won't be saying his prayers this night and sticking hard to his pallet."

"Yes, each one of them has learned that hard lesson: Monsters do exist."

The words rang with self-mocking. Aye, monsters exist, she thought. But only in a tortured man's mind.

"Marged," he said wryly, dropping his hand off his neck, "must be beside herself with all those bad omens splattered over the field."

"Oh, I think she'll have her mind on other things this day." Aileen leaned her hip into the edge of the table, remembering the tears on Marged's face. "If it wasn't a battle that had you tearing into the *llys,* then are you going to be telling me what happened to put that blood on your face?"

"It belongs to a puppy I slaughtered and ate for—"

"Stop it."

A cynical smile cracked the granite of his features. He slipped a hand beneath the neck of his tunic, then yanked out a puddle of leather.

"Dafydd would have me believe," he said, tossing the mask on the table, "that this is the work of your faeries."

She lifted the thick leather and ran her finger over a sharp cut through the skin. The top half of the mask dangled by a tendon.

"We rode through the woods toward the castle. Something scraped across my face." He trailed a hand over his jaw and looked at the blood on his fingers. "I didn't know I was wounded until I saw the blood drip onto the saddle."

"Dafydd was right, I'm thinking." The slash in the leather was razor-clean. "This looks to be the work of a faery-dart. And no surprise it is to me, with you building that tower despite all the trouble."

"My brothers can be just as invisible as the creatures of your imagination, and disappear into the forests just as swiftly. And the faeries," he added drily, "should have better aim."

Aileen thought of the piercing children's screams, the sight of the crowd racing away in terror over muddied ground in the bright of day.

Aye, aye. The faeries' aim was true.

"I've no skill with the needle," she said, "but I can do a fair enough job of it when I must. This can be repaired." *More easily than your heart.* She tossed the leather back onto the table. "Let me have a look at that cut."

"Come and look." A humorless grin stretched across his features, twisting the skin of his affliction tight over his bones. "Maybe you can prevent a scar."

She hated him talking like this, so full of cynical self-mocking. It was the children, she told herself. That could bring any man to his knees; surely it was enough to summon that strange hard light to his eyes, the mask of a man who pretends to care about nothing and no one.

"Maybe," he added, eyeing her as she approached, "you can even heal it."

A flush stole up her cheeks. Aye, wasn't he in the strangest of moods this day, icy-calm, world-weary, standing as if nothing could penetrate that shell while slinging stones that he knew would strike her at her most vulnerable? She knew she'd made no progress in the healing of his face, though she'd prayed with her knees hard against the stone floor of the chapel for her gift to return. But she'd stopped the spreading, hadn't she? And she'd thought, until this moment, that she'd done some healing to his soul.

"Don't be turning your arrows upon me, Rhys ap Gruffydd. I didn't command the faeries to sling that faery-dart."

She forced his face aside with a finger to the chin, then trailed her hand just under the cut. The blood dried in dark flakes between the ridges of his cheek. He was right; it was nothing but a shallow slash. Already, it had begun to heal.

Then she noticed something else. Her brows twitched together. In the mornings, they kept the draperies closed against the cold, so the light sifting onto the bed was hazy and uncertain. She rarely got so stark a look at his unmasked face as now. A purple mottling swelled from the edge of the affliction and ran in a thin line down his forehead and across one side of his nose; an inky outline of the border between the condition and his smooth skin.

She traced its path across his cheek. Soft, it was, tender to the touch. Like new leaves of a rosebush, ruddy and supple before hardening.

"It's growing, Aileen."

She dropped her hand from his face and met his gaze, hard and unreadable despite the mockery of a smile.

"It's just inflamed," she said. *It can't be anything else.* "Or a soreness from rubbing on the edge of that mask."

"It's growing."

"All it needs is a cleaning and—"

"I've seen this pattern enough these past five years. It needs a healing." He turned the muscle of a shoulder toward her. "A healing I will never get from you."

Her breath slammed in her lungs. Her heel crushed the rushes as she swiveled away. She yanked at the ties of her mantle which cut deep into her throat. "We've not had a healing session in months." Her fingers tangled in the laces. She struggled to keep them from shaking. "Now that spring is coming there'll be fresh herbs on the hills. We'll start with the salves again."

"Heaven save me from your salves."

"I'm no worker of miracles." She swung the mantle on a peg by the wall, then ran her hands over the fur, through the folds, not wanting to see the disappointment in his eyes. "But I've stopped it from spreading once before. I'll do it again."

I will. I will.

"Lies do have a way of coming 'round to a man."

Her fingers froze in the fur. "What are you talking about?"

"This scourge of mine stops spreading every winter." He stared into the flames sputtering in the hearth. "But with the coming of the cuckoos and the ploughing of the fields comes the flowering of the curse of Rhys ap Gruffydd."

"But . . ." She remembered a gurgling brook and the sight of Rhys's eyes. "You told me—"

"I told you what I needed to tell you to get you to stay here over the winter. I promised you what I could, to get you in my bed."

She crushed her mantle in her fists to stop herself from tumbling to her knees.

"The ladies of Graig aren't banging down the door to share my bed." He picked up a block of wood one of the men had dropped too close to the fire. "You proved an amusing enough companion. I had hoped our liaison would put some power into your salves."

She turned and pressed back against the wall, pressed back against her mantle, the fur cushioning her, brushing softly against a cheek stiff with shock. She remembered the first day, at the *hafod,* when he'd made her a woman, remembered what had transpired in that smoky little hut with nothing but a single blanket and their eager bodies to keep them warm.

"You were supposed to be the greatest healer in Ireland, able to heal my affliction with the pass of your hands. Did you even try, Aileen?"

She thought of the night she'd laid her bare hands on his

face and prayed for the healing energy. She recalled all the mornings she'd pressed her palm against the hollow of his heart and suffered the pain jarring her to her elbows.

"This," he said, gesturing to his face, "is what I get for listening to the words of tricksters who visit on pagan spirit nights."

"I made you," she whispered, her voice catching in her throat, "no promises."

"But I made you one." He tossed the wood into the flames. "I'm tired of waiting for miracles. It's spring. I'm sending you back to Inishmaan."

Seventeen

Once, when she'd been searching for bird's eggs on the cliffs of Inishmaan, she'd slipped upon a rock grown crumbly with salt and wind and knocked her head against a crag so hard that her ears rang and her senses dimmed and the sunlight faded and pain throbbed harder and harder in her head until she could hear nothing else.

She stood motionless while Rhys's words rang in her head, so loud that they made sense no longer, until she wondered if she'd even heard them, or if she'd just imagined he'd said them aloud to her . . . or if this were some fragment of a forgotten nightmare. He stood as still as stone watching the fire consume the block of wood in a flare of heat. The silence between them stretched thin enough to snap.

Not a word of remorse. Not a word of promise. Was he to sever this tie that bound them with the uttering of a few words, to relegate all those nights and mornings to some dark realm of the past?

No.

The word screamed in her head. She didn't believe it. It didn't make any sense. He'd spoken in haste. Men were queer enough creatures, but she knew something of this one. How much easier it was for him to push her away than to reveal the hurting pith of himself. It was the affliction flaring up again, that was what was doing this. Aye, the affliction.

"Come now, Aileen." He turned eyes of ice upon her. "Anyone would think you had been expecting a marriage proposal."

The scornful tilt of his lips shot daggers through her heart. Just this morning she had woken dreamy-eyed to the thought of the garden she was going to plant by the kitchens. She'd spent the winter spinning and weaving for clothes for the spring. She'd not expected a marriage proposal. She'd known better than to wish for the moon when she'd been happy enough with the stars. All along, she'd lived with the knowledge that this would have to end. Someday.

Not like this.

"I'm the son of Gruffydd," he said, "who was the son of Owen, the son of Roderic, the son of Mervyn the Great. I can trace my blood back twelve generations. Can you do the same?"

I am the daughter of Conaire. She tilted her chin, but it was an empty motion, a reflex of pride. She didn't know her grandfather's name, it had always been enough to be the daughter of Conaire.

"We had a bargain." He reached for a bladder of mead sagging by a stump and yanked out the cork. "I thought you too practical to hold to romantic dreams."

Her throat parched. It seemed as if her tongue shriveled in her mouth. *Dreams.* Aye, perhaps that was it. In Inishmaan, she'd buried that part of her that yearned for home and family, sure that she would never know it. But, in the cold of the Welsh winter, in the warmth of this man's bed, the seed she'd buried had begun to bud.

Now it began to bleed.

"We made a bargain," he said

She searched those eyes of blue, eyes as hard and emotionless as the cliffs of Inishmaan. The heat that had begun a slow burn in her chest rose over her neck to lose itself in her scalp. At that moment, more than any other time in her life, she hated the fairness of her skin which revealed her emotions to the world and stole from her any chance of pride.

Words surged in her throat. She had half a mind to tell him she loved him, to tell him she didn't want to leave. She had half a mind to beg him to let her stay. But she *did* want to leave. She wanted to see Ma and Da and her family, she wanted to smell the sweet breath of the sea again, she wanted to be somewhere where people loved her.

A trembling began deep in the core of her. She felt the trembling as if she were not a part of it, as if she were floating somewhere above her body watching herself shake like a leaf in the wind and knowing that there would come a time when she couldn't protect herself like this. There would come a time when she would feel the pain.

"If there's a child, send him to me." He tossed the bladder beside the stump and threw the last dagger over his shoulder. "In Wales, a man takes care of his bastards."

Rhys peered through the gnarled trees toward the mountain pass below. He stilled his horse so that not even the creak of saddle leather interrupted the silence of the morning. He strained his ears for sound . . . and heard it, the first crinkle of hooves in the moist spring litter.

He edged his horse deeper into the shadows of a boulder as Dafydd's mount came into view. Dafydd scanned the woods around him, then lifted his face toward where Rhys stood in the shadows. A scowl marred his brother's face beneath the twist of his scarlet hood. They'd nearly come to blows about Rhys's decision to send Aileen back. But Dafydd didn't understand. No man could.

Rhys wasn't sure he understood himself.

He waited for her to appear. A clutch of Irish workers clung together as they marched forward and glanced warily into the woods around them. Single-file, the mounted men he'd sent along to protect her urged their horses through the dark, narrow pass into the wider valley. Cattle had been stolen on the northern border again; with the coming of spring his brothers and half brothers emerged from their wintering places like moles blinking against the sun, and again mindlessly took up arms.

All the more reason to send her back to Ireland. She hated the killing, and in these bloodstained mountains it was as inevitable as the coming of rain. She'd be better off on peaceful Inishmaan, with her family, where he should have left her all those months ago instead of dragging her into the hell of his own life.

She emerged from the pass, riding the mare he'd given her, as straight-backed as if she'd been born to the saddle. Her red hair sprung from the netting she'd tried to stuff it into, and his hands itched for the feel of it full in his palms. The fur-lined cloak she'd taken to wearing, the only luxury she'd really adopted in all her time in Wales, swathed her figure. He wondered if she even knew she wore it, or if Marged had tossed it across her shoulders while Aileen wandered in the same silence that had gripped her since the day he'd ordered her gone.

A lump hardened in his throat. The silence, that was what got to him most. Aileen, as silent as one without a tongue, her gray eyes as bruised as a cloudy sky. Aileen, who never knew better when to speak and when to hold still . . . silent as the grave. If she had narrowed her eyes at him, if she had lashed out with that razor of a tongue and stripped him bloody with anger . . . That, he could have suffered. That, he could have fought. But she'd remained silent until the arrangements were finalized for the journey, and then she had left without a word.

He flexed his hands across the pommel of his saddle. His gaze clung to her hair, bright against the gold netting, bright against the gray fur. The first time he'd laid eyes on her on Inishmaan, he'd wondered if she were human. Now he knew just how human—how fragile of bone and heart. A heart he had not even known he had held, until he'd felt it break in his own hands.

He knew, in that deep, calm part of himself he'd come to

know these past days, that this was for the best. In time, the pain of the parting would fade in both their memories. He'd already come into the habit of taking memories out like jewels wrapped in silk, lifting them to the light and turning them this way and that to see the way they sparkled. The *hafod*. The first day she laughed in their bed as he struggled with their clothes. The kitchen and the sweet taste of honey. The sight of her honest face, with that gleam in her eye that spoke of intimate knowledge—gasps of pleasure, hands reaching out and taking him, willingly, openly, fully.

She'd given him his manhood again, this little Irish lass. He watched her stiff back as the procession advanced into the next pass. She'd stared him full in the face and seen beyond the mottling of his skin to the man inside. She'd shown him the true face of friendship, not only in herself but in the others around him. He'd seen that face in Dafydd, even as Dafydd cursed him and called him a fool for letting Aileen go.

She'd survive the pain. She'd find another lover, more worthy. There would be no new lover for him. Aileen was the last.

Rhys lifted a hand and traced the new growth beneath the edge of his mended mask. Aileen had given him a season of hope. But it was over. He knew with a certainty beyond questioning that there was no chance of ever returning to the man he was, to the world he'd once lived in. This curse upon his face would never be cured.

His horse pawed the stone, uneasy with the restraint. The smell of ripe earth rose up from the valley, the green scent of spring. He sucked the air deep into his lungs. It had taken him five years, but he'd finally stopped wrestling with ghosts. There was a freedom in resignation. He knew the path of his life; it lay before him.

This land . . . it would remain his exile. The castle he was building would be his home. There, the years would pass and the mottling of his skin would grow, and he'd have larger and larger masks made, to cover the horror from the simple, the superstitious. One day it would cover him, from scalp to toes, and he'd be nothing but a monster of a man. The ogre in the cave. A mythical thing lurking in the castle. Mothers would whisper about him to keep children in their beds.

No woman could look upon a man in such a state and feel anything more than pity. Not even a woman with the strength to look past half a man, could forever hold back the disgust.

So he sent Aileen away. He gave her her freedom.

In his heart he would hold the memory of her face. In his heart he'd remember those days when a woman had held him and lain beneath him, hot-blooded and eager.

He watched her retreating back until he could no longer see the bright swath of her hair between the trees. Then he lifted his hand in a silent farewell.

I love her.

A quiet sound gurgled from his chest, a sound like a laugh, though he'd not heard such a noise from his lips for too long to remember. A fool he'd been, all these weeks. How incredibly simple. Now, in this calm that had descended upon him, the knowledge drifted to him as easy as a summer breeze.

He loved her.

Because he loved her, he had to send her away.

The valley rang silent. They were gone. Rhys kicked his horse to the edge of the crag and raised his face to the rare spring sunshine.

Funny, he thought. Not a cloud in the sky.

Yet his face ran with rain.

Eighteen

Aileen gripped the rail of the merchant ship as Inishmaan loomed out of the sea, curling its craggy spine against the Atlantic. The wind battered her face raw and filled her head with the perfume of land, the first she'd smelled since the ship left Aberffraw in Wales. As they neared, the captain barked out orders and eased the battered ship around to the bay side of the island.

A softness brushed her cheek as someone draped a fur-lined cloak across her shoulders. She clutched the edges and dragged them under her chin, as Dafydd came to stand at the rail beside her.

Not again, Dafydd. She did not meet his eyes. Words quivered on his lips, but she did not want to hear them. Not now, not ever. She wanted to hear the lilt of Irish on an islander's tongue, to feel the coarse sands of Inishmaan beneath her feet, to smell new-bloomed primroses upon a sun-warmed rock-pile fence. She wanted to see Ma.

A sliver of a boat set out from a strip of sand on the lee side of the island. Seamus, no doubt, looking to catch this ship before it sailed through to Galway for fresh food and water. The old salt had always been the first shipside, and profited well from his diligence. Aye, he'd be surprised to see her on board, swathed in furs, and more than willing to take her to the island for a chance at the first bit of gossip.

Dafydd leaned an elbow upon the rail and twisted toward her. "Aileen—"

She held up her hand and closed her eyes. He'd lasted longer than usual this time. *Aye, Dafydd, you mean well, but each word you say about him is another needle in my heart. Can't you see that it takes all my strength to keep my knees from giving out, to keep my body breathing and moving about; or are you as blind to a woman's pain as all other men?*

"I won't go without saying my piece." His good hand whitened into a fist against the splintered rail. "Don't listen, if you can't bear it, but I will speak."

She knew what he was about to say. A voyage that should have taken a matter of weeks had stretched to a month as they had battled gales and currents, and so it seemed he'd said his piece a hundred thousand times during the journey. She braced her heart against the words she wanted so much to hear.

"I've known the man all my life, Aileen. I like to think I know something of him. No, you'll stand here, at least, and make a pretense of listening."

Dafydd seized her with his good hand and held her still. She swallowed the lump growing in her throat.

"He's not like me," he said. "He was not born with that thing that crawls across his face, as I was born without a hand. This scourge attacked him when he was at his brightest. He has watched it destroy his life."

She resisted the urge to press the flat of her palms over her ears. *As if I don't know what that scourge did to his heart, as if I didn't feel the pain jarring up to my elbows a hundred mornings as I placed my hands over his chest—healing hands, indeed. The faeries gave me a gift and then snatched it away when I needed it most.*

"Then you came," he persisted. "You came and gave him hope. Do you think I didn't notice the change in both of you? He came to life again, I saw it with my own eyes that night when he picked up the harp he hadn't played in years. I don't know why he's sent you away. But this I know: The man loves you. He'd deny it until his death, he'd say anything before he'd

admit any vulnerability to any other human being on this
earth—but he loves you."

*Fool, fool. You were as fooled as me, Dafydd. He doesn't
love, he doesn't know how to love. He knows only how to hurt
and kill and destroy, and I was a fool for believing he could
open himself to anything else.*

She gripped the rail again, not against the bobbing of the
boat, subdued now that they were well into the bay, but against
the weakness in her body, against the emptiness of her soul
that the sea breeze seemed to waft right through. She had no
strength left, no pride, nothing; nothing but the beating of her
heart and the rush of blood through her veins. That kept her
standing, as the *curragh* made its way across the waves toward
the boat, the *curragh* that would be the vessel of her last voyage ever off the coast of Inishmaan.

Ma waited upon that island, probably weaving a new blanket
from the spring wool-cuttings or chopping up the last of the
salted meat for a stew. Aileen wanted to feel those battered
old knives in her hands, she wanted to smell onion rising to
her nostrils while the sea breeze swept in through the open
doorway.

Dafydd's hand slipped off her arm. His warmth receded.
She heard his boots tapping on the deck behind her, the anxious rustling of his clothing.

"This ship is battered from the storms," he said. "We'll be
anchoring near Galway for repairs. Before we head back to
Wales, we'll anchor here off Inishmaan. You'll see us. If you
change your mind, and choose to come back, I'll be waiting
for you."

He walked around her and tilted up her chin. The sea-spray
sparkled upon his dark hair, misted in those sad hazel eyes.
Something moved inside her, a memory of another tall man
with dark hair, and she closed her eyes against the blurring
that could so easily change Dafydd's handsome features into
those of his brother.

"He's a damn fool, Aileen."

She pressed her forehead against his chest. As he wrapped his arms around her, she thought of Shrovetide, when Dafydd had played some ball-game with the men in the yard and had stumbled into the mead-hall covered head to toe in mud and so full of mead he could hardly walk. Her heart ached anew for the friend she was losing.

"I could have prevented all of this. I helped wrestle you into that boat."

She shook her head against his chest.

"Remember that I'll be waiting for you."

Something bumped against the hull of the ship. A greeting rose from the water. Aileen pressed away from Dafydd and leaned over the rail to call out to Seamus. His familiar sun-weathered face collapsed in disbelief at the sight of her. He muttered something to the gods.

After the commerce was done, Dafydd helped her over the rail onto the hemp rope. She felt his eyes upon her as she climbed down and settled in the wobbly *curragh,* turning her back to the ship and setting her sights on Inishmaan as the men dipped their oars into the water. The *curragh* bobbed like a nutshell upon the waves, and its boards reeked of mackerel. Seamus bubbled over with questions, but one look at her face and he kept his tongue. Out of respect for her she supposed, and for the first time she blessed the capricious gift that kept her separate from the others, that made them look upon her with a touch of reverence.

Aye, she was home. She sucked air deep into her lungs, and it felt like the first breath she'd taken since that horrible evening in the *llys.* She coughed, and coughed again, clearing her lungs of mustiness and filling them again and again with fresh ocean air, heaving as if she couldn't get enough, heaving like a woman suffocating, welcoming the splash of sea-spray upon her cloak, upon her face and limbs as they entered the rough surf, as they bobbed and waited for the ocean to give them leave to land.

Seamus watched the coming swells with bright eyes in sea-leathered skin, then called out his command and sent the *curragh* slicing through the surf, swift and clean, until its belly scraped against the sand. Then the men jumped out and yanked the boat away from the waves which crashed in its wake.

She took his hand and eased up and out of the boat, waiting for the wobble to leave her limbs. When she heard a voice coming from the path, she looked up to see a woman racing down it, her blond hair flying and her arms outstretched.

Ma.

Stumbling on uncertain legs, Aileen lurched toward her. The tide came then, the swelling she'd held back for too many weeks. It rose now, too hard and too fast to hold back, it surged to her throat, then lurched from her lips in a single tortured cry. Tears poured from her eyes as she raced across the sand, clutching her cloak away from her uncertain feet, staring at the woman racing toward her, blond hair flying, those familiar swirling green eyes clouded with tears; seeing in them all the knowledge of the world, all the sympathy only a mother could give. Then she was in her Ma's arms, sobbing, clinging to her, wanting her to smooth away all the pain, and knowing deep in her heart that couldn't be, that nothing could wash away this pain, that she would hold it in her heart for the rest of her life.

But at least she was home. Aileen buried her face in her mother's hair, breathing in the scent of stew and onions.

At least she was home.

The fog sifted over the island all morning, bathing the limestone cliffs black and sprinkling the scrubby grass with the clearest drops of dew. With an empty egg-basket slung over her arm, Aileen set off for the cliffs as soon as the first luminous light broke through the gray mist. She walked awkwardly, for despite three days of wear the calfskin of her old *pampooties* still stuck out at stiff angles. The edges dug raw blisters into the backs of her heels.

The fog dissipated to tendrils as she edged her way along the bird-cliffs. Below, the ocean crashed over the ledges of rock which shot out deep into the sea. Terns and gannets hovered in the air, cawing in a great confusion of wings as they shot down to the surf to pluck dinner from ebbing pools. Gusts of salt-wind edged beneath her skirt and lifted her hair wildly around her ears.

Aileen caught sight of the first knot of weathered twigs and seaweed sagging off the leanest of ledges; a tern's nest heavy with eggs. She plucked a few and gingerly placed them in her basket before edging along the cliff to the next. Aye, at least this hasn't changed, she thought, as the handle dug into her forearm. The nests were still here, and she knew the way to find them.

She hunkered down at a wide ledge and shifted her load off her arm, pressed her back against the smooth black limestone. She closed her eyes so all she could hear was the confusion of the birds, the roar of the sea, the howl of the wind through stone.

Aye, and she could hear *them,* too. They'd followed her from the house. She'd heard their swift tiny feet in the grass behind her as she made her way across the island. She'd sensed their muted whispering amid the rocks as she'd collected eggs. Now, she sensed them hunkering down on a ledge just over her shoulder, and in her mind's eye she noticed them leaning back and closing their eyes in an unwitting imitation of her own stance.

It seemed she was never alone on this island, not even on the most remote cliffside with rock at her back and sea at her feet. Not that she minded the company of the *Sídh.* At least they didn't chatter on about nothing and give her curious looks over dinner, or beg for stories about Wales at bedtime or try to get her alone like Cairenn and Niall to wheedle the true story of her travels out of her. Nay, the *Sídh* followed her about as quiet as a breeze, as if they were waiting for her to do something or say something and in truth she didn't know what to do or say. She didn't know whether to be angry at them for dragging her into their schemes, or penitent for not being able to save that sacred place upon which Rhys built a castle in Wales. So she simply ignored their presence and took some measure of comfort in their silent company.

She blinked open her eyes and stared down at the sea crashing against the rocks. It was still as wild as she remembered, and the mist-laden air above it just as salt-sweet, just as fresh. She filled her lungs with the scent.

This hadn't changed. The sea . . . it was always the same. Aye, it had been the same deep blue when she'd left the island. When the mist finally broke, she knew that purple shadows would emerge to the north—the outline of the mountains. She knew, too, that the whitecaps floating on the blue water in the distance would run higher and harder to ultimately crash upon the shore below.

Nothing and nobody could penetrate this island exile without everyone on the island knowing it. That was why Ma and Da had chosen this as their home. That was why she had loved it, too. Inishmaan protected her from the cruelty of the outside world.

Aileen shifted and tugged on the backs of her *pampooties*. She must have put on some weight over the months, she couldn't seem to find a comfortable perch upon this ledge. Didn't she once spend hours seated up here, watching the ebb and flow of the waves? Didn't she love to huddle in this wet little nook until the birds settled around her? Now it just made her restless and uncomfortable, it made her think of the things that lay beyond those waves, things she was determined not to dwell on, not yet, not until more time had passed and she had finally settled back into this life here on Inishmaan.

It's just the change, she scolded herself. So much had happened. Did she expect to come back to Inishmaan and have everyone be just as young, everything be untouched, as if this were some small corner of *Tir na nOg?* Babes had been born, people had married and others had died. Dairine had grown a full head taller, and wanted nighttime stories full of frightening things, when once the young lass would have had none of that. Aileen had spent six months living in a hall ten times the size of her own house, that was why the rafters of her birth home seemed so low. She'd never noticed before the smoke-darkened walls, or the work that needed to be done on the rock-pile fence. She'd lived too long in great open spaces, so she was forced to stifle the urges of her heart to race wildly and blindly, in fear that she'd drop off the very edge of the island.

She edged back to solid ground, her burden heavy on her arm. Small feet pattered at her heels. She paused at the height to look around at the whole of the island; the row of *clocháns* bubbling against the background of the glittering bay, the sweep of grass speckled with cows, the roll of the land down to the north island, and beyond, to the mainland lost in the mist. This was the whole of her home, this tiny speck of land in Galway Bay. For reasons beyond her comprehension she found herself thinking of a winter ride through the mountains with a steed firm between her legs, a ride that went on for hours over hills and through passes, while the landscape shifted endlessly around her.

What a contrary thing she was! She'd hated that place, the dead land, the forgotten faery-places, the lifeless earth. She set her feet upon the path.

Ma sat on a stump just outside the door, a basket of sewing at her feet. "Just put those eggs in the pail of water, Aileen," she said without lifting her head. "Then come out and sit with me."

Aileen bent her head under the thatch overhang and entered the cool interior. The peat fire crackled in the center hearth and curled sweet blue smoke up toward the smoke-hole. The room smelled of peat and fresh-cut onion. Familiar aromas which assaulted her senses as she slipped the eggs into the water.

Aileen emerged to watch the last wisps of fog dance across

the island. She settled back against the doorjamb, and lifted one foot upon her knee to tug at the back of her *pampooties*.

"You'll not be needing them for long, lass," her mother said, lifting the calfskin in her lap. "I'm making you a new pair."

"Aye, Ma, there was no need to go doing that," she protested. "They'll soften enough with time and a few dips in the sea."

"They've been abandoned too long. Once the calfskin hardens that much, there's no fitting into them again." Ma shrugged her shoulders. "Besides, new shoes for a new life, that's what you'll be needing."

"It's my old life I'm wanting back."

"Wouldn't it be a fine thing if we all could recapture that gentle moment in our lives we loved most?" Her mother pulled the twine through a hole she'd punched in the leather. "Nay, Aileen, you've been gone too long and you've felt too many changes. I can see it in your eyes. You're not the same girl who left this place. If you're staying, it's a new life you'll have to make here. I thought you'd be knowing that by now."

Aileen slipped the boot off her aching foot and massaged the arch. Leave it to Ma to place her finger on the heart of a problem. She'd thought she'd hidden it so well. But every night as she sat in her old place at the dinner table, she felt she was a hundred miles away, so separate was she from the old banter and the easy arguing she'd once been such a part of.

"Niall thinks you've a *Lianhaun-shee* living upon you, you're losing so much weight. And Cairenn thinks you were taken away by the faeries, the way you do be walking about in the gentle places all the morn and night, as if you're yearning for *Tir na nOg.*"

"Wales was far from *Tir na nOg,* Ma."

"So you've told me."

Aileen held her foot tightly. She'd told Ma the whole story when she'd first arrived on Inishmaan. It had come out of her disjointed, wrenched up from the deepest of sorrow. Only Ma knew the full truth, for Aileen could only bear to tell the story once. Ma had related the essentials to the rest of the family and had bid them not to question her about it. She knew that because everyone had been so careful around dinner time not to speak of her absence, tiptoeing easily around the subject while granting her curious, sidelong glances.

Ma tsked and shook her head. "It must be a poor, wretched place, this Wales."

"Not a bit of life in it," Aileen murmured. "So barren and devoid of magic. But for that one place. . . ."

"The one he was building the castle upon."

"Aberygaun."

"A pity." Ma shook her head over her sewing. "It sounds like a place tortured, a place that needs a bit of a healing."

Aileen looked sharply at her, but her mother kept to her sewing. *A place that needs a bit of a healing.* Wasn't that a fine way to put it. A land that needed healing, what kind of a place was that? What could she do about it, when she couldn't even heal the man she loved with the hands that had failed her?

Suddenly, she didn't want to talk about it. "What of the Widdy Peggeen, Ma? I've been meaning to visit her. I've not heard a word about her since I've been back."

"Och, lass." Ma reached across the doorway to pat her daughter on the arm. "Did no one tell you? Poor old Peggeen passed over last winter. Died as peaceful as a lamb, your father said, not one word of complaint out of her, she just slipped away."

A butterfly flitted by, white and pure, and it hovered for a moment in front of Aileen before it flittered off toward the primroses nodding on the rock-pile fence. Marged had once told her that butterflies were the souls of people sent off to eternal peace. A stab of something like homesickness pierced her heart.

By God, when would she stop feeling like this, torn between a home she couldn't recognize anymore and a place that had never really been her home?

"You know, Aileen, I've been thinking about that place you told me about, the one where he was building a castle."

Aileen wondered if she would ever stop flinching whenever his memory was evoked.

"It brought to mind an old tale a friend once told to me, so many years ago it's a wonder I even remember it."

"Ma, you'd think you were ready for the grave, the way you do be talking. There isn't a thing that passes by you without you remembering it."

"We're talking twenty-odd years passed, lass." She poked another hole in the calfskin. "Before Conaire and I came to Inishmaan. I was so torn, thinking about the gentle lands of Champagne . . . and trying to get used to this wild place. But I was with Conaire, and in truth he was my home, not a bit of land."

Aileen flexed her dirty toes. *Where is my home, Ma? Is it with a contrary Welsh prince in a tortured faery-place? Or can it be here, the land of my childhood?*

"But as for the story . . . It was told to me by a man I haven't seen since, a funny little Irishman who used to entertain me while your father glowered at me across a fire, in the time before he saw sense and decided to make me his wife." Ma's smile softened her face so, for a moment she looked like a girl of eighteen. "I started thinking about it last night, and I can't get it out of my mind."

Aileen planted her feet back onto the ground and reached into the sewing basket for an awl. "Give me that other strip of calfskin, Ma, and I'll set to me own *pampooties*."

"Seems there was this young man," her mother began, holding out the calfskin while her gaze roved over the wind-blown meadow stretched out before them, "an ambitious man, whose father held a good plot of land of his own and herds and herds of cows. As the young man grew his father taught him how to pasture the beasts in the low fields in the winter and the high ones in the summer. But in order to pass from one pasturage to the other, they had to make a long wide journey around a bit of wild land. The son questioned his Da about it, wondering why they couldn't cut right through, but his father said he'd been told long ago by a faery-woman who lived nearby that his family would only be prosperous if they left that bit of land alone."

Aileen settled back against the door post, lifting her work to her face to set the holes along the edge of the calfskin. Aye, this was what she'd come home for; to listen to her mother's stories while the sun made its way toward the horizon.

"This boy, being a curious sort, always wondered what lay along that land, and as the years passed he drove the cows closer and closer to it, peering at the mound in its midst and the river that curled along its edge, thinking it would be a fine place to build a house, with so much water nearby and such a commanding view of all about, and so conveniently located halfway between the summer and winter pasturage. He began to think his father a fool and the old neighbor naught but a jealous woman who wanted to deny his family the rich green pasturage that would make their cows fatter and the milk from them richer. But when the boy made mention of it, his father stood firm. 'That's faery-land,' his father told him. 'Don't you be thinking of using it or it'll bring nothing but grief.' "

Aye, Aileen thought, and why was the memory of Marged coming to her mind now? It was true, Marged spent many a morning over a bucket of turnips telling Aileen stories of the white faery-cow and the Lady of the Lake, but her mother had been doing the same long before. Why, now, did she hear Marged's voice on her mother's lips?

"Well, it's not a surprise to say that when the boy's father passed over to the other world, and the boy took over his land and his cows, it did not take long for the boy to forget his father's warning and look upon that faery-mound with all kinds of ideas swirling like a gale in his head. In the end, he determined to build a house upon the faery-mound, and pasture his cattle on the rich green fields by the river."

Aileen paused in the midst of setting some twine through

a needle. Was that what the story was about, then? A man determined to build a house upon a faery-mound? She stared pointedly at her mother, who calmly continued her sewing.

"He set to clearing it, and he began to get an ache on his back which he figured was from all the hard work clearing brush and weeds from the height. It didn't stop him, nay, no more than the bees that swarmed there though there were few flowers on the height and nearby lay a whole field of blooming purple heather.

"No one in the neighborhood would lend a hand and help him, for they all knew better. They even pointed out that his cow's milk this year grew thin and watery. But this only made the boy more determined, so he set out to hire some tinkers to help with the building. They never stayed long and always set off complaining about noise and lights in the midst of night and some such things, which the man thought was nonsense and an excuse for laziness. So in the end the young man determined to roll his rocks up the hill to build his house by himself, even though he found after each day's work that he could barely straighten up and his shirts were beginning to fit him oddly, on account of all the muscle he was making, so he thought.

"One day, as he went into town to buy himself a new spade—his old one broke in the hard ground of the hill—he noticed that people along the road were staring at him, and whispering to each other, and pointing."

Aileen lay the sewing upon her lap while her mother tilted her head against the door post, staring across the fields, lost in the story.

" 'What's that upon your back?' the blacksmith asked as the young man hobbled toward him. 'It's naught but a lot of hard work,' the boy growled, trying to straighten up. 'I bend over my anvil all day,' the blacksmith argued, 'and you don't see me with a lump on me back.' And with that the young man hobbled over to a helmet the blacksmith had been polishing for the local baron and peered into it. And by God, did he cry out fit to split the hairs on a woman's head! For sure as he stood living and breathing, a lump swelled on his back just below his shoulder, hunching him over as did the one on the village idiot, who had been like that since birth.

"He went to the doctor, of course, but what do doctors know of such things as that? The doctor made him pay dearly and gave him unguents and the like, but nothing got rid of the terrible swelling, nothing at all. And the young man began to despair, for he'd set his heart upon Bonnie Mary of the next town, and he'd been building the strong stone house all for her. Now, she'd have nothing to do with him, for all his riches."

The calfskin slipped out of Aileen's hands, tumbled over her lap, and settled into a pool on the flagstones. It came to her now, as plain as day, and she wondered why she hadn't figured it out the day she rode to see Rhys's castle rising from the sacred earth of the faery-mound. Sitting up straight, she searched her memory for what little she knew of the undertaking; when it had begun, when Rhys first noticed the affliction upon his shoulder . . . how it stopped every winter when snow and cold weather caused the construction of the castle to cease.

"It wasn't long before that faery woman came to see the young man, out of the goodness of her own heart, mind you, for the man had done nothing but scorn her to all the people of the land. She was still old, but she had a quick mind for all her slow steps, and took the boy to task."

"And what did she tell him, Ma?" Aileen jerked up and scraped barefoot across the paving stones of the path. "Did she tell him that he mustn't build upon the mound? That he must tear down all he had done and put it to rights?"

Her mother nodded sagely, a gentle smile softening her features. "The faeries had put a curse upon him for building with mortar and stone upon their sacred place. 'Twas the only way, the faery woman told him, to set all to rights."

"I suppose your story has a happy ending." Aileen hugged her middle, anger roiling up in her. "I suppose the young man does as he's told and loses his hump and marries Bonnie Mary to raise a passel of children and he never goes near the faery-mound again."

Her mother pushed her hair off her shoulder and picked up the sewing she'd abandoned. "You know, lass, it's the strangest thing, but I don't remember the end of the story at all."

"Aye, you're a sly one." Aileen swept up the *pampootie* she'd abandoned and dumped it in her mother's basket. "Do you think I didn't try to stop him? I knew he had no business building on such sacred ground." She plopped down on the stump to shove her feet into her old *pampooties*. "Is it a faery-curse, then? Is that why my hands couldn't make it all pass away?" She spun about, not waiting for an answer. "You should think of better stories."

She set off down the path, the wind blowing her hair wild and her mind spinning and tears pricking the back of her eyes. She set off to march clear across the island, passing the herd of cows they kept all year round while most summered on the mainland. The salt air choking her, and the hard earth cutting through her calfskin shoes, she set off for the horizon, for the wild part of the island where only the barest of grass poked between the bones of stone. And always, always, she came to an edge, until she'd covered the island and had no place left to walk, no place left to go but down to a ribbon of shore washed with surf strong enough to scour clumps of stone from the cliff, down to the end of her world.

There she paced, rubbing her arms against the wind, watching the glitter of Galway Bay and the boats bobbing upon it, seeing only Rhys's face as he sat upon his steed bathed in mist and pointed down the hill toward the skeleton of his castle, the child of his dreams.

She had told him it was sacrilege. He'd scoffed at her warnings. Would it make a difference if she told him that by tearing down his dream, he could once again be whole—as handsome and unmarred and unfeared as he'd been before the wretched thing had climbed from his shoulder to his face? He'd scoff.

He'd call it wretched imaginings, the talk of superstition and paganism. He wouldn't believe, not Rhys ap Gruffydd the unbeliever. He wouldn't heed *her*, his last hope. The woman who had cheated him out of a healing.

She collapsed into a bundle, then buried her head on her knees. She sensed the *Sídh* around her, trilling their soft music in the air, agitated, uneasy. Aye, she knew the pain of their cousins in Wales, she'd stood upon that tortured ground and heard the screams. She'd felt the vibrations in every stretch of skin and bone. She had tried to save them, not even knowing that with the healing of one would come the healing of the other.

You belong there.

No. She shook her head between her knees as the words drifted to her on the music of the *Sídh*. What was she to do? Go and live among the Welsh, make her living as a healer, always under the shadow of Rhys's castle, seeing him only from afar on feast-days, remembering the nights they spent in his bed? Away from her family, away from the only people who truly knew who and what she was, and made no bones about it?

She lifted her head and peered out to the western horizon, to the faintest stretch of masts and flutter of sail at the bay's inner end. Dafydd's ship, awaiting repairs.

I can't go back.

The *Sídh* eased their swarming, and settled down around her like thistledown riding off a breeze. Aileen took a shaky breath and whispered for forgiveness, over and over. The *Sídh* had given up convincing her. The battle was over.

Languor swept through her. She lay down upon the rock, curling her knees tight into her chest. She was so tired, so very, very tired. Weary to the marrow of her bones from healing others, from taking the burden of so much sickness and sorrow upon her shoulders. She was drained, broken.

Who, in this world, could heal the healer?

The sea breeze turned gentle and oddly warm over these

rocks. She listened to it rustle through the scrubby grass, then listened to the rock and heard hollow music rising from the secret caverns that riddled this end of the island. The gentle suck and ebb of the sea. The hush of sand sifting through stone.

Sleep gripped her in soft hands. Ma wouldn't miss her for hours, she thought. In the few days she'd been back, she'd noticed that there were hands enough to do the work. What difference would it make if she lay here for a while and bathed in the uncertain sunshine? Perhaps here she could finally sleep a dreamless sleep.

Strange, she thought, as she drifted into slumber. She heard no cawing or screeching, nothing but the rumble of the waves. . . . The breeze rushed so gently over her it was as if birds brushed the tips of their wings over her skin, as if invisible hands trailed her hair off her face.

Strange . . .

Nineteen

With every slap of his horse's hooves in the mud, Rhys cursed the north tower. What had possessed him to start construction on the marshy puddle of the northern edge of the island, instead of the solid rock of the southern end? And why was it that he'd never noticed how soft the ground was when he'd first walked the site? The earth caved deeper into itself with every load of stone.

He dug his heels into his mount. The horse lunged up the path that lead to the *llys*. Three months of work, for a tower that teetered over the river. A tower that threatened to topple all its well-hewn stones and hard-made mortar into the current before midsummer. True, his brothers' raiding had kept him on horseback night and day, and away from supervising the building. But he shouldn't have to be there watching the unloading of every stone. He'd ship that master-mason back to Ireland and search for another if it wouldn't take so damn long to find a replacement. Wouldn't Aileen have had a mouthful to say about this?

He leaned low over the saddle and set his horse to racing across the yard that led to the *llys,* his mind closed against the memory that surged . . . a memory of wild hair and silver eyes . . . a memory of vinegar on her tongue and honey on her lips.

He pounded over the wooden bridge and startled a clutch of dusty men milling around the stables. His gaze drifted over them. So they were back, he thought. He swung his leg off the horse.

It was finally over.

Dafydd burst out of the mead-hall. His thin purple mantle slapped back to reveal the yellow silk lining as he strode straightaway to Rhys's side. The tracks of a comb lined his damp hair. He smelled of soap and hazel.

"You look like the hounds have been at you, brother." Dafydd's eyes gleamed with a bright hardness. "I heard that you've been having some trouble."

"The same trouble we have every year. I grant you one night of rest." Rhys brushed by his brother and headed toward the mead-hall, choking down the question surging to his lips. She was gone. He didn't want to hear her name spoken aloud. He didn't want to think of her. Every thought was a nail in his flesh. "You'll be taking the evening patrol to the north tomorrow."

"And thank you for welcoming me back." Dafydd fell into step beside him, swinging his silken cloak aside. "Already ordering me to work. Don't you want to know that we fought gales every step of the way to Ireland? We were forced to port in Galway for nearly a week before the ship was mended enough to—"

"You can regale me with every lurch of the ship over dinner." Rhys lowered his brows. He remembered how battered she'd looked when he'd taken her out of the hold that morning on Aberffraw. "I've not eaten since morning."

"Aren't you going to ask about her?"

"No."

He'd done what he had to do. He'd given her her freedom. He'd sent her back where she belonged. For the first time in all these years, he'd righted a wrong.

No.

He wanted to shut it out, even the memory of it, every last thing that evoked her name, her scent, her voice. He wanted to close the door upon the light and the warmth that he'd never deserved. To think upon Aileen was to think upon a hope he could never hold, a magic he could never understand, a love he could never accept, a joy that he'd destroyed with his own hands.

That part of his life was over; the rest stretched before him like a dry and dusty road.

"We've done work on the castle." Rhys turned away from Dafydd's sharp eyes and pushed open the door to the mead-hall. "But next year I'm sending to England for a new master-mason. This one isn't worth the—"

He stopped in his tracks, waited for his eyes to adjust to the darkness, then blinked them to clear the illusion from his sight.

She had to be a new bondswoman sent to work in the kitchens. He'd redden Marged's hide for bringing up a woman with hair that unruly shade of red. He'd have her sent off immediately. Even as all these thoughts flew through his mind, he knew only one woman stood as stiff as that, only one could look straight back at him with eyes the gray of a winter sky, only one could cause his heart to stop in his chest for one, two, three beats until it throbbed finally on a spear of pain.

Figures moved around the mead-hall, slipped through the shadows, their footsteps furtive on the paving stones. Horns of mead clattered upon the table. Weapons jingled. Wool and linen rustled until the door eased shut for the last time and left them in an uncertain silence.

He'd forgotten how tall she was, had forgotten the jut of her jaw, the angular shape of her shoulders and elbows, the way her woolen tunic fell from her chest to her feet with only the jut of her knees and the sag of her belt to break the drape of golden cloth. He curled his fingers into his palms, stanching the itch to thrust them into that hair. Hair as soft as thistledown. That he remembered.

"She came of her own free will." Dafydd stood just behind him. "She has something she wants to say to you, and if you're any kind of man, my brother, you'll listen."

Rhys stood frozen to the ground as if she'd cast some witch's spell upon him. His tongue lay like lead in his mouth. She drifted toward the hearth, into the light. Color flooded her cheeks. Moments passed and her lips opened, then closed tight again, then opened only to close anew. His gaze fell to her abdomen.

A babe.

He'd sent her off with a knife in her back. She was not the type of woman to return to hand him the hilt. *A babe.* A son, perhaps. Illegitimate, yes, something he'd vowed he'd never have. But he'd never tried to stop it, not with this woman who scorched the sheets with her passion. He'd told her on the last day they spoke that any child of hers would be his heir—his *heir.* A lure no woman of practical mind could resist.

But she stood so straight and so thin. . . . He calculated back and reasoned that it was still early. A woman could easily hide her pregnancy at three or four months along. *A babe.* A child for the beast. A strange sort of wonder thawed his shock.

"You are with child."

Her gaze flew up to his, then fell swiftly to her abdomen. She ran a hand over her belly and drifted off in what seemed to be rapid calculations.

"No." She shook her head once. "It was no child that brought me here."

The elation barely born withered and died under the heat of his own scorn. Far be it for the powers that be to grant him a gift as fine as a child of his own loins in the long years to come.

"Why are you here?" *I wanted you gone, gone so you would never see what I will soon become.* "I gave you your freedom."

"You gave me something that had always been mine, Rhys ap Gruffydd. You were the only one who had ever taken it away."

He yanked his cloak off his shoulders. "So you've come all the way back to scold me for kidnapping you."

"Nay." A strand of her hair slipped out of the netting and

breezed across her cheek. "Nay, I've long learned that all my scolding falls upon your ears as it would fall upon stones. I've come to ask leave to stay here in your kingdom, my Lord of Graig."

The cloak slithered off his back. He caught it with a curl of his hand before it fell to the floor.

"I returned to Inishmaan," she continued. "But I found myself of little use there. My father is a fine doctor, and hale and hearty enough to see to the needs of the islanders, even some of the mainlanders when he's called upon. There's no need on Inishmaan for two healers, and seeing there's no chance that a woman of my age will find a husband, I felt myself nothing but a burden to my family."

"They turned you out."

"They did no such thing." Those gray eyes flashed. "They wanted me to stay." Her voice caught on a memory. "But I am not needed on Inishmaan as I am needed here, in Wales. A woman must look to her future."

His loins swelled at her words. He needed her here. Already the blood pumped hard through his body, the memories rose too fierce to ignore.

She's come back.

"There's not a doctor for twenty leagues from here." She stood steady by the hearth. "And the closest midwife must travel such hills that by the time she reaches a bondswoman in labor the child is already born—or both mother and child are dead. You've seen my work." Those lashes fell to hide her eyes. "I would be no burden to your estate. I'd make my way by healing. All I ask of you is a hut among those of the freemen at the base of the cliff, and mayhap a bit of land to make a garden by."

May as well ask for a pound of his flesh. May as well ask for a knife to thrust into his heart. He didn't want her here. He had sent her away. He had thrust her out of his life so he could retain the memory. Now she reappeared at his doorstep as winsome and practical as ever, asking for nothing more than a wattled hut upon his own land.

He waited for more, some sign of coquettishness, of weakening, anything to give him leave to cross this hearth and crush her in his arms, to take her over the trestle table as he'd once taken her in the kitchens, knowing even as he waited that he *couldn't* take her. He couldn't resurrect what he'd murdered.

"You think you can just live here," he said, "as if you were never my lover."

Those eyes of gray turned hard and fierce. "I'm not the first peasant to take to her lord's bed. No doubt I won't be the last."

The shaft of the knife sank deep into his chest.

"What is it, my lord? Are you ashamed of me?" Her chin jutted to the sky. "You don't have to worry, I won't flatter myself by strutting among the bondswomen as if I'd caught the tail feathers of a peacock. Nor will I go bragging about your skill between the linens, if that is what's got you so pale and stiff-faced. Or would you rather I did?"

"You've not learned to hold your tongue."

"I know my presence can't be pricking your conscience, for you've told me often enough you haven't one." She waved toward the north, toward some distant place outside these walls. "If you've no stomach to see my face each time you ride out of the *llys,* well, you've enough land to set me aside. Get me a hut beyond Arthur's grave, or in some isolated place in the woods. Do you think it matters to me where I live, so long as I live by my own hands?"

"And if I say no?"

"Dafydd has promised me safe passage to Inishmaan."

Rhys turned and glared at Dafydd, who stood there glaring back, like the conscience he wasn't supposed to have.

So she was to have a hut at the base of the cliff and a plot of land. He was to spend his life catching a glimpse of her hair amid the cottages, seeing her graceful figure as she made the rounds, mended wounds, delivered babies, and laughed with young bondsmen. She was strong and healthy enough, and she would grow wealthy enough with the skill she had, so rare in these parts. She'd marry in the passing of time. She wouldn't be the first woman who went to the altar not as pure as the day she was born. She'd bear another man's children. He'd see the pity in her eyes as she straightened from her labors, ripe in pregnancy, to watch him ride by on his horse, children at her skirts.

The cruel powers that be would not even allow him peace in his misery. Nay, those powers had brought her back to be his mirror; for each time he looked into her face he would see his own life crumbling. From now until the day he died, glimpses of her would be picks hacking away at the remnants of the memories, until they, too, were nothing but rubble.

"Tell the bondsmen we've a hut to make." Rhys seized one of the bladders of mead off the table and headed past Dafydd toward the door. "You have your place, Aileen the Red. Until it's built, you'll sleep in the kitchens with Marged."

The afternoon sun sifted in through the doorway of Aileen's new hut. Humming one of her brother's harp-melodies, she danced through the small house, brushing a twig broom across the paving-stones. Beyond the walls, cows lowed on the warm hillside as they made their way back to be milked. She smiled, thinking she could distinguish her own cow's lowing amid the herd.

Leaning the broom against the doorjamb, Aileen posed in the doorway, half in the warmth of the July sunshine, half in the cool interior. The fresh new thatch which hung over the door smelled of clover and sweet herbs she'd woven into it to keep away the fleas. Rich brown earth lay drying in the sun in the garden plot she'd only turned over this morning, and sprigs of precious herbs Father Adda had sent over to her fluttered nearby, waiting for their beds in the earth.

A fine hut, it was, overlooking a stretch of a cultivated field in the base of the valley, not far from the other huts which clung to the foot of the slope. Another woman tending her garden straightened and lifted a hand in greeting, and Aileen waved back while warmth spread through her heart.

She'd done right, coming back here to Wales. When she'd woken up that afternoon on the cliff of Inishmaan feeling as if she'd spent years asleep, it had all come to her so clearly. She had no place on Inishmaan, not really. And the gentle people of Wales cried out with their need. To stay on Inishmaan was to stay a child; to return to Wales was to face the consequences of her actions and to put the gift that rushed through her to good use again. To become a woman in her own right at last.

As for Rhys . . . She hugged the tip of the broom under her chin. She was a woman, full grown, not a silly child. He had never loved her, for all her imaginings. But she loved him, as sure as she stood at the doorway of her own home. She knew it the moment she'd set eyes upon those strong shoulders and those tortured eyes, and felt the floor drop off beneath her feet. A faery had brought her to this place and to this man. She held no hope that this love she felt for him would ever fade, or that any other man could come into her life and move her heart as he did. She would have to take what joy she could, knowing she had loved as few women ever did, and find some pleasure in his nearness.

As if by thinking of him she made him materialize, there he rode, clear across the valley as if chased by demons. Someone flopped over on the back of his steed. It didn't take long for her to realize that Rhys was riding a straight line to her hut, and the boy behind him was Owen, covered in blood.

She raced down the unpaved path and met them at the edge of the garden. "By the saints, Rhys, what happened?"

"An accident at the castle." Rhys swung down and caught Owen in his arms as the boy sagged off the saddle. "Hit by scaffolding that had rotted through."

Aileen raced ahead to direct him to the pallet. There was

only one in the hut now, but there would be a second, soon enough, when she got herself settled. No doubt many a night would be spent with someone ailing. She smoothed the hay with a blanket and rounded Rhys as he laid the boy down.

She fell to her knees at Owen's side. The boy's breath soughed shallow through cracked lips, and a pulse throbbed in his throat, but he did not wake to her gentle shaking. Blood matted his hair against his cheek. An ugly gash stretched just above his eye, and the skin around it swelled a threatening purple.

Rhys hovered behind her, as agitated as a bird with its legs trussed. He smelled of horse and leather, and his cloak brushed against her back with every pass of his pacing.

"Will he live?"

"How would I be knowing," she said, "with him just set before me?" She passed her fingers across the boy's temple. "It'd help if you'd give him some room to breathe, it would."

He drew back and light flooded over the pallet. A sheen of sweat lay on the boy's brow and his skin burned to the touch.

"How long has he been unconscious?"

"Not long. He was alert when I put him on my horse. He slumped against me on the way over." Rhys blocked out the light again. "Use your herbs, woman, make him come to."

Nay, it wasn't herbs she was thinking of using. She wondered why she hesitated before him. Hadn't she used the pass of her hands a thousand times in his presence, used it upon him? Didn't she know well enough how to pass her hands across an injury without it looking as if she were doing anything out of the ordinary? It was an old habit, this unease in the gut whenever she set to do her healing under the eyes of others. And there was a surge of defensiveness, for this man knew her gift and scorned it—with reason—for it had failed him.

She fisted her skirts and rose to her feet, finding him far too close for comfort.

Aye, far too close. He loomed over her, his nostrils flaring and his body smelling like man, all sweaty and strong and pulsing from the long ride across the hills, his cloak swung back to show the tautness of his tunic across his chest. That chest . . . she knew the feel of the skin under her palm, the taste of his sweat upon her tongue. A hundred thousand memories flooded her mind.

She stumbled back, but her knees bumped against the edge of the pallet. His blue gaze flared over her. He made no effort to step back. The moment of awareness rang between them like the single string of a lyre plucked in silence.

It wouldn't do, if she felt her insides melting like butter in the warm sun each time he came to her hut. There would be no profit in showing him the depth of her own weakness—only shame in it—and she would not be caught again in that sticky web.

"Have you thought, my lord, that the boy's body needs sleep for the healing?" She forced steel into her breathless voice. "And how am I to help him, if you won't let me move about in my own house?"

He turned reluctantly to one side, cast his gaze around the building. "This hut's not fit for a cow."

"It is fine enough for me, thank you very much." She bustled to the waning fire, filling her lungs with the air that he'd stolen from them. "It's no larger or smaller than any others built here."

"You need more room," he argued, waving his hand to the rafters hung with a few drying herbs, "for . . . things. Your plants. Whatever it is you use. What are you doing?"

She hung an iron pot over the fire. "Setting a pot of water to boil, if you don't mind."

"Set to the boy."

"What am I doing, if not that? He'll be needing some broth when he comes to, and a poultice for that wound after I see to the stitching—"

"Then do the stitching, and I'll set to that."

He seized the heavy pot from her hands, fiddled with the

tripod until the pot hung well over the weakening fire. Eyeing him, she opened her bag and pulled out her precious silver needle. Three times, she tried to thread the thing while her gaze drifted to the hulk of a man hunkering by the fire.

He stoked the flames and piled up the fuel until heat filled the house. "I'll get water."

Banging the wooden-lathed bucket against his knees, he strode out of the house and headed to the trickle of a stream which funneled its way down the slope to pool in a small pond just beyond the fields. Aileen took the moment to tug a fresh linen out of her bag and set to sewing the boy's gash together before he came to.

When she was done, she glanced over her shoulder, out into the sunshine, but saw no one coming up the path. Rhys's scorn of her powers still lodged in her mind like a splinter speared too deeply to be pulled out. Well, she wouldn't furtively hide it as if it were a disfiguring birthmark or a rotted tooth—not from Rhys.

Later, Rhys strode in with the metal rings of the bucket clattering against his sword, cursing the distance and the ruts in the path that had made him splash icy mountain water all over himself. As he poured the water into the cauldron, he fell into a sudden silence. From some distant place she sensed his gaze upon her. She forced that ripple of knowledge away, so it wouldn't affect the healing. Now it was the healing that engulfed her, the drawing away of poisons, the mending of tissues, the slow easing of the swelling pressure, the current of light and warmth. The boy had taken a solid bump on his head, not enough to kill him, but enough to keep him abed till Lughnasa.

She drew her hands away. The air swirled warm around her. The water bubbled hot and the wood-fire crackled loud in the silence. She could have been at the healing for a minute or an hour; she never could tell. The light in her hut had dimmed, but it only took her a moment to realize that something cast a shadow over her. Rhys stood close again, just beside the pallet.

He said, "He'll live."

"He should." She slipped by Rhys to tend to the pot. "It was a hard knock he took, but he's a strong young man. I'll know better by evening."

Rhys hovered over the pallet, frowning down at the boy, who now rested peacefully, a hint of color on his cheeks. "He's a foolish boy."

"You told me it was an accident."

"An accident meant for my head—not his." Rhys turned away and leaned against the doorjamb. "He saw the scaffolding give and ran clear across the island to push me out of the way."

Aileen twisted the wooden spoon in her hand. *Aye, it's a hard thing for you to understand loyalty, isn't it, Rhys ap Gruffydd?* "What was he doing at the castle? I thought his duties were in the *llys*."

"He got it in his head to take up a trade rather than tend to hounds his life through." Rhys shrugged. "So I took him to meet the master-mason, thinking he could always use a pair of hands."

"It was a brave thing he did, not a foolish one." She dipped the spoon into the boiling water. "Though of the two of you, your head is the harder, I'm thinking. I've no doubt that wood was for your head, Rhys ap Gruffydd. Mayhap to knock some sense into you."

He lay his back against the doorjamb. "You've much to learn, woman, about how to speak to your lord and master."

"We had no master upon Inishmaan. And I've never taken much to all that bowing and scraping."

"You think the scaffolding was meant for me, eh? It isn't the first time there's been danger upon that site."

"Nay, and it won't be the last, until you come to your senses and tear the whole thing down."

"I'll find the culprit first. The Englishman in our midst. Or the Welsh traitor."

"Well, I'll not be wishing you luck if you're thinking of getting rid of the faeries."

He seemed in such a mood this day, distracted by the wounding of the boy, all in a flux about something. There was no need for him to be hovering about. No doubt there were a hundred thousand things for the lord of the land to be doing right now, with a castle half-built and a household to run and enemies raiding cattle on the borders all times of the day and night. She'd seen little of him this past month when she'd lived in the *llys,* and less since she'd moved into her hut. Yet now he lingered, strangely uneasy.

"My mother told me a story," she said swiftly, before he could scoff, "when I was at Inishmaan. It got me to thinking about you and that castle in a way I'd not thought before."

She swept a horn of mead off a peg—a gift from Marged—and paced to the door to thrust the thing at him.

He raised a brow at it. "Is the price of this mead a bunch of faery-stories?"

"Will you be insulting me, Rhys ap Gruffydd, by refusing my hospitality?"

He uncorked the flagon and eyed her over the rim as he took a deep and healthy swig. While she worked around the center fire, pinching dried herbs into the water and then cutting up a pile of wild onions she'd collected on the hill, she told him the story as her Ma had told it to her, keeping her gaze on her work until she'd come to the end . . . only to look up and see him scowling at her, the empty flagon hanging from his hand.

"A fine story, Aileen the Red. Is your mother English, by the by?"

"Half-French and half-Irish, I'll have you know. And she knows naught of you and less of men's wars."

"She knows a good story." His lips curled. "So, break down the castle and I'll be cured, is that it?"

"There's no need to be scoffing. Aye, I don't know why I bother with you."

"It's a question I've asked myself."

She tossed the wild onions into the pot of water. The water slopped over the rim and sizzled upon the flames. Why had she expected him to take it to heart? Why had she expected anything but the scorn that dripped from his lips?

"My Ma heard the tale a long time ago."

"From a faery, no doubt."

"Aye, and what of it? If you want to be knowing the truth of it, he was a strange little man named Octavius, who used to work for my father, and only in the end did they know he was a faery."

"What was his name?"

He'd crossed the room in two strides and now stood across the pot, glaring at her through the steam.

"His *name,*" Rhys insisted. "The storyteller's name?"

She planted her hands on her hips and dragged her gaze from the open neck of his tunic, from the gleam of the strong chest beneath. "What difference, that? His name was Octavius."

Rhys straightened, his gaze unreadable. With two strides and a snap of his cloak, he was gone, leaving nothing but the potent perfume of man, leather, and steel.

Dafydd urged his horse toward his brother as Rhys emerged from the edge of the woods.

"The boy," Dafydd said, "how is he?"

"She says he'll survive."

Rhys scanned the rise of the castle walls. Scaffolding caged every stretch of stone. He watched the Irishmen and the Welshmen working in their *braies* at mixing mortar and transporting stones and hammering together fresh-cut wood for the scaffolding. He breathed in the scents of fresh-turned earth, of hay heating in the summer sun, of fresh-cut oak.

How many years had he planned the making of this castle? The number was lost on him now. He'd spent enough time warring in Southern Wales to see the English castles built there, to envy their strength, to revel in their majesty, even if it was not Welsh majesty. *There* was strength, *there* was beauty, *there* was something solid and immortal—something impenetrable, a bulwark against a world full of enemies. With those castles, the English had conquered the south of Wales, and had kept it. If the north of Wales was ever going to hold out against them it must build such castles of its own.

Here was his, commissioned by Llywelyn, the Prince of Wales. Here was stone and mortar of what he'd built, over and over, in the mud of the *llys* as a boy. Here was his own cage.

"We've rebuilt the scaffolding." Dafydd eyed him strangely. "And we've checked the other wood for rot or looseness."

"What of the north tower?"

Dafydd shrugged. "The master-mason thinks we can shore up the base with mortar, and thus stop the tilting."

Damned gray-eyed wench. Glowing like some ethereal thing every time she laid her hands upon a wounded man, looking like an angel hovering over the dead—utterly untouchable—bringing color back into a wounded man's face with nothing but the touch of her fingers and something else. Some abiding, rock-strong faith in things unseen.

The words tore from Rhys's throat. "Knock it down."

"Rhys?"

"Knock the damned tower down. To the bones, Dafydd. Right to the foundation and get rid of that, too."

Why not, Rhys thought. The tower would have blown over with the first winter gale. He'd start it over from the base and watch every moment of work. If nothing else, he'd have, at the start of winter, a tower that would rage up out of the ground straight and tall. Proof to hold up to that red-haired wench that magic was a thing for the ignorant . . . and hope was dead.

Twenty

"Up, Rhys." Dafydd threw the door to Rhys's bedroom open, strode to the huge bed, and thrust the curtains aside. "A fine example you are, lolling about in bed until far past cock's crow, without even a woman as an excuse."

Rhys winced against the light. He scowled in the direction of his brother's voice. From the open door flooded the noises of morning: men swilling mead and arguing, women bustling about, dogs barking, and harnesses jingling with the third changing of the guard.

"Come, there's work to be done, a castle to be built." Dafydd strode to the tray by the door and poked amid Rhys's breakfast. "How do you expect your men to give you a good day's work if you don't show your face before Prime?"

"The evening patrol for you tonight." Rhys rolled his legs off the side of the bed. "We'll see how bright-eyed you are, brother, when you don't ride into the *llys* until after Matins."

"Your oatcake is still hot." Dafydd chewed a wad to one side of his cheek and mustered an oaty grin. "Should be stone cold by now. I suspect that new girl delivered it here late."

Rhys pulled the chamberpot from under the bed and relieved himself in it. So that was what made his brother so light-stepped and foolish these past days. Another conquest amid the servants. Another woman he'd trail after moon-eyed for a few months, who'd have him strutting like a cock amid the hens, unbearable to all.

"I'll have to speak to her."

"The blond one."

Rhys finished the necessary and footed the pot back under the bed. He swept up his hose from where he'd thrown them the night before. He remembered the woman. Clumsy, but buxom. Attractive in the fleshy way his brother liked. That he himself had once liked, before he'd held the likes of Aileen.

Rhys snapped the hose clean. "See to it that the servant doesn't loll about in bed anymore."

"A task I'd be more than happy to free you from." Dafydd strutted across the room, grasped the two bedposts and leaned between them, a flagon of mead dangling from one hand. "In fact, I'll make it my personal—"

Dafydd choked mid-sentence. Rhys yanked on his hose and tied them to the belt of his *braies,* suspecting his brother had choked on his own swaggering. "The girl," Rhys said, "best be a better cook than a servant."

Dafydd's boots scraped against the floor. He crouched before Rhys. "By Christ's Heart."

Rhys scowled and tied the hose. What was this? A new pattern upon the old? A patch redder than the others? Another ripple? Rhys stood up, turned his back on his brother, snatched the dangling black leather mask from a post above the bed, and slapped it over his shoulder.

Dafydd jerked the leather out of his hands and sent it sailing across the room. "By Christ's Heart, Rhys, it's receding."

"My hairline? Or my teeth?"

"Look in a mirror, damn it, and see for yourself."

Rhys ignored him and wrestled into his shirt. He had no mirror—he'd cracked the last one long, long ago. Dafydd did his weekly shaving for him. He'd long given up the urge to peer into a glass, seeking the most infinitesimal change in the mottling of his skin, like a vain woman searching for age-lines.

It didn't matter anymore. His life lay before him, written in stone and tolerable enough. Rhys brushed by his brother and swept the mask up from the ground.

"Stop looking for trifles," he argued, "just to prove her right."

For a good two weeks they'd been tearing down the north tower of the castle. For a solid two weeks he'd been running his hand over his mangled face in the dark of night, scorning himself for expecting any sort of change.

"This isn't a trifle. This is half your face." Dafydd thrust the flagon in Rhys's free hand and searched the room. "What? Not a polished helmet, not a polished shield in all of this? Ah! I know . . ."

He was gone, breezing out of the room and calling out for one of the men. Rhys filled his belly with honey-mead. The bladder collapsed under his hand. He tossed it aside with a spray of drops. He slapped the black leather back on his shoulder and tied the strings tight under his arm, flung open his trunk and grabbed the first tunic he lay hands on. He jerked this over his head and fastened his girdle around his waist. He yanked his belt tight, tied the knots of his tunic, wrapped the laces of his boots firmly around his ankles and calves. When he had no more clothing to don, he stood in the light of the smoke-hole and flexed his hands, over and over. His face prickled with awareness.

This is half your face.

Foolishness. It was nothing but a castle, a pile of mortar and stones, upon a mound of grass. It was nothing but another valley in a kingdom of valleys. And this thing on his face . . . it was just another scabious disease that no doctor knew how to cure.

His fingers strayed up to his jaw.

His skin lay liquid beneath them, as if it had melted and swirled before being baked back onto his bones. Damn Dafydd for seeing things. Damn him for trying to justify bringing the lass all the way back to Wales. His brother was so eager to prove her faery-lore right, to see elves in the twilight and magic in nonsense.

Rhys thrust his fingers through his hair, rested the butt of his hand on his forehead.

And froze.

"Look. Pedr's helmet." Dafydd thrust a helmet into Rhys's belly. "He stole it from an Englishman all those years ago. He always keeps it polished to a shine, if only just to admire his mustaches in its sheen."

Rhys seized the rim of the helmet and tossed it up, one-handed, turning it so he could raise the seamed back before his face. He peered into the distorted surface of the scratched steel.

The face that peered back was the face of a man he'd left behind years ago, a man who had not yet fashioned the mask that was to become his only ornament—the face of a man one-quarter disfigured, the skin of forehead and cheekbone as smooth and unmarred as that of any man of his years, the creeping horror of what was to come just rising over his jaw.

The helmet chinked to the paving stones and rolled, flashing, a new dent along its side.

"The lass is right." Dafydd seized the helmet in both hands. "She is *right*. It was the castle all along."

Rhys glared at the helmet, but resisted the urge to snag it from his brother and stare in it again lest what he saw before turned out to be an illusion, one final mockery upon him. Dafydd's laugh filled the room, but Rhys didn't move. He couldn't. This could not be.

Fairy-rings and magic mounds. Screaming that he couldn't hear. Curses upon him for building on land that belonged to little creatures, the *Y Tylwyth Teg,* immortal creatures who could not be seen or heard, on creatures the church ignored or wrote off as the souls of virtuous Druids who could not enter Heaven. Faery-women so beautiful they could steal a mortal's heart.

Rhys brushed by Dafydd and strode through the hall, ignoring the gasps of the kitchen servants, ignoring the men's stares. He burst out of the mead-hall and knew the minute he strode through the dust that all of the *llys* had heard. Dafydd had made it known and the news had traveled like a brush fire on the slopes in mid-July. Now his people clustered. They watched him as he passed, as he seized the first mounted horse he could find and climbed upon it. He yanked the reins toward the portal, kicked the horse and bent over him to speed him down to the cluster of huts at the base of the cliff.

Was this why she had returned, then? To give him what he wanted when he no longer wanted it, when he no longer needed it. His face still stung with the prickling, and now with something else, with the unfamiliar feel of wind against it, blowing his hair free; the unfamiliar feel of the hot summer sun upon it. He'd ridden like this with Llywelyn on campaigns, bare-faced, unashamed, a frisky horse between his thighs and dreams in his head. Aye, he remembered it. Too well.

Dirt choked his passage, but did not discourage the women who peered out their open doorways at the sound of hoofbeats or the children who squealed at the sight of him on a horse. The new thatch of Aileen's hut glared flaxen where it hung over the edge of the roof, shimmering in the mid-summer sun. She kneeled in the plot of garden and stroked the dark soil between tufts of greenery, her hair caught up in a bit of linen. Catching sight of him, she rose to her feet and slapped her hands free of soil.

He dismounted and strode up the smooth, newly laid paving-stone. She stood in front of this tiny hut, her chin raised as if she stood before a castle, her hands firm on her lean hips, her woolen skirts streaked with mud. She looked as if she'd lived here all her life. She fit in so well with the peasants who fell into a cluster, in hushed silence, just beyond his horse. Yet she owned the carriage of a woman noble-born, and her eyes were bright with an odd twinkle as he stopped in front of her.

"Just what brings you to my home on such a fine, hot day, my Lord of Graig?" She dropped her gaze from his head to his toes and back again. "Couldn't be a bit of the ague at you now, could it? Or are you looking for an ointment for the sting of those black biting bugs that come out by the marshes this time of year?"

She stared him straight in the face with something twitching at the corners of her lips, her eyes full of mischief, full of *knowing,* as if this was nothing more than a broken bone set to rights, when the impudent little wench knew that five years of thwarted hope lay behind it.

"You're looking fine this day," she said, "but if you don't mind me saying, my lord, you're in need of a bit of sun." She drew her brows together as she clucked her tongue. "One part of your face is as pale as a breast of chicken, now I wonder how it got that way?"

She'd spoken in Welsh, loud enough for the audience just beyond his horse to gasp and choke upon chuckles.

"This," he growled in Irish, "is the work of your hands."

"You flatter me, my lord." She hefted a basket full of greens into the crook of her elbow. "It's been a fine long time since I've laid my hands upon you. Would that it were the work of me hands. That would have avoided more than a bit of trouble, wouldn't you say?"

"Tell me what you did, woman." He closed his hands into fists to keep from reaching out and wiping away the soil which streaked her freckled cheek. "Did you give Marged some of those herbs? Sprinkle them in my mead? Chant spells under a midnight moon?"

"Chanting spells?" She casually feathered her fingers over the greens to gauge the contents. "Aye, and here I was thinking you gave no mind to such things."

He seized her arm. "Then you *did* do something."

"Aye, aye, I did something." She shook her arm free. Mischief seeped out of her gaze. "I'm the one who told you to tear down the castle, I did, for all the mind you gave me. And by the looks of you, the north tower is near down to the foundations." His silence affirmed her supposition. She swiveled on one heel. "The day brings me double the good news, then."

She marched off to the doorway of her hut without a never-you-mind, her thin hips twitching with each step.

His mind fermented with suspicion. She was in league with the English. Or his wretched half brothers. There were enough people who didn't want to see such a strong castle raised in such a vulnerable place, people who would pay well for a witch to work her magic to their ends. Even as the thought passed through his mind he knew it was foolishness. If she'd known of a way to free him of this affliction, she'd have done it long ago, when he'd first kidnapped her. She would have done it for the price of her freedom.

Why now, why now? What magic did she use? How long would it last? What demon powers had she summoned for this little trick, what price would he have to pay, and how long would he be beholden to her for this unbidden magic?

He found himself striding after her. He dipped his head beneath the door post and entered the coolness of the hut, ripe with the scents of something sweet boiling in the pot, woodsmoke, and newly cut greens.

"So you've come looking for explanations, have you?" She clanged the rim of the cauldron as she thrust a spoon into the contents. "Aye, Rhys ap Gruffydd, you're like a child who cannot stop saying 'Why?' 'Why?' 'Why?' until a woman is like to grow as mad as a loon answering the unanswerable."

"I've no liking for witchery."

"There's that word again." She splattered herself with the hot liquid, but ignored the stains on her bodice. "I thought that was a word of the ignorant, eh? What would please you, my lord? Thrusting my hand in boiling oil to see if I scream out? Tossing me into the river to determine if I float or sink? Searching my body for a mark of the devil—"

She pulled out the spoon and turned away to clatter it on a table littered with herbs and wooden mortars and pestles. Even in the dim room, Rhys saw the color rising over her face and felt an answering surge of blood in his loins.

He'd searched that body already. He'd tasted every crease,

every curve, with his own lips, he knew the way the freckles tapered on her thighs and left a belly with skin as creamy as May-milk. There was devilry in that body, there was bewitchment in those loins; a man could lose himself in the earthy woman-scent of her, a man could lose a part of his soul.

But that had nothing to do with witchery. Rhys thrust his fingers through his hair, feeling again the unfamiliar smooth skin under the butt of his palm. No, that feeling between them had nothing to do with witchery. It had to do with a woman who opened all of herself to him, without asking for anything in return but the pleasure of his company and the warmth of his body during the cold nights. That enchantment had been a result of a woman's steady gray gaze upon a mottled face, a woman's strong heart and quiet loyalty, a woman's full understanding and gentle hands, a woman's piercing gaze into the heart of a wretched shell of a man.

It had been a love he'd never thought to feel again, a love he'd been afraid to keep for fear of disgust passing over her features one day as she looked upon him in his disfigurement.

But now that fear was gone.

"If you're here looking for explanations, the answer is the same as before." She tossed a few leaves into a mortar and seized the pestle to grind it into a gloppy green mess. "You've a faery-curse upon you, for daring to build a castle upon a sacred place."

He leaned back against the wall next to the portal and dug the butt of his palms into his eyes. There she went again, talking faery-nonsense, and thinking he would believe it, even after all this time.

"For all I know," she continued, "that island may be the last doorway in all of your wretched Wales between this world and the Otherworld—the world you know as *Annwn*. The faeries, they're doing whatever they can to hold onto this world, though only God knows why, with so many ignorant people walking about. They must get rid of the stone and mortar weighing down the mound."

"So they sent one of their own to me," Rhys argued, hating the sarcasm dripping in his voice, "to lead me to you."

"Aye, that's the way of it." She bustled to the cauldron and scraped the dark green muck into the pot with the edge of the pestle. "And they're not English, mind you. They don't care for the wars of our people and the struggles for land above the ground, so don't you go thinking there's anything else to this but a faery-curse."

"You haven't told me anything that any Welsh grandmother couldn't whisper to me across a fire. Why would they go to such lengths to send me to Ireland, to send me to *you?*"

The mortar and pestle clattered on the table. She lifted her chin and stared sightlessly at the wall. A piece of wood cracked beneath the fire. Outside, a cuckoo flitted across the garden and trilled its song in the thatch overhang.

"They sent you to me," she began, steadily, "because I'm one of them."

The fire crackled too hot. She felt it against her ankles, through the wool of her tunic and the calfskin of her shoes. She should turn and take care of it, pull some wood from the blaze, tamp it down so the unguent she was making, for that poor boy in the river valley with the burn along his thigh, wouldn't bubble over and be worth nothing. But for the life of her, she couldn't seem to move from her spot. She was afraid if she turned and faced the man standing stiff in the shadows of the portal she'd see a grin on his face or hear the first laugh, and she'd be hard put not to curse him to the bowels of hell.

She gripped the cool edge of the mortar and ran her fingers over the chips on the inside. Outside, his horse neighed, attended still by the curious bystanders whose murmuring drifted through the doorway of the hut, as did the laughter of the children racing about and playing games in the bright July sun. What difference did it make if she told him the truth now?

He didn't believe the evidence of his own eyes, the clearing of that handsome face of his after the destruction of part of the castle. He searched for other reasons, for herbs, unguents, treachery, or even witchery to explain it, so he wouldn't have to believe the unbelievable—so he wouldn't have to *believe*.

What difference would it make now? she thought, while the boiling liquid rumbled and sputtered. A fine, handsome man he was, Rhys ap Gruffydd, and with the affliction ebbed to just the curve of his cheek, she saw far too clearly what he had been before it had overtaken him. The kind of man who could steal any woman's breath away, with those clear blue eyes and finely sculpted cheekbones, that straight nose, and those black brows. It was a wonder he didn't have a passel of bastards roaming these hills. She was sure he would, soon enough, when the rest of the affliction faded and his world turned back to the way it had been before.

He'd get himself a fine young wife, a beauty, no less, and rich as he, with plenty of land for their herds of cattle. Another castle, on another place less sacred than the old. A seat in the mead-hall of the Prince of Wales again. He stood confused and angry in her hut now, not understanding, but soon enough he'd realize the consequences of what had happened this day. Then he'd visit her hut no longer.

"My father told me," she said, needing to fill the silence of the room with something other than the sound of her own breathing, "that one of my ancestors was a woman of high standing. A priestess, in Ulster. This was at a time long, long ago, when the church was just coming to Ireland and the veils between the worlds shifted easily."

She released the pestle and rubbed her hands together, balling the bits of columbine which clung to her fingers. "She loved a man of the Otherworld—a man of *Tir na nOg*—and on one *Samhain* when the veils thinned to nothing she lay with him by the light of the fires."

She remembered when Da had told her the story while they sat on the ledges fishing for bream, not long after she'd discovered her own faery-gift. It had all seemed so logical then, with the *Sidh* dancing around them whilst they pulled fish from the sea. But that was upon Inishmaan, where nothing was quite what it seemed and no one thought to question the way of the world. Now, in this silent place with just Rhys listening, she felt as if she were telling a tale rather than revealing the roots of her family, the secrets of her faery-blood.

"They created a link of flesh and spirit, of faery and human, which kept the worlds together even as they were drifting apart. And so all of us born of that woman have faery-blood racing in our veins."

"Aileen—"

"No, don't stop me now, Rhys, not when I've the truth to tell at last." She heard his footsteps brushing across the paving stones and rushed on to have done with this. "We all have faery-blood running in our veins, and thus a faery-gift." She flexed her hands in front of her. "Mine is the gift of the healing hands."

"That's a strange tale for a father to tell a daughter to explain a gift God-given." He stood beside her, his breath brushing her ear. "You're no faery, Aileen the Red."

She smelled him now, oh, such a familiar scent, and closed her eyes to breathe in the full of it, perhaps for the last time. "I've faery-blood in me, Rhys, that's why I have this magic in my hands."

"I can see you," he continued, his voice dropping, low and gravelly now. "I can *feel* you."

At that he moved close behind her, close enough for their bodies to brush and set her skin alight with each touch. Her mind screamed, *Pull away,* but her body paid the voice no heed.

"You don't believe me," she whispered.

"There was a time when I didn't know what you were," he said. His lips came perilously close to the nape of her neck. "But I know now that you are woman, flesh and blood, through and through."

"Where does it say," she retorted, her voice quavering, "that I cannot be a bit of both?"

He kissed the crook between her neck and her shoulder. Aileen let her eyes drift closed, let her head rest back against his chest. She turned and rubbed her cheek against the fine weave of his linen tunic, and wished again for the thousandth time that she could be nothing but a woman, flesh and blood, without the responsibility of her faery-blood, and the price she must pay—to always be doubted by this man, the only man she would ever love.

"Look at me."

He moved her as if she were naught but a wooden doll, then forced her chin up to face the blaze of his blue eyes. The air swept out of her lungs, for by the golden light streaming through the doorway he was Rhys ap Gruffydd, Lord of Graig, all but whole again, as vital and handsome a man as ever walked the earth. One part of her heart ached for the man she'd known before, the masked man with the distorted face, the tormented soul who had opened up under the touch of her hands. The man who once needed her.

He needed her no longer.

"It looks," she stammered, under the intensity of his scrutiny, "as if I've finally fulfilled my side of the bargain."

He didn't answer. Had he spoken she wasn't sure she would have heard the words, for as their gazes locked a roaring began in her ears, the rush of blood and excitement through her body. Flesh and blood she was—more than spirit by the heat which rose to her skin—and in the space of a heartbeat all the memories of those winter nights returned, a blur of sensation of flesh against flesh, the rustle of linens and the hush of indrawn breath, the endless yearning for moist lips against an open mouth.

Then it was a memory no longer, but a thing living and breathing between them, as his mouth captured her jaw and made a mockery of memory. Sensation swept away all rational thought: His sun-warmed hair sifted between her fingers, his arm banded around her back. He tugged the linen from her head so her hair sprang unfettered around them. His skin tasted of honey-mead. Too long, too long it had been since those cold winter nights in the cocoon of warmth of his bed. Now, the heat of the July sun set her hair aflame as he hefted her hips upon the table and leaned her back, sending mortars and pestles clattering to the floor. A spot of sunlight trailed over her face, drifted down her neck, and rested on the bare, freckled skin of her bosom where Rhys tugged the ties open to suck upon her skin.

She braced herself against his shoulders as his lips worked magic, telling herself with tears pricking her eyes that it was no sin to follow the urges of her body. She'd forgive herself later for being so weak in his presence. No woman of sane mind could look into those blue eyes hot with need and find a way to make her tongue say, *no, no, not like this, not without love between us.*

It was too late, even if she'd found the strength, for his fingers worked magic under her skirts, trailing the inside of her thighs, thrusting them open and seeking the heat and the ache. He ground the heat of his own hardened loins against her, stoking the flames in a mockery of the lovemaking to come, until finally, finally, as she hung her arms around his shoulders and let her head fall upon them, he tugged up his tunic and fumbled with his *braies* and gave her what she needed—what *they* needed—and filled her up with himself.

It's nothing more than rutting, she told herself as his breath soughed harsh against her ear. It's nothing more, she insisted to herself, as his fingers curled into her hair, than a lord finding his pleasure in the arms of a willing maiden. To hope for more was to hope for the impossible—it was to wish for the moon—and now Aileen the Red knew better than to reach farther than arm's length.

She held the thought tight through his senseless murmurings; she held it tight as sensation coiled in her abdomen, losing it only when the world whirled around her and all thought shattered and she knew only the powerful thrust of his loins, the surge of his seed deep into her womb, the blinding joy of sated need.

The world came back to her swiftly: the singe of the sunlight on the top of her head, the poke of an overturned bowl in the small of her back, the rustle of a bird in the thatch above. The door to her hut hung ajar, and she heard the bondswomen gossiping at the end of the path, the children still racing around, out of sight only by the grace of God.

A foolish thing, they'd done here, when all the world lingered outside and could have seen them writhing together on a table. A fine thing that would have been, for a respectable healer, a woman unmarried, a mistress sent away.

His arms tightened around her as she made to move away. She lifted her head and her heart lurched, for the faintest smile lingered about his lips—an easy smile, for all the stretch of the skin unused to so simple a movement.

"Stop your fussing." He wiped something off her cheek. "They will all know soon enough, Irish, that you're my mistress again."

"Will they, now?"

Another bowl overturned and clattered to the floor as she extricated herself from Rhys's embrace. Mistress, then? Just as she'd thought. He wanted everything back the way it was. It was so easy for a man, easier for a lord. She brushed her skirts down over her legs and wiped the backs of them, where they'd grown damp from contact with the washed herbs. She set to her hair which snarled every which way and made a mockery of her efforts.

Giving up on vanity, she rounded the cauldron, avoiding his gaze as she seized the spoon and stirred the bubbling mixture. "And who says," she murmured through lips still throbbing with the need to be kissed, "that I'll consent to being your mistress again?"

He ran his hand over the space she'd vacated as he turned

and leaned back against the table. "You haven't retied the laces of your tunic, Irish."

Her face flamed as she realized the sleeves still hung over her shoulders, and by leaning over the cauldron she'd given him a view clear down, to breasts still tight with sensation. Well, what of it, after the passion of moments ago? She was not so much of a hypocrite that she'd deny she'd enjoyed the moment.

"Is this the way of all men, then," she said, tossing the spoon aside and setting her fingers to the laces, "to think that just because a woman got her pleasure from him, she'll make it a habit of going to his bed?"

"Yes. If she takes as much pleasure as you, Irish."

The flush of indignancy nearly choked her. "For all your arrogance, there's no use in me denying it."

"I have the bites on my shoulder to prove it." His voice dipped to a growl. "It's not as if you haven't shared my bed before."

"That was *before,*" she argued, tugging the laces tight, "and that makes all the difference."

The smile on his face withered. Sweeping her hair off her shoulders, she picked up the spoon again and set to the stirring with vigor. Damned fool of a man. Did he really think she could return to the *llys* with her heart throbbing so close to her skin, lay with him every night whilst she watched his life open up again to the world? Did he think she could give up this freedom she'd bargained for—this house of her own, this calling, this life she'd determined to forge for herself—just for the uncertain pleasure of having him in her bed for a short time?

Nay. She swallowed a lump that rose to her throat. *Nay.* Before, she'd considered her time in Wales as a time outside her life, a short period of unrestricted freedom in which she could take risks which wouldn't reverberate beyond these shores, a period outside of her Inishmaan. But now, she had determined to make this country her home. Anything she did here would have consequences far beyond the moment. If she lay with Rhys every night, she'd be known as the mistress of the Lord of Graig—perhaps for the rest of her life though the affair might not last through the year. But if she stayed here, chaste, in her own home, she'd be the healer of Graig. A person in her own right, with her life firmly in her own hands. Her heart as whole as she could keep it.

She couldn't give that up. Not for a man who wanted her only to ease his loins. A man who didn't love her.

Even as the thoughts passed through her mind, she knew there was more to it than this. For if she believed, even for a moment, that he would love her, that there was a chance he would someday make her his wife . . . then she'd risk everything. *Everything*. But he was healed now, if only partially. She supposed he'd tear down the rest of the castle to rid himself of the rest of the affliction, and then he'd be the same man he was five years ago—handsome and full of new ambition, triumphantly returning to the world he'd left behind, and able to attract the richest of heiresses with the finest of bloodlines. That would be the end of Aileen the Red.

There was some strange mockery in it all: She had healed him, only to lose him forever.

"You prefer," he said darkly, "this flea-ridden hut to lying on smooth linens by my side?"

"I prefer," she retorted, "my own bed and my own life to an uncertain one with you."

"Uncertain?" He pushed away from the table and loomed over the cauldron. "I've taken care of you well enough."

"I'll take care of myself, thank you very much. I've no liking to be 'taken care of' in the way you're thinking, for all the temporary pleasure it'll give me."

"You were crying out none of this when you were on that table."

"You should spend more time at Mass." She clattered the spoon on the table and crouched down into the heat to readjust the fire. "A woman's flesh is weak, and I'm no exception to that. You come storming into my house, my lord, swaggering and as handsome as ever, and start nibbling at me—well, what's a poor peasant to do, will you be telling me that? A bit of madness, it was, what we did on that table, and mind you, I'll muster every bit of strength I can to prevent it from happening again."

She thrust a poker into the flames until they died a bit, then hustled around the fire to pick up the debris fallen during that moment of madness, keeping her chin high and her will strong, and feeling the waves of anger emanating from him.

"Women always want sweet words." He reached for her, but she swiveled out of his way. "I don't have the tongue for it."

"Keep your words," she snapped, struggling with an armload of mortars and pestles. "It's not words I want."

"What do you want, then?" His hands curled into fists by his sides. "Don't ask for more than I can give you."

His words shot through her heart as surely as an arrow, piercing the single bud of lingering hope she hadn't even known existed. She turned her back upon him and thrust the bowls upon the table. "It is precisely because I know you can't give me what I want, that I don't bother to ask for it." She planted her fists on her hips and dared to face him, dared to meet his gaze. "You've told me yourself we are of different worlds—and I'm agreeing with you. In my world, faery-blood is a thing honored and cherished, but in yours it's nonsense; for you value knowing the names of your ancestors back twelve generations instead. There can be no future for us, and I've no liking for the role you'd have me play. Now, if you don't mind"—she clanked one bowl off another—"I've a salve to make for a boy in the river valley who burned himself yesterday on the kiln stones, so good day to you, my lord."

He didn't wait to hear her last words, but stormed out of the hut so suddenly that a gasp went up among the people lingering around his horse. She heard the jingle of harness as he hefted himself upon the beast's back, the pounding of hooves fading in the distance. Despite herself, she drifted to the door and leaned against the jamb, watching the dust of his passing settle. A great sadness weighed down upon her.

It was over. By her hand, no less. She waited for tears to come, for sobs to tear her apart.

The ache throbbed too deeply for tears.

Out of the dust emerged the figure of another rider. Dafydd glanced over his shoulder at the path of his brother's passing, and nudged his horse to her door.

"What a rage," he commented, dismounting and coming to stand by her. "Don't take it to heart, Aileen. It's hard for a man to believe in magic after so many years of not believing."

Her throat parched, and she blinked back the dry sting of her eyes. It wasn't even in the clearing of the faery-curse where the magic lay. The magic lay in the love she felt for him, the love he couldn't accept, the love she was no longer willing to compromise.

"You were right, though," Dafydd continued. "It was the castle. Mayhap the man will come to his senses and tear the thing down. I've had a belly full of it, truth be known."

Dafydd glanced at her, and his gaze stopped at her throat marked with redness, at the wrinkling of her tunic, at the wildness of her hair; and Aileen tilted her chin away as knowledge came into his eyes.

She didn't need to hear it. She didn't want to hear it, not now. "Dafydd, don't you know when it's best to go see to the cows or something?"

"I'll say nothing, then."

"And won't that be an effort for a man who can't stop his babbling any more than he can stop a herd of frightened cattle."

He mustered a faint laugh, then shuffled his feet. "It's not really Rhys I came here to talk to you about." He squinted toward the far rim of the hills and leaned back against the stone wall. "Seeing what you've done for him . . . well, I'd another matter I'd wanted to discuss. With you. As a healer."

She filled her lungs with air and stiffened her back. A healer, she was; that duty she could fulfill sure enough. "What is it? Too much mead to drink last night?"

"I was wondering. . . ." He toyed with the sleeve of his handless arm, then gently shoved the cloth above his wrist. "I was wondering . . . after all you've done for Rhys . . . if there was anything you could do about this."

Her gaze fell to his arm. He bailed the ruddy end of it in his good hand. Sympathy flooded through her. Not once in all the time she'd spent here in Wales had she ever heard him complain of this. Never had she seen it limit him in any way. All this time, all his life perhaps, he'd hidden this hope in his heart.

A strange thing, it was, to have such different brothers: One who believed in nothing, and the other who believed too much in magic.

"Aye, Dafydd. . . ." She laid her hand upon the fingerless knuckles and held them tight. "There's no knowing God's will. But in some things, it cannot be changed."

He managed a self-deprecating laugh, then pushed away from the wall to flash her a grin. "Didn't think so. Wouldn't know what to do with all those fingers anyway."

She watched him lumber down the path. He eased himself onto his horse, and tipped his fingers to her as he nudged his mount toward the *llys*. Whistling a light tune, he wove his way down the path, the sunlight flashing off reddish streaks in his chestnut-colored hair.

We all carry a bit of sadness inside us, she realized, as her vision blurred. The trick, she supposed, was in hiding it . . . at the same time spreading a bit of joy.

Twenty-one

Her heel sank into a grassy turf. Aileen bit her lip on a curse and stumbled up onto a fallen log. She frowned as she gazed at the reed-strewn ground around her. Father Adda had been sure she'd find some meadowsweet around this lake, but she'd slipped and slithered halfway around the boggy edge and seen no sign of the wildflower, though it was well into the season of its blooming.

Despite all his learning, Father Adda was a nervous, scattered sort. He'd probably mixed up the name of one lake with another. Ah, well, there'd be no loss to the day if she made it to Mass before the offering. She stepped off the log and sank into another patch of dappled mud. She just hoped her calfskin boots were not completely ruined. It would do her no good to arrive at Mass looking scratched and dirty, as if she'd spent the morning rolling in the muck.

Aye, she knew what the people of Graig would think if they saw her in such a state. They'd wink and whisper among themselves, and grant her gentle, knowing little smiles. There wasn't a thing that passed by these sharp-eyed Welshwomen. They'd known the moment Rhys had stormed out of her hut that there'd been more than conversation going on between them. For a full week Aileen had been ignoring their sly-eyed questions with as much dignity as she could muster, whilst her wretched freckled skin flamed redder than her hair, making a mockery of all her denials.

Reeds clustered in the ill-drained valley. They caved beneath her feet as she mucked her way to a patch of dry ground. Let them wonder, she thought. Rhys himself would soon enough dispel any of their imaginings. He'd not set foot on her paved path since, and had only passed through the cluster of houses at the base of the cliff when riding to the borders in search of his brothers, who continued to raid here and there with no pattern to their mischief. She'd been told he'd put a halt to the castle-building, but he'd made no effort to tear down the rest of the foundation.

That, she knew, was but a matter of time. For what man could resist returning to the world of his youth?

Purple foxglove, harebells, and butterwort sagged out of her basket. Wiping hair off her cheek, she squinted up through the dense fencing of trees which blocked the top of the slope. She'd gotten to know the pathways of these hills well enough, but this way was unfamiliar to her, and overgrown enough to show few people took this roundabout way to the church. Squinting up through the trees, she gauged the direction in which she walked by the slant of the sunlight, then hiked her skirts above her feet and set off into the thick.

The cool scent of leaves and green bark enveloped her under the hush of the deep woods. Saplings stood stiff around the knotted bark of their mother's trunks, stretching for what little light pierced the leafy canopy. Aileen pulled her way up the slope, startling thrushes which rustled in the verdure of thorny thickets and sending jays screeching amid the confusion of greenery. Midway up she paused, curling her fingers around an oak sapling.

Her lips lifted into the faintest of smiles. Aye, she hadn't imagined it, though the rustling of tiny feet had ceased the moment she'd paused to listen for them. In the wood-spice fragrance of such cool dark woods, the *Sidh* dared to emerge from their hiding places and patter about in the soft summer litter. She noticed the gentle swaying of a fern, though no wind seeped down from the height, noticed the drift of a leaf too young to fall from the tree and, just beyond, an ancient standing stone covered with ivy.

A warmth curled into her heart. In all her time in Wales, she'd sensed the *Sídh* only twice before; on the edge of the battleground in a moment of terror and in the woods around the half-built castle on the faery-mound. Now, with some of the mortar and stone removed from the land, the *Sídh* grew bold enough to slip through the veils of the worlds to greet her.

The patter of their feet faded as she strode beyond the ancient standing stone, and the circle of oaks around it, but her smile lingered. This she had done. Her mother would call it a fine, fair thing. Perhaps it was worth all the sadness she must live through in the years to come, to feel the singing joy of the faeries dancing upon these once-silent hillsides.

Perhaps it was the joy of hearing the *Sídh*, or the steepness of the climb and the rasp of her breath through her lungs, but she did not sense the sudden silence in the woods until she stepped out of them, into a clearing of rock just at the height of the hill.

She blinked into the blinding white light of the mid-morning and came to a sudden stop.

Ma and Da had told her that the *Sídh* could take the form of humans so well you could pass them thinking they were as whole as yourself. These horsemen lined up before her were dressed strangely enough to be of the *Sídh*. Jerkins of skin hung from their shoulders, over thighs covered by the most threadbare of woolen leggings. Blue woad-smeared faces were heavily mustached and bearded, framed with long matted hair braided through with bits of shell and stone. Javelins and sheafs of arrows poked up from their backs. Bare feet clung to the bare backs of their mounts. Only one man stood out, for having draped a bit of boiled leather over his mount, and strapped grass about his own feet in a sort of prickly boot.

A shock of recognition jolted through her.

She'd met those eyes before, beneath the stretch of an up-raised javelin. In a dappled glade not unlike the woods through

which she'd just emerged. But then the trees had been bare
and the ground had rustled with autumn leaves, and the world
had erupted around her in a chaos of high-pitched war-cries.

In the second before her basket of herbs slipped out of her
hand, in that moment before her muscles bunched for flight,
she took in the cluster of warriors and knew she faced the
renegade fury of Rhys's half brothers.

"Get her."

She heard the words over the snap of branches under her
feet, over the rush of the breeze in her ears and the roar of
terror in her head. Branches of saplings snapped across her
arms, whipped into her face and jerked her head back as they
snarled in her hair. She raced blindly down the slope, ignoring
the tearing of her woolen tunic and the slice of an edged stone
through the sole of her boot. Their mounts would never make
it through these thickets, she told herself as she sprung side-
ways through a dense netting of saplings; they'd have to dismount and follow her on foot. She gulped lungfuls of air and
pretended not to hear the crashing of heavier feet behind her,
pretended that a woman could outrun a clutch of strong, war-
hardened, desperate men; she told herself she could swim the
length of the lake if she dared, rather than splash her way
around it.

Black spots exploded before her eyes as someone snagged
her hair and snapped her head back hard enough to launch her
off her feet. She lost her footing and slipped down the slope
until her captor hauled her up against him. He stank like a
wild thing, of sweat and urine and unwashed flesh. The odor
filled her nostrils as he swung a meaty arm around her neck
and dragged her back up the slope. She clawed at his arm and
struggled for breath, but it was like clawing leather for all the
harm her ragged nails did on his battle-scarred skin. Too soon,
he swung her into the brightness of the clearing and tossed
her like a sack of barley upon the stone, where she lay on her
knees with her hands braced against the rock, choking air back
into her lungs.

The toes of two grassy boots came into her vision.

"Where are your bees now, witch?"

She leaned back onto her knees, fighting back the panic. Screaming would do naught but frighten the deer and the rabbits. The nearest settlement was two valleys away; the church, where everyone headed this time of the morning, yet another slope beyond. At Mass, people might gossip about her absence, but she wouldn't be missed until long after. They all knew of her propensity to wander off herb-gathering on a fine day.

She tumbled back at the blow to her jaw.

"Speak! They tell me you can mumble your witchery in Welsh as well as in Irish now." The leader crouched on his haunches before her. "Where are your demons to save you?"

His face spun in her vision as pain throbbed on her jaw. Blue woad caked the skin above a matted blond beard, a blue that echoed in his eyes. He'd dressed his hair so it stood up from a low and wrinkled forehead, like two horns above his eyes. Crouched there before her, he looked half-beast, half-man like a creature she'd seen once jutting out above a doorway to the monastery on the north island.

A gleam of cracked yellow teeth shone beneath the tuft of his mustache. He threw back his head with a cackle of a laugh while his gaze roved over her from head to muddy toe.

"No witchery for us now, eh? Has my brother Rhys banged it out of you?" He seized the hem of her dress and flipped it up, to laugh at her threadbare stockings before she yanked the tunic back down. "Legs like a chicken. For all my brother's gold, he couldn't find a better-looking witch?"

Laughter rippled among the men, but it was a nervous laughter, and when she glared at them it died off. There was power in this fear, the only power she held against such men.

"I think," the leader continued, his smile dimming, "that you used up all your magic. Otherwise, you'd be summoning your demons to ward us off, as you did to me before."

She clenched her hand into a fist in order to resist the urge to rub her sore jaw. Aye, to be a witch . . . She narrowed her

eyes upon the leader with all the contempt she could muster
To be able to mutter a few unintelligible words and turn this
creature into stone, to be able to summon a flock of crows
down upon them. A frisson of hate shook her spine, and she
clutched it as a stronghold against the fear.

"You dare much," she said, "coming so close to the *llys*."

"I dare nothing." He tugged a piece of straw from his makeshift boot and clamped it in his mouth. "Not from my brother,
and not from you. God has long abandoned my brother, despite
your meddling. And now your demons have abandoned you—
to us."

A strange emotion, hate. She had only felt it once before,
facing Edwen for the first time. Now it rose again, gut-deep,
the urge to scratch the grin from this man's face for all the
pain he'd caused Rhys, for all the misery he'd caused the people of Graig. In that moment, she understood a warrior's code,
she understood the blood-lust that drove a man to reach for
his spear or a bow and arrow, that allowed him to aim his
weapon at another human being.

The intensity of the emotion shocked her, fortified her. Hold
this hate, she told herself, for it will keep you whole.

"You have an eye on you, I'll grant you that." The leader
settled back on his haunches. "More power than that, if you've
done what they say you've done. If you've cured our brother
Rhys of his . . . unfortunate ailment."

"News travels swiftly in these hills."

"More swiftly," he countered, "than the wind."

"You should whisper." She leaned forward, close enough to
get a whiff of his stench. "Voices carry over these slopes. He'l
hear you . . . and he'll kill you."

"If he can catch me. Three years he's been trying to do
that."

She sank back. She knew those eyes of ice blue. Rhys's
father must have had the same eyes. Something twisted in her
to see them glittering in this man's face. To see them filled
with such absolute fearlessness, soulless as an animal's. For

all Rhys's torment, never had he lost that touch of pain in his eyes, that wall that spoke of so much hidden torment. She thought, this is what it is to lose all sense of humanity; this is what it is, truly, to be a beast.

She could pick up a knife or a lance and have done with him, as she would slaughter a cow or a rabbit for food, or a predator for threatening those she loved.

"It's true. Rhys is cured." She brushed some caked mud from her tunic and rose to her feet, then focused all her attention on the men around them. "He's cured. No more a maimed leader rules the lands of Graig. Now you've no standing on your claim to his lands."

"You're a woman—an Irishwoman. You speak foolishness. We're all Welsh sons of a Welsh father—we are entitled to this land." He jerked up, yanked the straw from his mouth, and raised his voice. "What are we to do with our good fortune, eh, brothers? We've captured our brother Rhys's lucky charm—an ugly heifer, but a prized one."

"You overestimate my importance to my lord of Graig." The words rang with painful truth. "He'd pay more for stolen cattle."

"Ransom? I'd not thought of that." He tossed the straw into the dirt. "We have no need of gold in these hills, and we slaughter any cattle that we steal—our own cattle." His lips curled as he stared her up and down. "I'm of a mind to think Rhys won't part with a kingdom for the likes of your bag of bones, even if you are the only woman who cares to tumble him."

The men snickered, and this time they did not look away when she glared.

"There is our brother Edwen. . . . Now, that's a score to be settled."

The men nodded their agreement. An eagerness vibrated in the air. An acrid scent rose around her, emanating from these men and their desperation; a rustling, an uneasy fluttering movement of the air. A crow screeched. She tilted her chin as

something cold washed over her skin. She stiffened her spine
even as she began to tremble.

"But a brother's life avenged with that of a mere woman?
A peasant woman, at that?" The smile disappeared, the glitter
in the leader's eyes faded and revealed the smoky uninhibited
hate of a trapped creature. "It's not an even match. Could
hardly pay tribute to a man as fine as Edwen, a warrior as
bold as he."

She took no hope in his words. She knew from the moment
she'd stepped into this clearing what her fate would be. She'd
entered into the heart of darkness, where judgment and mercy
no longer existed.

"We've only one choice." His nostrils flared. "We'll have
to make your death . . . spectacular."

She hoped she wouldn't cry out, that she would show the
honor of the daughter of Conaire, a daughter of Inishmaan.
She hoped she would have the strength and the courage to spit
in his face with her last breath. She hoped Rhys would remember her.

"What do you think, brothers?" The leader folded his arms
and tapped his finger against his painted cheek as if choosing
a tunic for the day. "The only way to rid oneself of a witch . .
is to burn her."

She'd expected the burning, but not the mockery.

While some of the men gathered wood for the pyre, the
leader tied her hands behind her and forced her to kneel on
the rock. He set himself up as a man of the church, complete
with his brother's skins draped around him, a tall curl of birch
bark as a conical hat, and a straight stick with a knot at the
end as his scepter. He pounded the scepter upon the rock with
effect when displeased that she would not answer his questions
or rise to his statements.

*Have you ever turned yourself into a rabbit and sucked milk
from the teat of a neighbor's cow?*

We've received reports from good Christians that you've been seen flying through the air on Midsummer's Night.

Good Owen here says he's seen you do your magic with a dead man's hand.

All this, splintered with a good knocking from one of the other men who jerked her hair back whenever the "bishop" roared his ire. Her ribs ached from the whack of his "scepter" and warm blood dripped over her cheek from a gash above her eye. The sun shimmered high in the sky and blazed the rock beneath her knees hot, and her throat dried until she knew she couldn't speak even if she dared. All the while the men pranced about, laughing at the antics of the "bishop" while the pyre they built grew higher, and higher. When aflame, she knew it would be high enough to be seen from the *llys*.

A bladder of ale tumbled from hand to hand. The mockery grew ribald; the "bishop" rubbed himself as the accusations grew more and more lurid.

Seducer of priests and monks; a demon's tongue can have its uses, can it not?

Confess to laying with incubi, to bearing demons of your own, and we'll throttle you to death instead.

Do you deny laying with the devil while you said the Lord's Prayer backward?

She listened to it with half an ear, too dazed from the knocking to pay it much more mind. How many times had she dreamed such a scene which always ended with the heat of flames at her feet, consuming her, consuming her and all the devilry people thought her capable of? Here it was, the trial, the pyre, and it was all mockery, nothing but revenge against the man she loved, a man who couldn't love her enough.

Poor Ma . . . Should she hear of this, Deirdre would blame herself for sending her own daughter back to her death. *Aye, Ma, I chose it myself.* But she didn't have that kind of power, to send a thought across the seas. The words lingered in her head and no farther.

She lifted her face to the blue sky above, knowing it was

useless to pray for rain, knowing that now she was probably
beyond prayer but for the redemption of her soul. She had
made many choices these past months, difficult ones, and now
she wondered if she'd done the right thing. How short life
could be, how quickly it could be cut off, and no man or
woman could choose their own time. All she had was the here
and the now. It would soon be over with no more said between
her and Rhys.

I love you, Rhys.

The first tear oozed out from her swelling eye and trickled
down her face to join the blood spotting her tunic. The leader's
recitations droned in her ears. Her legs ached from kneeling;
her knees stung from scraping against rock. The cut on her
foot throbbed, and her arms stung with slashes.

Yes, she had loved in this life. Only a year ago she'd dismissed the idea that she would ever be loved. True, she'd never
heard gentle words from Rhys's lips, but she'd felt the heat of
his passion. She'd felt *needed,* and not for her healing hands
or for the herbs and comfort she could give—she had felt like
a woman desired.

When the "bishop" cast out his arms and called for silence
so he could render his judgment, she lifted her head of her
own accord and stared at him through eyes full of pity.

She had lived a fuller life than most, fuller, surely, than any
of these ragged, pagan-looking warriors scuttling about like
anxious wolves in a pack. She had healed and been healed,
she had loved and been loved, and she would leave this life
with a clear conscience.

"Guilty."

He thrust his face at her. The stench of his breath, tinged
now with rancid ale that had taken on the taste of the bladder,
filled her nostrils. Though she'd not had a drop to drink under
the hot sun, though it hurt to move the flesh of her throat to
swallow, she sucked through her cheeks and willed one last
bit of moisture . . . so she could spit it straight into his face.

She laughed at the enraged shock in his eyes, laughed even

as he backhanded her clear out of her guard's hands, and continued to laugh in big heaving gulps. Someone hauled her up by the armpits and set her on wobbly feet, then pushed her toward the pyre looming up in the center of the rock. She shook away from them and walked of her own power toward what she'd known was her destiny since she'd first discovered her gift.

Then she heard the first shout. Still, she didn't stop, for one shout was like another in this mockery of a trial, and the men had taken to making bloodthirsty war cries. So she stumbled forward and glared up at the pyre and wondered how on earth she was to climb the thing with her hands tied around her back.

She turned to spit mockery at the leader, and found the men scattering like so many rats. The leader stood clutching a flagon of mead, barking unintelligible orders and pointing at her, but the men mounted their horses and paid him no mind. She wondered what was happening as she stumbled back over a piece of wood and cracked her elbows on the ground.

The leader threw down his "scepter" and stormed toward her. He yanked a knife from his waist. Her heels scraped against the earth as she pushed herself back. The stakes of the pyre dug into her back and brought her to a fierce halt. Still he came, intent firm in his eyes, and she began to pray.

Our Father, who art in heaven. . . .

She wondered if the steel would seep in soft and cold, or if it would strike bone and singe as it sank. She wondered if Rhys would bury her among the Christians in the cemetery on the chapel grounds, or if he would leave her pagan body in an unmarked grave, thinking in his confused way that would be what she wanted.

Hallowed be thy name. . . .

How quiet the clearing, despite the rustling of horses and the pounding of hooves down the north slope. The world slowed down around her. She could chart the waving of each coarse summer leaf against the blue sky. She noticed the flutter of wind under a bird's wings as it dipped over the clearing. She watched the flying of the leader's laces around his shins as he approached.

Thy kingdom come. . . .

Aye, full of imaginings she was, for something tore through the shadows up from the southern slope, a snarling black thing flashing through the leaves, all teeth and foam. A blur of something Otherworldly, perhaps the *Sidh* . . . but it was too late to help, for the beast's shadow was upon her, blocking out the sight of the thing. She closed her eyes against the flash of the knife as it arced down.

Thy will be done. . . .

A weight collapsed upon her; crushing her against the staves. *Where is the burning? Where is the icy steel?* she wondered as she gasped for breath too thick to suck into her lungs. Something trickled warm over her shoulder and she knew it was her blood draining from her body. *Is this it, then? A crushing weight upon her, the slow choke into blackness?*

Then, in a moment, the weight lifted and a gust of cool air shimmered over her skin and the blue sky blinded her. With a rush she filled her lungs with air, and coughed and coughed, her body bucking with each spasm.

"Get them—*get them.*"

The words roared in her ears. A rush of breeze swung her hair out from her face as the earth rumbled beneath her. Hands fell upon her, rough and uncompromising, squeezing all the sore places on her body and making her cry out at the pain, a cry which died against something warm and hard, some textured cloth that smelled of hazel-bark and lye.

"You can't die, Irish."

Those hands trembled. She winced, one eye open, and peered up at the voice. She tried to muster a smile as she felt herself heaved up off the ground, up toward the blue sky with its soft, welcoming clouds.

How appropriate that she'd be taken off to Heaven in the arms of an angel. An angel with the face of Rhys.

* * *

Rhys pounded into the *llys* and swept off the horse before his mount skidded to a stop, then slid the bloody bundle of a woman into his arms. He strode across the yard and kicked open the door to the mead-hall.

"Water. Linens. Fetch Marged. *Now.*"

Mead slopped on his sleeve as he shouldered by a servant. Going sidewise through the portal of his room, he barked for fire, dropped to one knee, and stretched Aileen over the furs.

Gripping the edges of her tunic in both hands, he yanked until the cloth gave, then flattened his ear against her chest.

She was still alive.

He seized a fur and swept it over her body, tucked it tight around her legs, her hips, her waist, her arms. Keep her warm. Make sure she breathes. Check the bleeding. He yanked the fur off and ran his hands over her body. Cuts on her arms, her head, her jaw.

Find them, Dafydd. Find them and bring them to me so I can hang them all from the palisades.

He roared up to his full height and stared down at her, battered and bruised and for all he knew hovering close to death. He flexed his hands, raging at his own impotence. He knew nothing of healing, but what he'd learned by necessity on the field of battle, where most men died before their wounds were properly tended to.

"Don't leave me, Irish."

The words wrenched out of him. He didn't recognize his voice. What if that boy hadn't gone in search of a lost calf? What if that boy hadn't spied the horses on the hilltop? The lad could have headed to church instead of to the *llys,* where only by way of a broken harness Rhys tarried. And had Rhys raced up that slope a few minutes later, that pyre would still be belching smoke to the sky.

Luck. Nothing but luck had kept her from the razor's edge of death.

"By all the saints, my lord, aye, you did find her!" Marged hurried in. "We were all wondering why she wasn't at church. Father Adda was more than a bit worried, I tell you, for he was supposed to be giving her some herb for— Saints alive, what happened to her?"

"Tend to her."

"Of course, of course." Marged's jowls shuddered as she skittered to Aileen's bedside. "By God's Glory, my lord, look what they've done."

"Do something."

"I don't know the first of such things, but to wash her." Marged wrung her hands and glanced over her shoulder to the pitcher of water on the table by the door. "Aye, I'll wash her, then see to that bump on her head. Seems to me I remember her putting a cold linen upon Roderic's son when he stumbled on the hillside. . . ."

Marged's nervous chattering whirled to a whine in his ears. He dug his nails into the palms that ached to grab the soul of the woman he loved and drag her back to the living. *Don't drift off to your wretched faery-place. Stay here with me.*

I need you.

"Faith, my lord, she's laying there as if—" Marged jerked up from her perch on the edge of the bed. "You must send for someone. That doctor from Aberffraw . . . someone . . ."

"Myddfai." This he could do. "I'll send Roderic to Myddfai for a physician."

"That's too long to travel, and I don't know what to do for her but make her comfortable. What if—"

"Tie mint leaves around her wrist. Put a knife under her bed to cut the pain. I don't give a damn. Just keep her alive."

"My lord!" Marged's feet scraped against the rushes. "Where are you going?"

He set his eyes on the light streaming around the mead-hall door. "To get help."

The sun glowed through the summer leaves which feathered over the shores of Llyn Dyffryn. Rhys kicked his mount past vines of wild strawberries which sagged off tree trunks and crept across the grassy path. Lavender scented the crease of the pass, and teased him down toward the chapel of rubble-and-stone wedged between mountain and a gurgle of stream.

Rhys burst through the chapel door. Father Adda stumbled up from his seat by the altar, gripping the Eucharist cup and a piece of linen. Rhys strode down the nave, his gaze fixed on the cross hanging over the altar. His knees scraped the floor.

The cup clattered on the paving stones.

"Forgive me, Father, for I have sinned. . . ."

Twenty-two

The physician of Myddfai swept into the room in a stench of perfume so strong it set Rhys to choking.

"Ahhh, my lord, I've just the thing to put an end to that cough." The physician reached into his wide-sleeved robe and pulled out a small packet. He handed it to a young man hovering behind him. "Boil figs in strong ale, and add this to the liquid." The physician bowed and smiled wider. "The brew is good also for rheumatism and chillblains, my lord, and for preventing drunkenness."

"In such a Christian household!" Aileen said, straightening where she was propped up against the mound of pillows upon his bed. "We've no problems of the like here, Doctor."

Aileen ignored Rhys's scowl as the physician murmured all the appropriate remarks. Doctor number three, this one was, and perhaps the most ridiculous of all, with his long white beard and his white eyebrows oiled into curls. She was disappointed, for this one was said to be descended from the race of the faeries.

"This," Rhys began, "is the physician of Myddfai, known far and wide as the best physician in all of Wales. He has traveled far to see to you."

"I'm afraid you've wasted your time, Doctor, and my lord has wasted his gold." Aileen shoved up the unsewn sleeve of the linen tunic he'd given her to wear, and showed the bruises of earlier bleedings in the crook of her elbow. "This is by far the most damage this body of mine has suffered, and it was done right here in this room."

"Bleedings?" The physician pursed his lips. "It is clear by your disposition, my lady, that you have no need for bloodletting. Now if you were more melancholy—"

"Choleric is what I am." She tugged the sleeve down and glared at Rhys. "And getting more so by the minute."

"My lord . . ." The physician curled his fingers around Rhys's arm and drew him away from the bed. Bells jingled from somewhere beneath his cloak, and the light from the smoke-hole gleamed off the embroidered moons, stars, and suns scattered across the dark blue wool. A clear blue amulet flashed where it hung from his chest. She scowled at the two of them whispering with their heads together, as if she were some ignorant idiot and not a healer in her own right. She heard the physician discussing the color of her hair and the alignment of the stars and how much time it would take for a full recovery until she couldn't stand anymore of the hypocrisy.

"If you want to be helping," she interrupted, "then get me some of that wild cherry juice that last physician prescribed. Or put saffron in my milk—aye, I've developed a taste for that. And you won't see me objecting to almonds, or those sticky little red fruits the physician from Aberffraw brought from the Holy Land—"

"It's good to see you have an appetite," the physician said, his smile not quite reaching his eyes. "But we have a saying in Myddfai."

"Do you, now?"

" 'Supper has killed more than ever were cured by the Physicians of Myddfai.' "

She jerked upright on the bed. "Have the physicians of Myddfai killed so many, then?"

"It is more wholesome to smell warm bread," the physician persisted, "than to eat it."

She glared at Rhys, and ignored the flex of his cheek. "What kind of healer have you sent me, who starves a patient?" She tossed the covers off her legs. "I won't have it."

"Get back into that bed, woman."

"Get back in that bed, get back in that bed. Haven't I heard that enough from you, Rhys ap Gruffydd?" She swung her knees over the side and let the sweep of her hair veil her flush from his gaze. "Well, lord or not, I won't be eating the powdered poisons he makes, all the beetle's backs and the like. He can stuff them in his own mouth."

"Perhaps," the physician interrupted in the calm sing-song voice that made her hair stand on end, "it would be better if I stepped out for a moment."

"Step out and keep on walking," Aileen called after him, rising to her feet and slapping her tunic down her knees. "We have no need of you here in Graig, I'll have you know, I'd kill the patient myself before sending him to the likes of you."

The door banged shut behind the physician. Rhys turned on her with murder in his eyes.

"Don't you be looking at me like that." She hiked up the long tunic and nudged the fallen covers with her toe. "I've told you enough times—you're wasting your gold with those men."

"We've none of your skill here."

"You've no need of anyone at all. Your brother didn't stab me with that knife. All he left were bruises and scratches which only God and time can rid me of; and no stinging poultices, no poking and prodding, and no bleeding, will do a bit of good."

She crouched down and tugged up the fallen covers, searching for her tunic. Aye, she knew how battered she looked, with one eye swelling and her cheek purple with contusions, her arms and her legs streaked with angry scratches. Her ribs still ached and would for some time, she supposed. But she had to get out of this room with all its memories, out of this bed and the rasp of its furs, away from the pillows which smothered her with the scent of man and loving. She had to escape the fierce blue gaze of the man who'd hovered over her for days, touching her, always touching her, and making her yearn for things she had no right to want.

"What were you doing anyway, spending gold on such men? I'm naught but your subject." She seized her dress, shook it out, then cast him a glare. "Did you have them bleed me when I was weak, just to see if I would bleed green?"

"I knew the color of your blood," he growled, "when I dragged you from under my brother's dead body."

New heat flushed her cheeks. She didn't want to think of those foggy moments, else she'd be imagining things again. The tightness of his grip, the feel of his lips in her hair. The fierceness of his voice.

"Well, I won't have a minute more of this coddling. I'm no child, and I've work to be done." She tugged her old woolen tunic, stained with blood and snagged in a dozen places, over her head. "I'm going," she muttered under the cover of wool, "back to my home. You've enough to do in this house without having a sick woman in your room. It's a long voyage to Aberffraw. It's not good to keep a prince waiting when he invites you to his castle."

He flinched. "So you've heard."

"Do you think your brother boxed my ears so hard that I've lost my hearing? Of course I've heard. The servants talk of nothing else but the Prince of Wales's invitation."

The courier arrived two days ago, bearing an invitation for Rhys to join the Prince at Aberffraw to celebrate the knighting of one of Llewelyn's foster sons. Rhys hadn't mentioned a word to her. By now every sword, shield, every metal boss on every horse's harness must be polished to the brightest sheen in preparation for the trip. Part of her heart thrilled for Rhys, for now he would have his triumphant return. Now he could face the men who'd betrayed him, and be restored to his rightful place at the side of the Prince of Wales. He could again assume the life the affliction had stolen from him. The life she'd given back to him.

"I'm not going to Aberffraw."

The netting she struggled to sweep over her hair snapped out of her hand. Her gaze flew to him as hair sprang over her shoulders, and it was if she looked upon a stranger. Not because he stood before her unmasked, not because the affliction had receded to a ripple along his jaw and thus the true breath-stealing beauty of the man showed, not because he'd taken to wearing a blue silken tunic edged with braids of gold that made him look like the Prince he was . . . but because his eyes shone with the same bright determination she'd seen the day he'd kidnapped her off the coast of Inishmaan.

"I'm not going to Aberffraw," he repeated.

Her breath froze in her throat.

"Not," he said, "without you."

One day in late winter, Rhys had hunted with Dafydd in the woods just south of Moel Cefn. They'd trailed the path of a boar over a league, beating him out of hiding and chasing him across uneven ground. More than once the beast turned to fight his attackers, forcing them to retreat under the threat of those wild burning eyes and flashing tusks, but finally they trapped him in a rocky ravine. The beast turned on them, heaving. In the moment before Rhys set loose his lance, the creature stood proud, waiting for the death blow.

So he waited now, his heart pounding as if he'd raced through the winter woods, watching his woman across the length of this bedroom, waiting for her words to pierce him dead. She'd cast him away before, for airy reasons he had only now begun to grasp. In his arrogance he'd thought she'd want better than a hut that smelled of cow and a pallet of scratchy wool, that she'd want him for his wealth and his position. Strange woman. Uncommon woman. Born dirt-poor, she knew nonetheless that love was more important than the wealth of kings.

What did he know of love—damn her—of gentle things and

soft words? All he knew was he wanted this woman standing so proud by his bed. He wanted to bury his hands in that nest of hair, to tilt that face up to his and see the silver spark of her eyes, the softness that made her lips as moist as dew, and then taste them . . . taste them.

Then he was standing in front of her, not knowing how he'd got there, not remembering crossing the room, just suddenly standing there breathing in the scent of wild lavender rising up from her hair—so strong, so fierce he could be standing in a field of it with the sun warm on his back and the earth ripe under his feet. She did that to him, made him feel like a boy of fifteen eager for the taste of a woman, blind for it, his heart throbbing so hard in his chest and his loins heavy-hard with need.

It had ever been like this whenever he stepped within the circle of her body. All the thoughts of a triumphant return that had burned in his head blew away like ashes in the wind. She did this. She was the flame that burned away the rage that blinded him, showed him that it wasn't Aberffraw he lusted after all these years but something more basic, something he'd held in his hands before he'd sent her away, something he'd never find in that nest of vipers—something as simple as long winter nights and a bed warmed with Aileen.

She stood before him as mute as stone, her face swelling from the beating which only made her clear gray eyes all the sharper, all the more intense. Would she make him say it, would she make him fall upon his knees like a wretched pilgrim? What magic had she conjured around him to make his loins surge at the smell of her, while his head screamed not to touch her, not to hurt her anymore, to leave her to her life and her independence and her pride . . . to her own choices?

Her lips parted; a breath trembled between them.

Beware of faery women, he'd been told all his life. Don't let yourself be bewitched. They tempt a man with their fair tresses and uncommon beauty, they lure him into the faery-dance, then urge him to steal a kiss . . . a kiss that would capture a man in the madness of love and condemn him never to leave the enchanted faery-place.

Oh, but for one single taste of Paradise . . .

She lived a thousand years in the moment Rhys stood before her, searching her face as if he were searching for life itself in her features. She knew with that fierce, blinding knowledge that comes to a woman in such times that she would remember this moment for the rest of her life. The intensity of his eyes, a turbulent blue to rival the blinding waters of Galway Bay after a gale had swept away the clouds and the foam. The twitch of a muscle in his darkly bristled cheek. The stumble of a pulse in his throat. The fragrance of a green hazelshoot perfuming his ragged breath.

Every bone in her body dissolved into honey. She didn't breathe. She waited. For him to pull away. For that mask to shutter his eyes. She waited for the fantasy to stop and reality to finally wake her. She waited for things she didn't want to dream of; and even as she stood before him she found herself swept away in the river of her fantasies, for hadn't she curled up on that lonely pallet in her home every night since she'd returned to Wales, thinking about this very room, this very bed, this very man. Only in the darkness did she ever take out her hope and look at it; only in the night did she let herself imagine a handsome, mighty lord might love so fiercely as to take a spindly-legged peasant to wife.

Aye, but in her dreams her hair tumbled down in silken waves and her body softened to generous curves and her skin shone with pearly luminescence. . . . And didn't her breasts feel heavy now, didn't her hair cloud around her face, didn't her cheeks glow with the gentlest of heat? What a fine illusion in this harpstring's pluck of a moment, to feel more beautiful than the legendary Deirdre of the Sorrows.

She trembled as the still air crackled around them and the room pulsed with its brilliant, blinding white light, as it might

in the moment before lightning struck. He scraped a hand
along her jaw, then cupped it in the palm, while his fingers
trailed up to tug a strand of hair clinging to the corner of her
lips. Her body swayed toward his; their clothing brushed, cre-
ating sparks between them. He scraped a thumb along her
cheekbone, then pressed the swelling tenderness of her lower
lip.

Surely this was death, the blinding headlong race toward a
Paradise too beautiful to behold.

"Aileen."

The word a whisper, the word a dream, no harp's melody
had ever sounded so sweet.

She said yes before he even asked the question; she felt her
lips move though only a whisper of sound came out on a
breath. Her heart sang the word—*yes yes yes*—and she curled
her fingers into all that blue silk, tugging him down even as
she raised to her toes; anything, anything to feel his lips finally
upon hers.

He spoke as his hands scraped off her face and sifted
through her hair, as he gripped her head and held it still. He
spoke with his lips pressed against her skin, he spoke in a
voice broken and ragged and husky with passion.

"Aileen . . . be my wife."

She spoke her yes into his mouth.

Aileen stood in the circle of stones as the last of the summer
light streaked the sky purple. The first orange embers of *Lughnasa* fires flickered among the black crags of the hilltops.
Torches pierced the ground between each standing stone
around her, emanating the thick scent of pine resin and a mist
of blue smoke that rose into a sky just beginning to glitter
with stars.

The wind shifted. Aileen closed her eyes to breathe in the
salt-sweet warmth of the first breath of *Lughnasa*. She smelled
the honey-mead and the smoke of the soil fires—aye, and she

heard the music, too, the ringing of a harp, the happy wail of
pipes, the rustle of veils grown thin and blown about as the
air of each world mingled. Around her, the grass rustled. A
pebble clattered off one of the standing stones. The water lapping the reed-strewn shore of the island rippled with new intensity. She knew she was no longer alone.

The *Sídh* had come to give away the bride.

A shiver fluttered through her body, tightening the symbols
of blue woad painted upon her belly, her breasts, her legs. A
white silk robe fluttered around her calves, open partway to
the sweet summer air. Twilight cast its shadowy hand across
the valley. Soon enough, she told herself, with a weakening in
her knees—soon enough, Rhys would come and make her his
wife in the old way, as her father had married her mother, and
as her grandmother had married, before them. On this faery-
island in the midst of a river, on a sacred spirit night, she and
Rhys would finally become one body, one spirit, one life.

Outside the ring of torches, all lay silent but for the lapping
of the river . . . yet she heard the sudden shift in the gentle
gurgling. Aye, he'd wasted no time after the setting of the sun
to leave the opposite shore and join her. As moments passed,
something brushed into the forest of reeds by the shore, and
an oar knocked upon the wooden rim of a coracle.

Her heart trembled in her breast. She didn't need eyes that
could pierce the darkness to know those muffled footsteps belonged to Rhys. Nor did she need the knowledge that two
dozen of Rhys's bondsmen ringed the valley on high, watching
for a danger that wouldn't come, since Rhys's brothers had
scattered into England after the death of their leader. No, she
sensed with a sense beyond meaning that the swift shuffle of
those footsteps up the bank belonged to the man she loved
with a whole and tender heart.

So when he stepped through the fencing of torches and
standing stones, into the warm amber glow of light, she waited
for him with her arms spread wide.

He wore the white robe she'd sewn for him, out of linen

bought for her own wedding-clothes for the Christian ceremony which would follow hard upon this. His dark hair, unbound and shining with dressing, lay upon his shoulders. If it
weren't for the way he cast his eyes about the circle of stones,
she could mistake him for one of the Druids who once wor-
shipped in this sacred place.

Then he set his eyes upon her and the world faded away.

After all this time, she still woke by his side in the mornings
and gazed at his smooth, handsome face and wondered at the
absurdity of it all, that a woman as plain and unlikely as she
would be marrying a nobleman with the face of a fallen angel.
For it was all gone now, every last bit of the affliction. The
faery-mound they stood upon had once held the mortar and
stones of his half-built castle. That castle was destroyed now,
and he'd set the standing stones back in their places. By her
request alone, he'd torn down his dream, and with a shrug of
his shoulder had told her it was an old dream and the time
had come to build a new one.

Thus, he put all the world to right.

No more screaming rose from this ground, nay, and though
scars still remained upon the land from the hasty removal,
they'd soon heal over. Tonight, this joining of her faery-blood
with that of a mortal man, would be like a poultice upon the
land, the start of the healing.

He strode toward her with fierce intent, the *Lughnasa* wind
tossing his hair around his face, but as he neared his steps
faltered. He halted an arm's-length from her, while his gaze
scoured the robe from her body.

"By God's Nails . . ."

She breathed in a deep and trembling breath, for the shifting
of his robe revealed to her the fullness of her own power over
him. Aye, there was the wonder of it. Look what she could do
to the man. Here she was, Aileen the Red, nothing but a bony
lass from Inishmaan with a bit of a quirk—marrying a great
lord of Wales, a man so handsome, so powerful, so strong that

the very sight of him walking toward her stole her breath from her lungs.

Aye, Ma was right, all that time ago, when she'd said there are powers beyond this world with plans of their own, and there's no telling how they'll weave the path of one's life. What a wonderful tapestry they'd made of hers . . . and it was only just begun.

"It's a fine thing," he rasped, "that Father Adda won't be here to witness this."

"Father Adda will have his own ceremony, soon enough."

"A dull one it will be after this, Irish."

She let her smile drift wider, then shrugged her shoulders out of the silk so it sluiced down her naked body into a shimmering pool at her feet. His breath caught in his throat. His chest expanded. Her nipples tightened under the blue woad into sharp, exquisite points of sensation—throbbing under the brush of his gaze.

He reached out and traced the edge of a symbol painted upon her belly. "What's this?"

"Ancient things." Her skin tingled where he touched. The blue woad tightened. "Symbols. Prayers of a sort. For fertility."

"My pagan." He curled his hand under her jaw. "Good for you that the Christian ceremony is only in a few weeks."

"You've no need to fear for my soul, Rhys."

"No, and I've no fear for that. But tonight," he growled, lowering his face to hers, "I'm filling you with child."

"It always worked," she murmured on a throaty laugh, "for my mother."

He laughed, that joyous sound she'd still not gotten used to. A bright thing, of many shades . . . now rumbling and full of promise, leaving in its wake a smile so breathtaking. . . . It was as if she'd never looked upon the man before, as if she'd been blind and only now could see the joyous man who'd been trapped so long in this shell of his body.

"Well, Irish," he whispered against her lips. "Are there any words to be said?"

"Words?"

"A ceremony." He trailed a finger over her breast. "Something to chant under the stars. A pagan dance you'll have me do, and spend a lifetime teasing me about. Speak now, Irish, or there'll be no more talking."

She'd half a mind to set him prancing about like a rooster or play the randy bull, howl at the moonless sky . . . but her heart wasn't into the mischief. Her heart was too full of love. Truth be known, with his naked flesh so close to hers, with his fingers dancing over her breast and the salt-sweet wind of *Lughnasa* in her head, her body pulsed hot with the magic of the night. She was too full of wanting to wait.

"Love me," she whispered, stepping into the warmth of his embrace and holding his face in her hands. "Love me, and we shall be one."

His robe rustled to the ground. She wound her arms around those broad shoulders, broad enough for a woman to lay a lifetime of worries upon. Flesh pressed against flesh in the open air, their world defined by the amber glow of the torches off the gleam of standing stones. Through the haze of pine-smoke, the stars gleamed down upon them. The wind whistled music through the river-reeds.

He tasted of the honey-mead she'd told him to drink, tasted of passion and love . . . and she tasted him over and over, like a woman starved for love and finding it here, now, and finding an answer in the kisses he lay hot upon her. She'd never tire of the kissing. His hands lay everywhere upon her body, and as he pressed her down upon the grass she stretched herself open for him, welcoming his weight and his heat and soon, oh, so soon, the throb of his loins against her inner thigh, the very root of the man. There'd be no long lovemaking tonight, at least not at once, not while the heat of the *Lughnasa* fires pulsed in their blood. She'd felt this every season as a girl, when she'd lingered out of the light of the fires and watched the others dance and throw themselves through the flames and then melt away in couples into the shadows.

She'd never be alone in those shadows anymore.

But as she opened herself up for him, as he shifted his weight upon her . . . he paused to lift his head.

She spoke his name on a rasp of a breath. Getting no answer, she blinked her eyes open and followed the path of his gaze. They lay alone in the sacred circle, alone but for the gurgle of the river around the island and the crackle of the torch-fires.

"What is it, Rhys?"

"I don't know." He lifted himself up on his elbows, suddenly tense. "I hear . . . something."

She lay her hand against his chest and cocked her ear . . . and another smile tilted her lips. Aye, she heard it, too, the rustle of wind in the reeds, the patter of tiny footsteps reeling in dances, the high whine of faint and distant music—the celebration of the union to come, drifting through the thinning veils of the worlds. She took Rhys's head in her hands and lay the softest of kisses upon his lips, until he relaxed in her arms.

"Aye, Rhys. . . . I'll make a believer out of you yet."

Epilogue

The day had begun like any other summer morning here in the lands of Graig.

At the first sound of cock's crow, I poked my head out of one of the windows of the new castle. Below, mist curled up from the gurgle of the river. Silence swathed the valley, and even from within the lazy bustle of the castle itself I could hear the cows lowing on their summer pastures high in the hills. It was a fine, cool morning and so I set myself to get the first pail of water of the day straight from the river, to put some oats to boil, so there'd be nothing but good in the house all day. But first I was after bustling into the master's chamber and taking the little one from where he slept between the master and the mistress, then hefting him on my hip for the journey.

I take him in the mornings, you see, to give the mistress a bit of rest, though truly she doesn't get much of a respite. For I know the moment I leave the room my lord is upon her, for though they seem to sleep like the dead whenever I come in, I hear their laughter as I close the door upon them. Well, I suppose my lord must work as hard as he can to try to get another babe from her. The mistress doesn't take too quickly to child, you know—not from lack of interest from the master, I tell you—she's just that way, as some women are. The shameless truth of the matter is that I think neither she nor he complain about the labor a bit. They enjoy it as shamelessly as pagans, and the one child she has borne is so healthy that it's unworldly.

He squirmed on my hip that morning, all bright unearthly green eyes like his grandmother on his mother's side—and all full of mischief as was his way.

And so we set off through the grand castle gates with the sentinels standing so stiff on either side, and I sang a little Irish song I remembered from when I used to sing it to his father, God bless him. It was promising to be the finest day, with the cuckoos singing down upon us, and I saw a white lamb skitter across our path as swift as can be, and then I knew it was to be a lucky day.

So when I got to the river's edge I set Wiliam down beside me and gave him the ring of keys the master entrusted me with. What a bothersome thing, always jingling and jangling and banging on me hip, but I'll not be one to give back such an honor, not while I still draw breath. Still I wonder why we needed so many rooms in the new castle. No sooner had I turned around and dipped my bucket in the water when I was hearing a voice behind me.

"A bright morning to you, mistress."

I nearly fell headfirst into the water, I tell you, with the shock of it all; and I turned around to yell at the man, but the words stopped in my throat. No man of Graig, this, with his tattered and odd-looking clothes, leaning upon a gnarled knot of a stick and grinning his yellow smile at me, looking as if he'd topple over with the faintest of pushes but for the black, dancing mischief of his eyes.

"I wondered," he continued, as if he hadn't snuck up behind me from the very grass, "if you'd mind sharing a drop of that water in your pail. I'm mighty parched, you see, having traveled far this day."

Well, what was I to say? He was an old man, and so weak, and my heart went out to him. It was common enough for visitors to pass this way, now that we lived here in the valley near the river and a bit of a road, and no longer in that smoky

*old mead-hall on the crag only a single horse could climb.
Common enough for Irish to come, too, with the mistress's
relatives always making their way here and staying a while,
wild bunch that they are. I handed him the pail and let him
drink his fill of it. As I watched him, I wondered if my mind
was slipping, for there was something familiar about the man,
something I couldn't place.*

"Where'd you come from, traveler?" I asked.

*With the pail to his lips he pointed vaguely to the eastern
hills, to the peak upon which Lake Dyffryn lay, the lake where
that young boy went last year claiming he'd seen a faery-bride,
and came down months later as happy as could be, trailing
behind him the whitest cow you've ever seen. A cow that bore
two calves every season and the richest milk you ever set into
your mouth.*

*"A blessing on you, mistress," the traveler said as he handed
the pail back, though why he was blessing me for water when
a river of it flowed free behind me and no one would have
stopped him for kneeling over and drinking his fill of it. Then
he set his eye on the little one rattling the keys and asked his
name. After I told him, he grinned a wide grin and began
jabbering at Wiliam in Irish.*

*Now, it was no wonder the man set to the boy. The boy had
a light of his own that drew all people to smiling at him. So
it was the boy that caught my eye, for he laughed as if he
understood every word the man was after saying, when he had
not yet reached the age where he could even mutter his
mother's name. Then I thought—this must be one of the mistress's relatives, that's why the boy and the man took so well.
And I rattled my brain trying to loosen the man's name from
it and it just wouldn't come to me . . . strange. It's true, my
mind isn't what it used to be, years ago, but I'm not near as
daft as some of the new castle-servants would make me out
to be.*

*Then I spied two of the kitchen girls striding out of the
castle with their own pails. Wanting the first for myself I turned*

to refill mine, watching man and boy out of the corner of my eye. Thinking, how small the man. When he hunkered down like that he looked no bigger than Wiliam himself, and wasn't that a strange thing? And what was that sparkling around him, just a curl of mist gleaming in the first breakthrough of the sun?

It was then I remembered where I'd seen that man before. Disappearing into a puff of smoke in the old mead-hall, oh, so many years ago . . . Octavius by name, and the man who'd started so much mischief that ended in so much joy.

As sure as I stand here today I stood up and dropped my pail, splattering all the good morning water onto the ground. There was Wiliam, still staring off at the spot where Octavius had been, still laughing and gesturing, though nothing was there but a wisp of mist and a strange sort of flattening of the grass, nothing around the whole of the valley but mist and dew. When I asked the kitchen girls if they'd seen the traveler, they looked upon me as if I'd finally lost the last of my senses and said they'd seen no one. Surely if anyone had been here he couldn't have run away so quickly with the land cleared through the whole of the valley.

But I paid them no mind, and took my pail and filled it again with water. I hefted a gurgling Wiliam upon my hip to head back to the castle, a tingle at the back of my neck.

That's when I set to thinking. . . . Aye, and the more I thought, the more I was after knowing it was true. I'm old, aye; I'd seen more changes than a woman should in this place—from good to bad and then to good again—but I wouldn't let anyone be after telling me I'd lost the last of my mind.

For it was that day I realized the truth, and not a man, a woman or a child could convince me otherwise.

Since the coming of the mistress, God bless her, the faeries run free again on the hills of Wales.

A Note From the Author

I've always loved faery tales, and all their trappings: Leprechauns, magic spells, holy places in oak groves, princes in disguise, curses reversed by love's first kiss.

Wales is a land full of such magic. The country has been Christian since the time of the Romans, yet the Celtic pagan gods linger not only in the names of rivers and caves, but also in the popular imagination—in the stories the Welsh tell across the hearth fire.

Entrances to the Underworld yawn at the bottom of every mountain lake. The Celtic mother goddesses are remembered in the mountain called Moel Famau, in the Clwydian range. In Harlech, people still listen for the magical birds of Rhiannon. Dragons and winged serpents are said to inhabit the high crags of Gwynedd. Fairy islands are still spotted, now and again, floating in the fog of the Irish sea.

This is the land of King Arthur and Camelot. Merlin and Morgaine. The doomed love of Guenevere and Lancelot. The tragedy of Tristan and Isolde. Stories like that of Aileen and Rhys: Tales of otherworldly magic—and bewitched love.

Wales is not the only country gifted with such enchantment. Some of you may remember the tale of Aileen's parents, Dierdre and Conaire, from TWICE UPON A TIME (released in 1994). They, too, had their own tangled magic to work through before finding happiness upon Inishmaan, that wind-swept island in Galway Bay. Ireland—with its rolling green hills and mysterious forest ring forts—is also a place of wondrous enchantment.

I could speak, too, of the faeries of the French Pyrenees;

of the Celtic stories of Brittany; of the legends of the Algonquin Indians of North America. Faery tales exist in all countries, in all cultures, for they celebrate one simple, universal truth: That the greatest magic of all is the power of love.

I hope you enjoyed THE FAERY BRIDE. For those of you curious as to what happens to Aileen and Rhys's little boy . . . well, he, too, has faery blood running in his veins. He, too, has his own unusual gift.

But that is a tale for another day.

Lisa Ann Verge
Lughnasa, 1995

Lisa Ann Verge will be returning to Ireland with her next release, ENCHANTED HEARTS. This is the tale of Moreen, a determined foundling with a burning dream—and Colin, the vagabond minstrel with the enchanted heart, who shows her that the best path is not always the straightest one. Look for ENCHANTED HEARTS in your local bookstore in mid-February 1997. You may write to Ms. Verge c/o Kensington Publishing Corporation, 850 Third Avenue, New York, New York 10022.

ABOUT THE AUTHOR

Lisa Ann Verge is the award-winning author of eight historical and contemporary romances, including *TWICE UPON A TIME* (Conaire and Deirdre's story), *HEAVEN IN HIS ARMS*, and a novella, *"THE O'MADDEN,"* published in Zebra's supernatural historical romance collection, *UNDER HIS SPELL*, all of which are available from Zebra Books. A "Vassar Girl" who used to work as an environmental chemist, Lisa is an intrepid traveler who has explored Europe and Canada, occasionally solo and often with no more luggage than a backpack. She has lived in Boston, Manhattan, and San Francisco, but currently, she makes her home in New Jersey with her husband and two young daughters.

Lisa is currently hard at work on her next Zebra historical romance, to be published in March 1997. She loves hearing from her readers. You may write to her c/o Zebra Books. Please include a stamped, self-addressed envelope if you wish a response.

SURRENDER TO THE SPLENDOR
OF THE ROMANCES
OF ROSANNE BITTNER!

JANE KIDDER'S EXCITING
WELLESLEY BROTHERS SERIES

MAIL ORDER TEMPTRESS   (3863, $4.25)
Kirsten Lundgren traveled all the way to Minnesota to be a mail order bride, but when Eric Wellesley wrapped her in his virile embrace, her hopes for security soon turned to dreams of passion!

PASSION'S SONG   (4174, $4.25)
When beautiful opera singer Elizabeth Ashford agreed to care for widower Adam Wellesley's four children, she never dreamed she'd fall in love with the little devils—and with their handsome father as well!

PASSION'S CAPTIVE   (4341, $4.50)
To prevent her from hanging, Union captain Stuart Wellesley offered to marry feisty Confederate spy Claire Boudreau. Little did he realize he was in for a different kind of war after the wedding!

PASSION'S BARGAIN   (4539, $4.50)
When she was sold into an unwanted marriage by her father, Megan Taylor took matters into her own hands and black-mailed Geoffrey Wellesley into becoming her husband instead. But Meg soon found that marriage to the handsome, wealthy timber baron was far more than she had bargained for!

Available wherever paperbacks are sold, or order direct from the Publisher. Send cover price plus 50¢ per copy for mailing and handling to Penguin USA, P.O. Box 999, c/o Dept. 17109, Bergenfield, NJ 07621. Residents of New York and Tennessee must include sales tax. DO NOT SEND CASH.

ZEBRA'S REGENCY ROMANCES
DAZZLE AND DELIGHT

A BEGUILING INTRIGUE (4441, $3.99)
by Olivia Sumner

Pretty as a picture Justine Riggs cared nothing for propriety. She dressed as a boy, sat on her horse like a jockey, and pondered the stars like a scientist. But when she tried to best the handsome Quenton Fletcher, Marquess of Devon, by proving that she was the better equestrian, he would try to prove Justine's antics were pure folly. The game he had in mind was seduction — never imagining that he might lose his heart in the process!

AN INCONVENIENT ENGAGEMENT (4442, $3.99)
by Joy Reed

Rebecca Wentworth was furious when she saw her betrothed waltzing with another. So she decides to make him jealous by flirting with the handsomest man at the ball, John Collinwood, Earl of Stanford. The "wicked" nobleman knew exactly what the enticing miss was up to — and he was only too happy to play along. But as Rebecca gazed into his magnificent eyes, her errant fiancé was soon utterly forgotten!

SCANDAL'S LADY (4472, $3.99)
by Mary Kingsley

Cassandra was shocked to learn that the new Earl of Lynton was her childhood friend, Nicholas St. John. After years at sea and mixed feelings Nicholas had come home to take the family title. And although Cassandra knew her place as a governess, she could not help the thrill that went through her each time he was near. Nicholas was pleased to find that his old friend Cassandra was his new next door neighbor, but after being near her, he wondered if mere friendship would be enough . . .

HIS LORDSHIP'S REWARD (4473, $3.99)
by Carola Dunn

As the daughter of a seasoned soldier, Fanny Ingram was accustomed to the vagaries of military life and cared not a whit about matters of rank and social standing. So she certainly never foresaw her *tendre* for handsome Viscount Roworth of Kent with whom she was forced to share lodgings, while he carried out his clandestine activities on behalf of the British Army. And though good sense told Roworth to keep his distance, he couldn't stop from taking Fanny in his arms for a kiss that made all hearts equal!

JANELLE TAYLOR

ZEBRA'S BEST-SELLING AUTHOR

DON'T MISS ANY OF HER
EXCEPTIONAL, EXHILARATING, EXCITING

ECSTASY SERIES